DEEP RIVER PUBLIC LIBRARY
F MacD
Hell hath no fury / Ross-Ma
3 6039 00003 3999

P9-CDL-474

PLEASE NOTE

To save tax dollars, no overdue notice will be sent on this item.
You are responsible for returning it by the latest date stamped.
The next notice you receive will be a bill.

Deep River Public Library Board of Directors
Deep River, CT 06417 526-6039

HELL HATH NO FURY

Also by Malcolm Macdonald

A Woman Alone
An Innocent Woman
His Father's Son
A Notorious Woman
Honour and Obey
The Silver Highways
On a Far Wild Shore
Tessa D'Arblay
For They Shall Inherit
Goldeneye
Abigail
Sons of Fortune
The Rich Are with You Always
The World from Rough Stones

HELL HATH NO FURY

Malcolm Macdonald

F
Mac

Deep River Public Library
150 Main Street
Deep River, Ct. 06417

St. Martin's Press
New York

HELL HATH NO FURY. Copyright © 1990 by Malcolm Ross Macdonald. All rights reserved. Printed in the United States of America. No part of this book may be used or reproduced in any manner whatsoever without written permission except in the case of brief quotations embodied in critical articles or reviews. For information, address St. Martin's Press, 175 Fifth Avenue, New York, N.Y. 10010.

Library of Congress Cataloging-in-Publication Data

Macdonald, Malcolm Ross.
Hell hath no fury / Malcolm Macdonald.
p. cm.
ISBN 0-312-06994-4
I. Title.
PR6068.0827H45 1992
823'.914—dc20 91-41090
CIP

First published in Great Britain by Headline Book Publishing Plc.

First U.S. Edition: March 1992
10 9 8 7 6 5 4 3 2 1

for
Hugh Carr

Part I
Avowals

1

Change at Maryborough, change at Ballybrophy, change at Roscrea. The only thing that didn't change, Daisy reflected, was the quality of the second-class carriages; on main line, minor line, branch line, and whatever-this-was line, the seats were uniformly hard, the windows evenly smeared, and the decor an unvarying sea of brown, from pale dun to the darkest chocolate. Still, you had to see it from the coachbuilder's point of view. If they made it more comfortable, a lot of first-class folk would drop to second; and if they made it less, a lot of seconds would drop to third.

Dropping in class was very much on Daisy O'Lindon's mind that day.

She glanced across the narrow carriage at her companion for this journey. Fellow traveller, anyway. Mary Rourke. Now there was one who wouldn't grumble too much that only an inch of kapok distinguished a second-class bench from a third, not with those great blind-cheeks behind her. Poor little Mary – nature hadn't given her much, and where it had, it had gone too far. She hadn't a hope of getting this place, of course – nor of much else in life, either. The mouth on her could have been cut out of her face with an axe. You'd find better teeth on broken cogwheels. And whichever eye was right, the other wasn't; they couldn't even agree on which way to look. The left one caught Daisy at her survey. The gash below her squashed-potato nose broke into a gappy grin. 'Soon be there,' she said. Daisy forced a smile, nodded, and turned again to the window.

'Clare to God, it wasn't the prettiest part of Ireland, either. She thought of the Dublin Mountains, which rose behind her own home in Monkstown, and the Wicklow Mountains beyond, which she had seen on the parish excursion to the holy places at Glendalough. The contrast with this flat, boggy landscape could not have been greater. As far as the eye could see, through that grimy pane and the driving rain beyond it, there was nothing but bog, barley, and booreens. Hadn't Uncle Thomas warned her? 'What doesn't drown a man will break him.' He was one of the O'Lindons who had remained in these parts, so he should know.

Now and then there was a glimpse of a landlord house or a hint of something even grander. You wouldn't see the big house itself, of course, but the woodlands where the pheasants and foxes were preserved, they dawdled by every few miles. She wondered what Coolderg Castle would be like. When Aunt Kathleen, her uncle's sister, had written to say there might be a place for a good Protestant girl as lady's maid at Coolderg, it had sounded very romantic: a castle, the Lord alone knew how old, in wooded parkland, by a river, near a lough on the Shannon, with a mountain behind it. But she hadn't pictured it on a day like this, with the showers on each other's heels and a wind that could take you from any quarter at its whim.

A lady's maid – Daisy O'Lindon a lady's maid! And to the Lyndon-Furys of all people! Who'd ever have thought it? Her mother would be telling everyone she'd gone down to visit her relations in County Keelity, or 'O'Lindon Country,' as she affected to call it. That was going to be the worst – keeping up appearances whenever she went back home. For, although her transition from the middle to the servant class was, on the face of it, a step down in the world, it would, in fact, be a liberation of a kind. She'd have money of her own for the first time in her life, and not be forever having to endure her parents' lectures on the state of trade and her thoughtless extravagances and why couldn't she be more like her sister? And she'd be free at long last of having to be chaperoned everywhere – which, in practice, meant she couldn't put her nose out of doors without her mother at her side. Other girls, even if they didn't have their own maid, could always borrow the tweeny or the general for an hour or two; but Daisy's parents had no tweeny and they kept the one general at it from dawn till suppertime. So, all in all, Daisy was rather looking forward to her 'come-down' in the world.

The rain passed over and there was a sudden glory of sunshine. It revealed a few smudges of grey on the horizon, grey that was not cloud. Now she knew they must be drawing near the end of this brief but tedious journey. The smudges in the south were – whatever those mountains in Tipperary were called – the ones they had seen when they changed trains at Roscrea. But those pale blue humps away to the west, now, they were her native land. Or her father's native land: the Slieve Derg, the Beautiful Mountains, the ancient stronghold of the O'Laughlins until the O'Lindons drove them out in the . . . sixteenth century, was it? Not too long ago, anyway.

Daisy wondered what Madeleine Lyndon-Fury would be like. Never mind the romantic castle and the Beautiful Mountains, a mistress could turn hell to heaven on her maid, and heaven to hell. Miss Lyndon-Fury had just emerged from an academy for young ladies in Brighton, just outside London or somewhere. Susan Warner said those places could soak every last drop of the milk of human kindness out of a girl. Still, anything would be better than taking in sewing by the kitchen door after dark and seeing every penny vanish into the bottomless pit of her parents' pretensions; and hadn't her father promised that if the japanning business picked up soon, the first call on his purse would be to get her and her sister back out of service – only he hadn't said *if*, he'd said *when*.

And Uncle Thomas had said never mind what Miss Madeleine would be like; the one to watch out for was Herself, Lady Lyndon-Fury, she had a tongue on her would clip a hedge.

2

The six girls from the Union Workhouse stood in a bold group a little way down the platform, just beyond the large board that read: SIMONSTOWN. Beneath the proclamation a more artistically inclined hand had added the informative legend: *Turminus*. The girls were waiting to catch the 3.30pm from Simonstown to Roscrea, thence to Limerick, ultimately to Boston, Massachusetts. Immediately behind the board ran a tall pale of white-painted slats, behind which an avenue of dripping limes formed the station approach. And parked there, enduring the thunder of the large droplets hoarded from the latest shower by the trees, sat Lady Lyndon-Fury, waiting for the 2.30pm from Roscrea – which was, indeed, the very same train.

Her ladyship gazed at the paupers with undisguised contempt. They knew full well whose carriage was parked beside them, and what they owed its occupant. Where did they suppose the money came from to buy those serviceable gray dresses, the boots and shawls, and the stout wooden chests in which all their earthly plunder was held? Come to that, who had kept their parents alive during the famines, thirty years ago – so that they could breed these bold young hoydens? Why, they owed their very existence, not to mention everything that clothed and supported it, to the Lyndon-Furys – and now they could round it off with the £5 fare to America. But not so much as a half-inch curtsy out of one of them. There was gratitude for you!

There was a whistle from the region of the Cut. Lady Lyndon-Fury made one last survey of the female ingrates and decided that the New World was more than welcome to them. She could name each and every girl – and cost out the burden she had been, the harm she had done, the scandal she had caused, from the day of her birth until now; bold, impertinent, insubordinate hussies all. Good riddance!

The train that would rid the Simonstown Union of this small but permanent burden screeched to a halt on great skirts of steam. Lady Lyndon-Fury picked her daughter's new lady's maid the moment she stepped from the carriage. Indeed, the choice made itself. One of the girls was exactly right; the other was so plainly unsuited it was a marvel anyone had thought to send her at all. Macarty, her driver, had also spotted the pair of them. Well, wasn't he a veteran of these impromptu hiring fairs on Simonstown platform by now?

'Good man, yourself,' she murmured as he went up to the unsuitable one and spoke a few words in her ear – probably to tell her she might as well leave her boxes on the train.

And would you look at the shock in her eyes! Dear God, you'd think it was the end of the world!

3

Daisy simply could not believe it. She just stood there and gawped at the man until he repeated his astonishing statement: 'You'd liefer turn about now, miss, and leave your box in the van.' And this time he added the explanation: 'Her ladyship would no more have you in the house than Delilah and Jezebel themselves.'

'But surely . . .' She pointed at poor Mary as if words would be superfluous.

The man scrutinized Daisy as if he might reconsider his choice. He saw her chestnut tresses, her clear gray eyes, flecked with green, her slender nose and fine-drawn nostrils, her generous lips . . . he noted her firm jaw, her trim figure, her upright stance, and he recognized the mien of a young woman who is utterly confident of her own good looks and charm. In short, he could find not one redeeming feature that might secure her a place at Coolderg Castle.

Daisy drew a deep breath and, avoiding Mary's eye – indeed, both of Mary's seemingly independent eyes – said, 'She's a cripple, too, you know. Her left boot is built up six inches. I saw it when she got in the carriage.'

'Three and a quarter inches,' Mary said quietly.

'There! How's she going to stump her way up and down all those steps at the castle? Ask yourself now.'

The man just shook his head and, turning to Mary, said, 'Get your box from the van, colleen.'

'Well . . .' Daisy stared uncertainly about at her shattered world. 'I'll just see what her ladyship has to say when she hears of this. I don't know what it is, but you and this cripple girl must be cousins. There's no other explanation.'

Without waiting for a reply she marched toward the station exit. Her route led directly past a group of pauper girls being shipped off to the colonies. 'You're too pretty, miss,' one of them told her with a kindly smile.

In the normal way, Daisy would never have demeaned herself by hob-nobbing with such a bold creature, but the world had suddenly turned very far from normal. 'What does that mean?' she asked.

'Hasn't the oul' bat three lusty bachelor sons at the castle. All the maids are like that wan.' She nodded at Mary. 'You may come back when you're forty. Isn't that the truth of it?' She asked the question of her companions, all of whom confirmed it with a nod or an 'Aye'.

'I'll still have a word with her,' Daisy said, but her mood as she continued her brief walk was now more thoughtful than belligerent. In the vestibule by the ticket office she paused long enough to rearrange her hair across her forehead in the frowzy style of thirty years ago; she pinched and rubbed at her nose to make it red, and all the way down to the carriage she compressed her lips tightly, to make them seem pale and bloodless; and even when she arrived she kept them slightly puckered. *Your face is your fortune!* she thought glumly – her father's parting words at Kingsbridge that very morning.

She arrived at the carriage and curtsied deeply. When she rose, her muddied underskirts laid chill stripes across her ankles; a breeze soughed among the limes and a three-second downpour drenched her. 'Good afternoon, my lady,' she called up solemnly. 'May I speak with you?'

An obviously displeased Lady Lyndon-Fury dropped the carriage window six inches or so. 'Well?' her profile snapped, for she did not deign to look at the girl.

'If it please you, my lady, I understand very well why you have told your man to choose the plainest girl, but since there is one else here to speak for me, I must speak for myself.'

'There's no must about it,' her ladyship replied; but she did not close the window again.

'Nonetheless, I feel you should know that . . .'

'I'm not going to argue with you.'

'Nor I with you, my lady. But that girl is more than half blind and has one leg a good bit shorter than the other.' She paused and then, seeing the uncertainty in the other's face, added, 'And her teeth are so bad I shouldn't wonder if her breath might not poison Miss Lyndon-Fury.'

The other turned to look at her then, rather wearily. 'Never mind about her,' she said. 'The position is still not open to you. And do stop sucking in your lips like that! Nothing can disguise the fact that you are far too pretty for my liking – and, what is more important, for my household, too.'

'But your ladyship doesn't even know my name, I am Daisy O'Lindon.'

Her ladyship's stare became a good deal sharper.

Daisy pressed home her point. 'It's not a hundred years since our two families were united in the bonds of holy matrimony.'

The other smiled acidly. 'You're right. It is "not a hundred years". More like three hundred, in fact.' She did not add that everything else Daisy had said was a travesty of the real history; she did not think the girl important enough to bandy words with. Or, perhaps, history was *too* important.

'And the O'Lindons have been on the Fury side in many a faction fight since, I'm sure. But would they have fought with such valour, Lady Lyndon-Fury, if it had e'er crossed their minds that a descendant of theirs would be left penniless and without place when she crossed half Ireland to stand again on the very soil where they shed their blood for you?'

She almost brought herself to tears at the noble ring of this dignified plea; but her ladyship was swiftly in with a metaphorical handkerchief when she retorted, 'Stuff and nonsense! They fought for what they got – preferment – and the chance to squander it in some of the most reckless and profligate behaviour this county has ever witnessed. No, Miss O'Lindon, there is no udder of obligation left for you to milk. Not in 1885!'

'But how am I to get home again?' Daisy asked.

A silk-gloved hand wafted at the train.

'I spent my last penny in getting here.'

Her ladyship's resolve was beginning to falter. Thinking to tip the scales, Daisy added, 'My Aunt Kathleen from Loora, she swore the Lyndon-Furys would never turn an O'Lindon away.'

It was a mistake. The woman simply smiled and said, '*Now* I know the family you're from. Well my girl, penniless or not, the one thing you're rich in hereabouts is cousins. And if you think the Lyndon-Furys have nothing better to do with their money than to send big bold girls here, there, and everywhere about the world – think again! Half a dozen is quite enough for one day.' And she gestured toward the paupers, who were at that moment boarding the train.

A porter peered down at her through the pale. 'Do I bring the box off or what, miss?' he asked.

A few minutes later, her box beside her, Daisy stood at the station entrance and watched her ladyship's carriage draw away – with Miss Lyndon-Fury's new lady's maid sitting beside the driver.

' 'Clare to God,' the porter told her morosely. 'That oul' wan wouldn't even spend Christmas.'
'One day,' Daisy said, 'I don't know how, but I'll make her regret this afternoon's work.'
The man sniffed. 'I have a dog at home that I'm learning to read the papers to me aloud. We could make a race of it if you like.'

4

It was three weeks before Daisy returned to Dublin, by which time she knew exactly what she intended to do. It had required at least those twenty-one days to visit all her kinsfolk in the district, for Lady Lyndon-Fury had not lied as to their numbers. From them she learned that hers had, indeed, been a lucky escape, that her Aunt Kathleen must have been wandering in her mind to have suggested the place might be hers, and that there were better Protestant houses in every barony in Ireland. But most important of all, she learned that Napier Lyndon-Fury, third and darling son of her ladyship, was studying to be an artist in Dublin. After that it was mere politeness, and family duty, and an insatiable ear for gossip, that caused her to tarry there in Keelity, the county of her ancestors.

By early June she was back in Kingstown. Her father had received a good order for japanned boxes from an English tea importer, which had paid off all the most pressing of his debts and left enough over (he said) to keep his daughters out of service for another . . . well, a short while, anyway. Daisy's sister Maude, however, wrote from Avoca to say she was enjoying the certainties of her place as housekeeper to a retired clergyman there and would not be returning to the potluck of life at home.

Daisy allowed a couple of days to pass, so that no one would suspect her purpose, and then gave out at breakfast that she might like to go into Dublin that day with her father and see the factory again. It had been such a long time.

He pointed a warning finger at her over the marmalade. 'If this is just some excuse to spend money on ribbons . . .'

She assured him it was no such thing. The very idea!

They rode in together on the train. They were last through the barrier at the Westland Row terminus, so the ticket collector had time for some crack. 'And is it the poor horse lame again this morning, Mr O'Lindon?' he asked.

Her father shook his head in sad acknowledgement. 'Ah, Mr Donovan,' he said. 'My heart would never fit inside my purse, and that's the truth. He's eating his head off in the stables this minute, and the poor creature can hardly stand. I'd have him shot if I weren't so kindly.'

'God send he's improved by tomorrow, so.' The man leaned forward with a conspiratorial grin. 'Did ye hear the dirt on Fogarty?'

Mr O'Lindon smiled. 'The clerk of the works at the Dunleary coal harbour?'

'The same. You know the new pit they're after digging down between that and the railway? Well, your man was standing there talking to the quare fella, bragging as per usual. "Indade, Mr Scully," says he, "me and Mr Mangan's very tick, you know. Oh yes - very tick." And he crosses his fingers to show his meaning. Mangan's the clerk of the works in Dublin, of course. He wouldn't give the steam off his porridge to Fogarty.'

'Sure, I know Mangan well. I saw him only . . .'

'Wait till I tell you.' His grin invoiced the dénouement. 'Who was it down in the pit at his feet, only Charley Collins. And didn't every Christian and dog inside three hundred yards hear him mutter, "Begod, it's the truth - and I don't know which of yez is the *tickest*." And the only one who never heard a word of it was Fogarty himself.'

He was still dabbing the tears of laughter from his eyes as they passed out of sight down the grand staircase to the street. From there it was but a short ride by omnibus to Carlisle Bridge. Mr O'Lindon got into a desultory argument with a man about the merits of various racehorses, which lasted all the way.

'Who was that?' Daisy asked him as they walked up Bachelors Quay.

'Lionel Bell,' he told her. 'Racing correspondent of the *Dublin Herald*. And a bigger blatherskite never dipped quill in ink. What he doesn't know about bloodstock would fill an encyclopedia.'

'But he makes a living at it, all the same.'

He nodded morosely. 'That's Dublin for you. Find some trade at which you're manifestly incompetent and none can hold you. Look at me. No man in these islands knows more about japanning than me. And where am I today? Where I was twenty-five years ago - in a dirty little booreen off Bachelors Quay.'

'You're not going to drink at lunchtime, are you?' she asked.

His head jerked rapidly her way. 'Did your mother tell you to say that?' He answered his own question with a sad shake of his head. 'No. You're old enough to lepp to your own conclusions.' His gaze wandered on up the Liffey, past the Ha'penny Bridge. 'Well, those days are done.'

Not wishing to fall out with him, Daisy took his arm and led him up the alley to his factory - which was really no more than an old stables and coach house with a door knocked between them; his office was the former tack room. While he sorted out the bills, she stood at the window that gave out into the factory and stared at the work girls long enough for her question to seem spontaneous: 'Where in the name of God do they get all their pattrens from?'

'Don't swear.' He squared up the piles of paper and looked at his watch. 'They carry them in their heads by now.'

'Yes, but originally. Did they make them up?' Beneath the top sheet she saw the corner of a five-pound note.

'No. We have a whole book of them.' His eyes searched vaguely along the dusty shelves and then gave up. He moved between her and the papers on his desk, blocking her sight of them.

'And every other japanning factory would have the same book?'

'Or similar. There's half a dozen. What's the point of all these questions?' He played abstractedly with the papers, making sure he covered up the banknote.

She shrugged vaguely. 'I was only thinking . . . wouldn't it bring in more trade if we could offer our customers original designs for a change?'

His head wobbled this way and that, unwilling to nod or shake. He looked at his watch again.

'I'm sure it would,' she asserted. 'Couldn't you get the girls to make up their own?'

'In the name of God!' His hand darted forward and blocked her mouth with jocular violence. 'They'd want double what they're getting – which is already twice too much.'

She nodded at the justice of that. Then her crestfallen look gave way to a sudden inspiration. 'But then maybe I could sketch some for you – or for them to copy.'

'You?' he began scornfully, but she interrupted: 'And I wouldn't want a penny for it.'

He put his head on one side and asked, 'What d'you know about it, anyway?'

'Divil a thing,' she admitted jovially. 'But I was never more willing to learn. If I could enrol in art classes somewhere in Dublin . . . part-time, you know, in the afternoons, maybe. And in the mornings I could come in here with you. Spend an hour or so tidying your office. Just look at it! How you ever hope to impress our customers with a mess like this . . . I don't know!'

He turned away from her and leaned his head against the jamb of the door that led into the factory. 'Dear God!' he intoned, banging his head against it, hard and rhythmically. 'Dear God . . . dear God!'

She seized her chance and leaped to his desk. 'I'll bet there's money and everything among all these papers. Did you ever see such a higgledy-piggledy?'

'No! There's nothing there but writs and bills.' He sprang toward her, but it was too late. She was already holding up not one crisp fiver but four.

'Any one of those should pay my fees,' she said, smiling.

With wounded dignity he pocketed the notes. 'Now you'll tell your mother, I suppose,' he said morosely.

'What a mark of a fool do you see on me?,' she cajoled. 'Listen while I tell you now. We have a chance to make a real go of this place. And as for my mother, wouldn't she just *love* to be traipsing all over Kingstown and idly letting fall the fact that her daughter Daisy was studying aaart at the Royal Hibaaairnian Academy?'

'There's no such thing,' he said scornfully. 'I mean the Academy has no school attached.'

'When did that sort of thing ever stop her from embroidering a tale. There's half a dozen *academies* of art in this city.'

He stared thoughtfully at her, tugging his little goatee beard. 'God, it would get her claws out of me for a week or two.' He sniffed. 'And would a fiver cover it, d'you think?'

'It would be a start.'

'Wouldn't it!' His misery returned. 'The start of God knows what.'

'Sure, there'd be no harm in finding out,' she suggested. 'I'm not all that shtuck on it, not so's I'd curl up and die if I didn't, you know. But where's the harm in asking a question or two?'

'As the Serpent said to Adam and Eve.'

'Will I or won't I?'

His only reply was a fatalistic shrug.

At the door she hesitated. 'I'll be passing by College Green,' she reminded him. 'Will I bank that cash on my way?'

He consulted his watch. 'I have a little entertaining to do . . . an important order . . . could mean a great deal to us.'

She patted one of his waistcoat pockets, where two sovereigns clinked merrily. 'You're well set-up for that, then,' she said. 'I'll bank it, so.'

She did not leave until she had the fivers in the bag.

The clerk at the Hibernian Bank on College Green was so astounded to be at the receiving end of any O'Lindon transaction, let alone one of fifteen pounds, that he sent for the manager, Mr Fitzpatrick. 'Is your father quite well, Miss O'Lindon?' was his first question.

'He's on the baker's list again, Mr Fitzpatrick,' she assured him. 'Trade is so brisk the poor man's rushed off his feet. Just think – I found those three fivers pushed in among all his correspondence. Sure, that was never his strength. But I'll be seeing to all that, myself, from now on.'

'Will you, now?' he asked with interest.

'Indeed, I will. I'm to do all the correspondence and book-keeping in the morning and in the afternoon I'm to study the applied arts at the Academy or somewhere. I'm on my way to see about that now.'

He smiled. 'It's certainly an improvement on earlier plans for your future.'

She chuckled. 'Did you hear about that? I think it was done to frighten us. It was never seriously intended, you see. He took one look at the haberdashers' bills and thought he'd put the fear of God into us. You know yourself the sort of man he is. The quickest way over the Liffey is by way of North Wales – that's him.'

'There may be something in that,' he allowed vaguely.

'No may-bes in it at all, Mr Fitzpatrick. Why else would he send me to Lady Lyndon-Fury. Haven't they hated the O'Lindons ever since they incurred obligations to us in 1645. And didn't the whole of County Keelity, apart from me, know she wouldn't *look* at a girl with two legs of even length and two eyes that could hit the same target. Oh, he's as cute as a pet fox – though he's my father. And it worked!' She tapped the bank lodgement book, hinting that that was where the money would go from now on.

She screwed up her eyes as if a new thought had just struck her. 'The Lyndon-Furys, now, haven't they a son studying to be an artist here in Dublin? I'd want to steer well clear of him after the brush I had with his mother!'

His eyes adopted the unreadable cast of a bank manager wondering how much he might ethically divulge. 'I believe they do,' he said at length. 'I believe he's at the Academy School in Dawson Street.'

'I'll give that a wide berth, so,' she said heavily. 'Where else now would be a good place, I wonder? I want to learn applied decoration for the japanning trade, you see – flowers and cupids and such.'

He told her of a Miss Deasy, who had a painting school for young ladies on the south side of St Stephen's Green. Well pleased with her fishing and bait casting, she left. Life was only grand when you had a purpose in it.

She sauntered up Grafton Street, past all the fine shops where one day she'd surely have an account and the shopkeepers would come bowing and scraping their way to her carriage. To prolong the dream she walked the full length of the street, up to the Green; the quickest way to the Art Academy was, of course, through South Anne Street, but the detour had nothing to do with any nervousness she might feel at taking the first actual step in the unfolding of her design. Perish the thought! All the same, her pace dwindled to a crawl as she walked down Dawson Street, and she dawdled a fair time before the railings in front of the school.

Standing nearby, watching her with sympathetic amusement, was a stout lady of middle years – who eventually approached her and said, 'Thinking of applying for the place, are you, my dear?'

'Place?' Daisy echoed.

'They're looking for a model, or didn't you know? Were you just chancing it?'

'A model?' Daisy murmured speculatively. 'God, that might be better yet.'

She turned to her questioner. 'What does it involve? Would I have to go naked?'

'Nude, dear. It's different from naked.' She glanced at the clock over the tailor's shop. 'You have half an hour before the drawing master would see you anyway. Shall we take some tay while I tell you all about it? There's a baker in South Anne Street who'll serve tea to Academy students and models. Very comfortable. I'm Mrs Geech, by the way.'

5

It was the most fruitful half-hour Daisy ever spent in her life, or so she felt as she made her way back to the school. According to Mrs Geech, the drawing master, Mr Dairmid Trench, though strict enough as a teacher, was nonetheless sympathetic to the feelings of a well-brought-up young lady. He'd likely start her on for a month or two in the portrait class, where it was just a matter of donning some slightly theatrical costume and sitting fully clothed for the students. Next she'd graduate to the ladies' life class, where, although she'd be nude, there would be no men to gawp at her. And in any case she'd realize by then that all the students – men and women alike – were so absorbed in their work that amatory or impure thoughts were out of the question.

Mrs Geech had been an artist's model for almost thirty years. She'd been so nervous the first time, when she was sixteen, she'd almost fainted. But after only half an hour of watching the men as they studied her anatomy, she'd realized that was all she was to them: an anatomy. 'Could you imagine it?' she asked Daisy scornfully. 'Maintaining impure or lustful thoughts – for the same woman in the same pose – six to eight hours a day, five days a week, for a month or more? Don Jew-wan himself couldn't have done it.'

'And d'you get no chance to mingle with them at all?' Daisy had asked – thinking she might with luck pick up her art training as a sideline to this novel form of paid employment.

Mrs Geech's answer had made up her mind for her. Sure, couldn't she eavesdrop on all the teaching going on around her, and talk to the artists themselves, and look at their work? She'd have to be both blind and deaf not to pick up *something* – enough, surely, to knock out a few simple patterns for her father's use. Anyway, she could pose four days a week and enrol at Miss Deasy's on the fifth and cover her tracks that way.

Portrait modelling was fivepence an hour; full-figure modelling eight-pence. Five shillings and fourpence a day! Just over a guinea a week! Or more than fifty pounds a year! Many a clerk would be happy to get that. Why wasn't there a line of girls for this job, all the way down to Nassau Street? The Catholic Church, to be sure. Sinful to them; socially unacceptable to the other lot. And there she was, neatly in between, happily neither, except during one hour of matins on Sundays. She'd have to bank the money, of course. She could never spend it or there'd surely be questions. What incredible chances life hinged on, really, when you came to think of it! If she hadn't arrived at just that moment, and if Mrs Geech hadn't been standing there watching her, all her clever schemes would have come to nothing. For another of the things the woman had told her was that the Academy did not sully itself with the Applied and Useful Arts.

Her heart was leaping round her gizzard like a thing demented, but she kept a cool exterior and a level gaze on Mr Dairmid Trench as he led her into his office. Mrs Geech had advised her on the best way to deal with him, but the old woman had been wrong in one thing: Trench was taken with her *as a woman*. No doubt of it, and never mind your artistic saintliness. The beauty that had been too much for Lady Lyndon-Fury worked an opposite charm here.

It was all very well for Mrs Geech to say they hadn't an improper thought in their heads when it came to staring at a nude model; and maybe it was true in the second week of a pose – or even the second hour. But surely there must be that primal moment when Old Adam fought the artist for a peep?

The first question the man asked her was whether her parents knew she was applying for the place. 'Well now I want to tell you about that, Mr Trench . . .' she began.

Five minutes later, and all thanks to Mrs G's coaching, he was filled with admiration for her pluck. Here was a young girl of superior breeding whose father's business had hit a bad patch, whose mother had thought to send her into service – where at most she'd earn fifteen pounds a year toward their support; and now, off her own bat, she had hit on this courageous step. How could he do anything other than admire her for taking it? How could he deny her, and them, the chance? Of course her secret would be safe with him. Besides, she was such a beauty . . .

'And you know yourself now,' she concluded, 'there's nothing lewd or immoral in it.'

He agreed there was not. Indeed, there was not, but how rare it was to encounter a young woman of impeccable character with so open a mind. Would she care to start on a month's trial next week? There was a pose beginning in the portrait class on Monday.

She could already feel how her enthusiasm might wither in the icy blast of second thoughts . . . and third and fourth thoughts, between now and then. Somehow, having screwed her courage to this sticking place, she had expected to go in to bat straight away. She gave him a nervous smile. 'My father,' she said hesitantly, 'when he swims at the fortyfoot, always cries, "Take the plunge!" At the back of my mind, I suppose, I'd expected . . .' She let her voice falter as if she were already regretting her importunity.

He licked his lips and eyed her warily. 'I wonder?' he mused. 'Taking the plunge would be the word for it, all right. It so happens that the gentlemen's life class has been let down by one of our regular models. It ought to be the start of a three-weeker for them – but if you've never held a pose for that length of time, it would be sheer murder.' He continued to rub his chin speculatively.

'I'm game to try,' she offered.

He smiled and shook his head. 'But, come to think of it, we haven't done what we call lightning poses – in other words, half-hour poses – with those particular specimens of pond life for some time. What about that?'

Her heart, which had returned to its normal habits some while ago, made a sudden new leap into her throat. Before she could argue herself out of it, she nodded and proclaimed a firm, 'Yes!'

'Come on, then,' he said, before she could change her mind. 'I'll bring you to the female models' changing room.' He led her through several turns of a high, dusty corridor. Here and there were plaster casts of classical sculptures, several of which had attendant groups of acolytes in the form of students standing at easels or sitting at 'donkeys'. All were sketching away intently. In only one case was there a male and a female student working side by side – and she, Daisy noticed, was wearing a wedding ring.

The men she passed all eyed her in a way that had everything to do with being young men seeing a pretty woman – and little or nothing to do with academic art. Another thing she noticed was that the male statues, the Hermes and the discus thrower, gathered female artists about them, while the men clustered about the Venuses and the Dianas.

'There'll be four half-hour poses with three minutes' rest between them – and then we'll break for luncheon,' Trench told her as he paused at the female models' door. He nodded at it. 'You'll find an old cape or a cloak or something in there. And maybe a pair of slippers. Otherwise, just step back into your boots. I'll go and assemble your class. Actually, we've just walked past most of it. Five minutes, then, eh?'

In a daze she started to undress. One wall of the changing rooms was neatly partitioned off into half a dozen open-fronted lockers, three of which contained female clothing. Obviously no one was afraid of petty thieves here. Daisy took off her bodice and skirt and hung them up in the nearest empty locker. She avoided her own eye in the tall, ornately framed looking glass that was the central feature of the facing wall. To one side of it was a washstand with a basin and ewer; to the other a commode. She shouldn't have had those two cups of tea with Mrs Geech. How long was it now? Two hours to lunch. Still, there were the rests between poses. Experimentally, she untied her bodice and slipped it off her shoulders.

For the love of Michael and all angels! she told herself. *You do it every night without a second thought. And if you had a penny for every minute you'd stood before a mirror in your skin, telling yourself it wasn't a bad-looking arrangement altogether, there'd be no necessity to stand here now with the fear of God oozing out of every pore.*

That was the thing to do, she decided. Make believe she was alone at home, just admiring herself the way she often did. With fresh heart she stepped out of the last of her clothes and stood boldly before the looking glass. 'Now that's surely worth eightpence an hour,' she told herself aloud. 'I should get an illuminated address beside.'

She found an old cape, threadbare but serviceable, in one of the empty lockers, and an equally worn pair of velvet slippers with dragons on their tops. She stole one more admiring glance at herself as she passed the mirror on her way out. 'You're doing them the favour,' she assured herself with a wink.

In her mind she added the stage directions: *Chin high, our plucky heroine marches fearlessly to her first life class.* She omitted the slightly less heroic details: the tight clutch she maintained on the cape as she shuffled out of the room and the rather uncertain way in which she peeped up the corridor beyond. All the men had vanished. Hermes and the Discobolus still had their devotees, though. Daisy was just about to approach them when a cheery male voice behind her said, 'You're the new model, eh?'

She turned round and found herself faced by one of the handsomest young men she had ever seen, with deep-set eyes of the most intense turquoise. They, for their part, searched her face with undisguised admiration. 'It was no exaggeration, then,' he murmured. 'Have you a name at all?' He patted the plaster Venus at his side, saying, 'I shall call you the New Venus.'

'Would you ever stop all that!' she exclaimed in delight. 'Are you going to show me where the class is or what? My name is Miss O'Lindon.'

Having started to lead the way, he now spun round in surprise. 'But how extraordinary! I know your family well.' He resumed their walk up the corridor.

'You have a name, too, I'm sure,' she prompted. In passing she caught the eye of one of the female students, who said, 'It's Narcissus, actually.'

The young man nodded in cheerful agreement and continued walking.

'No, go on,' she begged, trotting in his wake. 'Tell me properly.'

'I will not. Or you'll never speak to me again.'

They reached the door then; if she hadn't been so bewildered with new impressions earlier, she'd have noticed the legend GENTLEMEN'S LIFE STUDIO in gold Egyptians on its midrail. The young man leaned confidentially toward her as he added, 'And I very much desire you to speak to me again, Miss O'Lindon.' He flung wide the door.

'Ah, good for you, Miss O'Lindon,' Trench called out. 'You found your way, then. I wish those present had one tenth of your powers of observation.' Then, to the young man: 'Lyndon-Fury! Last of all, I see.'

Daisy spun round and stared at him. He nodded and pulled a face, much as to say, 'What did I tell you?'

'Come on, young lady,' Trench said with peremptory kindness.

Some instinct told her that if she behaved as if all this were excruciatingly embarrassing, they would all become excruciatingly embarrassed. *Just as if you were alone at home*, she reminded herself. Then, taking one deep breath, she kicked off her slippers and let the cape fall until she held its collar in her left hand, trailing up the steps behind her. Thank heavens it was summer and the air warm.

She was just about to take the final plunge – turning to face them – when one of the men called out 'Yes!' There was a general murmur of approval and she understood it was a good pose just as it was.

'Hold that while I look,' Trench told her and leaped off the dais to see her from the students' point of view.

In that moment she discovered she somehow had the ability to imagine herself as she must seem from anywhere in the room. Not in any detail, to be sure, and not all of her at once. But if she thought of her arm, say – the left one, holding the cape – she could see what sort of line it made and how it would sit on a page. Instinctively she curved it a little more . . . so . . . bent the crook of her finger . . . and, in general, added that essential bit of bravura to the gesture.

'Could you try moving your . . .' one of the men began.

'Let her! Let her!' Trench called out. She could hear a sort of contained excitement in his voice. 'Go on, Miss O'Lindon.'

What she had done with her left arm was merely the beginning. That first student, the one who had called out 'Yes!' – what he had seen was the drama of her gesture: her arm drawn behind her by the inertia of the cape, and then the material spilling down over the steps. Now she sought to heighten it. She moved more onto her left foot, the forward one of the two, and lifted her right heel a fraction. That would curve her backbone just . . . so! She almost laughed aloud to discover how clearly she could picture it. Now her head ought to be twisted in . . . *this* direction. A bit more? She tried it. More still? Could she hold that for half an hour? She draped her right arm casually on her hip, a slack counterpart to the tension in her left.

There it was, then – her first pose. Only as she settled to it did she remember that she was, indeed, standing without a stitch on before a dozen young men, and all eyes on her.

And did it matter?

Not a damn!

Behind her you could have heard a pin drop. A model like this, with such an immediate understanding of the power and vigour of human gesture, didn't simply walk in off the streets every day. Were she wreathed in fat and sunk in years, they would nonetheless have flocked to draw her; that she had the figure of a sylph and the face of Aphrodite was the merest bonus.

6

For the last pose before lunch the students dragged a chaise longue covered in faded red plush up onto the dais, thinking to give her bones and muscles some ease. They had hoped to give her that the previous time, too, when they had made her sprawl across the dusty taffeta that draped the dais; but when Daisy sprawled it was like Salome writhing across the floor after the last of the seven veils had gone, begging for the Baptist's head and – by the glint in her eye – knowing she'd get it, too.

It was the same now in the chaise longue. Stretched out upon it, half sitting, half lying, she crossed her legs chastely and then threw up her elbows and twined her fingers behind her neck before she lay back upon the headrest. And once again, by this artless artifice, she created a scene full of contradictions and tension. The apparent lasciviousness of her gesture with her arms was belied by the modesty of her thighs; and when you turned to her face, to see which way her expression might resolve the issue, you found the mask of the basilisk – a remote, cool gaze that sent shivers down your spine and dared you to exaggerate any of those contrasts you might see in her pose.

The atmosphere in that life class was electric, and Dairmid Trench did all he could to raise the voltage still further, knowing that chances like this were all too rare. 'What in the name of God are you doing, man?' he would cry in horror as he sat at a student's donkey or stood before his easel. 'What d'you think drawing is, anyway? Casting a net of lines to imprison your subject? You come in here with your pencil to perform an act of worship. We are gathered here to pay homage to one of the profoundest of all God's daily miracles – the living human body. And what have you done instead? Flayed her into an anatomy!'

To another, who had perhaps taken these romantic urgings too much to heart, he'd cry, 'Where's your discipline, for the love of God? Is that a woman up there or some ethereal vision composed out of clouds? From this . . . this *froth* on your page I'm sure I couldn't tell. Look, that's a *hard* bit there – the collarbone. And there, the cheekbone. That's hard, too. Yet you've drawn it like a brussels sprout. And look at her elbow bone! By God, it's almost bursting out through her skin it's so taut there . . .'

And then, just when those whom he had not yet dismantled were starting to bless their luck, he'd look up and shout generally, 'When in the name of all that's holy are you people going to start learning to *draw*?'

In the brief intervals between poses, they would look at his little sketches, so simple, so pure, so competent beside theirs, and they would smile in patient despair.

During the final pose before lunch Daisy fixed her basilisk stare firmly on Napier Lyndon-Fury, whose donkey was at one o'clock, if her toes pointed at noon. To begin with he did all the proper, artistic things. He thrust his pencil at arm's length toward her and measured off her parts with his thumb and one eye. He squinted at her through half-closed lids to reduce her to a few simple tones of highlight and shadow. He ran his impersonal glance down the hithering-thithering movements of her flesh and translated them into the play of blacklead upon fine white cartridge.

But, moment by moment, that stare of hers contended with the artist in him for possession; and moment by moment it gained the edge. And yet never was a more impassive struggle waged between man and woman, for its winning depended on no sign from her, no response from him. Let her but smile and she had lost; let him but show the longing within him and it would mark his yielding. Whenever he looked up their eyes met, dwelled in each other's, and signalled an outward nothing. Hers did not move; his were not moved. And yet, when Trench's voice cut through that holy silence with his, 'Rest, thank you,' they had shared promises deeper than words. So that when he smiled at her and casually said, 'On fine days like this we usually go up to the Green and have an alfresco sort of luncheon,' it seemed the most natural thing in the world for her to accept.

In the changing room she met two of the other models, Nancy, a dark-haired girl her own age, and Mrs Wilmot, a small, wiry widow in her forties. 'Your first day?' they asked, and 'It's hard, isn't it?' They prepared to assure her she'd soon grow used to it. But she replied, 'I don't know. I seemed to fall into a sort of trance.' Then, seeing the remark put them in a quandary, she grinned and added that it was great fun, nonetheless.

The 'sort of alfresco luncheon' proved to be a picnic hamper of cooked meats, cheese, and fruits with a sparkling Italian wine to wash it down. It was brought to the Bachelors Walk side of Stephen's Green, at the top of Dawson Street, by a porter from the Britannia Hôtel. The things you could do with money! The fellow, however, did not accompany them into the gardens; most democratically they carried it between them to the grass near the bandstand – three young gentlemen and two other ladies, including, Daisy noticed, the one with the wedding ring. The man with her – who had also been at her side when they were sketching in the corridor, was now introduced as her husband: John and Bill (for Wilhelmina) Love. The other young man was Neville Joyce and the young lady was his belle, Rosamund Everett, known to all as Swan, for her beautiful Pre-Raphaelite neck.

It occurred to Daisy that the other four, being married or courting, had some kind of official or acceptable reason for being there; only she and Napier were there – as it were – for their own sakes. Then it struck her as an odd sort of thought altogether, in the context. Official or acceptable to whom? To some kind of universal, anonymous, prying, and prurient aunt who might pop out of the shrubbery at any moment with a cry of, 'And *what* do you suppose you're all doing here?' But such a creature was a figment, the creation, of an imagination that belonged in an altogether different world. Nobody here, she now realized, thought like that at all. In a curious way it was both a relief and a disappointment; for though it was now easier to accept that Napier's invitation carried no especial designs, it also lost significance for that very reason. She *wanted* him to 'have designs upon her,' as the saying goes. That had been her whole purpose in coming to Dublin today.

Of course, she had never dreamed that within a matter of hours she'd be lying on the grass in Stephen's Green, the particular guest of the object of all her machinations. Nor would she have imagined that her own feelings would be thrown into such a three-na-haila by it all. It was not simply that he was so handsome. She had known other young men, equally good-looking, who had stirred her much less profoundly than this. There was something compelling about Napier, too – something that in no way depended on his looks; all they did was make it easier to accept.

As they ate and drank, the other five chatted in a languid, desultory way about things that went mostly over Daisy's head – artistic things. From it she managed to glean that pictures which told stories were little more than tasteless jokes. Light was king. Surface and texture was the true business of the painter. Content was meaningless. Paint itself was its own hero.

Since they all agreed with each other, she couldn't see why they had to keep on with their assertions. She guessed that most people, even in their own little world of artists, wouldn't agree with them, so they gathered here when the weather was fine and kept one another pure in thought.

Except Napier. She got the feeling he'd be like he was even without the encouragement of his friends. They took their strength from him. It was a most satisfactory conclusion.

The repast was light and they were quickly finished. After that there was still a half hour left before classes resumed. Bill lay on her back, covered her face with her pale straw hat, and slept; her husband opened a little book and began sketching fragments from the scene before them – the ironwork of the bandstand, the filigree of leaves against the sky. Neville Joyce took out a penny whistle and began to play mournful, twiddly tunes from Connemara. Close your eyes and you could imagine some little rocky inlet far on the western shore, with the sun setting on a cold, wet day, and a ring of grey seals bobbing their heads up in surprise at the dolorous keening of the pipe. Anyway, that was what Swan said as she fished out a pocket edition of Rosetti and settled to read. Almost as an afterthought she looked up and asked Daisy if she had known Napier long.

The question was altogether too casual. Daisy peered more closely into her eyes. Swan returned to her book, flipped a page or two, and glanced up again.

'No,' Daisy replied. 'Why?'

'Oh . . .' Swan managed to imply a mild disbelief. 'Your name's O'Lindon, is it? I just wondered if there's any connection to the Lyndon-Furys?'

Napier laid a gentle hand on Daisy's arm. 'The O'Lindons justified our very existence,' he said grandly. 'Care for a walk?'

She laughed as she rose. He asked why. 'You said *walk* exactly the way my father talks to our dog.'

He pretended to accept it as a rebuke. 'Hereafter I shall always say, "A little stroll, milady?" Or is that the way he speaks to your mother, instead?'

'Don't call me milady,' she replied. 'That's a little too near the bone.' And she went on to tell him what had happened a few weeks earlier at Simonstown station.

He closed his eyes and clung to a tree as if for support. 'How can you even talk to me?' he asked morosely.

'You said that before,' she reminded him, 'about what out families did in 1720 or whenever it was. I don't think people are responsible for each other in that way, do you? Are you responsible for the way your mother behaves?'

'I'm affected by it.'

She gave a dry chuckle. 'I'm affected by the weather. That doesn't make me responsible for it.'

They were passing a bench on which an elderly gentleman sat reading – Dryden, she saw as she went by. He heard what she said, looked up, and smiled approvingly. If she were alone, she'd have stopped for the crack; she knew his eyes were still on her as they walked away. 'I want to know everyone in all the world,' she said suddenly.

He laughed. 'Even my mother?' The humour deserted him. 'Actually, one should cultivate their acquaintance. They're the last of . . .'

He hesitated so long she supplied what she thought was his conclusion: 'The last of the good wine?'

'Not at all!' he exclaimed scornfully. 'They're the last of that kind. The Old Ascendancy. Ireland can't go on being the way they'd like it – don't you feel that?'

'Another 'Ninety-eight?' she suggested jokingly.

'God, I hope not. But don't you feel that things have got to change?'

'I don't like to think about such matters,' she confessed. 'I only end up seeing *everybody's* point of view and it makes my head spin. And sure, won't it all get sorted out in the end no matter what I say and do.'

'You're right enough there,' he said fervently. They came to another bench, empty this time. He waved a hand towards it, offering her the chance to sit – which she took. 'I'm not really political, either,' he confessed glumly as he sat beside her. 'I haven't the patience with it. All those meetings that go on and on for ever. I've tried . I've been to them but I just end up taking out my sketchbook and not knowing what the hell I just voted for. Or against. I just wish it were over and done with, that's all. So we could get on with our proper business, which is art. Ireland has little enough to offer the world but by God we can hold our own when it comes to art.'

She cleared her throat hesitantly. If he talked like this at home, it was hard to see why he was still her ladyship's darling. And if he wasn't, then she'd made some extremely foolish decisions since breakfasttime this morning. She wanted to ask him about Swan – had there ever been anything between him and that one? 'I expect your parents are glad you're not the one to be inheriting Coolderg,' she said.

Again he laughed. 'There'd be no point in talking to them like this, anyway,' he retorted. 'Apart from which, what makes you think my brother Trapper won't get rid of the estate just as effectually by accident as I would by design? He's *born* to lose it all, and if it weren't entailed to him, I believe my father would rather see it go back to the O'Lindons than have it descend to him.'

'Well, I'm sure I know nothing about all that,' she repeated. 'Until a month ago I'd never even heard of Trapper Lyndon-Fury. And all I know now is that he has a wild reputation.'

He sensed she had tired of the subject. He glanced slyly at her and said,

'Anyway, what possessed you to go off down there, thinking you'd make a lady's maid to my sister? You'd have hated it.'

'I think my father knew the way it would be. He had no intention of seeing me in service. He just wanted to shock me into spending less.'

'Is this your revenge?' he asked.

She stared at him in alarm.

'Becoming a model at the schools?' he explained. 'The world doesn't see it as we do. Or does he approve, in fact?'

She went on staring at him, wondering how to cover her mistake in showing her disquiet at his mention of revenge. 'You're right,' she admitted at last. 'You frightened me – spotting it so swiftly. It was my act of revenge, of course. But how often do we start things with one motive in mind, only to be overtaken by events that make it superfluous.'

'You're a born model, I hope you realize? You could be a truly great model in time. I think it's an even rarer skill than being a great actress. When I'm emperor of all the world, it will be justly rewarded, too.'

Smiling with gratitude she rose and dusted nothing in particular off her dress. 'I'll get no reward at all if I'm not back on the hour. But I must say this: I never before attempted anything that felt so immediately *right* for me. D'you know that feeling – when something is absolutely right?' When he did not reply she turned and questioned him with her eyebrows.

He smiled lazily and nodded. She knew at once that he was thinking of his feelings for her; and though it warmed her to realize it, she was nonetheless glad he did not put it into words as yet. They strolled back by another path to the bandstand. At one point they passed the stump of an old tree.

'I'll tell you how important 'Ninety-eight was,' he said suddenly. And bending over the stump he jabbed his finger at the rings that marked its growth.

'That's 'Ninety-eight. That's when your ancestors lost Coolderg. That's when I was born. That's when you were born. And where's the difference in any one of them? Riddle me that, you Trinity scholars!'

It seemed wonderful to her to be able to relate such a small part of the world to all the rest of it in that electric way; by contrast she seemed to live her own life in a semi-conscious daze.

They covered the remaining distance in easeful silence – so close they occasionally touched. It felt odd to be walking beside a man who now knew every inch of her naked body (and in his case, or in the case of him-and-her – for the feelings were hers, too – it was naked not nude). For the best part of two hours he had studied her nakedness from every angle. If it was odd to walk beside him now, fully clothed and yet knowing that his mind's eye could disrobe her more completely than she herself, then how was it for him?

As they walked back to the school, Swan took Daisy's arm and they lingered outside the haberdasher's on the corner of Dawson Street, admiring the summer bonnets.

Daisy studied the woman's reflection in the glass. Superficially, they were quite alike – of similar height and figure, anyway. But Miss Everett's hair was a drab brown rather than chestnut, and its waves surely cost time and effort to produce. Her eyes, though as bright and as gray, were flecked with mud rather than green. Her nose was passable; Daisy would even allow that its slight retroussé was prettier than her own more classical line. But after forty the poor woman would start to look like a pug dog. And as for her lips . . . the top one was much too thin and severe, whereas the lower was uncomfortably sensuous and full. No, if Daisy envied Miss Everett anything, it was her small, firm chin and those high cheekbones, which gave her a little-girl-lost appeal. On the other hand, she reflected, those same features would give her a mutton-masked-as-lamb appearance in her thirties, and in her old age she'd look positively death-masky.

'I hear you put other models in the halfpenny place, Miss O'Lindon,' she said.

'What would I know of that?' Daisy replied uncomfortably. 'Sure, I never did such a thing – nor dreamt of such a thing before this morning.' And she went on to explain about learning design and paying her way.

'I knew it!' Swan crowed.

'Knew what? We ought to be getting back.'

'You're so different from our usual. Most of the young ones . . . well, they're from Irishtown, you know, and they imagine it'll be easier than the other thing.'

'Easy is it!' Daisy exclaimed, pointedly ignoring the rest of Swan's innuendo. Then, by way of divilment, she added, 'But you're right in one way, Miss Everett. I mean, there is *one* thing makes it easier than it might have been, and that's the attitude of a fine gentleman like Mr Lyndon-Fury.'

She knew she had drawn blood when the smile on Swan's face froze to the iciest that politeness would allow.

7

Throughout the long, balmy summer of '85, Daisy continued to model at the schools on the first four days of each week, and to attend Miss Deasy's academy every Friday. On randomly chosen evenings and every Saturday morning she would be at the japanning works, tidying up her father's desk, completing his correspondence, filling out the books, asking where this or that sum of money went, and generally – as he said – making his life a misery. His complaining, however, was the empty ritual of the once-free man caught and confined at last by a woman he could no longer outwit.

It hadn't taken Daisy long to realize that for years her father had run the place at a level where ruin was an ever-present threat; but he was cute enough never to let the axe fall. If he had money in his pockets to stand his round and lay a small bet, a customer could go hang; but if all they held was fluff, he could conjure trade out of nowhere. She saw then that he did not actually wish to be the proprietor of a japanning factory, or indeed the proprietor of anything; all he desired was a proprietor's income. So she abandoned her efforts to reform him and instead capitalized on his grudging willingness to grant no more than three hours a day to the business. She saw to it that he devoted those precious hours to the two things at which he excelled: checking the quality of the previous day's output and bringing in new orders. And since half of the latter was traditionally done with one elbow resting and the other bent, she got a good day's work out of him most of the time. She herself managed the rest – the things he had always let slide.

She discovered they were owed at least £600 by as many as two dozen trade debtors. Much of it, of course, was unrecoverable by now but she put a collector onto it and got in over £200 before the summer was out. It was the sort of thing her mother ought to have done years ago. Unfortunately, the poor woman had spent most of her time denying the very existence of the factory. Her attitude toward Daisy's efforts had that same ambiguity. She enjoyed their unexpected affluence even while she continued to deny its source. Daisy longed to take her by the shoulders and shake some sense into her – make her realize what a gold mine she'd been ignoring these twenty years and more.

But, as with confessing to them what she was really doing with her days, she put it on the long finger. She could see her mother's point, of course. She had been the sixth daughter of a shopkeeper in Goatstown, a good Catholic family, comfortable, if not exactly prosperous. There had been a lot of headshaking when she had starting courting with this handsome but dubious Protestant who spoke like one of the Lord Lieutenant's entourage, yet turned up with lacquer under his fingernails, borrowed the cab fare home, and wanted groceries at wholesale rates. But a sixth daughter is a sixth daughter and when you're only comfortable-if-not-exactly-prosperous, you can't say much. The poor woman was now self-condemned to spend the rest of her life talking up the pretensions with which she had gilded her choice all those years ago.

Still, Daisy realized, it couldn't go on for ever. When the time came for her to marry, things would have to change. And that time was no longer some infinitely remote possibility on the longest finger of all.

On Saturday afternoons Napier would hire a two-horse car and turn up at the O'Lindons' house in Monkstown, usually with the Loves and Neville and Swan aboard, and take Daisy off for a ramble in the mountains, which was anywhere their fancy might lead them between Shankill and Mount Venus.

Since that day on the green Swan had pointedly – too pointedly – ignored Napier, though she had said to Margaret O'Connor that she could 'get him with one crook of her finger' – and Margaret had naturally told Miss Geech, who had, of course, passed it straight on to Daisy.

The Loves, being a married couple, were nominally their 'daisy pickers' or chaperones, but it was only for the look of the thing. No sooner had they arrived at some suitable hostelry, where they could stable the horses and later return for tea, than they would pair off and wander into the woods and fields for an hour or two of whatever took their fancy.

In those early weeks in June, what took Daisy's and Napier's fancy was talk. They roved the slopes above Sandyford and Fernhill, squandering the lexicon and setting all the world to rights. It was the perfect, godlike eyrie for such activity, since you may sit on those hills and, if the haze does not settle, look clear across the Irish Sea to Wales. By the time of their third visit the conversation descended from lofty universality to their own particular prospects.

'That's where we're all headed soon enough,' he said with a laconic nod toward the distant mainland. Today only one minute triangle of white – the icecap on Mount Snowdon – hung ghostlike above the purple vagueness of the horizon. 'London and Paris.'

He took off his jacket and spread it on the sere, yellow grass for her comfort. That was all they had done so far, sat beside each other and talked. And held hands once on the way back down. Last week, that was.

Today, as always, she sat on his coat; he on the grass. 'Won't you sit beside me?' she asked. 'In case I'd get a blast of the cold. You never know what sudden winds can blow up here.'

He chuckled and did as she suggested. 'London and Paris!' he repeated, with more enthusiasm than before – seeing she had not exploded in derision the first time.

She lay back in the grass and put up a hand to shield her face from the sun – also to see him without having to squint. 'I don't want to think about London and places like that. You have a whole year before you need talk of emigration.'

He plucked a stalk of shivery grass and caressed her nose and cheek with its pendulous seeds. 'No, little Venus, *this* is my final year.'

Her eyes opened wide in shock. 'But I thought . . .' She faltered, being unable to remember a moment when they had discussed it. Time had seemed so infinite; something . . . some casual remark from one or other of them, must have misled her into thinking next year was his finals.

'My diploma show is at the end of July,' he said solemnly. 'Five weeks. I've no right to be here at all at all. I should be back in my rooms concocting my history picture. And I'm short a figure painting, too. And a still life.'

He went on caressing her face with the grass. Her upraised arm fell slack across her breast; she just lay there, sick with the news. One more month only! What was she going to do? Her original plan – to ensnare him if she could, to make an abject creature of him, to punish his mother through him for that humiliation at Simonstown – all that had long since gone by the board. She was now more in love with him than . . . well, there was no comparison. He was the love of her life; she would follow him to the gates of hell and beyond.

One more month!

'I could help with the figure painting,' she offered hesitantly. 'I mean' – she swallowed – 'I could come to your rooms and pose for you . . . tomorrow if you want. I could say I'm going to the service at Christchurch with Hilda Talbot. She'd back me up.'

'Aren't they Catholics, the Talbots?'

'The ones at Malahide are, but some of the others are Protestants. You know how it was.'

'It's all cod, anyway. In Paris nobody cares.'

'I thought they were all Catholic.'

'So they are. But they don't care the way people do here. London's the same. We'll be well off out of all that.'

What did he mean by 'we'? She was afraid to ask. 'What about it, anyway?' she prompted him. 'Tomorrow, I mean.'

The shadow of his head darkened her vision. Her eyelids flickered, about to open, when his fingers fell lightly on them. 'No,' he murmured. 'Keep them shut. You're so beautiful like that. You're the most beautiful girl I've ever known, Venus. I long to kiss you. I've wanted to kiss you from the moment I saw you. But I'm afraid.'

She opened her eyes then and found his, only inches away. She smiled reproachfully. 'Why?'

'Because beauty as great as yours is always frightening.'

'Ah, gwan!' She laughed and, lifting her head slightly, gave him a quick peck on his cheek – enough to blunt the edge of his solemnity without stealing from that most wonderful moment in any such affair: the First Kiss.

She lay back again and closed her eyes. A moment later his lips grazed hers, and parted almost at once, then grazed them again, parted again . . . and on and on, with each such contact firmer and longer, but never long enough . . . until she was in a frenzy of wanting him. And then at last he put his lips to hers and did not move away.

Her arms stole up around his head and pulled him to her with an urgent ferocity that forced him to change position, to lie across her, to put the weight of his chest on hers and then share it with the elbow he placed beyond her arm, pinning her there to the ground – and all this without breaking that magical touch of their lips. She pushed out the tip of her tongue and gingerly explored the portal of his mouth, something she had read of but never done.

She seemed to divide into two people. Part of her was lost in a passion of such depth and tenderness that she wondered how she would ever survive it and return to ordinary, humdrum life. Her innards turned over and fell away inside her. Ice and fire contended in her veins. She felt her whole body dissolving in a whirl of arousal. And yet part of her simply lay there and observed. It noted the curious sensation of his warm, wet teeth, which, from her tongue's point of view, arched the wrong way. It felt how the beating of his heart interfered with his panting breath. It caught the harmonics of their breath as it rushed in and out of their nostrils – hers pitched low while his were like the banshee. The reek of his sun-hot skin was like bread from the oven.

His fingers moved into her hair. His nails raked her scalp with maddening gentleness. Suddenly it was no longer possible to draw enough breath; she felt herself drowning in a rising tide of sensations and desires. At last she had to break from him and gasp for air, lungful after lungful of warm summer balm. High above, tethered on gossamer, a solitary skylark held its manic auction of the land where they lay.

'I love you, Venus,' he murmured as he settled his face in the furnace beside her ear.

The words tickled and she snuggled her head tight against his.

'I think of you all the time,' he went on. 'You haunt me, day and night. When I wake up – just for a fraction of a second – I get the feeling something stupendous is about to happen to me, something more wonderful than I ever . . . and then, it hits me: *You!* You are there, somewhere in my world. In my life. My Venus! I've been so afraid to tell you, in case you'd laugh.'

'Silly!' She turned onto her side and rubbed her nose against his. 'Surely you knew?'

He nodded and gave a rueful little laugh, a whisper of a laugh. 'But in such a painful case as mine, knowing is not enough. All I know is your smile, your tender glance, your melting stare. But what I really want to know . . .' He sighed at the impossibility of explaining it. Then he put his forehead against hers and pressed. 'I want your mind to be somehow inside my mind, or alongside it, or fused with it, so that I know what prompts the smile and the tender glance. I want to be you, and you to be me, even while we go on being ourselves. I want our souls to flow into each other and coalesce until there is no you, and no me, but only the hard, burning, gem-like flame of *us*! I want . . . I want . . .' He subsided.

Until he relaxed like that she had not been aware how tense he was. 'The impossible,' he concluded lamely. After an easy silence he said, 'What do you want?'

'I want to help you get your diploma.'

He drew away and raised himself on one elbow. 'Really?'

When he stared into her eyes like that she felt like turning cartwheels. She nodded.

'Tomorrow?'

She smiled at his incredulity; couldn't he see she'd do anything he asked?

'The world might take note,' he warned. 'The world might not understand.'

'It's the world's loss, so.'

'Oh, Venus!' He leaned into her and gave her one more kiss. 'Will I ever be one tenth the man who deserves you?'

'I *also*,' she said. 'want to plant a sweet pea.'

He laughed and let her go for that.

8

There was little fear of the world doing much noting, the following day. Napier's chambers were in a little court off an alley off Dame Street, in that curious area between the Castle and the Liffey, which began life in great respectability, then went to the dogs, and was now on its way back up again. The street that led to his court was a haunt of ragpickers, hoors, and sweated labourers of every degree; yet the court itself housed two widower merchants from Wellington Quay, an antiquarian, a crammer of medical students, and an elderly widow who told fortunes by correspondence.

Daisy went up the hill to Christchurch first, to catch sight of the hymn boards and to learn who conducted the service and read the lessons. One never knew.

'It's a quare sort of place, this,' she told Napier as he helped her off with her coat. 'You wouldn't want to look too much to right or left.'

'If you had money to spare,' he replied, 'you could do worse than buy up property round here, I'll tell you . . .'

She put a finger to his lips and smiled. He took her in his arms then and kissed her. She felt the ground beginning to sway beneath her feet. But abruptly he broke away and held her at arm's length. Indeed, his holding was more of a warding off. 'I can't,' he said. 'I mustn't.'

'What?' She tried to move close to him again but his arms remained rigid.

'I can't separate . . . I mean, I *must* separate you, my darling Venus, the world's most beautiful girl, from Miss Daisy O'Lindon, the world's finest model. If we start this, I'll do no painting today.'

'I don't mind,' she offered.

He closed his eyes, shutting out the invitation. 'I must paint.'

It amused her to see how properly they managed it all. She disrobed behind a screen, in whose direction he did not even glance – at least, whenever she peeped, he was looking assiduously elsewhere, busying himself with his easel, his palette, his canvas, his brushes.

'God, I've grown to love that smell,' she called out to him. 'Linseed oil and turps.'

'Mmmm,' he agreed abstractedly.

'The one is so drowsy and creamy and the other is so . . . I don't know. It has such a tang. Like walking in a pine forest.'

'I've grown used to it.'

'D'you want an heroic pose? I hope not. I could be Joan of Arc for your history subject. I'll lie flat on the floor as if I'm writhing in agony and you can add the flames when I'm gone.'

He laughed. 'I gather you want a lying-down pose.'

'It is the day of rest.'

'I think I may oblige you there. Lord, isn't it sickening to have to paint a *subject* at all! What the hell have subjects got to do with painting?' His face creased in an impish grin. 'Actually,' he murmured, 'I wonder?'

'What?' she asked as she emerged from behind the screen. 'I can't find any slippers.' It seemed absurd to be apologizing for her naked feet when the rest of her would be in the same condition in a minute or so.

'I just had an idea.' He threw back the covers on his bed. 'Luckily I put on clean sheets today.' He avoided her eye as he spoke the words but turned to her with that same saucy smile as he went on, 'Joan of Arc, eh? Just slip onto there . . . no, keep the dressing gown on. Sit up and lie against the pillows . . . so! I'll give you a couple more. Are you comfy?

'I'll fall asleep,' she warned.

'Wait till I've done with you!' He unfolded yesterday's *Irish Times* and put it into her hands. 'Find a page that interests you. Open it right out.' From somewhere he produced an antique pair of wire-rimmed spectacles, frames without glass. 'I wore these in the last rag,' he explained, fitting them over her nose and ears.

She stared up at him through the unglazed frames, quizzically lopsided. 'By all the holy,' she asked, 'what has this to do with the Maid of Orleans?'

'You're the woman herself,' he explained, jokingly solemn. 'It's the third day of your trial. You've just woken up and the first thing you do, naturally, is read your reviews! How did you do yesterday? What are the critics all saying? Will you bamboozle the English or burn?'

She laughed and told him to be serious.

'I am,' he protested. 'Never more so. I'll teach them to demand that a painting should have a subject. I'll give them "Joan of Arc Reading Her Notices on the Fourth Morning of Her Trial." You can't say that's not a subject and a half! Never before attempted – not even by Leighton. Now! All good history paintings are filled with bare bosoms, so – it's a hot day there in Orleans and you're warm from your bed . . .'

Daisy obliged by loosening her, or his, dressing gown and letting half of it fall to one side. 'Perfect,' he told her. 'Now show the right one a bit. That's it! How does it feel?'

'Cool.'

He chuckled. 'Think of the fires to come!' He surveyed her critically and added, 'Still not enough flesh. Below the waist.'

Again she obliged with a tweak here and there.

'Grand!' he exclaimed. 'One thing the Maid was not, and that's coy.'

'Did you know the Mahdi was dead?' she asked in surprise. 'In the Sudan, you know.'

He began jabbing at his canvas. 'Never having known he or she was alive, I have to answer no.'

'It's your paper.'

'I bought it to see how Guinness's had done. I may need to sell a few.'

'And Lord Salisbury has formed a new administration. If you're going to London, you should know these things.'

'Mmmm,' he said – and she knew she had lost him for an hour or two.

They broke for lunch at two. 'I told my mother Hilda and I might go on up to Phoenix Park and listen to the band,' she said as she slipped off the bed and stretched. Only in the middle of the gesture, when she saw him running his eyes up and down her half-clad body, did the incongruity of the situation strike her. She smiled lazily at him and added the words she had in any case meant to say, 'So we have all afternoon.' Now, however, the tone was different.

She came up behind him and leaned against his back, pretending to look at the painting but actually marvelling at the beauty of his neck . . . leaning down to kiss him. In the last moment she raised her eyes to the painting – and gave out a little cry of shock.

He was a good painter. Of course, she already knew that. Even though still a student he was outstanding. But something had happened during the last two hours to raise him to an altogether higher level. It was everything they ever talked about during their lazy picnics on the Green and on the long summer rides to and from Sandyford. Though unquestionably a painting of her, in that particular bed, and in that precise light, it also possessed those timeless and universal qualities that make a painting great. This was as yet a sketch, of course, but already she could see that light was its hero and texture and colour its medium.

'I don't know what happened,' he murmured, staring at it as if emerging from a trance.

'You've found your own voice,' she told him. 'There's no one else in Dublin paints like that. No one else in the world, is there?'

'I don't know.' He shook his head sharply as if to clear his vision. 'It's like nothing I've ever seen. I'm going to do away with the spectacles. It's not a joke any longer.'

'What makes you pick those colours? When you see them there, it's all so exactly right. And yet if I sat down in front of an empty canvas, I'd never in a million years achieve them.'

He leaned his head until it touched hers. 'It's you,' he said. 'Being with you is like . . . coming home at last. I never felt I belonged anywhere until I met you.'

She reached across him, took the palette from his hands and laid it on the table. Then she slipped the dressing gown from her shoulders and waited. 'There'll never be a better moment, my darling,' she whispered.

9

It was inevitable, given the way life goes on in Dublin; the only odd thing about it was that it took so long. An English artist once told Daisy that hers was the only city he'd ever been in where people didn't read newspapers on omnibuses and trains – they preferred to gather the news at first hand by staring out the windows. As with any observation about Ireland, it was at least half true: Dubliners – indeed, the Irish in general – do prefer to see life in full colour; the other half of the truth is that they also prefer to see it in black and white. What happened over 'Joan of Arc Reading her Reviews on the Fourth Day of her Trial' was a case in point.

It was the *succée de scandale* of that summer's show. Dairmid Trench, who knew a good painting when he saw one, gave it pride of place, directly facing the visitor on entry. If he had 'sky-ed' it somewhere over the door, it could have been passed off as one of those unfortunate exuberances to which students are prone . . . just playing for attention . . . best ignore it and he'll go away. But stuck where it was, blaring like the trumpet fanfare in *Saul*, it became a rallying point for exhausted warriors who thought they had fought one another to a standstill years ago. Classicists and Romanticists, Traditionalists and Modernists – most of whom had forgotten where the battle lines were – came wheezing hotfoot from studios as remote as Rathgar and Mountjoy Square to enlist once more in the Grand Oul' Cause.

The really scandalous thing in Napier's painting was the behaviour of the sunlight. Normally, it's a very handy commodity. What happens is that the painter arranges for a convenient break in the clouds so that a single shaft of it pierces the scene (which is otherwise given over to a teeming sort of gloom) and picks out the hero or heroine. If that central figure is doing something more active than simply being a hero or heroine, shafts of feeble illumination from a secondary sun can be arranged. Thus a saint may confront his tormentors, or a king a beggar mind, and everyone can see what's supposed to be happening. And the artists can order up all his paints in advance.

But what did the sun do in Napier's monstrosity? The lowermost portion of it ran in a diagonal across a patch of torn linoleum ('if that's what that coloured vomit's supposed to be,' as one octogenarian put it); then there was a vertical climb up a disordered array of crimson blanket and whitish sheet. From there a second diagonal finger went snaking across the bed, illuminating three inches of the calf of a seminaked female – 'and the least interesting three inches at that,' said a thirty-year-old octogenarian with a thriving trade in portraits around Ballsbridge to defend. This impudent band of sunlight went on to pick out an equal width of purple dressing gown before it fell into a gulf behind her. It finally re-emerged as a vivid vertical slash upon the brown wallpaper beyond – except that when you looked into it, there was no brown at all but a trickery of pinks and greens.

The immediate impression was thus of a brightly coloured zigzag climbing from bottom-left to top-right of a large, dark rectangle. It was only when you peered into those darks, 'vibrant,' said one defender, 'with the tumbling restlessness of life itself,' that you realized what was really going on: A striking young woman was lying on a bed, reading the *Irish Times* and exposing much of her skin to the coolth of summer. 'A work of haunting and disturbing beauty,' said one critic. 'A blasphemy against God and Art,' cried another.

A Roman Catholic priest wrote in a later number of that same newspaper (which was to all intents and purposes the house organ of the Other church) with proof that the female in the painting had no connection with Joan of Arc (adding the parenthetical reminder that she had been martyred at the behest of the English for her faith and that there was a powerful worldwide movement for her canonization, of which, as it happened, he was secretary to the Irish branch). The proof lay in the errant behaviour of the sunlight, which refused to single out the Holy Martyr as it would do in any decent sort of a painting. An Anglican dean replied with the tactless reminder that it was the Holy Inquisition under a French bishop who had burned Joan for heresy and sorcery. A Jesuit weighed in to the rescue (both of his coreligionist and the original point) by asking if God was really to be thought of as a kind of Theatrical Lighting Manager and Arranger of Celestial Pyrotechnics to the Guild of History Painters. A brass bed manufacturer added the information that the bed in the painting had been manufactured by his firm in 1847 – some four centuries too late to be of any use to Joan, sainted or not. A greatly improved version of the bed was now offered to all patrons of that sort of thing. A Protestant pyrotechnics manufacturer said that his was a serious business which, if pursued with the levity revealed by a correspondent with the initials SJ after his name, would result in tragic loss of life.

And then, for Daisy and Napier, the laughter stopped. For when the manufacturers of brass beds and of pyrotechnic devices were flocking in their twos and threes to scrutinize this work of art, it was only a matter of time before one or other of the O'Lindons' friends in Monkstown began remarking on what a striking young woman Daisy had turned out to be and of course there was nothing wrong not really wrong in taking off your clothes in the cause of art and they were sure it was all extremely respectable or else a nice young girl like Daisy wouldn't be in it at all at all.

10

Gray-faced and trembling, Mrs O'Lindon walked down Dawson Street and into the side door of the school, where a hand-painted notice, 'illuminated' to a blinding degree of illegibility, pointed her towards the summer exhibition. One glance around the walls, from which her nude daughter stared down at her in a dozen renditions of varying life but unmistakable life-likeness, confirmed her worst nightmares. Without pausing for thought she advanced on Napier's monstrosity.

This was worst of all. The others at least showed her in poses that were recognizably artistic and classical; moreover, you could see other students and their easels in the background; no one could imagine that improprieties either had taken place or were about to. But *that* great . . . diarrhoea of colour and light was another story altogether – a naked hoor (no point in mincing words) lying with everything showing, waiting for the man to leap aboard her. It was plain as a pastry board. And it was undeniably Daisy.

Sick with a kind of fatalistic dread, an instantaneous knowledge that no form of words was ever going to explain away this catastrophe, she turned on her heel and drifted out into Dawson Street. All the way down to Nassau Street, past Trinity playing fields to Westland Row, she wandered in that same unfeeling daze. *How could she?* The words repeated themselves so often in her mind that they lost all meaning; Daisy herself ceased to exist, or, rather, began to merge with those odious flourishes of pigment that now mocked twenty-two years of marriage and the unending struggle for respectability.

At last, as she boarded the train for Kingstown, that was the thought which penetrated her stupefaction: It had all been wasted. A week after her marriage to Aloysius, when they returned from the honeymoon in Bray, he had tentatively suggested that she and he might work side by side in the japanning factory and make a real go of it together. But she had said no. A married lady, she thought, should be a *lady*, and so she had scrimped and saved all these years to maintain at least the outward trappings of that ambition. And where had it got her? In a few heedless months her daughter had ruined it all. There weren't enough years left – not if she lived to a hundred – to undo the harm Daisy had done.

She got out at Blackrock but instead of walking straight up the road to Balaclava Terrace, she crossed the line and went down to the beach. How seductive the water looked! Its calm, gently rippling surface invited her to walk in, dressed as she was – to walk and never stop. In her imagination she felt the cool line of it advancing up her body until it closed over her shoulders, hugged her neck, caressed her chin, dabbled at her lips, and at last flowed in by her nostrils. It wouldn't take long. It was a quick and easy way to go. Like the drowned sailor on the beach at Howth when that big iron merchantman went down off Lambay. 'An easeful death,' someone said. And looking at his face you'd believe it.

Serve that wicked girl right, too – to live with that on her conscience for the rest of her life. The trouble was, you couldn't knock Daisy down like that. She was the same as her father, never down for long. She'd mope for a day or two, tell all the world she was the wickedest and most miserable of mortals, then she'd spy a chink of daylight and next moment she'd be out in the sunshine again saying it wasn't a bad old life if you didn't weaken. Six months from now her dead mother would be just an item on one of Daisy's lists: 'Buy flowers for Mammy's grave.'

The thought – the certainty – of such a fate put all ideas of an easeful drowning from her mind. What was needed was a positive gesture. Something to show the neighbours – so that when two or three gathered to scoff and snigger they'd not be able to ignore it.

She stepped out for home now, full of purpose. Daisy's meagre belongings were soon packed; indeed, some of them had not yet been unpacked since her visit to O'Lindon Country. It took almost longer for her and Mrs Mooney to manhandle the trunk and two boxes into the front porch. Then Mrs O'Lindon went out into the road to look at the effect. It was disappointingly small – indeed, the casual passer-by might even imagine that this was the luggage-in-advance of some new lodger.

Burning with shame at the very thought, she re-enlisted Mrs Mooney and they dragged it further, right out into the street. Then she took a cloth and wrapped it round her finger and dipped it in some blacklead and wrote on a piece of pink card: MISS DAISY O'LINDON NO LONGER RESIDES HERE, and pinned it to the trunk with a small pebble from the rockery. Now let the neighbours ignore that! She withdrew to the dark recesses of her drawing room and watched.

Faces soon appeared at windows. Curtains stirred discreetly. Opera glasses were sent for, then bonnets and shawls. Small errands to unobservant neighbours were run – all requiring, for some reason not immediately apparent, a detour across Balaclava Terrace and past the evicted paraphernalia. Those unobservant neighbours, in their turn, sauntered casually close to their windows. More opera glasses were sent for . . .

Smiling to herself, Mrs O'Lindon retired to await the explosion.

11

Daisy had spent the afternoon on the slopes of Mount Venus, a fittingly named location for her and Napier's employment in those balmy days of post-diploma relaxation. They had planned to go on to Glencree and back by way of Shankill and Foxrock, making a circle of it, but Daisy had whispered, 'Again?' once or twice too many, so they had to return by the direct road along the foothills of the Dublin Mountains, between Stillorgan and Leopardstown.

'From Mount Venus to Stillorgan!' Napier could not help pointing out, with rueful jocularity. 'Talk about symbolism! It's like everything else in this damned country.'

'What do you mean?' she asked dreamily.

'Nothing is ever just itself. You can take everything two ways.'

An indelicate reply occurred to her but she quelled it. 'At last I understand why they're so insistent on chaperoning us everywhere,' she murmured. 'When we have a daughter, I shan't let her out of my sight.'

He scratched his head with the stock of his whip. 'There's a flaw in that logic somewhere. Why is it all right for us but not for her?'

'Because her chance of finding as daycent and considerate a man as you, my darling, will be too low to make the risks acceptable.'

He transferred the reins to his whip hand and put the other arm about her. 'You're taking no risks with me, my precious Venus. You know I'm going to marry you.'

She leaned her head against his shoulder.

He gave a little sigh of surprise and said, 'There can't be another like you, either.'

His tone suggested he had some particular meaning in mind; she asked him what.

'How often have I said I'll marry you? At least a dozen times, I'm sure. And how often have you asked *when*, eh?'

'I don't know,' she lied, recalling how often she had bitten her tongue off on the point of putting that very question.

'Not once,' he told her admiringly. 'I don't suppose there's another girl like you in all the world; one who could show such restraint.'

'But it would be like saying I didn't trust you,' she objected – casting yet another net of weightless, invisible, unbreakable thread over his soul.

He gave her one further squeeze and then resumed more responsible control of the horse. 'D'you think it spoils it or makes it better?' he mused. 'We'll never know, of course.'

'What?'

'Jumping the starter's flag, as we have done. Most couples have to keep themselves continent for years . . . I mean, that's how long most engagements last.'

'Well, men can always go off and find themselves women of . . . you know, *those* women.' She faltered and blushed flame red.

He chuckled. 'You think it's the same?'

'I wouldn't know, would I?' She glanced at him archly.

Now it was his turn to blush.

'Is it?' she goaded.

He shook his head crossly and stared at the road ahead, refusing to glance at her. She gazed into the prosperous, well-tended gardens beside the road and said, 'You've been brought up so free and aisy, you can't imagine how wonderful it is for me.'

'What?' He was jovial again.

'To be able to talk about anything – anything one likes. It makes me realize how I've lived all my life with a sort of little black ball of fear sitting on my shoulder, guarding everything I say. I mean, we all think one line of thought, don't we, and we speak another. There's no honesty in it. That's what's marvellous about you – that we can be so completely honest. Don't you think?'

For a long while he peered at the road ahead, a light smile on his lips.

'Don't you?' she prompted at length.

'It cuts both ways,' he said reluctantly. 'Sometimes, when I'm holding you in my arms, I look down at your head and . . .'

'I'm not that much shorter than you.'

'All right, don't quibble! I look slightly-down-and-mostly-sideways at your head. And I wonder what's going on inside there. But, actually, I don't really want to know. Part of the wonder of you is that utter mystery . . . your exciting unknowability. Oh, it's impossible to describe! You read all those things poets and so on write about love and you say, "Can't they see what fools they're making of themselves? How absurdly overdone it all is?" And then you go and fall in love yourself and you suddenly understand that *no* form of words, however far-fetched, is anything like adequate to describe it. I feel I'm on the point of bursting with it all the time. Don't you?'

'I feel I want to tell everyone. It's like finding a wonderful secret that's been kept from us all these years – all our lives. I shiver with pleasure even when I just think of you . . .'

'Don't!' he pleaded.

'D'you think Swan and Neville do it? I'm sure they do. I keep wanting to ask her if she thinks it's just as . . . miraculous.'

'I hope you don't,' he warned with amused alarm.

'Why not?' her smile grew roguish. 'D'you mean especially not her? Or not anyone?'

He hesitated a moment too long before he said, 'Not anyone.'

'But more particularly not her.' Daisy no longer made it a question.

'She's not noted for her discretion,' he replied lamely, when silence would have been stronger.

'She'd claw my eyes out.'

'Lord, don't you give yourself airs!' he declared in a heavy rural accent, to show his attack was jocular. 'You'll take wing and fly next.'

Following his pattern she tossed her head and shrugged him aside. 'Begorrah, sorr, you should go down on your knees and bless that colleen, so you should. Were it not for her jealousy, sure I wouldn't have given *you* a second glance.'

He chuckled and slipped his arm about her again.

'Did you think it your charm alone that won my heart?' she asked in the same tone, though she did not shrug him off now.

He laughed again and let the topic die.

She returned, as if there had been no break at all, to the thread of their earlier conversation. 'Don't you want to tell everyone how splendid it is?'

He shook his head. 'Only you.'

She snuggled against him. 'Tell me then.'

'What?'

'About us. That we're doing nothing to be ashamed of. That we're right and the world is stupid and wrong. That it'll go on like this for ever and ever.'

He leaned his head briefly against her and said, 'I don't know! You baffle me.'

'Why?'

'Are the words truly so important to you?'

'Yes. Aren't they to you?'

He shook his head. 'You remember poor Billy Walsh's painting of you?'

'Don't start talking about painting,' she said crossly.

'I'm not. Listen. Poor old Billy put everything he knew into that bit of work – and he's not bad when it comes to the old technique. He got every little detail right, yet when you stood back and looked at the thing as a whole . . . what was it? Dead as mutton. To me, when it comes to *talking* about love, the finest words by the greatest poets are just the same – dead as mutton. They get no closer to describing the glory of an afternoon in the long grass with you than Billy Walsh's sterile mess of pigments got to depicting the most glorious model of the century. That's all.'

She dug him with her elbow, half-delighted, half-dissatisfied. 'That's not the sort of talking-about-love I mean. Not all that high-flown poetic stuff.' She fell to silence.

'What, then?' he asked.

'It doesn't matter.' Then, feeling this ending somewhat bleak, she butted his arm playfully with her forehead and added, 'Nothing matters as long as we're together.'

They turned into Balaclava Terrace. Daisy saw the pathetic little pile of her belongings at once. She was filled with a sudden foreboding, even before it registered with her exactly what it was. Before their gig was half-way down the hill, she was no longer in any doubt. Keeping her face pointing rigidly ahead she allowed her eyes to flicker this way and that, taking in all their neighbours. Pale ghosts swam in the net-curtained gloom of interiors, staring out with intense but reticent curiosity.

'Drive on,' Daisy muttered, forcing her lips to move as little as possible; upon them she fixed a fierce, if rather vacant, smile.

'What?' Napier asked in bewilderment.

'Never mind now. I'll tell you when we get round the corner. Just do it – please!'

He had been looking at the baggage, too. As they drew closer his abstract interest in it grew suddenly sharper. 'That's your house,' he said. 'I say, Venus . . .'

'No, don't!' she said vehemently. 'Just drive on. Oh, I say – look at that lovely clipper out there!' Knowing exactly what sort of picture she was cutting – not to say etching – in the eyes of all those neighbours, she raised one hand to clasp her bonnet and pointed the other with a dramatic flourish toward the horizon, for they were near the Dunleary road and the whole of Dublin Bay was now spread out before them.

'What clipper?' he asked, now even more bewildered than before.

'The one that damn well ought to be there at a time like this,' she replied and, bursting into genuine laughter, clutched at his arm and hugged her head against his shoulder.

They swept past her luggage without so much as a glance.

12

There was a hesitant knock at the door. Daisy turned over in bed and groaned. The next knock was firmer. From under the blankets came Napier's voice, muffled, disengaged: 'No one I know, I'm sure.'

Daisy slipped a toe out into the chill of a summer's morn, shivered, thought of pulling it back again. There was yet another knock, this time peremptory. 'Coming,' she moaned, inaudible to their visitor, as she groped among the tangle of clothing on the floor, seeking her dressing gown. Or Napier's dressing gown . . . their dressing gown, anyway. What did it matter? 'Coming!' she repeated, loud enough to carry, as soon as she felt its cool silk about her.

How swiftly it turned warm. Art silk wasn't like that. She'd never wear art silk again. Barefoot she glided toward the door and opened it a crack.

'You!' she cried, trying to shut it again the moment she saw who it was.

But her father, a veteran of many a doorstep in his day, got his foot there first. 'Would you slam the door in my face?' he asked bitterly.

Through the chink she said, 'I know you've got to back her up, Father. I don't want you to have to take sides.'

'At least let me in, woman. I can't stand out here talking.'

'There's nothing to talk about.'

'What d'you know about it? Are you going to let me in or what?'

'Let him in,' Napier muttered, still entombed in the blankets.

'I will not,' she whispered vehemently. Then, to the crack in the doorway, 'I'll meet you down on Essex Bridge in five minutes.'

'I know your idea of five minutes,' he answered scornfully.

'Well, it'll be even longer if you stand there gassing on.' She closed the door against him and waited for his footfall on the stair before she relaxed again.

Napier came up for air. 'Why didn't you let him in? Don't you think I've a right to meet my future father-in-law?'

'I know what *he* wants,' she said angrily, more to herself than him, as she hooked her petticoats around her waist, all three at once.

'Dear God!' Napier groaned, unable to take his eyes off her. 'Why can't our desires be trimmed to our capacity?'

'Well, I'm not going back,' she went on. 'We're going to England now and that's all settled. Did you write to your parents?' she asked sharply.

'I will. I will. I'll post it tomorrow, just before we sail.'

Her angry shrug indicated she couldn't go over the argument yet again – what was he so afraid of, anyway?

Ten minutes later she stepped onto Essex Bridge. Her father was in the exact middle, on the eastern, or downstream side, facing the morning sun. There was the first touch of autumn in the air. A woman was selling flowers by one of the stone balusters. A tug from Guinness's went by, towing a barge from the brewery up by Kingsbridge to the port, a mile downriver. The master gave a whistle and waved to the flower lady. 'Bring us back a parrot,' she called out to him. Then, with a wink to Daisy as she passed, she added, 'He won't, of course. Just another bloody bunch of bananas.' And she burst into wheezy laughter that ended in a fit of coughing.

'What was that?' her father asked as she drew near.

'Dublin,' she replied sadly. 'That's what I'll miss.'

He looked back at the rippling waters, combed to show its dirt by the bow wave of the tug. 'Then it's true,' he said.

'How did you know?'

'I asked at the school. The Hibaaaairnian Academy! They said you'd already gone over the water.'

'That's what I told them.'

'But there was a girl there collecting her paintings and she . . .' He sighed and nodded toward Napier's rooms.

'We're going tomorrow,' she said.

He nodded but made no other reply.

For a while they stood there, side by side, not close, leaning on the broad stone parapet, staring down the river. After a while she said, 'Will you still manage without me?'

'I'll have to.'

'This could be a big opportunity.'

'For you?'

'No! For *you* – you and Mother. She's no call now to persist in her idiotic pretensions.'

'Have a care,' he warned, but there was no heat in the words.

'I've seen to that! And there's nothing I've done, down there at the works – nothing she couldn't do better.'

Suddenly he turned his back on the river, as if the sight of it had become unbearable. Leaning against the parapet he folded his arms and stared across the bridge, idly letting his eye be caught by anything that passed – a dog, a brewery dray, a pretty ankle. 'Oh Daisy!' he exclaimed. ' 'Clare to God, I'd forgotten how easy everything is when you're young! How's your mother to change at her time of life? Can't you understand?'

'You could do it on your own, then. You could be one of the foremost businessmen in Dublin with very little extra effort.'

'Hah,' he exclaimed coldly.

'If you didn't have to keep rushing here there and everywhere to stave off collapse . . . I mean, one tenth of the effort you put into all that would see you and Mother on the road to prosperity. Why can't you understand that?'

An ugly little dog squatted in the gutter, eyed them guiltily, then fled, leaving behind a bright yellow pile. 'God knows why we tolerate them,' he murmured.

'Aren't I right?' she insisted.

'No,' he replied morosely. 'Yes! You're right for you. You're one of those people who can get things done. God knows who you inherited it from. Not the O'Lindon side, anyway. You could walk into Guinness's itself and set them to rights.'

'Father!' she cried in an odd mixture of vexation and delight. 'This is your old blarney.'

'It is not. You don't know how rare a thing you have. If you were a man . . .' He shook his head ruefully and sucked a tooth.

'Well, I've never been happier that I'm not,' she said defiantly.

He looked at her and nodded.

'Not a man, I mean,' she added, thinking he might not have grasped the point.

Again, all he did was nod.

'Doesn't it make you angry? Me living with Napier and so forth?'

He smiled at last. 'Dear child! D'you think the only reason parents guard their daughters from all that sort of thing is just because we want to make your lives a misery? That we want to stop you having your fun? D'you think that's all?'

'Why else?' she asked uncomfortably.

'Well, the rate you're going, you'll find out soon enough. They're different, men of that class. They're not like you and me . . .'

'Father!'

But he went on imperturbably. 'You'll see. They don't think like us.'

'We're as good as them any day of the week.'

'I'm not talking about that. I'm talking about outsiders and insiders. People like the Lyndon-Furys, they'll close ranks on you in the end.'

She turned away from him angrily. 'I don't know why I came out to see you at all. What did you want of me, anyway?'

'To say goodbye,' he told her simply – wrong-footing her completely. 'Properly, you know.' Then, just as she was struggling to apologize gracefully, he added, 'And to tell you to marry the bugger as soon as you can.'

They parted amicably enough, a short while later. On her way back to Napier she pondered her father's strange use of that indelicate word. He had never spoken to her like that before. Yet it had been no mere slip of the tongue, of that she was certain. It was as if, at the last, he had acknowledged her equality, almost as a partner. A crony, anyway. And there was no way to convey it except by use of that word.

But there was even more to it than that. If he had simply told her to marry Napier soon, she might have taken it for her mother's urging, with her father as the mere errand boy. The word also served to disabuse her of any such suspicion. It was not her mother's prayer: 'Make me respectable again in the eyes of our neighbours.' It was a wisdom altogether more profound.

If Napier didn't name a day soon, she'd have to start doing something about it herself.

13

The first pea-souper of the year settled over London on Friday evening just after the middle of October. For Daisy it had seemed to start around three o'clock, when thin fingers of autumnal mist came snaking down the Thames, cutting Battersea Bridge from its foundations, rising to engulf Albert Bridge, and finally spilling out into Chelsea, where, in Margaretta Terrace, she and Napier had found lodgings. For more experienced Londoners it had begun much earlier that day, when the wind dropped to a zephyr and the outpourings of the city's myriad chimneys started spreading a sulphurous pall over the face of the sun.

The effect by mid-morning had Napier in an ecstasy. He walked in the thin, golden sunshine all the way down the Embankment to Westminster, and back again via Battersea. 'It's turned the Thames into the Venice Lido,' he said. 'You suddenly see what Canaletto was all about.' But by four, when the rising miasma off the river met and mingled with the brown overhang, creating a twilight that was three hours premature, he was less pleased with the effect. He had to abandon his painting – a portrait of Daisy – and take up his sketchbook instead.

'What's for supper?' he asked.

She wet her lips and smacked them. The taste of sulphur in the air was faintly medicinal. Unappetizing, anyway. 'Are you very hungry?' she asked. 'Why don't we go out and walk around and see if we can get lost and buy a hot pie or something from that shop in the Fulham Road?'

He stared at her fondly and shook his head.

'What?' she asked in a mildly wounded tone.

'Let's get a pie. Let's go to a café. Let's buy a quart of cockles and mussels . . . What have I married?'

'You haven't married anything yet,' she reminded him, with less humour than usual.

'As good as,' he said easily.

She made no direct response but a hard glint crept into her eye. He saw it and held his tongue. An artist, she reflected drily, always has the perfect excuse for holding his tongue. Then, when he felt the silence was easeful enough, Napier asked, 'What would be the great attraction in getting lost in the fog?'

He knew it would touch that nerve of enthusiasm which, in Daisy, was never too far beneath the surface. 'Oh!' She closed her eyes and smiled, miming an ecstasy. 'To feel the terror of it and yet to know we were perfectly safe, really. I mean, you couldn't *actually* get lost in London, could you. There'd always be someone about.'

He took up the game: 'But what if everyone you asked just turned to you mournfully and said, "I'm sorry, I'm a stranger here myself"? Suppose we asked a dozen people, and they all replied in exactly that vein!'

He watched her shiver with delight at the thought; yet again her capacity for instantaneous pleasure, both in reality and in her imagination, bowled him over. She was the embodiment of everything he had ever read, or thought, on the subject of hedonism – but without any moralistic overtones. With Daisy it was so direct, so immediate, so utterly thoughtless, it left no room for moral qualifications. And yet she was not a thoughtless person. Far from it. She paid more heed to the morrow than he ever did or could; the number of lodgings she had inspected before accepting these rooms was prodigious.

In one, the landlady had no portrait of her late husband on display. Daisy couldn't say precisely why, but it simply made her uneasy. In another, the sheets on the bed had been of good Irish linen, but the replacements in the hot press had been of thin, washed-out cotton. She noticed everything. And yet, side by side with that sharply observant trait of hers was this rash, hedonistic streak; but the truly wonderful thing about it all was that she managed to contain them both and to make them equally *her*. When she was in that mood, he could deny her nothing.

'Would you really like to?' he asked. 'Go out and get lost?'

Her eyes gleamed and she sprang up from her seat; she had on her coat, muffler, and gloves while he was still looking for his boots.

As they closed the front door behind them, a lamplighter materialized out of a gloom that was neither day nor night. They paused to watch while he deftly raised his pole, inserted it under the open glass skirt of the lamp, and drew down the lever of the gas valve. The lamp was of the new type, with a brightly incandescent mantle instead of the old naked flame from a fishtail burner. 'A regular, right-down London Pertickler,' he commented as he cycled off into the fog again.

'Good luck!' Napier called after him. The brilliance of the lamp had the peculiar effect of turning the surrounding twilight into night. 'Which way?' he asked her.

'Let's do it like the maze at Hampton Court – left, right, left, right, at alternate turns.'

'But it didn't work there,' he objected. 'That's how we got lost.'

When she chuckled he saw the point. She took his arm and they set off to their right, north toward the Fulham Road. She hugged him tight, relishing his solidity and warmth. One of the things that allowed her to go on tolerating their unmarried state was the feeling that they were already married in all but formal name. The very feel and touch of him was that of a husband rather than of a lover. She remembered how he had felt only a few months ago in Dublin – exciting, alien, slightly threatening, enticing; but now the touch of him was something more profound if less superficially thrilling. Rather than feeling alien he was almost an extension of her; to lose touch with him would be to lose a new-grown part of herself.

'Hark!' he said. 'I hear footprints!'

They paused and strained their ears. Total silence. They laughed at the eeriness of it all. The fog hedged them about, reducing the great city to a small cocoon of travelling privacy that advanced silently before them and drew itself in behind. And she was suddenly overwhelmed with a feeling of overpowering love for this man at her side, who was now so much part of her own selfhood. She pulled his arm about her and leaned her head against his shoulder.

'Feeling lost yet?' he asked.

The other good thing about their growing familiarity was that the touch of him no longer automatically stirred those elemental passions in her. Time was when all he needed to do was rake one fingernail down any two inches of her skin and she could think of nothing but racing out of their clothes and entwining with him in that most ancient and thrilling of all embraces. But no longer. The touch of him was now a universal rather than a particular delight.

'Eh?' he prompted.

There was a smugness in the question, implying that he would never get lost. And unfortunately it was true. He had an uncanny ability to make a map of anywhere he walked, even just once. And as for real, printed maps, they were meat and drink to him. The first thing he'd done when they'd taken these present lodgings, was to buy the Ordnance Survey sheet for Chelsea. And whenever Mrs Fortis, their landlady, called out, 'You going to be in there much longer, Mr Lyndon-Fury?' you knew he was reading the map. Hence the smugness.

And hence, she suddenly realized, the challenge.

Swiftly she withdrew her arm and skipped out into the middle of the road. Even in those few paces he had become invisible.

'Don't be silly,' he called out crossly.

She giggled and ran all the way to the far side. 'This is very aggravating,' he cried as he started after her.

When she was sure he was following she called out, 'Can't catch me-ee!' and ran back past their lodgings, all the way down to Phene Street. There she paused and listened for him. Not a sound. 'Napier?' she called. Still there was no sound.

Then, suddenly, from very close, came a cry of 'Damnation!' He must have walked into a gatepost or an overhanging bush or something. Like a flash she was off again, over the road and into Oakley Crescent. At the end she beetled across the Crescent and, hitching up her skirts, ran on tiptoe all the way back to where she had last heard him – feeling sure he must have passed her on the far wing. There she paused and shouted out his name – to be rewarded with a cry of vexation from what was probably only twenty paces away into the crescent, though the muffling of the fog made it sound like a hundred. 'Daisy, do stop this tomfoolery!' he called out angrily.

Laughing again she skipped off toward Oakley Street.

After two more turnings she had passed beyond the bounds of her own limited knowledge of the area. From there on it was just . . . Chelsea: endless terraced streets of almost identical houses, built for people like her mother, with more pretensions than income. Every so often she paused to make sure he was following – always slipping away when he drew close.

She grew bolder, running faster and farther between pauses. Then he changed tactics. Whenever she stopped, he stopped, too. She listened for his breathing. Surely he was as much out of breath as her? But he must have muffled it into his scarf or up his sleeve or somewhere. She called out his name but he wouldn't reply; yet the moment she moved off, she heard his footfall behind her. Perhaps its was only her playful terror, but it seemed nearer each time.

'Very clever!' she called out next time she paused. 'I know exactly what you're doing and it won't work. I'm going to run on now and not stop until you catch me. D'you hear? Napier?'

A couple squeezed past her. The man asked her if she needed assistance. She laughed guiltily and explained it was just a game.

'Irish,' the woman said to her companion as they moved off. 'Did you hear?'

'Top of the morning to ye!' she called after them.

This time she ran until not an ounce of breath was left. Curiously, it was probably safer to be out in the streets in these conditions than at any other time. What few wheeled vehicles there were tended to crawl along by the kerb, with the driver leading his horse and feeling for the gutter with his nearside foot. She ran across streets and doubled back and back again and blindly took whatever new road might offer itself. And all the while she could hear Napier running behind her, pausing when she paused, running when she ran.

At last she came to a blank wall and realized she had strayed into a cul-de-sac. It was, in fact, the lane leading into the Roman Catholic presbytery off Park Street – though it might have been in Timbuctoo for all she knew or cared by now. Far more worrying than the thought of being so ignominiously trapped was the fact that Napier had not pursued her down here.

Of course, he was just showing off how well he knew the area. He was standing there at the entry to the lane, mentally twirling his villain's moustachioes, chuckling to himself, 'Now, me proud beauty! You'll just have to turn tail and come creeping out again.' And he'd be waiting there to pounce.

'Oh!' She grasped the railings and shook them in her frustration.

'Are you in distress, miss?' came a soft whisper from the garden beyond. 'Don't worry now. I'm Father d'Arcy. You're by the presbytery in Park Walk.' He spoke in the unmistakable accent of Dublin.

'I am, Father,' she said, taking a chance. The words came out in breathless spurts. 'There's a culchie behind me not three months off the bog, whom I have the misfortune to be sparking with these days, who thinks it the greatest sport on earth to pursue me like a jack o'lantern through the fog and frighten the lights and liver out of me.'

'And how may I help, my child?' came the calm rejoinder.

'I was just thinking,' she said, swiftly doing precisely that, 'if I was to be let in here and out by your front gate, the way I could creep up on him – well, all the saints in heaven would surely smile.'

The priest chuckled and, a moment later, she heard the faint squeak of the hinges. 'Just one thing now,' he whispered as she fell in by his side.

She wished she had not dressed so warmly. She was sweating from her exertions and no matter how deep she breathed she seemed unable to get enough air. The sharp tang of sulphur did nothing to help, either. 'What would that be, Father?' she asked.

'You'll vouchsafe me one little kiss between here and the gate.'

'Father!' she exclaimed in alarm, whispering like him – and now she understood why, for in a densely populated area like this he'd be only one of several priests in the house.

'Ah, g'wan!' he wheedled. 'Just the one.'

'What of your vows?'

'Did you never kiss a priest before?'

'Indeed, I did not!'

'And yourself from Dublin, too. Well, well, well! I'll not be letting you go without it, you know,' he whispered vehemently – yet she thought she detected a sort of cat-and-mouse mischievousness in it too. It was hard to tell what his mood might be when all he'd do was whisper, though.

'A very devotional kiss,' he promised. 'Sure, it's only a venial sin. The confessional would moulder without all the kissing that goes on.'

'It may be only a venial sin to you,' she replied. 'But what about my immortal soul? Isn't it a mortal sin worth a thousand years in purgatory to tempt a man in holy orders?' That much she knew from what her mother had said.

'Jesus, Mary, and Joseph!' the reverend father whispered angrily. 'Is that all that stops you? I'll forgive you that now. And your next ten sins into the bargain, if you like.' The words were hardly out before he threw his arms around her and covered her face in kisses, seeking her lips. A moment later he found them and, crushing her tightly to him, stuck his tongue deep into her mouth.

And a moment after *that* she drew back and punched him hard in the chest, crying out, 'Napier!'

Howling with laughter, he ran off toward the front gate, whose outline was now faintly discernible against the dimly glowing fog beyond. Behind her a window was thrown up and a man's voice called out, 'You down there! You must go to the priory in the Fulham Road. Father Kelly will see all callers at the chapel there.'

'Thank you, Father,' she called back, to set his mind at rest before she turned again to kill Napier. But when he let her catch up, she was so pleased to see him again that all she did was throw herself in his arms and half-hug him to death.

'No more silly tricks?' he asked when she had got her breath back.

For reply she pulled his arm about her waist and resettled her head on his shoulder, until they were in the precise positions they had occupied when she had first slipped away. 'I suppose you know *exactly* where we are and *exactly* how many paces to go until we're home again,' she said with disgust.

'I do, I do,' he agreed playfully.

'All right, then – tell me, what's in this street we're in? What's the name of it?'

'It's called Park Walk and there's an RC presbytery and school in it.'

'Very clever.'

'In a moment we'll come to the Fulham Road and Ma McGreevey's pie shop, and, after the next street, the Union Workhouse. And there's one question I'd like to ask.'

'What?'

'Why did a young heathen like yourself pretend to be an RC to that old reprobate of a priest back there?'

'Ah!' She laughed. 'I want to tell you about that. Didn't I get the plain feeling he was such a lecherous old goat that if he knew my immortal soul was already damned to hell as a Prod, there's no telling what he'd have done.' She felt Napier shaking with silent mirth.

A full minute before they reached Ma McGreevey's there was no doubting he was right; the aroma of beef and kidney and hot piecrust was only scrumptious; she was slavering at the lips by the time they paid their threepences (for the double-meat version) and returned to the fog. There, safe in its muffled anonymity, they tore aside the paper wrappings and ate ravenously. Daisy finished hers by the time they reached the next corner. 'I could eat another, so I could,' she announced. 'Straight off.'

'Does it seem to you that the fog is thinning?' he asked.

Thinning was a relative term; instead of passing into impenetrable gloom between one lamp and the next, they could actually see the pale ghost of the one looming up just before the equally pale image of the previous one was extinguished. 'There is a bit of a breeze,' she agreed. 'D'you know what I'd really like? That sour German cabbage we had last week. Where did we get that? I've thought about it ever since.'

'That little shop next to the pub down on the Embankment,' he reminded her. 'We could go back that way if you like.'

They took the next street to the left, leading down to the river. The fog was growing thinner in the breeze; they could just discern the light from the upper windows of the workhouse, which loomed over the ordinary domestic terrace on the opposite side of the street. They came upon a group of tramps, waiting for the doors to open at half past six, now only minutes away. Napier still had half his pie, which he plainly no longer relished. He gave a replete sigh, patted his stomach, and offered it to her. But she saw one of the tramps eyeing it hungrily and gave it to him instead. He snatched it and vanished into the fog without a word before any of the others might wrest it from him.

'I say!' Napier remonstrated with her when they had passed the rank-smelling rabble. 'That was an extra-meat pie, remember? Far too good for the likes of them. I thought you were hungry, anyway.'

'Not after I saw that poor fellow's face. Didn't you feel sorry for him?'

'I hardly saw the brute.' He took her arm again. She remembered the expression on Lady Lyndon-Fury's face when she looked at the workhouse girls on Simonstown platform.

'Don't you feel sorry for them?'

'I suppose so. Sour krout, that stuff's called, by the way.'

'D'you think it's their own fault they're like that?' she persisted.

She felt him shrug. 'I think, in any sort of humane and decent society, such poor creatures wouldn't exist. I was sketching a group of them at Victoria a few days ago. They're good subjects because they're so drunk and lethargic they hardly move. So I was able to observe them for an hour or more. And I couldn't help thinking, "What use are such wretched creatures?" Their lives can have no value or purpose whatsoever. I felt quite miserable about it, actually, because, of course, the moment I folded up my sketchbook, I became like everybody else – I just walked away from them. When the history of these times comes to be written, I don't suppose we're going to cut a very good figure, you know.'

'The poor ye have with ye always,' she quoted.

'Therefore do nothing, eh? Because Jesus says it's all right? No, love. In a decent society there'd be people-catchers as well as dog-catchers.' He felt the shock of her reaction and laughed. 'I don't mean they'd be put down like dogs. Good heavens, no! They'd be taken to a warm, clean, comfortable house . . . bathed, fed, pampered. Plenty of rum or whatever's their tipple. And once they're unconscious . . . well, they'd just never come to again. Ring down the curtains.'

'Napier!'

'I know, love,' he said easily. 'Shocked me at first. But think about it. Think about the alternative. Think of condemning such wretched creatures to spending the rest of their lives in that condition – starved, verminous, their minds rotted out with liquor – only to die miserably in rain or snow, five or ten years from now. And then what was the point of all that misery? Year after year. Pointless! Think about it, that's all.'

When they arrived back in Margaretta Terrace, spiced sausage and sour krout in hand, they learned that two telegrams had come for Napier. He read one, frowned in bewilderment, read the other, turned pale, placed it on top of the other, and handed both to her without a word.

The first read: ALEXANDER MISSING PRESUMED DROWNED STOP MEMORIAL SERVICE NEXT TUESDAY 18TH STOP WANT YOU HOME STOP MAMA.

And the second: FOR SURE OUR DEAR MAMA DID NOT TELL YOU ALEX WAS ON HIS WAY TO MAKE YOU SEE THE ERROR OF YOUR WAYS AND REPENT STOP BE WARNED OF A FIERCE COLD RECEPTION HERE STOP TRAPPER.

14

A week after Napier returned to Ireland for his cousin's funeral, Daisy received a visitor. 'Why, Mr Trench!' she cried. 'What an unexpected pleasure.'

'I came over to stock up at Cornellisen's and while I was there, who should I bump into but John Wardle. He gave me your address. I hope I call at a convenient hour?'

Wardle must be a friend of Napier's, she thought; the name meant nothing to her. 'Indeed, you were never more welcome. Come in, come in.' She smiled and stepped aside. 'I want to know everything that's happened in Dublin since we left. You'll take a cup of tea? Or there's something a mite stronger in the medicine chest. Bushmills?'

'Where's the harm?' he said easily. 'There's a nip in the air. Is himself . . . er?'

'Did you not hear? His cousin Alexander was drowned. He's back home for the funeral – or memorial service. He'll be furious to have missed you.'

He stared at her, first one eye, than the other, trying to gauge the degree of bereavement so as not to overdo his own response. 'Tell him how very sorry I am to hear that.'

She slipped off his overcoat and told him to go in and sit by the fire. In the doorway to the studio he paused, taking in its details with approval. She joined him and said over his shoulder, 'The landlady hates it, but as we haven't damaged anything she can't really say much. Sit down, sit down.'

The only two seats were a bentwood chair and an artist's donkey; he chose the donkey and, leaning his elbows on the upright, stretched his hands toward the fire. The familiar seat, the glow of the coals, and the informality of the arrangement eased the atmosphere, which, until then, had been slightly tense. On the far side of the room the dresser had been covered with oilcloth and newspaper, upon which stood an array of bottles – turps, linseed oil, copal varnish, white spirit . . . and Bushmills whiskey. She found two glasses, rinsed them at the tap, wiped them dryish, and carried them and the bottle to the mantelpiece. Trench chuckled. 'Everything a painter might require. I envy your husband. He was born with a silver paint-brush in his hand.'

'D'you want water with it?' she asked, handing him a generous measure. 'I don't like this London stuff. The best water I ever had was at my aunt's down in Keelity. Straight out of the limestone. If you left a tumbler beside your bed at night, it'd be furred white by morning.'

'I'll take it as it is, thanks. *Sláinte.*' He raised the glass toward her and took the merest sip, which he let trickle slowly down his throat, savouring its afterburn and peering at her with lazily hooded eyes. 'The only news from Dublin worth reporting,' he said, 'is that the whole school is in mourning at the loss of its finest model in years.'

'Ah, g'wan!' she retorted, flushed with pleasure at the compliment.

'I tell you no lie,' he assured her, taking another sip. Then he caught sight of her sketchbook, which she had pinned to the wall behind the whiskey bottle. 'What is that?' He rose and put a finger to it. 'May I?'

'You can, of course. It's nothing. Just whiling away the time sketching out some designs for my father – O'Lindon's japanning works in Bachelor's Walk, you know.'

He nodded. 'I do know, as it happens. I saw him talking to Swan on Stephen's Green and she told me he wanted your address but she didn't know it. I say, these are pretty good, you know. I couldn't do things like this at all.'

His egocentric measure of excellence amused her. 'I've always liked doodling patterns and flowers and things.'

He flipped the pages and stopped when his eye caught a different sort of sketch. 'What's this, then?' he held it up with a smile.

'Oh!' She set down her glass and stepped lively to him to close the book. 'That's nothing.'

He dodged it away from her. 'It looks like the plan of a house to me. An artisan's dwelling or what? Are you going in for this competition on the sly?'

She paused. 'What competition?'

'For model dwellings for artisans. Sponsored by the Royal Society.'

She shook her head. 'I didn't know about that. If you promise not to breathe a word to Napier, I'll tell you.' She was, in fact, longing to show it off to a sympathetic audience. 'It's the house we're going to build one day when he's rich and famous.' She resumed her seat in the bentwood chair and watched him closely.

He turned and reassessed it in the light of this information. 'He's rich already, of course. And you don't have to be famous before you build a house.' After a pause he added, 'It's not a rich man's house, either. That's why I thought it was for an artisan.'

'So it is,' she responded stoutly. 'A painter is an artisan above all else, surely?'

He nodded at the justice of that.

'Anyway,' she went on scornfully, 'what *is* a rich man's house? A museum full of bric-à-brac that needs an army of servants, all guzzling their heads off and smashing the place up very, very slowly – telling you it came apart in their hands or they were over the other side of the room when it just lepped off the whatnot all by itself – I promise you, Mr Trench, I'll never be the mistress of that sort of household.'

'Ah!' His smile was sardonic, sceptical. 'You're a "New Woman", all right, Miss O'Lindon. It'll be interesting to observe – what happens to a "New Woman" as she grows less new?' His eyes returned to her plans. 'It would certainly take very few servants to manage this household.'

'I'm thinking we'd get by very well with only four,' she told him proudly.

He suddenly fixed her with those eyes that seemed to observe everything. 'And why should Napier not know of this just yet? I'm a bachelor myself, but I always heard there should be no secrets between man and wife.'

Something about those eyes, something in the intensity of his gaze, made Daisy tell him: 'Actually, Mr Trench, Napier and I haven't quite tied the knot just yet.'

15

Dairmid Trench held the winebottle over Daisy's glass and lifted a questioning eyebrow. She smiled. 'Sure a bird never flew on one wing.' He refilled her glass, forbearing to point out that *this* particular bird already had enough wings for a small flock. He had never met a woman with such a head for the stuff. He was pretty good that way himself. The decline into incoherence was long and gradual with him; he wasn't one of those fellows who went from sober to fluthered between the third and fourth refill. But Miss O'Lindon had him bet all round the town; she was as composed and watchful now as she had been at four that afternoon, when he had first knocked at her door.

The discovery that she was *still* Miss O'Lindon had subtly changed his perception of her. It wasn't that he was now bent on seducing her – at least, not in the sense that a seduction was now the entire purpose of this evening's tête-à-tête by candlelight, here in this dark and delightful Soho bistro. But the possibility was something to toy with. And though it would almost certainly come to nothing, it would nonetheless spice their few hours together.

Daisy was in a similar frame of mind. She knew she was too much in love with Napier even to consider another man; and yet, so secure did the conviction allow her to feel, that, paradoxically, it became quite safe to imagine the impossible – to picture herself enjoying a 'fling' with Dairmid Trench.

One thing was certain: He was not just 'another man.' Given different circumstances – if she had not met Napier, for instance – who knows what might have happened between them? His interest in her, even at that very first interview, had been more than strictly professional. No doubt of it.

She recognized the dangers, of course. And the awareness reached deep enough into her to prevent the wine from having its usual effect. She had never drunk so much and felt so little giddiness. She also knew, without ever having experienced it before, that if she went on drinking, she would pass from this cool watchfulness to complete oblivion without ever traversing the more familiar stages of giggliness, sentimentality, and passionate desire. Was it the same for him, she wondered?

'Aren't we the strangest creatures?' she mused aloud. 'People in general, I mean. Human beings. We never speak our real thoughts, do we.'

'Ah!' He smiled. 'But we give out little clues all the time. Which is much more fun.'

'Fun,' she echoed. 'That's all it is, really, isn't it. Everything we do is in search of fun.'

He shook his head, not wishing to be diverted onto this new line. 'What made you say that – about not speaking our real thoughts? D'you not speak them even to Napier?'

'Oh, I can say *anything* to him, but he doesn't seem like a separate person any longer. He's more like a new bit of me that's just grown up lately. The bit that makes me complete at last. So he doesn't count. But what I was thinking . . . it was that couple over there put the notion into my head. I'm sure they're not married. Don't stare at them, for heaven's sake! I'm sure that's an assignation going on over there. And I saw her looking this way and wondering about us. And then I realized we don't look like man and wife, either. Nor even like a betrothed couple, I'm sure. So that's what she was wondering. And of course it set me thinking, too. And then I realized I could never pass on the thought to you.'

'But you are. You're doing it now.'

'No, I'm not. Not the actual thoughts. I'm doing what you said: giving out clues.'

'As huge as high Olympus!'

'And then it also struck me – even if you were thinking the same, you'd never say it, either. And it just seemed very funny. Two people dining together, both thinking the same things, and neither of them saying a word about it. Just wondering about each other. D'you know what I mean? The unknowability of other people. I think it's desperately sad, actually.'

His smile had an edge of melancholy. 'You make me feel old at times, Miss O'Lindon.'

'You find my sentiments naïve?' She was quite prepared to believe it and would not have felt offended.

He shook his head. 'You can do with words what Napier does with his brush: show me an entirely novel world and at the same time convince me it's been there all the time. Only I've been too blind, or too conventional – which is a kind of blindness – to see it until now.'

'You admit it, then? Thoughts of that nature have crossed your mind this evening?'

He grinned and closed his eyes. 'Thoughts "of that nature," dear young lady, cross every man's mind every waking hour.' He stared at her suddenly, raising his eyebrows and leaving the obvious question on the air between them.

'Me too.' She giggled. 'But it's only for codding ourselves, isn't it. Like being in Grafton Street, all hot and bothered on a roasting summer's day, and suddenly thinking of being in the sea at Bray. There's nothing to stop you getting on the train and going out there. Or even walking to Sandymount for a dip. But you don't bother to do it. You just think about it for the cod. It's what I said before – we're just looking for fun all the time, aren't we.'

Again he did not wish to pursue that notion. He half-refilled her glass once more and said, 'To be serious, I'll tell you another thought that's cropped up in my mind from time to time – and one that, in the normal course of events, it would be impertinent to voice aloud.'

'What's that?' Her eager smile pardoned all presumption.

'My only excuse for raising it at all is that I do feel partly responsible for what's happened to you since we met last summer. I mean, if I hadn't engaged you at the school, your life might have taken a very different turn.'

She nodded solemnly. 'You mean, but for you I wouldn't now be the grass widow, or grass-mistress to be honest, of a young artist in Chelsea? But then, if I hadn't met Mrs Geech first, I wouldn't have met you. So why not blame her? And if my father had been a better provider, I wouldn't have met Mrs Geech. So actually, he's to blame for it. Where does one stop? I didn't *have* to say yes to Napier . . .' A faraway look stole into her eyes. 'Except that, of course, I had no choice.' She jerked out of it just as swiftly. 'I'm sorry!'

'Not at all. In fact, that's what I was going to mention. You strike me as a thoroughly sensible, far-sighted young woman. So why . . . ?' He shook his head in vexation. 'No! Forgive me. It's no business of mine.'

She asked it for him. 'So why have I allowed myself to get into this position?' She sighed and shook her head. 'I don't know. It just happened.' She drew a bold breath and added, 'To tell the truth, I'm beginning to think Napier has no intention of marrying me.'

He stared at her in shocked alarm.

She nodded sadly. 'I don't mean he'll desert me or anything like that. But I don't think he has any opinion of marriage at all. It's not part of his vision. In his mind it's as if we are already bound together in a union ten times more indissoluble than anything a ring on this finger might signify.' She stretched forth her gloved hand, void of any ornament.

He gave it a token squeeze. 'It's all very well.' he said dubiously, vaguely.

She knew what he meant: *Until the children start coming along*. She closed her mind against that nagging fear. Suddenly she wanted to be alone, in her bed, in the dark, clutching Napier's pillow to her face and breathing Napier's name into its softness. She wished all the hours or minutes between now and that moment could pass over in a flush. And then, because the wish seemed so churlish, she gave Trench a radiant smile and said, 'Why are we talking just about me and Napier all the time? Tell me about you. Napier said you'll have three paintings in next summer's RHA.'

It was the right thing to say to an artist, of course, and for the next three-quarters of an hour he described his work and his dreams. Not until they were in the hansom, on their way back to Chelsea – where he also had lodgings – did he return to more general themes. And now, at last, he took up her notion that all human activity was aimed at enjoyment. He told her she was being too youthful, too hedonistic.

'What d'you think people really want, then?' she asked.

'Power,' he said morosely. 'Or – more precisely – control. The painter wants pigments to behave the way he dictates. The parent wants an obedient child. The government wants a docile citizenry that pays up and doesn't grumble. The lover wants the beloved to conform to his or her desires. It's all a question of control, you see. If you want true happiness, study how to gain control.'

Sometimes in the middle of a pose it had struck her as extraordinary that there was a connection between this strange activity (or inactivity) and the money in her fledging bank account down at College Green. She would watch the clock carve out another ten minutes and a voice would say in her head, 'That's another penny in the bank.' It was meaningless. She *knew* of the connection but she couldn't *feel* it.

And it was the same now with Trench's words. She knew he was right. She knew the words had meaning. Yet she could not feel it. Instead the thoughts rolled on and fell into that mental bank called 'wisdom,' where one day, perhaps, she might redeem them.

His next words were even more bleak. 'What follows from all this is not very pleasant, of course. Love is too unreliable to ensure control. All religions talk about it but none dares trust it. Instead they rely on the old faithfuls – fear, hatred, envy, greed, vanity – and our infinite capacity for self-delusion.'

They sounded like terrible words for an artist to be using, but they sounded even more like a mere list – something that would make sense only after careful study. There was a silhouette on the curtain of a passing window. An old man. She tried to imagine his features but could not. 'The awful unknowability of people,' she murmured.

When they arrived at her lodgings the landlady bustled out with a letter for Daisy. 'Came in the last post,' she said portentously. 'Just minutes after you left. You must have walked past him.'

It was from Napier, written from Coolderg Castle; she knew his hand even without the return address on the back of the envelope. She could hardly wait to get to their room and open it. She had forgotten she'd asked Trench in for a cup of chocolate. When she heard his footfall behind her she turned and stared at him in astonishment.

He grinned. 'No point in asking who it's from. Just show me where everything is and I'll make the nightcap.'

She left him in the large cupboard that served as their kitchen and retired to the bedroom, where she tore open the letter and read:

My Darling Venus,

The family is being abominible. Alexander was on his way to persaude me to leave you. He got drunk on the boat and fell overboard but I am to blame for it all because if I had not run of with you, he would not have been send after me. That is what they're all thinking, anyway. I see it in their eyes and hear it in their tone of voice, but we are all much too well bread to say it out loud.

Anyway, they've stoped my allowance, so I can't return for the moment. I must talk them out of it somehow, for it goes without saying we could not possibly live in London without an income . . .

'Oh, Napier!' She dashed the letter from her and hastened to the door. Trench was advancing toward her, a steaming mug of chocolate in each hand. 'A drop of whiskey would be the crowning of it,' he suggested.

'I wouldn't mind,' she replied glumly. 'I could do with the oblivion.' Immediately she changed her mind. 'No! Tell me, when are you going back to Dublin?'

'What does the dear boy say?' he asked over his shoulder as he poured a couple of tots into each mug – apparently not having heard her question.

'I don't know. I'm too angry to read it all. His family is coming down on him like a hundred of bricks. And he's just letting them do it. When are you going back to Dublin?'

'Tomorrow. I have to get back for Monday.'

'I'll come with you, so,' she told him grimly. 'Someone has to put the spine back into him.'

16

Daisy sensed defeat the moment the train pulled into the Simonstown terminus and she saw that she was to be met, not by Napier, as had been arranged, but by Lady Lyndon-Fury herself. The carriage was waiting in precisely the same spot beneath the now leafless lime trees, faced ready for departure, just as it had been last May. And Herself was there at the carriage window, in profile, glancing neither right nor left. Daisy envied her that absolute self-control.

All the way up the platform and then all the way down the avenue she turned over a dozen opening sallies, from the blunt, 'Where's Napier?' to the sweet, 'Why, Lady Lyndon-Fury, how very kind of you to come and meet me!' By the time she drew level she was still undecided, so, willy-nilly, she did the one thing she had not planned: She swept past without a word.

She was immediately buoyed up by a dry chuckle from Macarty, the coachman. She drew a deep breath of exultation and stepped out with fresh heart. Though it was all of ten miles to Coolderg Castle, the road would now surely rise to meet her. She thought of her ladyship sitting in impotent rage in that cold, lacquered box of a carriage and a tingle of pleasure ran down her spine. Not deigning to turn round, she re-created the scene in her mind's eye: the low winter sun striking the tree trunks, laying dark bars across the avenue, up over the coach and horses.

She heard the scrinch of the iron tyres on the gravel, the measured plod of hooves. One of the pair had a loose shoe. 'And where d'you suppose you're going, miss?' The well-bred, commanding voice scythed the air above Daisy's head.

Without breaking or even retarding her stride, Daisy turned and looked up. The open window framed the woman as for a portrait – a study in angry uncertainty. 'Lady Lyndon-Fury,' she replied in the flattest, remotest tone. And that was all she said.

In the brief moment she allowed her eyes to linger she noted with surprise that Napier's mother was much older than memory had painted her. From this angle you could see she had white, fleshy wattles beneath her chin; and the downward-sloping folds of skin over the external corners of her eyelids were most pronounced. Her father said all the Ascendancy had those folds of skin – it was a badge of membership. Even Napier had them in an incipient fashion.

'I asked *you* a question.' Her ladyship's stress on the word turned every vertical inch between them into a mile.

'I had expected to be met by my husband,' Daisy replied without looking at her.

'Husband! Why, you . . . baggage!'

In that moment Daisy opened a book of reckoning with Lady Lyndon-Fury's name on its cover.

'At least we must talk.' Consternation was seeping in at the edges of the older woman's imperiousness.

Daisy made no reply. They had reached the main road by now. She paused to let a dray laden with malt go past; two grinning urchins, stealing a ride, hung like dirty fruit beneath its tailboard.

'Oh *do* get in,' Lady Lyndon-Fury said crossly over the click of the carriage doorlatch.

'I will not,' Daisy replied without heat, almost abstractedly. 'If you send your carriage back for me when you get home – with Napier in it – then

I'll ride.' By way of afterthought she added, 'The land my ancestors trod is good enough for me.'

How grand a thing it was to have known ancestors, she thought. Normally she would have given a farthing for the lot of them, but they were handy enough at a time like this.

Lady Lyndon-Fury slammed the door, cried out, 'Drive on, Macarty!' and drew up the window with such a vicious tug at the leather that it strained her elbow. She determined to nurse the pain all the way home, using it as a device to keep at bay the nagging realization that, in prejudging Daisy O'Lindon, she had made one of the gravest errors of her life. For, if only the girl had been of the right background, she was *exactly* what Napier needed to keep his life in order and make it lead somewhere.

Too late, Augusta Lyndon-Fury now recognized Miss O'Lindon's type – not least because she herself was of that same mould. She was born a d'Olier, of Huguenot stock. 'Not,' her father had always stressed, '*those* d'Oliers,' meaning the rich branch of the family. And that had certainly been true. It still made her shiver to remember the insolent tradesmen calling to the house for money and refusing further orders until present bills were met. And the needlework she and her sisters had been forced to take in from O'Gorman the draper's after dark – and the arrogant way Mrs O'Gorman, who would drop them a curtsy if she saw them by daylight, would pick on every little fault and make them feel like incompetent worms.

Augusta d'Olier had grown up with no illusions about the world. She had stalked into the marriage market with one single aim: to find a landed family, as yet unencumbered by serious debt but going that way, and shake it back into vigour and prosperity. In short, to do with her husband what her mother should long ago have done with her father. And she had managed it, too. But for her, Sir Lucius would now be a latter-day replica of her father – cowering behind shuttered windows, running out into the grounds and lurking behind bushes at the approach of every tradesman's dogcart up the drive.

So she had every cause to know the type of girl whom she now recognized in Daisy O'Lindon. What had prevented her from realizing it at once, the moment Napier had dropped his bombshell, was that the object of modern female ambition had changed. In her day it had been land, land, and more land. Without it there was no position in society. You could be rich as Croesus, like the Jewmen in Dublin, and you'd still have to bow and scrape before bankrupt squireens whose lands and very lives you held in mortgage. Yet if you tried to foreclose and gain title, the families would rally round and buy out the debt rather than admit you among them. That was when land was sovereign.

But nowadays it was almost an encumbrance to advancement. Smart professional men, big wholesale traders, the rentiers of industry and the railways . . . they were the vulgar 'New Men' for this vulgar 'New Age'. Beside them a gifted and fashionable painter was almost an aristocrat – at least, that was the thought which had, after much heartsearching, reconciled her and Sir Lucius to Napier's most shocking choice of profession.

Though still nursing her pained elbow, Augusta Lyndon-Fury now began to feel much calmer about Miss Daisy O'Lindon. As soon as the girl's unpardonable arrogance could be seen as the clear-sighted, sinewy sort of toughness that her ladyship herself might have deployed, it became eminently pardonable.

Now the consequences of having underestimated Miss O'Lindon began to nag at her. What would the young woman do next? She'd camp in Napier's ear – that was plain enough. She'd obviously gone directly back to Dublin after their last meeting, seething with rejection and thoughts of revenge, and had set her cap at the lad. But why him? The third and youngest son is the most expendable limb of any family – no secure perch on which to launch an attack on the main body. That would be Trapper, of course, as heir to the entire Coolderg estate.

Had it gone like this: She took up with Napier, telling him nothing about that absurd journey to Simonstown last May. In the normal course of things she would hope to get an invitation to stay at the Castle sometime in the summer or autumn – around now, in fact. Once there, she could transfer her supposed affections to her real victim: Trapper. Well, she'd have been in for a disappointment with that one! Trapper wouldn't even notice a girl who couldn't sit a horse over a five-bar gate – and she doubted if Miss O'Lindon had done more than ride the ass on the sands at Blackrock when she was four. But never mind. The plan had, in any case, gone awry long before that. Either she had fallen genuinely in love with Napier, or she had seen that his artistic talent, properly cultivated by a woman with a good eye and a clear sight of the goal, would made an even better, because subtler, vehicle for her revenge.

By the time they reached the gate lodge to Coolderg Castle she had completely reversed her earlier plans. The simple '*No*' and the crude cold shoulder would no longer serve. Miss O'Lindon was to be treated more subtly than that. She was no longer to be snubbed. Indeed, she was to be encouraged in the delusion that Napier might soon marry her. Of course, he never would. Augusta Lyndon-Fury fancied she knew her son rather better than did young Miss O'Lindon.

She smiled to herself as her nimble mind began rehearsing the arguments that would make it seem no more than the mildest change of course.

17

Daisy saw the carriage a good half-mile off, as it came down a hill on the skyline to the west. 'You may put me down now, cousin,' she said in a jocular tone to the man who had eased the way for her. 'Thank you for your trouble now.'

'Sure it was no trouble. We're three miles yet from the Castle gate, you know.'

'I don't want them to see I got a ride on the way.'

'Ah, is that the way of it.' He reined in his pony; the lightweight trap stopped with a jerk. He turned to her with the oddest expression – what would have been a broad grin but for the fact that his lips were pursed as if to whistle. And he was shaking his head slowly. The whole gesture lay ambiguously between astonishment and admiration. 'Good luck!' he called over his shoulder as he drove off, leaving her standing on a rime of frost in the unthawing shade of the ditch.

'And you!' she called after him, feeling a little sad at the necessity that had made her descend, for Stephen O'Lindon had been excellent company.

He was, as it turned out, a third cousin to her – which had taken some time to establish, once they discovered they were of the same clan. They had worked back through their respective fathers and grandfathers to arrive at Hugh O'Lindon, their common great-grandfather, a water bailiff on the Clanricarde estate, who had died in 1850. Daisy, a city girl to the very nails in her boots, thought it an amazing coincidence, but O'Lindon said it was a long family. He knew a dozen third cousins and supposed there must be more than a hundred scattered throughout Ireland – and as many again in America and England. He said everyone in these islands would have a bit of William the Conqueror's blood in him or her.

Though not yet thirty – twenty-eight, she'd have guessed – he was already a master-carpenter and joiner. In fact, if there was a call for it around here and if there weren't so many machines these days, he'd take up cabinet-making full time and drop all his jobbing work. At the moment he was a full-time servant of the Castle estate, doing all their running repairs and new building; but he was thinking of starting up in a small way on his own. He had a notion for a new kind of woodworking machine.

She'd told him about her father's japanning works in Dublin. At first she had tended to suggest it was a large and thriving establishment, to support her opening remark that she was going to the Castle. But then she heard her mother's tone, and even her mother's phrases tripping off her tongue, and had swiftly veered back toward the truth. Then she spoke of the difficulties her father had always had, getting in the debts, and how she'd tried to help him last summer. Jokingly he'd told her that if she had no luck at the Castle – he must have assumed she was going there as a companion or something – she could come and be debt-collector for his new 'undertaking'. She had used the same word, with the same slightly grand sonority, in starting to describe the japanning works, and she recognized his return of it as a gentle dig. It was all the gentler for being delivered in his mild Midlands drawl, which rolled out each syllable with almost even stress: un-der-*ta*-king.

She would have liked to talk with him longer. He had one quality in common with Napier – a total absorption, amounting almost to an obsession, with the material of his trade. In Mr O'Lindon's case it was wood; in Napier's, paint. But the quality of their infatuation was unmistakably the same. You only needed to look at the trap he had been driving to know he was an artist in wood. He had made every bit of it himself, even the wheels – as he had admitted with a most engaging mixture of shyness and pride, and after very slight inquiry on her part. It was this latter that reminded her of the artists she knew.

Napier leaped from the carriage when it was still a hundred yards off and came racing ahead of it up the road. 'Venus!' he cried, spreading wide his arms.

She ran towards him and threw herself into his embrace. For a moment or two, heedless of the crows and wrens, they covered each other's lips and cheeks with kisses, murmuring endearments and fighting for breath in between.

'What a stubborn thing you are!' he said at last. 'And then to insist on coming all this way on foot! I hope O'Lindon took you up? I shall speak to him sharply if he didn't. Oh darling, darling, darling – it's so wonderful to see you!'

The carriage caught up with him. 'Turn about in that gate,' he told Macarty.

'No, don't!' she said. 'Just wait there.'

'What now?' he asked, not entirely pleased.

'Let's go straight on to Simonstown.'

'But why? Macarty can take the trap and get your bags any time.'

'Let's catch the next train for Dublin and then go straight on to London. Hell to Coolderg Castle! Hell to your family!'

'Oh Venus, we can't.' He shook his head. 'It's all to be arranged now.'

'You're not even considering it,' she said angrily. 'What's all arranged?'

'Our wedding. Not quite arranged, but *to be* arranged.'

'Ha! I've heard that before.'

'No! My mother wants to arrange it. I don't know what you said to her. She went to Simonstown determined to put a flea in your ear, and she came back talking of nothing else but our wedding and my settlement – even though she left you behind. I can't understand it.'

Daisy felt the blood drain from her face. She couldn't understand it, either, and things she couldn't understand frightened her. 'It's a trick,' she said. 'Your mother hates me. You've only got to look in her eyes.'

'Well you come and look into her eyes now. You won't see any hatred there, I promise you.' He smiled and kissed the lobe of her ear, making her shiver. 'I always thought you were a bit of a witch, Venus, but now I'm sure.'

His jocular flattery did nothing to soothe her suspicions. In the end, curiosity got the better of her – also the thought that she and Lady Lyndon-Fury could now talk to one another absolutely without humbug; it was too enticing a prospect to pass by. Even so, as the carriage turned in at the lodge, a shiver ran through her and she implored him once again to turn about and put all his past, his family, their pretensions, their machinations . . . put it all behind them.

'What would we live on?' he asked.

She knew what she ought to reply. They could live on her earnings as a model. And he could sell his paintings. He already had one tentative portrait commission that only needed a little more persuasion to turn firm. They'd get by. It'd be a long time before they could once again enjoy even the simple luxuries they'd come to take for granted – whiskey ad lib, flowers and chocolates, dining out, the services of the laundry. But what matter? They'd get it all back sooner or later, and under their own steam this time.

That's what she ought to have said. But in the simple defeatism of those five words: What would we live on? all her questions were answered. She now knew exactly how his mother had taken his place at Simonstown station.

It was the first time since she had known Napier that he appeared something less than godlike to her. In a way she was glad of it. Their enforced separation had made her realize how much she worshipped him, and the thought had nagged her that it should be possible for a mature woman to love a man in quite a different way – clearly seeing all his faults.

She eyed him coolly enough now, yet without feeling that it threatened her love. He smiled back with pursed lips. Perhaps it would be no bad thing to see him at home – the baby of the family and monarch of nothing he surveyed.

'You didn't answer me,' he said, 'when I asked if O'Lindon had given you a ride.'

She smiled. 'I didn't take it for a question. Of course he did. He's my third cousin, you know, though I never heard of him before. It shows how families break up doesn't it, in only four generations! He's a master-joiner, I gather.'

'He's a master everything. When a bit of the castle wall started breaking away last year, he was the one who solved it. The masons hadn't an idea. Nothing under a thousand pounds, at least. But O'Lindon's way cost no more than fifty.'

'I hope you rewarded him well.'

Napier smiled at her earnestness. 'Nothing to do with me. But people like that, people whose families have been part of the estate for generations, they don't think like you and me, you know – always with one eye on reward. They feel part of it, like a family. The continuity is their reward. I've got no patience with it, mind – all that feudal nonsense. But I can't deny it's how *they* think.'

Daisy remembered how earnestly Mr O'Lindon had talked of striking out on his own, but she held her peace. 'Tell me about your sisters,' she said. 'Madeleine and Rosina, isn't it? Are they both at home?' She chuckled. 'To think I was once going to be Madeleine's maid.'

'I trust you'll have the good taste not to mention it,' he said in alarm.

The warning stung her. As if she would! Well, only if Madeleine started being offensive.

'Oh Venus, I'm sorry.' He put an arm about her and shook his head. 'I don't know what made me say that. Nerves. I suppose.'

She leaned her head on his shoulder. 'Poor man! It can't have been an easy time for you. Everyone getting at you . . . all that silent accusation.' She moved beside him and ran a fingernail lightly up the inside of his thigh, where she knew it drove him wild. 'I hope they don't expect us down for breakfast tomorrow?'

His eyes went wide with shock. 'There can be no question of that,' he said.

'Don't be absurd!'

'Honestly. Don't even think of it.'

She shook his arm in her anger. 'Don't you understand?' she cried. 'By giving way to them like that, you allow them to make all the rules. But there's no need for it. We make our own rules now and they must accept us. You tell them straight out that we're going to sleep together. And if they say no, we'll just pack up and go. We don't *need* them any more.'

He just sat there, shaking his head, staring into her eyes, hoping for her to burst out laughing and admit it was only a joke. 'Apart from anything else,' he said at last, 'just think of the example it would set the servants.'

18

Sir Lucius Lyndon-Fury, his two elder sons, Trapper and Cornel, and his elder daughter, Madeleine, had spent the day at a point-to-point organized by the Galway Blazers on the Marquess of Clanricarde's estate at Portumna. Trapper had lost two hundred guineas, which did not improve his temper. Cornel was too jarred to remember whether he had won or lost anything – but he knew it must be one or the other. Sir Lucius had won five hundred and was ready to embrace the world. Madeleine had bet nothing; but Peter Carroll, who was supposed to be sweet on her, had wagered a hundred guineas at her suggestion and lost it all, which was a hundred guineas more than he could afford.

'A satisfactory test of the fellow's affections, wouldn't you say?' Trapper gave her a squeeze too hard to be friendly.

Angrily she shrugged him off.

'Ah, but do you like him any the better for it?' Napier asked her.

She had to admit she did not.

Daisy listened to Napier joking with his father and siblings; asking all the right questions about the horses and riders, picking up their admiration or scorn, and wishing hypocritically that he'd joined them after all. It was a Napier she had not seen before. He was, she realized, making tiny sacrificial offerings of his principles to propitiate these gods of his hearth and home. He hadn't the slightest interest in the Blazers, nor bloodstock, nor betting – at least, not on horses. She remembered how he'd regaled the life class last summer with his account of his Uncle Guy, 'who had given all his money away to sick animals' – adding that, 'of course, he didn't know they were sick at the time he bet on them.' It was a far cry from the Napier she now saw at Coolderg Castle.

The others, after brief, informal introductions while they hopped about, trying to pull off their riding boots and gaiters, ignored her – a neglect to which Napier showed himself sensitive the moment they were alone again. 'Don't pay them too much attention, Venus,' he said, slipping an arm about her. 'Horse people aren't like the rest of the world. Something you'd take for out-and-out rudeness in a Claddagh fishwife is everyday behaviour among them.'

She folded herself into his embrace, hugging him tightly.

'You're shivering,' he said, slightly surprised. 'Are you cold? This wretched place never heats up properly, I know.'

She shook her head and clung to him even tighter. 'Too many unknowns,' she murmured.

'You needn't worry about them, my darling. It's just a matter of handling them properly.'

'Not truly being oneself, you mean?' she asked.

He chuckled, slightly uncomfortably. 'They weren't being truly themselves, either, you know. When they left here this morning, you were persona absolutely non grata according to my mother. You were to be turned around at Simonstown and sent back to Dublin with a flea in your ear . . .'

'Napier,' she interrupted.

'Just a mo'. Instead, when they come back, they find you a guest under our roof. And yet did you notice even the slightest flicker of surprise? Even from Cornel, drunk as he is?'

It occurred to Daisy that they weren't actually interested enough in either Napier or herself to feel any emotion, one way or the other. She said, 'Have we got time for a stroll before supper?'

'Dinner,' he corrected. 'I should think so.'

He helped her on with her coat and muffler and they strolled out into a frosty twilight with the first stars kindling. At the end of the carriage sweep she turned and took her first unhurried look at the place – a hodge-podge of buildings and styles if ever she saw one.

The dominant feature was a tall, square tower of the common Irish kind, this one rather larger than most. The high, crenellated wall that had once surrounded it was now slighted on two sides – to the west, facing Lough Cool, and to the east, facing the mountains. Built hard against the southern wall of the tower was a large, three-storey house whose roof was some two-thirds the height of the tower.

'There's still a bit of an old Norman wall round the side,' Napier told her. 'Or so people say. You never know how true these things are. Round here they'll swear there's a secret underground passage right across Lough Cool to Linford in County Clare. You know the history of the place, I suppose?'

She chuckled. 'Only my family's version of it. What's yours?'

They walked on into the deerpark, pausing to turn occasionally when he pointed out some particular feature. 'The castle itself, the big square tower, was built by your kinsmen around 1500. That was when Fergal O'Lindon got pushed out of Galway and took refuge up in the Slieve Derg. There he formed an alliance with the O'Laughlins' – he pointed northeast, toward the western end of King's County – 'and helped them drive out the O'Carrolls.' He pointed southeast, toward Tipperary. 'He claimed much of the O'Carroll lands as his reward. Everything on this side of the Slieve Derg. It was too much, in fact, because he then fell out with the O'Laughlins. Naturally, since this is Ireland, he turned to the O'Carrolls and formed an alliance with them – to drive out the O'Laughlins.'

'But why would the O'Carrolls agree to that?' Daisy asked. The way she had heard the tale, the O'Laughlins had *invited* her forebears across the

Shannon to help deliver a mortal blow to the O'Carrolls, promising them all the O'Carroll lands in Keelity by way of reward; only when they reneged on the promise did the O'Lindons switch their allegiance. Which version was true? Both probably.

'I don't know. Fond of a good fight, I suppose. Anyway, the loss of so much land had left the O'Carrolls weaker. It paid them to see the O'Laughlins cut down a bit, too. And that's how the O'Lindons got hold of most of County Keelity. And Fergal built that huge tower of a castle to make sure they kept it – which they did for six generations. D'you know the walls at the base are nearly twenty feet thick!'

'What happened after six generations?' she asked.

'Cromwell. Or the dreaded Hardress Waller.' He changed direction, leading her across the park on a path that would skirt around the house to the north and approach it along the Shannon callows, which were flooded at that time of year, doubling the size of Lough Cool. 'And some very long memories,' he added.

'And that big house that's been added on to it,' she said before they lost this view of the place, 'would that be Georgian?'

'Yes, I don't know who started calling it that. We always called it classical.'

'It's beautiful. Why wouldn't you just knock that ugly old tower and keep the classical bit?'

He pretended to be frightened, clapping his hand to her lips. 'For the love of God, don't let him hear you or he'll murther you in your bed tonight.'

Laughing, she struggled free of his hand. 'Who? Your father?'

'No – though he wouldn't have you in the house, either. But I'm talking about your unquiet ancestor – Fergal O'Lindon. Didn't you know he haunts the place? Him and about fifty others. Cromwell's men pushed a couple of dozen O'Lindons off the battlements. They're all buried under the ballroom floor. Anyway, the classical house is a bit of a sham, really. It's just one vast ballroom-cum-drawing room on the ground floor and family bedrooms above that. And guest bedrooms.' He paused and pointed at the house. 'See the very last window up there on the left? That's your room.'

'And which is yours?' she asked archly.

His finger traversed the entire eastern façade and rested on the main tower. 'The very last, topmost window on the right.'

'That's about half a mile of floorboards,' she said in pretend horror. 'Do they creak?'

He hugged her awhile in silence and then murmured, 'Please. Don't tempt me.'

'Let's go into that woodland now,' she said. 'There's time, surely? Lord, but I've been desperate for the want of you.'

He closed his eyes tight, shook his head, and sighed. 'There'll be gamekeepers on the prowl. It's terrible, but there's nowhere here, indoors or out, where we'd be unobserved. I hate it. This place. This whole way of life. It isn't real living. We're just "Example Setters", not people.'

She sniffed. 'And what about Cornel? What sort of example is that!'

'Oh, you can get drunk. You can fight. Swear . . . commit murder. But you don't commit the two really unforgivable sins: fornicating within the county boundary and seating Roman Catholics at table. Don't say anything about your mother being an RC, by the way.'

'Well, what do I say?'

'Just avoid it. It's to be kept from them at all costs. Especially the Pater.'

Easily said, she thought glumly. 'Which would have been my room if I'd been Madeleine's maid?' she asked.

He refused to take the question seriously. 'You'd never have been that,' was the only answer he'd give. 'There now.' He pointed out a straggle of buildings inside the dilapidated north wall of the castle. 'That's what they say is the original Norman wall. The one that forms this side of the kitchen.'

'What was it in those days?' she asked. 'A Norman castle?'

He shrugged. 'Or an abbey. They say that's why the farm buildings are so extensive. Those monks certainly knew how to look after their bellies.'

In the last of the twilight she could just about see what he meant. South of the castle demesne, all along the edge of the callows, was a straggle of stables and farm buildings that dwarfed the big house itself – in extent, if not in height. They could hear the lowing of cattle, for milking was coming to an end and the cows that had already been turned out were bellowing for their turnips and hay. A lantern, borne by a hand no longer visible, went swinging across a pasture. 'Locking in the hens,' Napier commented.

'Who?' she asked.

'Haven't the foggiest.'

The ghost of a limestone wall loomed up before them. 'The northwest tower,' he informed her.

'Is it used?'

Reluctantly he answered: 'By the ladies' maids.' A moment later the lights from the drawing room in the Georgian wing revealed what he had brought her to see – namely, that the whole outer wall on this side of the keep had been removed. 'Slighted by Cromwell,' he said.

'Wouldn't you ever build it back?' she asked, gauging the distance between the ladies' maids' tower and the much smaller, half-derelict turret at the south-western corner.

'For fear of the populace?' he asked, in a tone that dismissed the notion.

'For fear of the O'Lindons,' she said solemnly.

'Ah, well, now there you may have a point,' he allowed.
'You've sort of skirted over that bit of the history.'
He cleared his throat self-importantly.
She dug him in the ribs. 'No. Properly now.'
'Well, it's never been any great secret, I'm sure. The Furys, who were linked by marriage to both the O'Carrolls and the O'Laughlins, got in cahoots with Cromwell's men. Actually, it wasn't so simple as that. Did you notice a very tall tree – it's too dark now – but did you see it over there to the north? A Noble Fir.'
'I think so.'
'Well that's on the bank of a little tributary of the Shannon called the Flaxmills River. It's got some old Erse name, too, but everyone calls it that from the Quaker flax mill that used to work off its power. It's a distillery now, in fact.'
'And still Quaker?' she asked in surprise.
'Lyndon-Fury,' he said. 'Like everything else around here. Anyway, all the O'Lindons north of the town of Flaxmills were Protestant. All the ones this side were Roman Catholics. I don't know why. And Lucius Fury the First – I don't suppose he was actually the first, but he was the first of this Coolderg dynasty – he married a Caroline O'Lindon, one of the Protestant O'Lindons from Flaxmills town. In fact, there's a huge stone on top of that tower you're so keen to pull down, and it has Caroline's monogram on it and the date 1689, the year that she died – the famous O'Lindon Stone . . .'
Daisy yawned. 'Does any of this matter, Napier? I didn't think it was going to be . . .'
'Matter?' he exploded jocularly. '*They'll* expect you know all the family history, seed breed and generation. You won't understand half the things they talk to you about unless you know at least these rudimentary . . .'
'All right, all right. Caroline O'Lindon, the Prod, married . . .'
'Don't say Prod. Anyway, the point was that her father, William O'Lindon, felt he was the rightful heir of Fergal's body. He'd emigrated to England in James I's time, converted to Anglican, and come back under those first Stuart plantations, expecting to be given Coolderg as his reward. Instead, he got a very nice estate in Flaxmills called Sharavogue. But it rankled with him, so when Cromwell went storming through Ireland, booting every Roman Catholic landowner in sight out into Connemara, it seemed natural for Lucius Fury to marry Caroline O'Lindon and, with the treachery of the O'Laughlins and the O'Carrolls thrown in, take over the Coolderg estate from the papist usurpers. In those days the estate comprised four-fifths of the entire County Keelity, but gamblers like my father, huntin'-lunatics like Trapper, and drunkards like Cornel have whittled it down a bit.'
'And how did it became *Lyndon*-Fury, after all that?'

'It was in the marriage settlement. Only the clerk left off the *O* and spelled it with a *y* when they did the letters-patent.'

They started strolling across the lawn, where the slighted wall had once stood, making for the garden door into the ballroom. 'What happened to the O'Lindons of Sharavogue?' she asked. 'I never heard tell of them.'

'They made the mistake of joining in the rebellion of 'Ninety-eight. We own Sharavogue now but the house stands empty.'

'But the O'Lindon are *all* Protestant, surely. At least, all the ones I know are.'

He sucked in his breath in agreement. 'But they converted too late to do themselves much good – in the way of being given lands and titles. Still, it's ensured them steady work down the years. We've never employed any Roman Catholics on any of our farms, nor in the distillery, the sawmills . . . any of those places. Scullery maids and things like that, of course, but none of the upper servants.'

Her silence puzzled him. When they paused at the ballroom door, he gave her a squeeze and said, 'Sadder and wiser, eh?'

'God!' she exploded vehemently. 'Wouldn't you sometimes just wish Ireland would go away and leave you alone?'

He roared with laughter and kissed her warmly on the neck. 'Oh, Venus!' he murmured. 'You're the best of all. I do love you so.'

19

Sir Lucius, still warm with his winnings, carved Daisy a generous portion of roast beef – having told her that the Hereford which furnished it was reared on the finest pasture in the Irish Midlands, which therefore made it the best beef in all the world. 'You,' he told her, 'are the first O'Lindon to be seated at this table since the fifteenth of September, sixteen eighty-nine. That's not too bloody for you, I hope? I know how you Dubliners like your beef well ruined in the oven.'

Daisy's smile accepted the almost raw slices on her plate. Watching her, Napier, at his father's left, admired her ability not to reply, not to rise to these little probing challenges the family flung before her. 'Would that have been a Thursday?' she asked.

Madeleine, to Daisy's right, burst into laughter, which she quickly suppressed.

'Hanged if I know,' Sir Lucius said. 'Why?'

Daisy shrugged jovially. 'It's a shame to have so many details and just to miss the last one like that.'

'Hmph!' He eyed her warily, but still with some amusement. 'Aren't you curious what happened that day, Miss O'Lindon? I mean – as to *why* I may be so sure?'

Daisy screwed up her eyes and took a wild guess, blessing the inspiration that had led Napier to prime her during their walk. 'Isn't that the day Caroline O'Lindon died? The one who married the first Lucius Lyndon-Fury?'

'Good girl yourself,' murmured Cornel, to Napier's left.

All three sons were on that side, facing the two daughters and Daisy. In some curious way it produced a more belligerent atmosphere than the conventional mixture of alternating males and females would have done. But Daisy was glad of it, since it put the two sisters on her side in every sense of the word.

'Someone who actually knows the family history,' Madeleine said approvingly.

'Only from the O'Lindon point of view,' Daisy assured her.

'Well,' Sir Lucius cut in, 'without Caroline, we'd have had no very legitimate claim to this estate. Not that that ever stopped anyone with the sense to stay on the right side of Cromwell, but still it's nice to have that extra bit of legitimacy. Caroline was my fourth-great grandmother. I wonder now – what would she be to you?'

Daisy shook her head. 'I don't know that we're related to her at all, Sir Lucius. Except in the way all O'Lindons must somehow be kin. My father's a third generation Dubliner.'

'He's a rare animal, so.'

'Indeed. But both his brothers are back here in Keelity. They have the big builders' providers in Borrisokane – O'Lindon Brothers. Perhaps you know them?'

An anxious ripple passed round the table. 'We know them,' Sir Lucius said curtly. 'We used to deal with them quite a bit.'

'One of them married a papist, didn't he,' Napier said, and though his tone was conversational, his eyes warned her that that was why the topic was so delicate.

'I have no idea,' Daisy replied.

'Are you fond of fish, Miss O'Lindon?' Trapper asked suddenly. Of all the family he seemed the least amicable toward her.

'If it's fresh.' Daisy replied, more than a little mystified. 'Is there good fishing in the lough?'

Napier forced a laugh. 'There's better fishing at this table. What he's really asking – in view of your uncle's unfortunate lapse – is which foot you kick with, dear?' He stared wearily at Trapper. 'As if it needed asking.'

Daisy glanced swiftly around the table. All eyes were upon her. She turned to Sir Lucius. 'I'm more or less the same as Napier,' she told him, using her most bewitching smile.

Madeleine laughed. 'Best to inquire no further, then.'

'Dairmid Trench asked me what am I,' Napier cut in. 'Nothing in particular, says I. Ah well, says he, in Ireland that would *count* as Protestant.'

Sir Lucius stared at him coldly, but the moment of danger had passed.

Trapper passed on a bit of crack he'd heard at the races, about how Colonel Brailton had let off Tully Hall, his family's old town house, into lodgings. 'But he couldn't abide the thought of knowing that some of his lodgers would be living in taller rooms than he himself – those big rooms on the first floor, you know. So he got Stephen O'Lindon to divide that entire floor *horizontally*. It's now a four-storey house, plus basement.'

'But those rooms weren't so very tall,' his mother objected.

'Thirteen foot,' he confirmed. 'That's the joke. They now have ceilings a mere five-foot-eleven high. Poor old Scully, the plasterer, nearly crippled his back.'

'But where's the point?' Cornel asked. 'Who can live in such rooms?'

'Scotch judges,' Madeleine suggested. 'They'd get free powder on their wigs just by standing up.'

'No, wait!' Trapper cried over the laughter. 'It's even better. They're for people of diminutive stature! That's the Colonel's orders.' When the laughter died he added more seriously, 'They'd have been only five-foot-six if O'Lindon hadn't put iron rods under every other joist. He didn't cripple himself either. He put up the plastering lath before the floorboards – so he could poke his head up between the joists.'

Sir Lucius sucked shreds of beef from between his teeth. 'Yes,' he mused. 'You'd want to be up early to catch *that* one out.'

20

If Daisy had entertained any hope that Napier might come night-crawling to her, despite the creaking passageways of the old castle, they were dashed the moment she realized that the other bed in her room was Madeleine's, and not, as she had assumed, spare.

Madeleine at once dismissed the two maids who had been sent to help them undress. One of them was Mary Rourke, the cripple-girl who had beaten Daisy to the post last spring; she gave no sign of recognizing her travelling companion of that day.

'It's not where I usually sleep,' Madeleine informed Daisy with a knowing grin, 'but Mama thought you'd prefer some company. I confess the same thought had crossed my own mind though I had not seen myself as a candidate for the office. I warn you – I snore, or so Rosie says.'

'I'm sure I'm most obliged to you both.' Daisy spoke guardedly, being uncertain as yet quite how to take her future sister-in-law.

The knowing grin was broader and even more knowing. 'Would you come out of that! We both know the company you'd prefer, so, as far as I'm concerned, if Napier wants to freeze his feet off between his room and here, I'll just snore on.'

'Madeleine!' Daisy laughed in shocked discomfort.

'What? Sure, haven't we all cut that caper. And anyway the damage is done now . . . isn't it?'

Daisy swallowed hard, glanced down at her belly, and then looked swiftly elsewhere.

'Yes,' Madeleine added. 'I'm talking about *that.*'

'How did you know? I didn't even tell him yet.' She closed her eyes and slumped on the bed. 'Oh God! Is it so obvious?'

'Not at all,' Madeleine patted Daisy's arm and sat on the edge of her own bed, facing her.

Another small terror crossed Daisy's mind. 'Does your mother know, d'you think?' she asked.

'If *I* can guess it, you may be sure she has. Perhaps that's what changed her mind. When you wrote to Napier, saying you were coming here – you didn't mention it then?'

'Not the vaguest hint. Does it *show*?' She flattened her bosom and peered down at the dress over her belly. 'The thing is, I don't want Napier to say he'll marry me just because of this.'

'Which he would, of course.'

'Quite. So don't you be telling him.'

Madeleine lifted her eyebrows and shrugged. 'Well, I think you're a fool. But then' – she smiled sweetly – 'you've already proved that, haven't you!' She laughed. 'Don't mind me. When they dished out the tact I was lost at sea.' She frowned. 'Why *did* my mother change her mind? Perhaps she hasn't guessed, you know. She sallied forth this morning, bayonets fixed, ready to send you back to Dublin or Hades. Then she does a complete volt-face and brings you back with her . . .'

'No, she did not!'

'Oh?'

Daisy lowered her voice and glanced nervously toward the door. 'I told her I didn't give a damn whether she wanted to see me or not. I'd come to talk with Napier, not her. And then I set out walking.'

Madeleine's eyes seemed to thrust forward in their sockets.

'And when her coach caught up with me, she offered me a ride and I said no thanks.'

'Ah!' Madeleine relaxed into satisfaction at that. 'I think I have it now. She probably realized that you are just what Napier needs.' She started to unhook her bodice. 'I shouldn't have sent those two away. Would you ever undo those two for me?' She lifted her arm and turned sideways on.

'Mary Rourke and I travelled down together to Simonstown last May, you know. We were both . . .'

'Yes. I heard.' She chuckled. 'Dear Mama's policy of rejecting pretty maids may not be the wisest, after all. They only come back to haunt her in another form. Shall I do your top hooks?'

Daisy, though perfectly capable of dressing and undressing to the last hook and bow, let Madeleine oblige her – and to go on to her corset strings. 'Is it wise to have done them so tight?' Madeleine asked when the stays creaked at their release.

'It doesn't feel like a sickness to me, so I shan't treat it as such.'

'Oh, I'd be just the contrary,' Madeleine sighed, stretching herself luxuriously as Daisy returned the favour and loosened her corsets for her. 'I'd try and make sure it was summertime and I'd have a swinging seat put up in the summer house and I'd sprawl there on cushions and drink sherbet and read romantic tales all day long. We get little enough consideration as it is. It becomes almost a duty to milk our few privileges for all they're worth.' She shivered at the cold, damp touch of her calico nightgown; when she stood, her corset fell with a thump; she stepped out of it and left it just where it lay.

An instinct for tidiness made Daisy stoop to pick it up but Madeleine laughed and placed a cold, stockinged foot lightly on Daisy's fingers. 'You *didn't* get the position,' she said in a tone she might use for a simpleton. 'Remember?'

Daisy, feeling a mite awkward about her own much grander nightdress of silk, folded her underclothes carefully.

Madeleine, meanwhile, was holding her toothbrush in her hand and staring at it in consternation. Several times she gave her teeth a rub or two and then stared at it again.

'Something wrong?' Daisy asked, wetting her own toothbrush and shaking a little powder into its tufts.

'It won't foam.'

Daisy glanced briefly at the heavens and then, grasping Madeleine's hand, pulled the brush toward her and shook a little powder upon it, too. 'Try it now,' she said.

Gingerly Madeleine gave her teeth a rub or two. 'Amazing!' she exclaimed among the bubbles that were already gathering on her lips.

'You never knew that?' Daisy asked as they swilled their teeth and spat out into the old jordan.

Madeleine pulled a rueful face and shook her head.

'Does that mean,' Daisy went on, 'that this is the first night in your life you've got undressed without the help of a maid?'

'I suppose so. I always thought toothbrushes foamed of their own accord, you know.'

'By magic?'

Madeleine shrugged. 'I never even questioned it at all at all.'

Of all the novel insights she had gained that day, none so clearly revealed to Daisy how vast a gulf separated her from these people and their way of life. It began to worry her that Napier, for all his love of slumming and the artistic life, might only be playing at it; deep down, in his soul, he might not be as free of it as he liked to think.

So when Madeleine leaped between her sheets and shivered and suggested they should share the same bed for the warmth that was in it, Daisy agreed readily enough. She and her sister, Maude, always used to cuddle together in winter, since the number of occasions on which they could feign sickness and claim an all-night fire in the bedroom was limited.

But warmth was not her motive now; she hoped that, in the intimacy of a shared bed, Madeleine might be a little more forthcoming about Napier than if they were feet apart.

Perhaps Madeleine sensed something of her intentions for her first words were, 'I wonder if Napier knows this amazing fact about toothbrushes?'

'Well *I* certainly never put his powder on for him.'

'A very diplomatic answer, my dear.'

'In what way?'

'It leaves me unable to deduce whether you and he ever actually shared the same abode. Either you're hopeless at twigging when people are asking you questions – like Trapper asking if you're fond of fish – or you're a veritable genius at it and say these artless things to brush the matter aside.'

'Well, to set your mind at rest – Napier and I never lived together in Dublin . . . well, only for a day or two before we took the boat. But we did in Chelsea. God, I was there only last week and already it seems months ago!'

'I wonder what it's like, being with a man all the time. Night after night.'

Daisy, not liking this turn of conversation, said, 'I never thought about it.'

'Never?'

'No.'

Madeleine gave a single, rueful laugh. 'D'you suppose, Daisy dear, that if we remain friends for the next sixty years, we might eventually come across some teeny little thing we have in common?'

Daisy laughed and let the topic expire in silence.

'You *are* a veritable genius,' Madeleine decided.

'Talking of that particular man,' Daisy said, slightly clumsily, 'he's . . . I don't know . . . he's a different person down here.'

'Everyone is, surely, when their parents are around.'

'Yes, but even when they're not. In any case, I don't mean that kind of difference. If you'd met him in Dublin, you'd know what I mean. He was the leading spirit of his year – of the whole school, in fact. Even Dairmid Trench treated him more like a colleague than a pupil. I mean, in the artistic world he's . . . well, you couldn't say he's *somebody*, not yet. But he will be. But what I'm saying is he's not *nobody.*'

'And here you think he is?'

'That's how you all treat him. And he just seems to accept it. He doesn't *need* this wretched allowance. He doesn't *need* any of you.'

'Is that what you came all the way from London to tell him?'

'Yes. It's almost as if he were two people. Gay and self-reliant when he's on his own . . .'

'And little brother back here. You do surprise me, Daisy. I can't imagine him standing up on his own two feet in the way you say.'

After a silence Daisy murmured, 'I've got to get him away from here, then.'

And after an even longer silence Madeleine responded, 'Despite all their endless bickering, he is inordinately fond of his mother, you know.'

In its desultory way the conversation turned to life in Dublin and London, cities that Madeleine knew only from brief visits during the season, when, of course, she had been up to her eyeballs in chaperones, as she put it. The notion of strolling by herself in either place was unthinkable; picnicking in Stephen's Green or promenading down the Chelsea Embankment, were events so far beyond her horizon that she could only marvel at the ordinariness of Daisy's accounts of them. 'When you're married to Napier,' she said, 'may I come and stay with you and we can do all those things? It would be quite respectable if you were a married lady.'

Daisy felt a passing awareness that her own life was, after all, not as devoid of privilege as she had thought. 'Of course,' she said.

And so, with ever-lengthening pauses between their words, they pipedreamed their way to sleep once more.

Later that night, well into the small hours, Daisy came suddenly wide awake, filled with the certainty that Napier was creeping down the passage toward her room. Madeleine, despite her assertion, was not a snorer – at least, she was not snoring at that moment. Gingerly Daisy slipped from between the sheets and went tiptoeing toward the door. It opened on well-oiled hinges, unlike several other doors she had had cause to notice since her arrival, so Napier must have sneaked down here with an oil can at some moment in the past few days.

She saw him then, standing in his nightshirt in the moonlight at the farther end of the passage. He was staring out through the window, down at something on the ground.

'Napier!' She whispered his name as loudly as she dared.

He turned and stared at her; but still he made no move.

A moment later she jumped as something gripped her elbow.

'Only me,' Madeleine whispered at her left ear. 'Looking for ghosts?'

Daisy pointed at Napier – or, rather, at where he had been standing, for, the moment he saw his sister there, he had retreated out of sight.

'He probably tried it and gave up. There's only one way to get along this passage without making a floorboard creak.'

'How?'

The woman dug her in the ribs. 'Caught you! You *do* think about it sometimes. Tell him he must sort of edge along like this.' And she made a stiff diagonal of her body, resting the palms of her hands against the inner wall and the soles of her feet against the skirting board on the outer wall, with only her toes on the actual floorboards, at the very edge. She sidled crabwise for a demonstrational pace or two and then stood upright.

The floorboard gave out a resounding groan. A moment later Sir Lucius was at his door, peering suspiciously up and down. 'You two?' he barked, seeing no more than two pale shapes in the moonlight. 'What's going on?'

'Nothing's going on, Papa dear,' Madeleine replied wearily. 'Daisy's after seeing Fergal O'Lindon.'

'Ah!' His tone was at once more alert and interested. He shuffled toward them down the passageway; the floorboards giving out shrieking proof at every pace of the impossible journey Napier had begun. 'Tall fellow?' he asked. 'About Napier's height and build? Long white nightshirt? Standing by that end window, staring down into the park?'

'About Napier's height and build,' Daisy agreed cautiously.

'And you were standing . . . ?'

'Here.' She showed him.

He stood on the spot for a moment, hoping for a repeat of the manifestation, but they saw and heard nothing – beyond the occasional groan of a floorboard as it returned to its usual position.

He went on his way happy enough, though, saying that old Fergal hadn't been seen for at least five years and that it would bring her good luck.

As soon as they were back in bed, Madeleine cuddled up to her tightly and gave a theatrical shiver. 'Suppose it was old Fergal, after all!' she whispered. 'And you're the rightful owner of the place and all that. Ghosts would know that sort of thing – especially when one of their descendants turns up.'

She shivered again.

'Ghosts!' Daisy echoed scornfully. Outside a floorboard creaked, and Daisy could not suppress a little shiver.

21

The following morning they woke up to a white world. Some six inches of snow had fallen between the events that had disturbed Sir Lucius and the coming of the dawn. The maids brought hot water and stayed to help them dress. Daisy decided that she could happily grow used to the system. It surprised her to hear Madeleine talking to them more as junior members of the family than as servants. She knew all their personal histories and troubles. When Bridey Finn, the young girl who assisted Daisy, mentioned that her mother had an ague, she was told to take the rest of the day off and to bring home some pie from the castle – and to say that her ladyship would call with something else tomorrow.

'You're very good to them,' Daisy commented on their way down to breakfast.

'Sure what does it cost?' Madeleine replied. 'A slice of pie. She'll catch up on her work, anyway. They've got to feel they belong more up at the castle than down in the town. Next time someone gets the brilliant idea to hamstring one of our horses or fire our ricks, word will somehow get to us.'

'D'you mean she'd inform?' Daisy asked in horror.

Madeleine, eyes flaring in mock alarm, clapped her soap-scented hand over Daisy's lips. 'Would you houl' your wisht!' she cried. 'An informer is one who works for the other side.'

They arrived at the breakfast table to find themselves the first down. 'Not the first *up*, you understand,' Madeleine joked. 'Papa and Trapper and Rosina will be in the saddle even as we speak, laying a trail of halfbred hoofprints all over the park.'

'Wouldn't you have preferred to be with them?' Daisy asked.

She shook her head and shivered.

Napier came in at that moment, rubbing his hands against the cold.

'There is a stepmother's breath in the air, this morning,' he declared. His sketchbook was still under his arm. His pale skin and flushed cheek showed he, too, had been out and about.

'Let's have a peep,' Madeleine begged.

He passed it over without a word, not taking his eyes off Daisy, whom he kissed tenderly while his sister pretended to have her nose buried in the book.

'Not bad,' she commented, passing it back to him. 'A shilling a piece, I'd say.'

'Half a crown,' Daisy corrected her evenly, causing Madeleine to remember her quaint assertion that Napier could, in fact, live off his art.

Daisy glanced over her shoulder and then lowered her voice to ask him, 'Weren't you kill't with the cold last night?'

His jaw dropped and he stared at both women in consternation.

'There's no point pretending,' she went on, 'I saw you.'

Some secret glance must have passed between him and Madeleine for his alarm was replaced by a kind of playful vigilance. 'Saw me where?' he asked.

'You know jolly well.' She gave the porridge a miss and helped herself generously to the kedgeree.

'She saw old Fergal in the small hours but she's convinced herself it was you. The pater came out with a nightlight and blunderbuss.'

'Ha ha,' Daisy said in a yawn. 'I know jolly well it was Napier, so you can stop all that.'

A commotion in the hall was followed by the irruption of the three riders, who left a trail of mud and slush behind them. It took long to melt in the cold castle air.

Sir Lucius eyed Daisy over the tops of glasses he was not, in fact, wearing at that moment. 'Miss O'Lindon,' he said in mild but jocular surprise. 'I didn't expect to see you up so bright and early.' He turned to Napier. 'She saw old Fergal last night, you know.'

He behaved as if it were a complete surprise, turning to her with excited eyes and saying, 'No! Did you really?'

'Sure I never saw anything worse than myself, thank God,' she said, pointedly closing the subject.

Her annoyance at these stupid games soon evaporated, however, when she and Napier went strolling in the park after breakfast; in fact, she forgot the whole episode, having far more important things on her mind just then. The winter squalls that had whipped up the snowclouds overnight had died. They were only three days short of the solstice and the low sun, though it shone down through a cloudless sky of a quite startling blue, brought almost no heat with it. Their breath hung in gilded wreaths against the deep blue pools of snowshadow. When they came to an old forked elm Napier wedged his sketchbook into its crutch, peeled off his gloves, and began to make snowballs and pelt her. Laughing like a child again, she ran a little way off and then turned to give him two for one. She proved to enjoy the better circulation for in the end it was his fingers that cried mercy; and tears of unfeigned agony sprouted in his eyes as he tried to suck life and sensation back into their icy tips.

'Serves you right,' she sneered while she shook her hair vigorously to get out the snow where his shots had landed. She took up his sketchbook and offered it to him, but he shook his head. 'Let's just walk. We'll pick it up on the way back.'

Idly she flipped through its pages, marvelling, as always, at the richness of his talent. 'They're worth more than half a crown,' she said vehemently as she wedged it back in its place. 'I wasn't just joking.'

'I forgot to tell you, I had a letter from Trench yesterday. Or the day before. They're going to start a new society of artists in London – people like us who are sick of academic art. He thinks I ought to submit the Joan of Arc painting.'

'But that's wonderful, Napier! You will, of course.' She grabbed his wrists and thrust his hands under her arms. 'Warms them there,' she said.

His eyes gazed into hers. 'Oh, Daisy,' he murmured.

'Let's go back to London, darling. Today. You don't belong here any more. And I *certainly* don't!'

He gazed over her shoulders with half-closed eyes.

'Napier?' she prompted.

'I don't think anyone has ever painted snow properly, you know,' he said. 'We think it's like a blanket, covering the earth, but it's not. It's not a *thing* at all. It's pure light.'

'Shall we?' She withdrew an inch or two, bringing his hands onto the sides of her breasts.

He became aware of it, of the echoes of her last question, and a different look stole into his eyes. 'Here?' he asked.

'I said let you and me go to London. Today.'

His hands fell to his sides; he tucked them in his pockets, feeling for his gloves. 'Can't do that, old girl.'

'Why not? You don't belong here any more. Surely you can see that? You've outgrown it.'

He smiled wanly. 'I haven't outgrown the need for my allowance.'

'Divil take your old allowance! You *have* outgrown the need for that, too. That's what I keep trying to tell you. Besides, I don't like you here.'

'Oh really?' A slightly frosty edge to his voice.

She closed the small gap between them and laid her head briefly upon his shoulder. 'I don't mean I don't like *you,* silly. I mean I don't like what this place does to you. It changes you. Can't you feel it? They treat you like an amusing . . . I don't know. Almost as if you're the simple one of the family. It's more than baby brother. They just don't understand . . . you . . . anything. I mean any of the things you believe in. *We* believe in. It's right over their heads.'

'I think Madeleine does.'

'Don't be quibbling, now. Anyway, she doesn't. To her, art is just a grand trick for getting to Dublin or London or somewhere away from' – she waved a hand over the frozen landscape – 'all this. God, I'd not need to tell her twice. She'd be up with her maid now, packing every last boot-lace.'

He caught her hand at the end of its dramatic sweep and raised it to his lips. 'Dear Venus,' he said. 'Dear, darling girl. God send you'll never change. But one of us has to be practical. Suppose we did as you say – pack up now and go back to London. What are we going to live on? Bread and cheese and kisses? It's fine in a book. It'd make a lovely operetta . . .'

Daisy had to count down her impatience, to force herself to talk as calmly and reasonably as she could. 'Isn't it what I'm after telling you, these weeks past? I can work again as a model . . .' He drew breath to protest but she raised a finger and touched his lips. 'I can and I will. You know yourself now that I can earn enough to keep body and soul together – and on something more than just bread and cheese. And you can sell your paintings. And drawings.'

He was aghast. 'Commercialize my art, you mean?'

She stared at him in bewilderment.

'You mean, actually *live* off it,' he added.

She nodded. 'Like Rembrandt, Titian . . . Michelangelo. Why are you looking like that? Isn't it what you want?'

He shrugged awkwardly.

'Were you going to give your paintings away, then?' she pressed.

'Of course not. And very well you know it.'

She turned and walked a few paces, still moving away from the castle. 'All of a sudden, Napier, I feel I know nothing.' After a pause she strolled on.

He moved toward her, maintaining the gap rather than closing it. 'Of course I hoped to sell them. But not actually to live off them. Not to depend on it, you see. It's the difference between a gentleman-professional and a commercial-professional.'

Her eyes raked the heavens. 'And that's more important to you than all the rest? More important than being a painter? More important than marrying me? More important than . . .'

'No!' he cried angrily. 'They're *all* important. It's only you that's turning it into a question of either-or. Before you came rushing over here and . . . before you came here, I was working quietly away at it – getting them to agree to my living in London, continuing to develop my painting – which, you're quite right, they don't understand at all – but I was working on it. Drip, drip, drip. Like water wears away stone . . .'

'And I came rushing in like ten elephants, I suppose. Is that what you were going to say?'

He smiled wanly and laid his head on one side, unwilling to agree openly. In his troubled eyes she sensed what pressures he was struggling against, from her, from his upbringing as a gentleman, from his love of his art. She quelled a soft impulse to relent and, with a jerk of her head toward the castle, said, 'All I know is you're ten times the fella away from that place. A thousand times. I hardly recognize the little wee man you are at home.'

For a moment she knew she had almost swayed him. He stared into her eyes, first one, then the other, rapidly, and she knew he was testing the idea in his mind, framing himself to the decision. What images flickered past his image-fertile inner eye? Did he see himself and her leaving their lodgings in Chelsea for somewhere even cheaper – Whitechapel, say? A dingy little backroom in a street full of hoors and mendicants . . . the long, slow struggle to establish himself in a world that always had been and always would be glutted with aspiring artists . . . the sheer daily grind of it all, and knowing that it was sell or starve – or go on living off your wife's earnings?

Even Daisy, speculating about those images, and feeling their force, as it were, by proxy . . . even she felt her boundless confidence begin to wane – especially when she remembered the one vital fact she had so far concealed from him. But she was in that do-or-die mood which would not be turned aside. She had set her hand to the plough and would see this furrow to its farthest headland.

He closed his eyes, as if admitting he could speak his piece only by blotting her out. 'I think,' he said slowly, 'I must decide what's best for us. It isn't either-or. We can have the best of all worlds, and in the long run you'll see it, too.'

He waited, still with his eyes closed, for a reply. But he opened them when he heard the deliberate scrinch of her footfall in the snow. 'What now?' he asked plaintively.

'I'm doing no good here,' she called back over her shoulder. 'Don't forget your sketches.'

'What are you doing? Where d'you think you're going?'

'To my aunty's. I'll send back for my things.'

He ran and caught up with her. 'But you can't walk in those shoes.'

She stopped briefly and laughed, more in despair than with humour. 'Is that the truth of it? Were I to pull on galoshes, I could go?'

'No!' He struck his forehead angrily. 'The whole thing's just so stupid.

You know what I mean.' She resumed her angry departure while he walked at her side, trotting every few steps to keep up. 'No, I do not, Napier. I don't know anything any more. Yes, I do! I know that I came down here to bring you back where you belong, and instead, somehow, it's turned into a situation where I'm to win your father's approval and your mother's approval . . . and Mary Rourke's approval for all I know. And I'll have none of it, so there!'

He took her arm and held with just sufficient force to make her stop, relaxing his grip at once. Then he put his arms around her, kissed her neck and ear, and murmured, 'Venus . . . it's not like you, all this.'

'How would you know! How would I know? Oh, Napier, I just feel so afraid.'

'Of me?'

'Of the whole . . . everything.' She looked over his shoulder at the castle, so smug and solid in its possession of its acres, and struggled for the words to express what she could so clearly feel. 'The way it . . . sort of captures you.'

'What?'

'That place. That way of life. All those demands that are never spoken but that doesn't mean they're not pressed. I was almost beginning to think yes, I must win your father's approval. Well, my dear, I'm leaving before *it* wins.'

'But what's wrong with trying to gain my father's approval? What's wrong with wanting the best of all worlds?'

'What's wrong with standing on your own two feet? What's wrong with making your own world by your own efforts – instead of just meekly wanting the best of other people's?' She stopped when she felt him shaking with laughter. 'What's so funny?' she asked.

'Your sentiments.' He laughed openly now. 'They're very Coolderg Castle, did you but know it. I can hear my father saying those exact words.'

After a thoughtful pause Daisy said, 'Can you now!'

'Indeed,' he told her. 'Now where are you off to?'

'You're right,' she called back, fitting toe to the heel of her earlier tracks. 'I can't walk far in these thin shoes. I think I'll risk the castle a while longer yet.'

22

Lady Lyndon-Fury never showed her face before eleven, at which hour sherry and biscuits were served in the 'library'. It proved to be a dark-panelled room furnished with a motley collection of bookcases above the main guard. A grille in the floor, through which boiling lead might once have been poured upon intruders, now ensured that it kept well aired – even though the air itself was chill and dank. Today, as a concession to the snow, a sullen turf fire was permitted to smoulder in the hearth, but a hundred such would not drive out the mildewed damp that had taken up permanent home there. An enamel pail in the corner, beneath a dark stain in the ruined plaster, revealed at least one of its sources.

Her ladyship watched Daisy's eyes discover the room, noting how quick they darted this way and that, compiling an inventory of everything; she saw them alight on the pail. 'That one's a bit of a mystery,' she confessed. 'The floor immediately above is as dry as a bone.'

'Is there an old water main badly stopped off inside the wall beyond?' Daisy suggested.

'I never thought of that. But no, it only drips when it rains.'

'It's coming in from outside, so.'

'Ah!' Lady Lyndon-Fury handed her a sherry. 'What it must be to understand these things!'

Daisy could not be sure whether the remark was sarcastic or genuine.

'Is Napier not with you?' the woman went on.

'He went to sketch the hunt.'

'Ah, yes. They're out cubbing today, I understand.' She stared at the white world beyond the windows and shivered. 'Love may laugh at locksmiths, eh, but not at four-thousand acres of cold, clammy snow.'

Daisy smiled. It would be closer to the truth to say that she had engineered this meeting by insisting that Madeleine should accompany her brother. 'I had hoped to see Cornel here,' she lied.

'Cornel drink sherry? Only if the next choice were surgical spirit. No, he arranges his own refreshments.'

Daisy nodded contentedly and waited for the older woman to make the opening she knew must surely be in her mind. And indeed it was not long in coming.

Over the years Lady Lyndon-Fury had devised a number of strategies for dealing with an awkward situation. Among them, Absolute Frankness – or the appearance of the same – did not rank very high; but there were times, and this she felt was one of them, when nothing else would serve. 'I owe you an apology, Miss O'Lindon,' she said affably, 'which I hope you'll accept. I cannot think how I allowed myself to misjudge you so.'

Daisy was taken momentarily aback by this approach. 'Ah,' she said, and then, recovering, 'if any apology is due, Lady Lyndon-Fury, it is surely mine – for acting on my mother's and my aunt's absurd proposal last spring. Of course, I didn't even know of Napier's existence then.'

The other smiled. 'Yes, wasn't it extraordinary that you should have met him *so* soon after! Well, perhaps not. Ireland really *is* a small world.'

'He was the first person who spoke to me at the school. The first student, I mean.'

'Ah. *He* spoke to *you.*'

'Yes. To be honest, he spoke to a statue of Venus who happened to be handy. He patted her on the flank and told her to retire. He called me the New Venus.'

Her ladyship laughed. 'He was never bashful. I'll give him that. Well, I appreciate your candour, young lady – may I call you Daisy?'

Daisy nodded warily.

'Let me be equally candid. Napier has always been something of a worry to me. A cat with half an eye could see he doesn't belong here.' For some reason she lingered on the statement, canvassing Daisy for a response.

Daisy gave a curt nod. She was on the point of saying more – the sort of things she had been saying to Napier himself and Madeleine – but instinctively held back.

'I don't believe he could live and work here,' the other persisted. 'Not happily.'

Daisy felt a small twinge of alarm, 'Has he spoken of doing so?'

'Not lately, I must confess. There's a villa a little way down the lakeshore. Friends from England use it in the mayfly season but otherwise it's empty all year. I know he's always had his eye on that place, or he always used to. Has he never mentioned it to you?'

Daisy shook her head. 'He always spoke of London and Paris. Dairmid Trench says that's where a painter really ought to be. A young painter especially.'

'Is he one of the Trenches of Clonfert, I wonder? I didn't think they had an artistic atom in their blood. Still, nor do the Lyndon-Furys, come to that. He thinks very highly of Napier, I know.'

'He wants him to exhibit a painting of me at a new English art society they're talking of forming.' Daisy was pleased to see that this was news to her ladyship, though the woman did her best to conceal the fact. 'The Joan of Arc one.'

'Ah yes. Tell me, would he become a member of this new art society? Would he live in London then?'

Daisy placed her empty glass on the salver and declined a second. 'It's very hard predicting *what* Napier will do, Lady Lyndon-Fury. I was surprised he didn't return to London immediately after the funeral.'

The other cleared her throat and murmured, 'Yes.' She cleared her throat again. 'Let me put all my cards on the table, Daisy, dear. And I hope you'll do the same with me. *I* am entirely to blame for that. I thought he ought to stay at home and put all this artistic nonsense behind him. We only let him take it up in the first place in the hope of getting it out of his system . . .'

'When you say "we" . . .' Daisy interrupted.

She nodded. 'I mean "I," of course. His father couldn't give . . . I mean, is much more tolerant. Napier's the third son, so, as long as he doesn't shoot foxes . . .' A shrug and a smile completed the thought; then, as if it were part of the same pleasantry, she added, 'Or marry an RC, of course. So, yes, it was I who let him go to Dublin, in the hope, as I said, of letting him work it out of his system. I could not know that he would meet you there, of course. And the circumstances of your meeting, coming so soon after our little contretemps at Simonstown in the spring . . . well, you must realize how it seemed to me. I therefore thought it my plain duty, after the funeral, to keep him and you apart. By whatever means.'

She smiled at Daisy, who felt this gush of honesty making its intended effect upon her; but the reflection that it was, indeed, intended helped preserve some remnant of her caution. 'May I ask what has changed your mind?' she responded.

'Two things. First, Napier's behaviour since he has been home. He has actually become quite intelligent. There was a time when he wouldn't care tuppence what we thought or said. He'd go his own sweet way in all things – especially where his art was concerned. But no longer. He's actually trying to curry the family's favour now – pretending to share our interests, trying to be one of us. I ask you! But to me that's a clear sign that his art is far more important to him than I had ever suspected.' She smiled at her own astuteness and rang for a servant to come and throw more turf on the fire.

'You said two things?' Daisy reminded her.

'The second is you. Your character. It is not at all as I supposed.'

'And how was that?'

'Oh, it would be profitless to rake over all that now. I'm sure you can imagine it. The important thing is, I now see how I have erred and strayed . . . ?'

Her ladyship's strange intonation turned the statement into a question; her lifted eyebrows seemed to invite Daisy to complete the thought.

Daisy responded in the most neutral way that came to mind: 'Really?'

The other seemed dissatisfied with this reply, but she went on: 'It is now clear to me that the boy *is* serious about his art, that nothing will deflect his pursuit of it – and that without someone like you at his side he will probably make the most dreadful hames of it all. There now! Could I possibly put it plainer?'

Daisy swallowed hard and shook her head. She was filled with a sense of danger and yet could find nothing to which it might apply.

'May I hope you will now be equally candid with me?' the other prompted. Her eyes seemed to hold Daisy in a spell.

Daisy rose and went over to the window, where the draught between the sashes had cleared some of the frosted panes. 'They're coming back,' she said. 'Napier and Madeleine. Too cold, probably.'

Lady Lyndon-Fury cleared her throat.

'I want to marry Napier.' Daisy scratched a single vertical 'I' in the frost. 'I want us to live in London, where he can develop his art.' She hesitated slightly before adding, 'And sell it.' She scratched a second 'I' beside the first. Then, grasping the nettle, she added, 'And I'd like you to stop making him an allowance.' She scratched a diagonal between the two verticals and spun round to face her ladyship, who was staring at her in bewilderment.

'*Stop* his allowance?' she asked.

Daisy nodded.

'D'you mind telling me why?'

'Because it has him like sheep at a crossroads.' She chuckled as she picked up on her ladyship's earlier remark. 'Erring and straying like a lost sheep!'

'Ah!' The words seemed to please the woman inordinately.

'He doesn't know whether he's a painter or a gentleman first,' Daisy explained. 'But he'll be ten times the painter if he knew it was that or nothing.'

'But what would you live on?'

'The allowance keeps him one-foot-here, one-foot-there, like riding two horses in midstream – or whatever the saying is. But you know what I mean.'

She nodded. 'Yet I have to repeat the question – how will you manage?'

Daisy explained, saying nothing about the baby, though she came within an ace of blurting it out. A servant came and added two damp sods to the steaming smoulder in the hearth.

Lady Lyndon-Fury nodded at Daisy's explanation though she plainly did not accept it. 'Well, then,' she went on, 'to practicalities. There is one thing I have to ask you before we can make any public announcement. Forgive me, but it is absolutely necessary. Are there any Roman Catholics in your immediate family? I don't mean second cousins or batty old aunts. Every family is tainted in that way. I mean near relatives.'

'My mother is from a Catholic family in Goatstown,' Daisy said flatly. 'But she's lapsed, I think. My father was Church of Ireland . . .'

'Was?' she echoed in tones of foreboding.

'Well, he joined the Quakers when he thought it might put a bit of business his way. But it didn't. I don't think he's anything now.'

'What church d'you attend?'

'None. We're not a religious family. My father said some people say there is a God and some say there isn't and for his part the answer's in between.'

'So, he's still an Anglican, then. Sure that's what most of us believe. A good Sunday-morning faith, and none of your daily offices and mumbo-jumbo.'

But she was whistling down the wind, trying to fabricate a faith where none existed. Daisy just shook her head sadly.

'What church were they married in, your parents? That would be important.'

Daisy tilted her head awkwardly. 'You see, my father was in a bit of a financial pickle at the time . . .'

'But what church?'

'And there was a good dowry went with my mother, which he wouldn't have got if . . .'

'So it was an RC church.'

Daisy nodded. 'St Francis Xavier's.'

For a long, uneasy silence Lady Lyndon-Fury sat and stared at the sour little fire. 'I should have asked you first,' she said at length. 'It changes everything, of course.' She closed her eyes and shook her head angrily.' Why *didn't* I ask you first?'

A thought struck Daisy. That was why the woman had said 'erred and strayed' like that – from the Church of Ireland prayer book; it had been a test. Suddenly she felt sick of the whole business.

'No Lyndon-Fury has ever married a papist,' the older woman exploded.

'You say let's be candid,' Daisy told her. 'Cards on the table, et cetera. Well, I have no patience with any of this. I intend to marry Napier and I intend that we shall . . .'

'Miss O'Lindon.' Her ladyship rose and rang the bell yet again. 'I know that to you, if you are the heathen you say you are, it must seem the most trivial of causes. But we take our faith seriously in this family. You have become our guest under false colours. I must ask you to make other arrangements as soon as convenient – no, as soon as possible, whether convenient or no. And you must understand there can be no question of your forming any kind of an alliance with our son.'

A maidservant entered; but for that Daisy would have blurted out that she was carrying Napier's child.

'Miss O'Lindon is leaving us before lunch,' the woman told the maid. 'Have the dogcart brought to the front door in half an hour.' When they were alone again she turned to Daisy. 'No doubt you'd like to supervise the packing of your things?'

Daisy, her heart leaping about like a frog in a bag, sat down again. 'I'll wait for Napier,' she said.

'I was right all along, then,' the other said vehemently. 'You are nothing but a grasping little hoyden. A tuft-hunter out for what you can get.' She gave a sneer of a laugh. 'You're also a fool if you think you can get Napier like this. He knows what it would do to our family if he were to marry an RC. You must have kept it well concealed from him.'

'On the contrary, Lady Lyndon-Fury, he knows all about it. He has met my mother and he knows everything I have told you.'

The woman turned pale. 'Never,' she murmured.

'Here they come now. Ask him yourself.'

23

Complaining, arguing, laughing, Madeleine and Napier came sloven-footed up the spiral stairs to the passageway outside the library door. There they paused and their voices fell to a whisper.

'Well, do come in, if you're coming at all,' their mother called out.

Laughing once more, they burst in, rubbing their hands, seeking the sherry tray with their eyes – 'Are we too late? Have you left us any?' Then something in their mother's rigidity alerted them that all was not well. 'Rosie's horse went lame on her,' Madeleine said.

Nobody took it up.

'What's happened?' Napier asked, looking from one to the other, even to his sister, as if she might have a sixth sense.

'One guess,' Daisy told him.

Lady Lyndon-Fury drew breath to say it but Daisy called out, 'No, let him guess.'

Napier frowned at her, shaking his head as if to say, *surely not*?

She nodded.

'Your mother?' he asked aloud, as if he still could not believe it.

Daisy smiled triumphantly.

'Napier!' cried his mother.

He paid her no heed. 'You mean . . .' he went on, his gaze riveted on Daisy. 'But why did you have to tell her?'

'Napier!' The anguish was doubled in his mother's cry.

'Because I could not live a lie.' Rather pointedly, thrusting the words at her ladyship, she added, 'I have no training for it.'

He put his hands to his forehead. 'Aiee, aiee!'

'I cannot believe you knew,' his mother told him. 'Not from the beginning, surely?'

Madeleine raised her eyebrows at Daisy. 'Is your mother . . . ?' She made a motion of crossing herself and raised her eyebrows.

Daisy nodded. 'By birth. She's nothing at all now.'

'Say it's not true!' his mother commanded him.

'It is true,' he responded wearily. Then again he turned to Daisy, walked toward her. 'You should never have mentioned it . . .' As he passed his mother she gave him a stinging slap on the cheek. It took him so much by surprise that the tears sprang to his eyes before he could control them.

He mastered himself before it affected his voice but it was too late then to call back the actual water, which now coursed down his cheeks. Awareness of the indignity made him harsher than he would have been. He took the two remaining paces to Daisy's side, held out a hand to raise her, and said, 'Come on, old girl. We're done with this place.'

'And the allowance?' she asked, not stirring, although it cost every ounce of her will to remain.

'Daisy!' Madeleine cried out.

'What?'

'Think!'

Daisy, whose colour had returned at the sight of Napier's bravery, blanched again. 'Don't you dare!' she warned.

'But you're not thinking,' Madeleine insisted.

Mother and son, temporarily allied in their bewilderment, stared at the other two. 'What is this? What do you know? What are you concealing now?'

Daisy rose swiftly to her feet, her hand still in Napier's. 'You were right.' She jerked him toward the door. 'Let's leave before . . .'

'If you don't say something, I will,' Madeleine warned.

'We'll accept the allowance, then,' Daisy snapped at her (at the same time secretly crossing fingers on her free hand). 'Satisfied?'

'If you continue to associate with that creature,' her ladyship warned, 'knowing what you do, and knowing how we feel about it, there can be no question of a continuing allowance.'

'Come on!' Daisy urged, tugging at Napier's hand even harder, and begging Madeleine with her eyes to be silent.

But Madeleine refused to meet her gaze. 'You can't stop the allowance because she's carrying Napier's child,' she said just as they reached the door.

It took a second for the words to register, so that Napier actually returned to the room from outside – now dragging Daisy behind him. 'It's true,' his sister told him. Then, turning to her mother, 'I'm surprised at you. Not noticing it.'

The woman sat down abruptly, then stared about her as if only half-certain of where she was. 'Sherry,' she murmured.

Madeleine darted to her side and refilled her glass. 'I think we could all do with one,' she said, businesslike now. 'Then we must sit down and talk this over calmly.' Now, too, she dared meet Daisy's gaze. 'It was very wrong of you to conceal it, my dear.'

Napier put his arms around Daisy and hugged her for all he was worth – then, remembering why he was doing it, he pulled away in consternation. 'Is it . . . ?' He nodded toward her midriff.

Now she could not prevent the smile that rose to her lips.

'But why didn't you say? It changes everything.'

And she, thinking she knew what he meant, smiled triumphantly at his defeated mother.

24

Napier drew level with the dogcart before it reached the gate lodge. Daisy ignored him, staring straight ahead at the wastes of snow and the ragged black filigree of ditches and walls. The sun had set ten minutes earlier and already the world was darkling. 'Be reasonable, Venus,' he pleaded. 'Nothing lasts for ever. They'll come round. You'll see.'

She continued to ignore him.

'Venus?' he prompted.

'I said everything I have to say to you back there. If it didn't sink in . . .'

'We can't possibly talk like this.'

'I agree.'

'No. I mean . . . oh!' He rode ahead and grasped the reins of the cob that was pulling the little cart. 'You ride this mare of mine, Kelly,' he told her driver. 'I'll drive.'

Pointedly Daisy seized the reins from the man.

'I'll sit beside you, so,' Napier responded.

'It's a free country.' She shook the reins and the cob started off again.

'Won't you even try it?' he asked.

'What is there to try? It's a . . .' She sought for a word, one of Dairmid Trench's favourites. 'It's a grotesque suggestion.'

'But it wouldn't even last a month. They'd come round to our way of seeing it.'

'Our way?' she echoed scornfully. 'We haven't got *our* way, Napier. I don't understand what happened to change you. When your mother slapped you, you were all ready to . . . I've never felt so proud of you as I did at that moment. But now!'

'I don't wish to hurt them if there's a way around it. I explained all that.'

'Hurt them!' She laughed. 'You couldn't hurt them with a hive of hornets. They're tougher than a goat's gizzard. Come away with me now. Why won't you give *that* a try?'

After a pause he said, 'All right, I will.'

She turned to him in ecstasy. 'Honestly?'

He nodded. 'I'll make a bargain. You try their suggestion for a month. Just one month – now what would that cost you? And if at the end of that time they haven't relented, if they're not calling the banns and sending your mother their guest list, then I'll do it your way.'

He argued for this course all that long twilight journey, all the way to Simonstown. When he put her into her *Ladies Only* coach, he half-conceded defeat. 'Give *me* a month, then,' he begged. He was no more than a dark silhouette against a misty haze from the platform lamp beyond. 'Let me try and talk them round. If they haven't caved in by a month today, I'll collect you in Dublin and we'll go straight to London. That's a promise.' He reached a hand in through the window and tapped her belly lightly. 'And don't do anything foolish with that little fella,' he added.

She realized he had not noticed the nun sitting in the far corner of the dimly lit compartment. She signalled the warning with her eyes and nodded her head almost imperceptibly in the woman's direction. He gave her a quick kiss and withdrew in confusion. 'A month,' he repeated. 'I promise.'

It was a through coach to Dublin, coupled to the main line train at Roscrea junction, so the nun was her companion all the way. Several times Daisy wept softly to herself. The nun, thinking she could guess at the cause, and surmising from Napier's West British accent that the comforts of her faith would not be welcomed in any case, kept a self-congratulatory silence all the way to Kingsbridge.

25

'Like a cod my doubled-up head and tail,' Daisy said, thinking of herself and her situation as the days lengthened into Napier's promised four weeks. Christmas came and went with little cheer. Her mother took every sly chance she got to come out with remarks in the 'how are the mighty fallen' category. Her father, on the other hand, gladly accepted her back into the works, where, she was pleased to notice, not all of her reorganizing had gone by the board. Had it not been for that – for the fact that she was still of use *somewhere* – the bog-dark waters of the Liffey might have seemed a pleasant prospect.

And yet there were often times of darkness, especially when she reflected that her real testing was yet to come, when the signs of her carrying could no longer be concealed; then she could imagine herself taking a midnight leap off the Ha'penny Bridge. Work was sovereign, not for its Protestant ethic but for the exhaustion it brought – and the oblivion that soon followed. She knew it was probably harmful to her baby to drive herself so hard but, in the way people do, she placated it with vague promises of making everything up to it later. For the moment her overwhelming need was for the anodyne of fatigue.

Often her mental exhaustion would outpace that of her body; then she would take the omnibus or tram no farther than the Merrion Gate and walk home to Monkstown past the Booterstown marshes and through Blackrock. She realized how morose she must seem to others, for few who passed her bade her a cheery goodnight or gave out some comment on the day that was in it – 'There's another cold night for us, now!' – and so forth. Her thoughts turned round and round in her head: a miller's wheel, grinding the seeds of hope to a powder.

It was like a grief that could find no object, for she had not lost Napier. He wrote to her almost daily, and she to him. He had a fair italic hand but his spelling was atrocious. 'I feel,' he wrote in one of his letters, 'like the old garnled aok at the end of the aveneu.' But his drawing of the same old tree made his meaning clear. In an odd way his inability to spell depressed her more than anything. In his letter from London it had seemed no more than a charming eccentricity; now it served only to remind her of his essential childishness.

On those dark, cold, lonely walks her thoughts of Napier would tail off into dissatisfaction. Then, idly, she'd run her mind over some part of the business she'd set to rights that day – a debt recovered, a payment successfully banked. Then suddenly some memory of him would return and overwhelm her with a force to take her breath away – a walk through the London fog, an afternoon on Mount Venus, an evening in Jury's. At such moments their separation seemed bitter indeed. And it occurred to her that love itself is very like a currency. Not only had it the power to move and change the world according to its own unbending laws, but – and more disturbingly in her present mood – it could be changed for a different currency, of equal power, when it could not itself be tendered.

She learned this when she felt her love for Napier becoming increasingly tinged with anger at his obstinacy and the lack of self-confidence that lay behind it, telling him he 'had' to have his wretched allowance or he'd go under. She realized how hard it must be for him. He'd grown up in that world where there was *always* money coming in from somewhere: money you didn't have to work for, money that was yours by some strange ancestral right. The prospect of losing that right was a terror to all of his class; they learned the fear of it with their wet nurse's milk. To give it up voluntarily must seem the very height of folly. She understood all that and yet she could not feel it in her bones. Her request to Lady Lyndon-Fury, that the allowance should stop, was not mere foolish bravado – which was how it had been interpreted. Deep inside her she knew such money was corrupt at its source and could only corrupt those who took it. This was nothing like a political sentiment. Socialists and anarchists who would abolish such rights by law left her as cold as those puritan parties that arose from time to time, clamouring to abolish other sins by statute. For her it was a moral sentiment: To accept what you had not earned was like accepting what you knew to be stolen. To refuse it was a choice for each individual to make; what society might do about it by law was neither here nor there.

When she marshalled these thoughts and set them down calmly in a letter to Napier, some three or four days before his promised month was up, it provoked a resounding silence. The flow of his letters to her simply dried up. Unwittingly he had produced the very situation in which the currency of her love could no longer be tendered – there was nothing to tender it for. Hour by hour, as deliveries came and went, with nothing from Coolderg for her, she felt it being exchanged for the coin of that other most powerful emotion of the woman scorned. Not all at once and not completely, of course. One moment she felt her contempt for Napier's weakness welling up into a blazing hatred; moments later, that very weakness would melt her heart and bring out every protective instinct she possessed, so that there was nothing she would rather do than love her darling man and help him see how well he might stand on his own two feet.

But – and this was the truly frightening thing – that fiery hatred held a seductive sway over her. Like an ardent spirit liberated in her veins it could bring a thrill every bit as strong as its opposite. Self-righteous, self-justifying, and ultimately self-destructive – she knew it was all of these, and yet she could not deny herself the occasional luxury of its indulgence.

When five days had passed in silence from him, three of them beyond his promised month, she could stand it no longer. Apart from anything else, the danger of seeing her love turn to hate was too large to ignore. She told her father where she was going and why, and, early one Friday afternoon toward the end of January, took the tram out to Kingsbridge station.

You were supposed to get on at the front and off at the back, but this was Dublin. So, although she had boarded the vehicle at its origin by Carlisle Bridge and, in her usual curious way, had inspected everyone who got on and off at all the stops, she did not see him until they both got off at Kingsbridge. And even then it took her some moments before she placed him.

Oddly enough, he recognized her at once; but he turned away, half-hiding his face from her, without making the action too obtrusive. He's bashful, she thought, approaching him with a smile prepared. 'Mr O'Lindon?' She put just enough question in her tone to suggest uncertainty.

'Yes!' He turned round as if he had been waiting for her to speak first, then stepped aside and ushered her to the ticket-office window first.

She took a return to Simonstown; all he wanted was the new timetable.

'May I carry your bag?' he asked as they made for the platform. Then, with a poker face: 'You remember my name, then.'

She laughed.

26

It would have been churlish for her to have insisted on the *Ladies Only*. They found an almost empty compartment near the front of the train. The only other occupants were a snoozing priest and a grubby little boy who appeared to be in his charge. Mr O'Lindon handed her into a window seat on the south side, where she'd catch the thin, wintry sun. He took the seat opposite. The train started almost at once and they sat for a while, staring out at the passing suburbs. The first, Inchicore, was one of Dublin's poorest.

'That's a strange thing now,' Daisy said suddenly. 'I've lived in Dublin all my life and I don't suppose the sights and sounds of the place would have changed all that much. I remember the tramlines starting when I was a little girl. That was a new sound, all right – the trams. But I don't mean that. I mean the people. I wouldn't imagine they'd changed much. Yet I was never so aware of the poverty as I was this time. Did you see them on Carlisle Bridge? Three and four deep, and in clothes you could scarce call daycent. What in the name of God do those people live on at all?'

'I saw them,' he said. After a while he added, 'I've seen worse. I was hardly ever in Dublin before this.'

'You don't come often, then. I wondered. It's not a regular thing.'

'Ah, it could be.' He turned away and grinned at the window, as if he had said more than the words implied.

She took the chance to inspect him unobserved. The overwhelming impression he gave was of strength. He was a big man – not especially tall, but solid and muscular – the sort of man you'd want on your side in a fight, and at your side if he were.

But his strength went deeper than that, for it was strength of character, too. You could see it in his very features. His fair hair, luxuriant and thick, framed a clean-shaven face that was a pleasure to dwell on. It was his eyes that mainly held her. Deep set and dark blue, they were intense, not so much in their colour as in their intelligence and power. They were observant and shrewd. *Protestant* eyes, she thought.

Now there was a funny thing: Napier's eyes were shrewd and observant too, but not in a Protestant way. His were artistic. You didn't have to *be* a Protestant to have Protestant eyes. Any policeman had them, looking for suspects in a crowd. Even dogs could have them – in those moments when they square up for a fight.

That was the quality she now saw in Stephen O'Lindon's eyes. By God, you'd think twice before you squared up for a fight with him! She caught herself wishing Napier might have just a bit of that same quality.

'Are you going back to the castle, Miss O'Lindon?' he asked. 'Will I lighten the road for you again?'

She wondered why they didn't call each other by their Christian names, which, as third cousins, they'd be entitled to do without its meaning anything; in fact, by an odd sort of reversal, their use of their common surname carried a hint of a provisional intimacy that a more intimate form of address would have lacked in their particular circumstances.

'Why, that would be more than kind, Mr O'Lindon. Are you sure it won't be out of your way?'

'As it happens, it won't,' he replied. 'Not today. I'm to meet Mr Woods, Sir Lucius's agent, tonight.'

Something in the way he spoke hinted that this was no casually dropped remark; he was willing her to pursue it. But, as always when she felt herself nudged like that, she resisted. 'I heard about what you did at Colonel Brailton's house in Borrisokane.' The name just popped into her mind like that.

'Tully Hall.' He laughed. 'Wasn't he a fierce man – apartments for the Little People! Well, this job for Sir Lucius is different altogether.'

Again she resisted the hint. 'I suppose by the time you retire you'll be able to drive about the whole of Keelity saying "I put that up . . . I made those windows . . . I did that roof." It can't be dull.'

There was a gleam in his eye, for he realized she was deliberately resisting his baits. He settled back and drew from his pocket a bag of mint humbugs, which he offered to her. She saw the grubby little boy's eyes light up and drew Mr O'Lindon's attention to him with a nod of her head. He diverted the bag that way. Then, when the boy turned a pleading glance at his guardian, he stretched his arm diagonally across the compartment and said, 'What about yourself, Father? Won't it wash away the taste of Dublin.'

The priest chuckled. 'Well . . . just the one. I'm obliged to you, sir.' Then, more sternly to the boy: 'Just the one now or you'll burst out in spots.'

The boy took one – but it emerged with a second stuck to it. Again those pleading eyes turned to the cleric, who shrugged and looked away. Triumphantly the boy stuffed his gob, as he would have put it.

That's how they keep them faithful, Daisy thought. Preach hellfire and turn a blind eye.

The bag nudged her arm. Her acceptance was like one more step into an impromptu conspiracy that had begun when he set about subverting the priest's dominion over the boy. She bit a mint in two and parked a half in each of her cheeks, where neither was large enough to distort her face. 'We're both lucky, so,' she said with a tilt of her head towards the lad. 'Me getting a ride the whole way.'

'The luck is mine,' he assured her. 'Didn't I think I'd be on the next train to this and have to drive to Coolderg like the Earl of Hell. But it's held all day, so it has.'

'You concluded your business early, then? And to your satisfaction, from what you say?' It occurred to her that he might think it unmannerly to talk of business with a lady, so she began to tell him how she had passed her time since leaving Coolderg – reminding him how she had reorganized her father's business last summer.

When she had last spoken of it, that time he had given her the ride, he had seemed only mildly interested. Now, however, he started to question her closely. And the nature of his questions intrigued her.

Most men, like Napier when she had taken him to the little factory one day, were interested in the japanning process itself (and, to be sure, in the comely young females who did much of the work there). But Mr O'Lindon, deprived, perhaps, of that interesting stimulus, was much more concerned to know about the routine of the office, the book-keeping, the acquiring of new clients, the maintenance of old ones, and the collection of debts. Especially the collection of debts.

At last she asked him why that subject so fascinated him.

He sighed. 'Could I but get in all I'm owed, I could put my feet up for two years.'

She thought it a shame she hardly knew him, or she could offer to do it on his behalf, for it was work she truly enjoyed. Yet, in a curious way, she felt that was not what he wanted or was hinting at. 'You wouldn't, though, would you.' She grinned. 'Put your feet up, I mean.'

She expected him to smile back at her but instead he withdrew into some inward struggle with himself. His eyes were fixed on her, but nine-tenths of his mind was elsewhere. Whatever the struggle, he resolved it at last and drew from an inside pocket a long manilla envelope, marked, in a church-book hymnal sort of lettering, Registrar of Patents. 'It'll be published soon enough,' he said, as if concluding his argument with himself. He passed it to her and watched keenly for her response.

She took it gingerly but still did not like to open it.

'That's what brought me to Dublin today,' he added.

She slipped her fingers inside and drew forth a long parchment or deed. It was all couched in terms considerably more jaw-breaking than the twinned humbugs with which the little boy was still struggling, but as far as she could make out – and the attached drawing was a great help – it was a patent for a machine to be used in some branch of furniture making. Of the patentee there could be no doubt whatever. The anxiety with which he awaited her reaction proclaimed him at once; but so did a flourish at the top of the first page: Stephen Everest O'Lindon of the County Keelity, Ireland.

'You'd build that,' she guessed.

He nodded.

'It looks a fierce thing altogether. What does it do at all?' She turned the drawing this way and that.

'It will bend wood to any shape . . .'

'*Any* wood?'

'Properly treated. Sallies mostly. It bends it and holds it while you attach . . . for instance, it would bend the back of a chair and hold it while you attach the seat and a cross-brace. Then that would hold it permanently.'

'But aren't there other such machines?' she asked.

'Dozens. But none so small nor so handy. That would also bend oak planks for ship's clinkers – *and* put a twist in them. That's where the idea came to me to start with. I was at George Dowd's in Killaloe and there were two men all day boiling up planks of oak in cast-iron pipes. Ordinary rainwater chutes, they were, laying in a turf fire with a cork bung at each end. Boiling up planks of oak inside them. And it took them all week to do one side of a boat.' He tapped the document in her hand. 'With that you could do the whole boat in a day. The outer skin of her, you understand.'

Daisy whistled. 'You'll hardly be the most popular man on the Shannon – with the other boatbuilders, anyway. You'll be needing good locks and bars.'

He chuckled and shook his head. She asked him why. 'You're so practical,' he said, as if the discovery surprised him.

'Everest?' she asked, handing him back the document.

He pulled a face. 'My mother's idea.'

'You don't like it?'

He pulled the same face again.

'Look on the bright side,' she told him. 'What if the only mountain she knew was the Sugarloaf.'

He laughed and the priest joined in. 'She has you there, right enough, my son,' he declared.

The rest of the hour to Roscrea passed in amiable crack among the three of them, while the boy was allowed to gorge on humbugs to his stomach's content.

It was pitch dark by the time they arrived at Simonstown. Only when they were upon the road did Daisy remember his business with Mr Woods – or, rather, that he had tried to make her ask him what it was. She relented at last.

'Oh yes,' he said, as if he, too, had forgotten it – though she knew very well he had not. 'In a way it's the very opposite of the job for the Colonel. I'm to make a grand little place grander yet.'

'On the Coolderg estate?'

'Down by the lake. They have a villa in a townland called Glaster, right on the lakeshore.'

'The villa they let to friends from England for the mayfly?'

'The very one. I'm to make it into the grandest little home ever – for Mr Napier, you know. And, or so I believe, yourself.'

27

Napier stared morosely out through the window, letting his eyes stray down across the lawn, over a small pasture, to the rushy, stony shores of Lough Cool, where his rowing boat bobbed and nudged the rotting little jetty. Beyond the wind-whipped waters, half lost in the haze of a soft

February day, rolled the blue-gray hills of the Slieve Bernagh. 'It's a grand view, anyway,' he offered.

'At this particular moment,' she told him, 'I'm more interested in prospects of a different kind.'

'I know.' He nodded. 'I know.'

'I don't see how anybody could think this is an improvement,' she went on. 'I'm not talking about the house but about our situation. I have to know, darling. I mean, where do I stand now?' She tried not to sound shrewish but it was not easy.

He turned and folded her in his arms. 'It's very unsatisfactory for you, I know. Well, it's unsatisfactory for me, too, come to that.'

'Except that nobody's going to be pointing the scornful finger at *you* in four or five months' time.'

He clenched his eyes tight. 'Is that all there is?'

'They'll nudge one another and call you no end of a dog.'

'Four months!'

'I don't know. I wasn't too careful, counting. Something like that. What's the odds, anyway?'

'Time is all-important. It's all a question of giving it time. They'll come round to it in the end, you'll see. I mean – even agreeing to do up this place and letting you stay here . . . that's a big concession to . . .' His voice tailed off as he saw the scorn in her eyes. Then he rallied. 'Oh, I know what you'd like. The grand gesture! Shake the dust of this place off my heels. Go running off to London for the fine, free life on bread and water! Well, it might just have been possible if there were only the two of us to consider.'

'Napier!' she exploded. 'How can you say such a thing! Even before you knew I was expecting, you wouldn't even think of it. So don't pretend now. You're just . . .' She shrugged herself out of his embrace and turned her back on him. 'You're not man enough. That's the top and tail of it.'

'You won't provoke me,' he told her evenly.

'Why can't you have more faith in yourself? *I'm* willing to give it a try. And I'm the one who'd suffer most. But you . . . you just haven't got it in you.'

He came to her side and opened his arms again but she took a further step from him. He touched her elbow and said gently, 'In years to come we'll look back on this as our blackest moment. You'll see. Before the baby's born they'll come round to it and we'll be married and there'll be a proper settlement and we can start life together as God intends – not in some rat-infested slum in Whitechapel . . .'

'This desert were a heaven wert thou there,' she murmured. 'Something like that.'

'The difference between poetry and real life. A desert's a desert whoever's there.'

He kissed her again, promised to return tomorrow, told her to keep a good blaze in the hearth – said there was no shortage of firing – and made her promise to send the maid if there was any sort of difficulty at all. She watched him striding down over the meadow to the jetty, where he turned and waved before setting off to row back upwind to the castle. Every movement he made was so strong, so full of confidence, and yet it was an illusion, a mere trick of his body. Why couldn't he let some of that accidental self-assurance seep inward and infect his spirit, too – where it really counted?

More to the point, why had her own perceptions waited until now to make this rather important discovery about him!

As he grasped the oars he waved up at her the final time. She waved back – and vented one small scream of frustration. Did she still love him? she wondered. Not in the heedless way she had done last summer and autumn; it had turned into such a complicated emotion, something that could coexist with anger and even . . . well, she wouldn't want to call it hate – it came and went too quickly for that. But it was something close. She could murder him at times. And yet the feelings she had thought of as love persisted, too – so perhaps that's what they really were.

There was a scraping of heavy boots in the hall, then a voice she recognized as Stephen O'Lindon's. A moment later Bridget, the maid, announced him and said he was looking for Mr Napier.

'She says I missed him,' he spoke as he entered. 'But I don't see how. I'm after coming directly from the castle.'

She pointed out the dark little matchstick figure down on the lake, just vanishing behind a stand of pine on a headland by the shore.

'Ah, they didn't say.'

'Was it important? Will you take a dish of tea?'

'No, thanks. I have the estimate. That was all. There were one or two things I wanted to go over with . . .' He nodded toward the lake. ' 'Clare to God, a man could *walk* faster against that wind.'

She moved away from the window, prompting him to do likewise. Then she realized that had been her purpose; she didn't want Napier, when he emerged from behind the pine trees, to look up and see O'Lindon here. But why not? That sort of thing seemed to be happening more often these days – she'd do something or other quite instinctively, then realize she had a purpose in it, simple enough in an immediate sense, but complex and mysterious in its origins.

'Shall I look at it?' she asked.

'I don't know I'm sure.'

'It's going to be my place, too, after all.' She grinned. 'At least . . .' But whatever qualification had half-entered her mind, she let it drop, unspoken.

He passed a large unsealed envelope to her. On it a small, neat hand had written, 'Villa at Glaster'. Inside, in the same self-effacing copperplate, was page after page of specification and quantities, all of which added up to the final line: Grand total: £98. 17*s*. 4*d*.

'That *is* a grand total, too,' she said, handing it back to him. 'Just the right side of a hundred.'

His reluctant smile conceded it was no accident.

'What were your questions?' she asked.

He led her from room to room – that is, to seven of the villa's eight principal rooms – pointing out small defects and problems in each and explaining their implication in terms of money and time. Her admiration for his thoroughness deepened. 'The bedroom has passed your inspection unscathed, it seems,' she commented as they went back below.

'Ah, well . . .' He cleared his throat. 'There's nothing there that . . . I mean, your answers to the rest . . . no, nothing particular there. Will I write it all down and add it in or what?' he asked.

'I'd let them get used to the ninety-eight-odd pounds first,' she counselled.

His laughter, warm and slightly relieved, carried him to the door.

After he had gone it struck her that his response to her question about the bedroom had been . . . well, odd, to say the least. He had come to the house as a tradesman on a matter of trade; but his response to that question had been more . . . social, to put it at its most neutral.

Suddenly she saw the incident, trivial in itself, as a little peephole into something much larger. What sort of carpenter would be disturbed when his client, or the wife-to-be of his client, merely asked if there had been no defects or problems in the bedroom? Either an extremely shy man – and O'Lindon, now that she knew him better, did not strike her as being remotely shy – or one who did not see her simply as his client, or his client's betrothed. It was the first intimation that he had feelings of any kind about her, other than as a person who had shared the road with him a time or two.

She crossed the room to the window. Napier had passed out of sight by now but O'Lindon was moving near the edge of the pine plantation, surveying the timber with a professional eye and, every now and then, tapping one of the trunks with his ashplant, listening to the ring of it.

It amused her to think that Napier, the idle rich man, was probably sweating blood with his exertions against the wind by now; while O'Lindon, the artisan, was down there, sauntering through the wood, as leisurely as you'd like. It was a topsy-turvy world at times.

28

Of course, the whole of County Keelity *knew*, and what it lacked in certainty it made up for in tongues of invention. Daisy was the daughter of one of the high-ups at the Castle, *the* Castle, in Dublin. Sent here to hide her shame. Just wait, now. She'll start to show it any week. Trapper was the real father; Napier was only doing the daycent thing by him. Or by her.

From the Castle is it? From the moon more likely! Would you look at her – sure, anyone with half an ear could see it. She's one of *them*. Hadn't Liam O'Keefe seen her in Irishtown – and all the world knew what *he* was doing there. She's twisted that poor young fella round the finger that lacks the ring, may God come between him and all harm.

If you'd believed that, then here's another – it'll rain Spaniards this evening. True, the poor colleen's not from the Castle, not from inside it, if you follow me. But there *is* a connection. Oh boys, there surely is! Wait while I tell ye. She's only giving out she's a Protestant – to throw off the hunt. Her father's one of them Castle Catholics. I'd tell you his name only I'm sworn to it. That's the connection, d'ye see. It had nothing to do with the Lyndon-Furys at all at all, except someone tipped them a nudge and a wink. But I want to say this – there's a peerage in it for Sir Lucius, d'ye see. Except for her being a Catholic, the lad'd marry her like a shot off a shovel . . .

People who knew very well that Daisy O'Lindon was, indeed, Daisy O'Lindon nonetheless passed on this farrago, not as *the* truth but as one of many possible alternatives – one of those luxuriant hybrids of reality that flourish so mightily in Hibernian soil.

It annoyed Napier more than it did Daisy. You'd have to be very high up in Dublin before a scandal could really ruin you; in a village it would scar the meanest soul. So when it touched one of the county's leading families, it did more than graze the flesh. On his daily visits to the villa he grew increasingly morose. At first he used to pass on the latest outrage, but as imaginations and tongues probed the limits of the credible he gave up and sank into moody silence.

Daisy, though she naturally wished to see him cheerful again, was pragmatic enough to welcome his melancholy. It would, she thought, make him more willing to shake off the dust of this stuffy old county and go back where he belonged, taking her with him. She no longer argued with him about his stubbornness. She began to doubt her earlier judgement that he simply lacked the self-confidence to strike out alone; it was more complicated than that.

Just as the land and title would one day be Trapper's, by right of blood and descent, so the allowance was his, Napier's. Perhaps he *could* manage very well without it, but that wasn't the point; to give it up would be to renounce his rights. That was at the heart of his struggle, not the actual cash.

He could not express it so clearly, though. All he would say – on the few occasions when the subject arose – was, 'What gives them the right to cut me off? Why should I just tuck my tail in and run?'

Except for Madeleine's visits the days would have been dull indeed. She brought all the news of the district – gospel truth and first hand, most of it – and therefore barely tarnished in the telling. Hers was a way of life of which Daisy had only dreamed. Once the almost-daily duties of visiting the sick and the deserving poor of the villages were out of the way, Madeleine's time was completely given over to pleasure. In Daisy's world, a dance, a visit to the zoo, an outing to the Gaiety, was something you planned and looked forward to for weeks; even calling on a neighbour At Home could not be contemplated at under two days' notice – for the bonnet and the gloves and the trimmings it would entail. But Madeleine's life was one steady round of such pleasures, or their rural equivalents. And it required no forethought at all, for every other aspect of her life was geared to it . . . her wardrobe, the duties of her maid, the daily harnessing of carriage or gig – all presupposed that pleasure was her daily round.

The Keelity Hunt took up two full days in season and a ball each month. There was at least one other private ball a week and a dinner or two beside. There were sketching trips on Lough Cool when the weather permitted . . . more At Homes than you could ever attend . . . private theatricals, concert parties, church suppers, the occasional fit-up from Dublin, recitals by wandering operatic stars who had somehow failed to land a part at Milan this year – stars with Kerry accents and Italian names. What astonished Daisy was not so much that all these entertainments were going on all the time – for, of course, her native city could offer ten times such riches – but that Madeleine's first waking thought was to arrange her day around them.

It was flattering, too, that, in the midst of such a heady round of amusements, her sister-in-law-to-be not only found time to call at the villa but actually seemed to enjoy doing so. Even more flattering, she seemed to assume that Daisy had lived the equivalent sort of life in Dublin and was therefore infinitely advanced in the enjoyment of pleasures that would make her own rustic amusements seem picayune by comparison.

'But you *know* what my father does,' Daisy pointed out. 'You know we teeter at the edge of gentility. You know I even thought of applying for a place at Coolderg . . .'

'Yes, yes,' Madeleine would answer testily, shooing away the facts with a waft of her hand; a new hybrid was in the making and facts only got in the way.

'The world's gone mad altogether,' Daisy was reduced to saying. 'When the populace wants a myth in this country, it's God help the Recording Angel.'

Madeleine, to be sure, brought her the same gossip as Napier, but in the very opposite spirit. They would giggle over the wilder reachings of local fancy, yet when Daisy pointed out that Madeleine's picture of her life in Dublin was just as far from the known facts, that was different altogether.

'Did I do right, coming back here to torment Napier?' Daisy asked one day. 'That's not why I came, mind, but it's the way things have turned out.'

'You hadn't really an alternative,' Madeleine assured her – causing Daisy to realize the woman had given the matter not the slightest thought.

'Oh, indeed and I had. I could have gone on in my father's office. Should I go back there, I wonder, or what d'you think?'

'What about the baby?'

'I didn't come back here to hang that round his neck.'

'No, but there's no one in Dublin would give a tinker's cuss for it, one way or another. If your mother turned you outdoors for just showing yourself to artists, what on earth is she going to say to this! Surely your father would have to turn you out, too, this time?'

Madeleine was still not truly thinking about the situation – merely coming out with the most natural and obvious responses – the sort of thing any woman might say. It struck Daisy as doubly odd, then, that she herself had never once had such a thought. Was she, therefore, lacking in the natural and obvious responses of womankind?

'Why did you come back?' Madeleine challenged.

Daisy had to think. 'He stopped writing.' And but for that, she asked herself, I'd have stayed in Dublin? She had to admit it was not so. 'Actually, I suppose I saw myself persuading him to come away . . . thumb his nose at this allowance.'

Madeleine shook her head. 'The allowance isn't the important thing.'

'I'm beginning to agree.'

'Oh are you!' Her eyebrows shot up. 'You're more perceptive than I'd be in your place. I'll say that.'

'There's a principle involved, isn't there.'

Madeleine shook her head. 'Ah no. That's not your fox.'

'What then?'

Madeleine noticed that the door was an inch or two ajar. She rose and pushed it firmly shut. 'One never knows,' she said as she returned to her place by the fire. 'What I was going to say is . . . the way we pass on our land – the gentry, I mean – we deserve to lose it every fifth generation. Did you know the average landowning family only holds its land for five generations? Small wonder when you think of the lottery that's in it.'

'I don't follow,' Daisy said. 'I mean, I don't see how it applies here.'

'Don't you? How d'you think the Coolderg estate is going to fare once Trapper gets a-hold of it?'

Daisy frowned.

'Let me start the other end, then. Suppose the descent didn't automatically go to the eldest son. What if it could go to any child, son or daughter?'

Daisy thought a moment and then said, 'It'd be like Act One of *King Lear* in every landlord house in Ireland, by God.'

Madeleine laughed. 'So it would. I hadn't thought of that. But don't you believe the badge of ownership would be safer if each possessor could choose his followers? Don't you think I'd make a better steward of Coolderg than Trapper ever will? And don't you think Napier'd knock the lot of us into a cocked hat at it?'

'Indeed and I do not!' Daisy protested at once. 'He's an artist born.'

'Fiddlesticks!' Madeleine said cheerily, not the least abashed at Daisy's vehemence. 'His art is a way of owning this place. Wait till I tell ye. I was in the nursery the very day Napier realized he wouldn't grow up like Papa – he wouldn't ever be the owner of Coolderg.'

Daisy laughed. 'How can you possibly know such a thing – you a child and all?'

'Well now, he didn't just *realize* it, not just like that. To be honest with you, Trapper taunted him with it. Of course, Napier broke down in tears, and then Trapper was satisfied, and peace descended for at least another minute. And what did Napier do then, from that day on? Drawing! He drew desert islands with himself as Robinson Crusoe. And what was his home there? Coolderg Castle! He drew adventure stories of himself exploring for lost cities in the African jungle. And always, when he discovered them, the poor ignorant blackamoors would think him a god and invite him onto their throne. And what was the royal palace? I'll give you one guess! So that's what art is to Napier, let him dress it up how he will. I've watched it from that day to this. You could fill the main guard with his books of drawings of the place.'

Daisy could hardly believe that a simple little fact like that could change her whole perception of her darling man. And yet it did.

No longer did he seem merely stubborn; he became a man possessed – and so deeply possessed, too, that he himself was barely aware of it. She did not try to tax him with the accusation that was implicit in what Madeleine had revealed, for she knew he would pooh-pooh it and ridicule her; but that only made the whole idea more credible. She had far less trouble with the notion that a person could act for motives that were obvious to others (not least when a kind sibling went to the trouble of pointing them out!) and still be perfectly ignorant of them himself. After all, she thought, the same was probably true of her. She did lots of things without ever pausing to ask herself why. That probably boiled down to the same thing in the end, didn't it?

A constant and somewhat laconic observer of these goings-on was Stephen O'Lindon. When she had no visitors, he was usually to be found out in the turf shed he had converted into a workshop, repairing a door or making a new casement. But when Napier or Madeleine called, he came into the house to fit these items or remove the next one for refurbishment. At first she thought this was a fairly blatant excuse for eavesdropping, but then it occurred to her that it was all part-and-parcel with his earlier actions. He was behaving as if *he* – not she – needed a chaperone to be in the house with her at all. The thought began to intrigue her.

One morning Lady Lyndon-Fury herself called; O'Lindon almost trod on her heels as he came in to start stripping the old varnish off the panelling in the hall.

Her visitor was so unexpected that Daisy grew quite flustered; it annoyed her not to be glacially calm and correct – as she dearly wished she were – but there was nothing she could do beyond wait for her heart to settle and her tremor to subside. Her ladyship, however, misread it as a sign of weakness and became a little overconfident.

'I'll not go all five ways to Tipperary, Miss O'Lindon. When you decided to return to Coolderg, no one was more pleased than I. Well' – she smiled – 'except, perhaps, Napier. I fought, I may tell you, even harder than he, if such a thing were possible, to get my husband to agree to your staying here. The thought that his first grandchild might be born into a household that was half Roman Catholic was . . . well, you may imagine.'

'It was extremely good of you to take my part,' Daisy responded coolly – glad to notice how calm she had become.

The woman saw it, too, and became more wary. 'Not at all. Indeed, I do not think I took your part so much as my son's. I believe you and he are admirably suited to each other in every way . . . bar one. But, alas, it is that one I have come to talk about, for it has proved an insuperable objection.'

'To you?' Daisy was gaining in confidence with each moment that passed.

'To my husband – and therefore to me. I had hoped that, by getting to know you, he might soften . . .'

'You mean once he saw you can't even find the scars where they rooted out my horns!' She touched her brow as if in demonstration.

'There's no need to mock it, Miss O'Lindon. These matters are of the deepest significance to him. To us both, I mean. However, he remains adamant. You could be the Good Fairy herself but as long as your mother was what she was, there can be no question of an alliance between our two families.'

'Are you going to ask me to leave?' Daisy cut in.

Lady Lyndon-Fury held up her hand and shook her head. 'So impetuous! Of course I'm not. I know better even than to try.'

'Well, what then?'

'If you'll just . . .' She sighed. 'Listen and I'll tell you. You can, of course, continue to persuade Napier to forgo his allowance, run off with you, and marry you. It would mean he would never be welcome back here, even though it broke his father's heart to forbid him the place.' She broke off and stared into the fire. 'I think it might kill his father,' she murmured. 'However, I would not make my appeal to you on those grounds.'

'Oh!' Daisy was stung. 'D'you think I'd be insensitive . . .'

She held up her hand. 'I have better ones.' Her eyes looked Daisy up and down, assessing her carefully. 'Has it ever occurred to you that there are . . . liaisons other than marriage?'

Daisy swallowed hard but did not trust herself to speak.

The other let out a small head of pent-up breath. 'At least you don't explode. You do know what I mean?'

'Perfectly.'

'Had you considered such a course? Please be completely frank with me, my dear. I am on your side – at least to the extent that I wish to help you as far as the situation allows. Has it ever crossed your mind?'

'Yes,' Daisy said cautiously.

'Good!' Her ladyship relaxed again. 'The disadvantage of such a course is, as I'm sure you've already realized, that, should anything go amiss, you would be left in an extremely vulnerable situation. You've considered that, too?'

Daisy nodded.

'I thought as much. Well, far be it from me – I mean Sir Lucius and me – to condone immorality . . . though it's the lesser of two evils. But we, too, have given the matter some thought, and it seems to me – to us, I mean – that if we were to draw up a proper legal settlement, guaranteeing your rights and position . . . well, you might consider a liaison with our son that stopped short of marriage.'

'Here?' Daisy asked in surprise.

Lady Lyndon-Fury was surprised, too. 'How interesting that that should be your immediate question,' she observed.

'I have particular reason for asking it, I assure you.'

The other smiled. 'The answer is, of course, only until you've had the baby. After that, one of the conditions for our support would be that you never set foot in Keelity again. And, while we cannot stipulate that you remain out of Ireland entirely, we would appreciate it if you were to live mainly over the water. However, I think that was your wish in any case.'

'And Napier?'

'He would be free to come and go – and the grandchild, naturally.'

Daisy was on the point of asking what Napier had thought of this brilliant notion when a different form of the same question occurred to her. 'What did Napier say?' she asked. 'When you put this proposal to him.'

29

Daisy stood at the window watching Napier pick his way with care through the quagmire of the pasture to the mudfield of the lawn. All her frustrations were suddenly focused in him and she had to rein in her feelings, tell herself that nothing in life was ever meant to be simple . . . she was probably as much to blame, and so on – all the ways in which people manage to rub along together without resorting to murder.

A light drizzle, warm for the time of year, fell steadily from a sky of uniform gray. He passed Stephen O'Lindon on his way to the turf shed; they exchanged a word or two. Probably O'Lindon said, 'A soft day!' to which Napier would answer, 'Thank God.' The weather, too, was not meant to be simple; people also needed ways of coping there.

He made energetic noises out in the hall as he took off his oilskin and brushed the mud from his boots. 'A soft day,' the maid commented as she took his coat. 'Yes, thank God,' he replied.

Daisy grinned. 'A soft day,' she murmured, holding forth her arms to embrace him.

'Bloody awful,' he growled, giving her a perfunctory kiss. 'There are lunatics out there hunting and fishing, you know.'

'They probably think the same when they see you sketching.'

'And you sitting beside me.'

'Ah.' She smiled sweetly. 'But they know I don't belong here. Outsiders like me don't get judged in the same way.'

He knew what lay behind such apparently light badinage and wisely let her comments lie. 'If I go sketching this afternoon . . . it might ease off a bit after luncheon. If I do, don't feel you have to come too.'

'What else is there for me to do?' she asked evenly. 'Madeleine isn't coming today.'

'But that's all you ever do. Come out and sit by me if I'm sketching, or gossip with her.' He sat on the padded seat of the hearth fender and reached his hands toward the glowing turf. 'I must be mad,' he added, 'even to think of going out on a day like this.'

'Shall I repeat the question?' she asked.

He slumped. 'No.'

'I know very well what *you* want me to do,' she went on. 'You'd like me to be discussing every little detail with O'Lindon and choosing colours and looking at samples of papers . . .'

'And why not?' he challenged.

She seated herself in a chair, three-quarters facing him. 'I'm not going to go over all that again.'

He stared at the fire a long time. 'Well,' he said at last.

'Well,' she echoed – and waited.

'What my mother said . . .'

'Yes?'

'She really is on our side, you know.'

'Hurrah!'

'I mean, that was her best offer. *Their* best offer.'

'Napier!' She stretched one hand across her forehead and massaged it energetically. 'You persist in manoeuvring me into a situation where I must seem to treat with them. I told your mother – and I presume she told you – I'm not in the least bit interested in offers . . . acceptances . . . legal agreements. Dear God but I thought it was the last straw when she said that the King of Bavaria or Bohemia or somewhere got around the difficulties of marrying a Catholic by this . . . what was it? Automatic marriage?'

'Morganatic.'

'That sounds even worse. It sounds like some way of restraining violent lunatics. Listen while I tell you. I'm no longer concerned if we're married or not. Of course, I'd like to be married but' – she smiled wickedly – 'we must all be prepared to make sacrifices, eh? All I really want is for the two of us to be away from here, and the farther the better. I want us to go back to London – even to a slum in Whitechapel, if you want to put it that way. I never want to see this place again.'

'But it doesn't have to be that choice,' he cried, half in anger, half in pain.

'It does,' she replied calmly. 'For me it does. They've turned you into nothing better than a remittance man. In fact, worse than a remittance man. He usually gets told to go off to New South Wales or somewhere. But you've put yourself on a short chain.'

'That's a most unfair way of describing it.'

'No it isn't. It's how I see it. I hate women who dish out ultimatums to their men and I always swore I never would, but now I've been patient long enough. Now I have to tell you: either you come away with me and we go back to living as we were, married or unmarried . . .' She let the rest hang.

'Or?'
Still she kept her silence.
'I see.' He pursed his lips angrily.
'I hope so.'

30

It was as if she had never spoken. For a day or two, then three, then four, she held her fire, thinking it reasonable to allow him time to come to terms with the enormity, the all-or-nothingness, of her ultimatum. Madeleine told her she was wasting her time. Napier would happily let four days turn into four weeks unless she kept up the pressure on him. But then Daisy knew how much the woman wanted a ready-made pied-à-terre, especially in London, and the alleged chaperonage of a married (or alleged) sister-in-law to sanctify her visits there – which would doubtless be as frequent as her brother's patience allowed.

But when Napier's silence on that particular topic stretched toward the full week, she came round to Madeleine's view. She gave way once more – not to him, this time, but to his mother's wishes. 'What if I swallow my pride?' she asked Napier. 'Agree to this legal rigmarole. Will you also . . . ?'

'But it means agreeing that we'll never marry,' he protested.

She shrugged. 'It looks like our only way out of this impasse.'

'Well, I won't have it.' He slipped his arms about her. 'Darling! We'll win in the end. We just have to hold on and not lose heart. When they realize we truly mean it, in throwing their offer back in their faces, then they'll also understand they have no other choice than to give way. Please? Just hold on a little longer?'

'How much longer?' she asked, already hating her own weakness.

He licked his lips and drew a deep breath. 'I think we should be prepared to hold out until . . . well, even a week before the baby is due.'

'And then?'

'Ah . . . well . . . if they haven't yielded by then . . .'

'Are you going to say you promise you'll marry me no matter what? I hope not, Napier, because that's an old, old song with you. You sang it in London. You sang it at Christmas. You sang it when I came back from Dublin. And you've been . . .'

'I know, but this time I really, really mean it. Honestly. Cross my heart and hope to die.'

She struggled out of his embrace and walked to the door. He asked where she was going. She left the room without a word, closing the door behind her.

He caught up with her on the stairs and again asked where she was going; again she remained silent. At the stairhead Stephen O'Lindon stood aside to let them pass. 'About this kingpost, Mr Napier,' he began.

'Later!' Napier snapped.

In her bedroom she reached for her one battered suitcase. Unthinkingly he leaped ahead of her and fished it down. Then it dawned on him. 'I see,' he said icily.

A tear gathered at the rim of her eye. She sniffed it back and framed herself to what she now knew was inevitable.

'You might at least talk,' he went on. His tone was exactly poised between anger and conciliation.

'I did,' she replied wearily. 'In September, October, November . . .'

'Oh, very funny!'

Silently she began to pack her things, but as fast as she put them in he grabbed them and clutched them to his chest. 'I mean *now*! Why can't you do as I ask? Why can't you wait just a little longer? They *will* give way, I promise you.'

'Promises!' she said contemptuously. ' 'Clare to God, the gombeen man must have been around with a wagon-load going cheap.' She put a chemise in the case, which he at once snatched up – letting go of one of her stockings in the process. She caught it, folded it neatly, and packed it once more. When he snatched it up, its partner fell.

At any other time the absurdity of these events would have sent them into hysterics. But now, by some strange alchemy of the emotions, it unleashed all their anger and bitterness. She flung the stocking at him and shouted, 'Your father will never yield, and well you know it! He's that sort of Protestant. And you're the same – as stiff-necked as fighting bulls.'

'And how many times have you met him?' Napier sneered.

'How many times would I look at the Shannon to know it wasn't dry?'

'Oh God, aren't you very quick!'

'No, I'm not, Napier. I'm slow. I should have done this weeks ago. I should never have come back at all. That was my mistake. You'd have come to Dublin yourself by now. But having me incarcerated in this mausoleum – that's made it too easy for you.'

'Easy?' he mocked.

'Yes. Easy to go on deluding yourself that you can get it all in the end – me, the child, your allowance, and your father's blessing. You needn't sacrifice a thing.'

'Needn't sacrifice unnecessarily,' he corrected.

'It's this place, isn't it,' she said bitterly. 'You'll never be free of it. Well, I'll tell you something. You never will be. As long as you're here, you never will be free of it. And in the end it will destroy you. Me. Both of us. We have to get away.'

The anger went out of him. He dropped her clothes and, seeming now to be a little embarrassed at handling such intimate things, walked away to the window. 'You're the one who's going to destroy it all,' he said. 'We could have a bloody marvellous life here. Look at it. Every painter I know – and his wife – would give their eye teeth to have a little haven like this. I could paint in peace and you could run the whole world around us. But you can't share me. That's really it, isn't it: You can't be big enough to share me.'

A strangled gasp of exasperation escaped her. 'Lord, I might as well be whistling jigs to a gravestone! The truth is exactly the opposite, only you're too blind to see it. I want to share you with the whole world. I want people to *know* you.'

'The way they know Rembrandt?' he asked pointedly. 'From his languid drawl and his brilliant wit and the beautiful descriptions of the grand pictures he's going to paint one of these days? Or the way they know Jimmy Whistler? From his monastic dedication to his art?'

The sarcasm – or, rather, the truth at the heart of it – dented her assurance. He saw it and came striding to her, gripping her arm and shaking it gently in time with his words. 'You see? An artist doesn't have to live at the Café Royal and be up on all the gossip. Trust me? Please? We'll do far better here than there. This is the world for a real artist to live in. London's just . . . opium.' He shrugged apologetically that he could find no better image.

For a moment she was convinced, but then all her experience came to buoy her up, to show her how impossible it would be. One argument alone would answer all his; the fact that it had not occurred to her immediately only showed how persuasive he could be, after his fashion. She put it to him now: 'Your parents will never allow it. The one condition they've clung to, through thick and thin, is that if we live together, we cannot do so here.'

He grinned lazily. 'Let's cross that bridge when we come to it, eh?'

She stamped her foot in rage but he persisted. 'What are they going to do? Evict you? Send round the bailiffs?' He shook his head at the impossibility of such a thing. 'They'll huff and they'll puff – and then they'll do exactly the same as me.'

'What?'

'Nothing.'

Looking into his smiling face she suddenly saw all her tomorrows mirrored there – a life of masterly procrastination, where every decision was put on the long finger unless it were about the placing of marks on paper or canvas. Life with a genius. And in that same instant she knew she was not up to it. She gathered her fallen underwear, folded it thoughtfully, and started once again to pack.

And this time he did not stop her.

'Devil take you, then,' he said quietly as he left the room.

A moment later she heard the front door slam.

31

When her bag was packed – a process that should have taken moments though, in fact, it dragged on a whole weary hour – Daisy wandered out to the stairhead. O'Lindon was offering up a repaired kingpost to the stumps of the balustrades. 'I suppose I've missed the last connection to Dublin, anyway,' she said, rubbing her hand over the smooth knob of the post. 'I say! Have you a lathe out there?'

It piqued his curiosity. 'And what may you know of lathes, Miss Daisy?' he asked with interest.

'Oh.' She preened herself in jocular fashion. 'We use them in the japanning business, too, you know. For circular lines and things. That's beautifully turned.'

'Ah, it was a grand piece of wood to start with. Red deal from the far north of Sweden. It must have been a hundred and fifty years a-growing. See how close the rings are?'

'Oh yes.' She moved her fingernail across them, a fraction of an inch at a time. 'What year was 'Ninety-eight, I wonder? And when was I born?' Her voice broke.

'Ah, you have the imagination,' he said admiringly.

She nodded, blinked, smiled. 'Have I missed the Dublin connection?'

'Not at all. Will I take you now?' He reached for her bag.

'What about your work?'

'My time's my own.'

It was a matter of moments to catch the pony and harness him up. They set off at a gentle trot over a road mottled with pools; the pale ridges between them were already turning to dust. 'There's good drying in that wind,' he said. The sun broke out from behind a bank of clouds over Lough Cool.

They came to a little booreen that ran up into the hills to the east. He checked the pony and she realized he was going to turn into it. A moment later she realized why – to avoid the sight of Coolderg Castle.

'No don't,' she said at once. 'Stay on this road.'

It was one of those small, impulsive decisions – the kind that people make all the time – which, it seemed in retrospect, determined the rest of her life.

After a mile or so they came to a sharp bend, where a pretty little gate lodge marked the back entrance to the Coolderg demesne. 'I carved those barge-boards,' he told her, adding unselfconsciously, 'the first jobbing joinery I ever did. Aren't they the crowning of the place?'

She agreed that they were.

'But they'd want to renew the paint this summer,' he went on. A sad edge to his tone told her he was thinking of the passing of the years.

As they took the sharp right-hand bend he said, 'Years ago, now, the old ones will tell you, that road went straight on. And there was a village in there. But the Lyndon-Furys evicted them all and enlarged the demesne. So that's why the road goes to Tipperary and back now.'

'And here's me evicting myself,' she commented.

'You were on about the rising of 'Ninety-eight. What chances would you give this new Home Rule Bill, I wonder?'

'I'm not great on politics,' she confessed – and then immediately fell to thinking what that bland statement actually meant.

He, meanwhile, continued talking. And as she listened with one ear and harkened to her own reasoning with the other, she became aware of an uncanny resonance between their two minds. It was as if he spoke aloud the thoughts that rose from within her.

'There's politics,' he said, 'and then again there's politics. I'm not great on all that gas over the water. But when it's happening down that lane or over that hill, then I'll sit up and take . . .' He hesitated. She thought he was going to say notice, but the word he used was, '. . . part.'

'In what way?' she asked.

He withdrew slightly into his former shell. 'Ah, there's a fierce need for land reform. A great spleen will go out over that if nothing's done.'

For most of its meandering way, the road gave no view of the castle, despite the fact that it passed along the flank of the hills that ringed the enlarged demesne. A high stone wall confined the eye. 'Can you imagine the labour of building that,' he said. 'My father worked on that. It was in the famines, for relief of the starving. When they saw the height of it, they knew the famine would be long. "God bless the English," he says. "But for them we'd all have died." That's his idea, now.'

'Does he mean the Lyndon-Furys?' she asked 'But they're not English.'

He nodded in ambiguous acceptance of that point of view. 'Sure, you wouldn't know what they are.'

At that moment they came to the gateway to the home farm, one of the few gaps in that long, high wall. He reined in the pony and for a while they sat there, staring down at the castle. The sun was now fully out, though, this being a late afternoon in winter, it was low in the sky and beyond the lough, whose waters were dark with reflections of the hills on its farther shore. Upon that blackness the sun etched the silhouette of the castle roofs and battlements in a burning line of silvery gold. A fitful breeze plucked at a pennant with the Lyndon-Fury arms; it rose and fell, rose and fell – the only moving thing in sight.

By now, of course, Daisy knew the castle from every angle – from the main drive, from the deerpark, from the lake. She had always seen it as a focus of beauty in the landscape, a symbol of permanence and continuity. Her own family's 'claim' to the place had become little more than a nostalgic jest – a friendly tease between her and Madeleine, and Napier, too. But now, into that complex tapestry of feelings that any such place is bound to evoke, she became aware of a new strand, weaving itself in of its own accord. Part of her could still acknowledge the picturesque charm of its ancient stones; but a new eye, sour and disillusioned, saw the arrogance with which it held its dominion there.

'Yours,' he said. 'And mine.'

She laughed but without humour. 'That wall your father built – we're the wrong side of it, look.'

He clucked the pony back into motion. 'Who was the last O'Lindon on the right side of that wall?' he asked with rhetorical emphasis.

But she took it as a genuine question. 'Caroline, I suppose. The one who married the first Fury and started the Lyndon-Furys.'

'Ah, but who was the last to own it? Caroline just married into it.'

'I don't know. What does it matter?'

'I was only thinking – when he came into his inheritance – when he stood on those battlements and looked out over the O'Lindon acres, did he ever imagine he'd be the last? And was there ever a pair of Furys went riding by, thinking to themselves wouldn't it be a fierce thing altogether to own that place?'

She pondered the question a while. 'It's a quare world, indeed,' she said at length.

'There's a thing I meant to ask you,' he went on after a silence. 'You remember that evening in Dublin? Or on the train? When you were after telling me how you got up a bit of credit for your father with that man at the bank?'

'Yes,' she said warily.

'Well, I was wondering, like, would you ever see your way to giving me a letter of introduction to that fella?'

His tone suggested it was a matter of little moment but she could feel him holding his breath. 'Is this about that invention of yours?' she asked.

'It is.'

'Well, I will of course. But there's one thing you should know. I've little enough experience of those men myself, but one thing I did learn – they'll not lend you a farthing until you can prove to them you don't need to borrow at all.'

He gave out a surprised grunt and frowned at her.

'It's the God's truth,' she went on, giving him a morosely encouraging smile. 'He wouldn't advance a penny at first, and then just as I was leaving – empty-handed, you understand – he asked wouldn't the landlord help. And when I told him my father was his own landlord – I mean, his father bought the freehold back in eighteen-fifty-something – well! You never saw the like of the change that came over him! Up he springs and ushers me back into my seat. "By all the holy!" says he, "why did you keep that back till last? Are you sure there's no mortgage on it?" I said how would I know and he asked if I'd seen the actual deeds and I said they were in a tin box in the office that minute and he said then there was no mortgage on it. Anyway, the upshot was he took the deeds and he lent my father a quarter of their value. That's how those fellows prosper.'

'Is he a Jew-man?'

'Not at all. He's a good Protestant like you and me. A Jew-man would have lent us the money without the deeds, but, of course, he'd want more interest on it.'

He shook his head wonderingly at the complexity of the world out there. 'You know a lot about it,' he commented.

She chuckled and jerked her head at the great wall to their left. 'When you lose a fine place like that . . . sure, it's a great teacher.'

Impulsively she seized his arm and gave it a squeeze. 'Ah, God love you, Stephen,' she cried. 'Aren't you the crowning of all comfort at a time like this!'

His eyes sparkled as he overcame his astonishment. He darted a glance at her, drew breath to speak . . . and then thought better of it. Whatever hurdle he saw between them, his spirit balked at the last moment. Then he merely nodded, as much to the road as to her – and as much in rueful admission of his own inadequacy as in delight at her outburst.

The muscles in his arms were so tense she made some excuse of adjusting her skirt so as to let go of him. It suddenly struck her that he wanted her. By some strange means of human communication, which cannot be explained – but cannot be doubted, either – she knew he was longing at that moment to turn to her, take her in his arms, kiss her. She knew it was so because, also at that moment, it was what she desired, too, more than anything.

They teetered on the verge of that possibility. Would he? she wondered. And would she?

Then he cleared his throat, clucked the pony to a smarter pace, and she knew the moment had passed. Cursing her own impulsiveness, she wondered how long it would be now before he would work himself so close to a declaration again. Knowing him, it would be weeks, or even months. Like the careful craftsman he was, he'd re-lay a good foundation first.

After a mile or two they joined the main road between Simonstown and Portumna. And a mile or two beyond that, away from the Coolderg gate, he pointed up a winding booreen to their left and said, 'Speaking of ancestral acres, I'm after being a bit of a landlord myself, did you know?' His grin warned her he was joking. 'Will I show you?'

'Have we time?' she asked, intrigued.

He turned the pony's head into the narrow lane, saying, 'The man who made time made plenty of it.'

A furlong or so up the lane there was an abrupt change in the flora, where thistles and nettles marked a site of recent cultivation. 'There!' he exclaimed, sticking his thumbs under his braces and snapping them in a parody of pride.

'What in the name of God is it?' she asked. 'Or *was* it?'

He became serious again. 'From here to that hill beyond it's all cutaway bog. Would you ever think there were eighty families here once? And in living memory, too?'

Looking at the landscape more closely she could see it was a patchwork of dereliction. Beneath the weeds were squared-off boundaries and, here and there, the last remains of old stone walls.

'The whole village got up one morning and rode to Shannon Harbour.'

'They went to America?'

He nodded. 'And that man there' – he pointed again at the plot beside them – 'for some reason he owned three acres there. He was the big farmer of this village. And he sold it to my father for five pounds and the passage money.'

'Your father was robbed, so,' she said.

He nodded in agreement. 'He had a softness for the old fella. He courted his daughter until she died.'

'Ah.' Her eyes roved this way and that over the weed-drowned acres, trying to fathom what emotions must once have charged this desolate place. 'And how do you come to own them?' she asked. 'Surely your father's still alive?'

'Thanks be to God.' He backed the trap into the brambles where he knew there had once been a gateway and the standing was hard. 'He told me – when I was fourteen, I'm talking about now – he told me that if I bet Tommy Kelly to first prize in the Bible Study class, he'd give me that land.'

'And plainly you did.'

He glanced back over his shoulder. 'Me and the lads built quite a castle there that summer. There was more of the house standing then, of course.'

'There's none now.'

'Ah, you'd be surprised.'

She was silent until they reached the main road. Then she said, casually, 'Have you the title deeds and all?'

Their eyes met and they laughed.

'God, it'd never work,' he said.

But she was vehement. 'Why not, I'd like to know? Is that man going to come all the way down here to look at three acres? Listen! I'll stay with me auntie tonight. You find those deeds. And we'll go to Dublin tomorrow instead. Sure what's another day when the man made so many of them.'

32

Mr Fitzpatrick turned the patent grant over, then over again, then yet again – as if, like a playing card taken from a conjuror, it might change each time. 'You must understand, Mr O'Lindon,' he said, 'we are not a merchant bank. This is really something more in Baring's line, or Rothschild's.'

Stephen O'Lindon cleared his throat dubiously. 'Merchant,' he repeated and let the word hang.

'I think,' Daisy cut in, 'Mr O'Lindon has it more in mind to be a manufacturer than a merchant. At least, that's my understanding. Like my father, you know. That's why I thought of you at once, Mr Fitzpatrick.'

He bowed his head gracefully. 'And a charming thought it was, too, Miss O'Lindon.' Then he explained what a merchant bank really was.

Stephen said he supposed it was like the difference between a carpenter and a joiner. Daisy, who could see that he was preparing himself for rejection, interrupted once again. She remembered a fragment of an earlier conversation with the manager and took a flying chance on it. 'Are you a sailing man at all, Mr Fitzpatrick?' she asked. 'You never struck me as someone who'd be entirely happy to be shut away indoors all the time.'

He chuckled. 'Now how could I afford to go sailing, Miss O'Lindon?' His eyes recruited Stephen's amusement at the divine impracticality of the fair sex. 'Though it's true I have my eye on a little rowing boat in Howth, where I could row out and fish off the head in good weather. And she'd take a sail the size of a good shirt now.'

She nodded sympathetically. 'You'd be wanting to put aside a fair few shillings for an item like that, I suppose? The boat, I mean. Not the shirt.'

They all laughed and he agreed it wasn't cheap.

Daisy jabbed a finger at him. 'And that's the whole beauty of Mr O'Lindon's machine, d'you see. He can make a boat at *half* the price of anyone else.'

She heard Stephen draw breath to protest and added firmly, 'Or even less.'

The banker lowered his eyes and stared again at the patent. He glanced briefly at her and scratched his chin. She chuckled. 'Have you half the price saved up already, then?' She turned to Stephen, as picador to matador. And he had the nous to take her up. 'You shall have the first one I make, Mr Fitzpatrick,' he promised.

'The first one that doesn't leak,' she added, as if it were a serious and necessary qualification.

Again they all laughed but now both she and Stephen knew it was a mere matter of time before he yielded. However, his next question caught them unawares.

'Forgive me if I seem to trespass beyond the strict compass of a banker's remit,' he said, 'but may I ask you, Miss O'Lindon, if you will . . . ah, how may I put it? In the shaping of this Mr O'Lindon's business will you be playing anything like the part you have already played in the reshaping of another Mr O'Lindon's?'

Daisy breathed in, caught Stephen's eye, and blushed furiously – at the same time she was angered at her lack of self-control. 'Why . . . ?' she stammered. 'I mean why d'you need to . . . what difference does it make?'

'A great deal. My directors are most grateful for what you did there.'

'Away!' Embarrassment made her more scornful than she intended. 'Anyone could have done it.'

'You may think so. The fact remains that it was not *anyone* who actually did it. It was you.'

Now poor Daisy did not know what to say. If she said no, O'Lindon might not get his loan; if yes, he might reasonably assume she'd gone to these elaborate lengths to trap him into employing her. Suddenly she knew that the most important thing in her life at that moment was that he should not think her so deceitful. 'No,' she said decisively.

But at that very moment Stephen said, 'I was going . . .' He paused as her answer struck home.

Mr Fitzpatrick smiled. 'Yes?' he urged.

To Daisy's astonishment Stephen's ears turned bright red. 'I was only going to say that if I got the capital to start up, I was surely going to ask Miss O'Lindon . . . to . . . what you said.'

Shyly she reached across and touched his arm. 'You don't have to,' she told him.

He stared uncomfortably at his boots. 'I do,' he mumbled.

The banker picked up the title deeds. 'In a formal sense, of course, the loan would be secured against these.' He grinned. 'I know there's little point in asking any Irishman to describe his own land, so, Miss O'Lindon, tell me what you think of it?'

'Killderrin Farm is it?' Daisy asked, giving that patch of secondary wilderness its full title. An image flitted through her mind of her father praising a consignment of japanned boxes that had yet to be painted – though he'd swear they were only after being packed and despatched that very moment. 'Ah, Mr Fitzpatrick, it's easy to tell you're not from County Keelity at all, for there's not a man, woman, or child west of the Slieve Derg who'd ask such a question. Wasn't the luxuriance of its pasture praised in the annals of Clonmacnoise? And didn't it pass to the Bishop of Clonfert, who fought twelve years with the Bishop of Killaloe for the title to it – the very title that's before you now.' She paused for breath and pointed dramatically at the country lawyer's scrawl upon the desk.

Seeing her set to go on as long as he'd let her, Mr Fitzpatrick raised a hand and stemmed the flow. He knew now that the place was more than likely worthless – but he also knew that wasn't the point. The deeds were a formality, something to pacify his directors; he, however, made up his mind on quite different grounds. Still, he thought, he'd give her a run for the money. 'I'm surprised you didn't go straight to a local bank,' he commented. 'With land of such enormous value, they'd surely leap at the chance to lend.'

She thought furiously. Tell him those banks had lent to competitors in Portumna and Killaloe? They'd see their investment vanish overnight? No. He'd only ask their names. She smiled her most engaging smile. 'To be honest with you now, Mr Fitzpatrick, I brought Mr O'Lindon here out of gratitude to you. For the way you've helped my father over his difficulties.'

'Don't think us too noble,' he warned her. 'Our supposed generosity has been handsomely repaid.'

'And don't you think that'll be the case here?' she challenged. 'Don't you see that Mr O'Lindon is going to have the biggest business in the whole Midlands before he's done?' She glanced at Stephen to quell any astonishment he might vent – and was herself astonished to see him nodding in solemn agreement.

Mr Fitzpatrick was silent awhile. He drummed his fingertips upon his leather-topped desk; he placed them together and pursed his lips between them; he stared intently at Daisy, then at Stephen. Finally he said, 'It's the risk of my lifetime, I know, and I shall possibly live to regret taking it. Yet I think not. I have a feeling about you, Mr O'Lindon, and you, Miss O'Lindon. And I trust it as implicitly as I'm going to trust you. If this enterprise of yours' – he spoke that word to Stephen alone but the ambiguity was not entirely dispelled – 'should by some misfortune fail, it will not be for lack of grey matter, nor of your willingness to work.' He smiled at both. 'So my answer is yes! My head clerk will draw up the necessary documents. If you return tomorrow, you may draw your first tranche.' He turned to Daisy. 'And if I may now have a brief private word with you, Miss O'Lindon, concerning your father?'

He rose and accompanied Stephen to the door, where he shook him warmly by the hand. Returning to his desk he asked offhandedly, 'He is a Protestant, I suppose? You'd hardly have brought him here otherwise?'

She nodded. 'Is my father all right? He's said nothing in his letters.'

He dipped his head as a reluctant concession that he could not actually point to anything amiss. 'I just wondered if you might find time to run up here . . . once a month, say? Just to do the books and . . . well, you know the sort of thing. He lacks your genius at getting in the bills.'

'He'd rather meet his debtors and drink five per cent on tick,' she agreed savagely.

'Quite. So you do understand? I mean, it's in your own interest, really. With this new boat-building venture ahead of you, the last thing you want is the distraction of your father's firm collapsing.'

She promised to do what she could.

He rose to his feet.

'About Mr O'Lindon,' she said. 'And me. I mean, that's the point. There's nothing between Mr O'Lindon and me. We're just distant cousins. We hadn't even discussed . . .'

He reached out a hand to help her rise and kept a gentle hold on her arm even after she was standing – all the way to the door. 'I know,' he said. 'I should apologize for that. I rushed that fence a little. Still.' His smile broadened. 'In years to come, it won't seem so heinous a crime, I believe.'

33

They went round the corner and up into Trinity Lane before they dared give vent to their delight. Once there, however, they grasped hands and, flinging decorum to the winds, danced an impromptu jig upon the pavement. 'We've done it!' Daisy cried. 'We've really and truly done it!'

Breathless with the excitement and exertion, he gasped, '*You've* done it! That Dublin jackeen hadn't the hair of a chance.'

'Careful!' She laughed and panted at the same time. 'I'm from those parts myself.'

He slowed down enough to reply, 'Well, that's to be decided, I'd say.'

Their gyration came to a halt. The stares of the passers-by made them suddenly self-conscious. They let go of each other. He dry-soaped his hands, caught her eye, looked away. She smoothed her dress, glanced casually across the lane – and saw a face from the past.

'Swan!' she called out. 'Yes, it *is* me.' She had no choice, for the woman had clearly recognized her and was only hesitating on whether or not to approach. As Swan crossed the road to them, Daisy quickly explained matters to her cousin.

'I thought you were in London with Napier,' Swan said cheerily as she drew near. She glanced at Stephen with brief but pointed curiosity.

'Too many fogs,' Daisy replied vaguely. 'Let me introduce Mr Stephen O'Lindon from Carrig, who's third cousin to me. This is' – she hesitated – 'Rosamund? Rosamund Everett? We only ever called you Swan – I'm sorry.'

She laughed as she shook Stephen's hand. 'I'm amazed you remember at all. Nobody else ever does. How is Napier these days? Did you know I'd got married? Well, obviously not. I'm Mrs Mercier now.'

'No!' Daisy leaped avidly on the news to avoid the prior question. 'Do I know him? I don't recall the name.' At the back of her mind, unspoken, was a vague memory that Swan was a Roman Catholic; but Mercier was surely a Protestant name, of old Huguenot stock. With that delicate bit of the landscape prepared she went on to ask, 'Is he an artist?'

'God, no! I needed someone who can keep *me* in pigments. He's with the Bank of Ireland round the corner. I'm after doing some shopping and I'm to meet him for luncheon at O'Donoghue's. Look, why not join us? I'm longing to hear all your news, too.'

Daisy started making all the proper dubious noises as she turned to Stephen, who, to her surprise, said, 'Why not, indeed? Sure haven't we something to celebrate?'

'Oh?' Swan's amused, alert eyes darted from one to the other.

'*You* have,' Daisy said. And then to Swan, 'Mr O'Lindon is going into the boat-building business on Lough Cool. I met him when he was refurbishing a villa belonging . . . a villa down in Keelity, where my family came from originally.' Daisy realized she was talking far too much, explaining too much. She cast about for a way to curtail her account. 'I'm just the go-between. I introduced him to my father's bankers – the Hibernian, you know – opposite your husband's.'

'Mr Fitzpatrick.'

'Yes.'

'We know him well. They dine with us.'

'Oh Swan!' Daisy laughed and squeezed her arm. 'It's so funny to hear you saying things like that: "They dine with us." You of all people. Whatever happened to the decline and fall of the bourgeois family?'

'My father stopped my allowance and I suddenly noticed the incline and rise of the price of oils and canvas. Mercier was always keen on me, *so* . . .' She pulled an amused-pugnacious face. 'Let's start walking or we'll be late. D'you think I'm awful?' She put herself between them, took an arm each, and thrust them back toward Dame Street. 'You do think I'm awful, don't you. Well, I don't. It's an arranged marriage only with this difference: *I* did the arranging. My parents still haven't recovered from the shock of it. A better phrase would be marriage of convenience – which is what all good marriages should be, don't you agree, Mr O'Lindon?'

'There's a lot to be said for it,' he replied guardedly.

'You never told me about Napier Lyndon-Fury,' Swan reminded Daisy.

'Nor I did,' she agreed. 'At this particular moment there's nothing really to say. He's gone back home for the summer, doing a lot of painting and drawing.'

'His home.' Swan very nearly made it a question, but not quite.

Daisy said nothing.

'Isn't it funny how things like that often happen,' Swan went on.

Daisy bristled. 'Things like what?'

'There he was at the Academy, the golden boy, sure to win the Prix de Rome, destined for great things altogether. But the big wide world's a different place. The big fish in a little pond is a minnow in the ocean.' She sighed at the ineluctable sadness of things and waited for Daisy to leap to Napier's defence – or not, as the case may be; either would be informative. When Daisy held her tongue, she turned to Stephen. 'D'you know him, Mr O'Lindon? You must think us terribly rude if you don't.'

'Mr Napier? Weren't we at the same parochial school till he went away to St Columba's,' Stephen told her. And there was his religion stated. 'He was always sketching and drawing even then, I remember.'

'Born to it,' Swan said vaguely. 'Ah well, sure he's not left the Academy a year. I'm a mite hard on the poor man, maybe. Dairmid Trench thinks highly of him, I know. You met him in London, too, he said. Oh Daise, there's so much crack to catch up on. And now here's O'Donoghue's and I have to transmogrify meself back into a proper young banker's proper little wife.'

Stephen pushed open the door and ushered them in.

Mercier, already seated, saw them and rose at once. He was no longer what Daisy would have called young – though banker she could certainly accept. In his dark morning coat and go-to-hell collar, he was every inch a man of that calling; he was also of the conservative breed who still kept a hat on when dining in a public place – in his case, a well-brushed silk topper. Stephen, who had doffed his humbler bowler on entering, replaced it at once.

While the introductions were going round, Daisy studied Swan's new husband. In his mid-thirties . . . darkish hair already receding . . . and a permanently watchful air about him. He had a sharp nose, a slightly receding chin, and small, alert eyes. He was not particularly pleased with his wife's impetuous invitation to the two interlopers but he was well-mannered enough not to make them aware of it – only that Daisy was studying him so closely did she catch sight of his brief glance of displeasure. Swan herself seemed impervious to it.

And for all his reserved Huguenot ancestry he was Irish enough to start quizzing his guests in the most shameless manner. An English importer had once told Daisy's father about straying onto some private land at Malahide and being greeted by the owner with the belligerent declaration: 'You're trespassing!' followed immediately by a much gentler: 'Where are you from?' It had greatly amused the Englishman but her father, in retelling the tale, had said dolefully, 'Those half-dozen words are Ireland's epitaph.' She didn't know what he meant – and nor, she suspected, did he. But she remembered the tale now as she watched Mercier dismantle his reserve and become almost as involved in the new venture as Stephen himself.

She chuckled. 'There must be a book somewhere that gives out what questions a banker must ask a prospective man of business,' she commented. 'Aren't those the very same answers Mr Fitzpatrick was after seeking not an hour since?'

He bowed his head as if accepting a rebuke – which she had not intended. 'I'm sorry. I get carried away.'

'You're in good company, so.' Daisy nodded significantly in Stephen's direction. 'That one can talk of nothing else, too.'

'Fitzpatrick's a good man. You did right to go to him, since you're known there, Miss O'Lindon. But you could have approached us, too – which I trust you'll remember.'

'There's very little land in it,' Daisy pointed out.

He shook his head. 'Land is a poor investment these days, I fear. You'd get short shrift from us if it was a loan to buy land, I can tell you.'

'Doesn't the time fly when you're having fun!' Swan said suddenly.

Mercier smiled indulgently and squeezed her hand. 'You're quite right, my dear. This is disgraceful.'

He kept a hold of her hand while the waiter took their orders – which was easily done since there was only roast beef or salmon on the menu.

'What d'you do when you're not being a banker, Mr Mercier?' Daisy asked.

'Wildfowling mostly,' he told her. 'And fishing, of course . . .'

'Very very mostly,' Swan chipped in – then reversed their hands and squeezed his briefly. 'I do not complain, my dear.' To the others she added, 'It is his absolute ruling passion.'

'Around Port Marnock,' he added. 'And up in the Wicklow Mountains. I've never been in the Midlands but I hear it's only marvellous?'

Stephen described the callows around Lough Cool – the water meadows that comprised the flood plain of the Shannon. He told how in winter, when the river rose, they became home to hundreds of thousands of water-fowl, every duck and goose and swan in the almanac.

'Except one,' Swan pointed out primly.

Mercier employed his laugh in order to remove his hand from hers.

Stephen went on to describe the same callows in summer when the water was down and they became the breeding ground of teal and golden plover. 'I've seen that entire land rise up and darken the sun. Sure, an aimless stone would down a dozen.'

Mercier's eyes shone and he licked his lips at the very thought.

'It's but two hours by train and another half in a gig,' Daisy told him experimentally.

He responded with a rueful nod. 'I don't know what it is – but you're a Dubliner yourself, as I can hear, so you'll know what I mean. But when you're talking about that land beyond Lucan – or Maynooth, say – it might as well be Timbuctoo as Tipperary. It's the old Dublin Pale, so it is.'

'And which side of the Pale do you belong these days, Daise?' Swan asked archly. Then, catching the echo of her words, she laughed. 'Days, Daise,' she repeated in case they had not heard it.

'I don't know,' Daisy said heavily. 'I suppose you could say I'm in a bit of a *daze* myself.'

How they all roared with laughter! After that the conversation roamed at will and without reserve, except, to be sure, upon the question of Home Rule and who kicked with which foot. They parted with many a protestation of renewed and continuing friendship. Daisy would surely never come to Dublin without sending a p.c. ahead to warn of her arrival, and they were never to *think* of staying at an hôtel, and a Friday-to-Sunday wild-fowling in Keelity might very well be on the cards before long.

'I wonder will we ever meet them again?' Daisy asked as she and Stephen strolled off down Dame Street, looking in all the shops.

34

Stephen stayed at an hôtel on Ormonde Quay; Daisy spent the night at Monkstown with her mother, her father having gone to Belfast to rake in a debt. To her surprise, she found her mother as nice as pie to her. She was not, however, deceived, recognizing it as cupboard love of a fairly blatant kind. The benefits of Daisy's 'spring cleaning' at the japanning works were beginning to show in the great amelioration of their domestic life. The last thing Mrs O'Lindon wanted was to go back to the old uncertainties.

Daisy, never one to let a sleeping dog lie if it could be poked and played with, decided to tell her mother about the baby; in a few weeks there'd be no hiding it anyway and it was better to grab the bull by the horns than to let the beast choose where to place them.

Mrs O'Lindon almost fainted at the shock. Even so, as she collapsed into her chair and asked for her smelling salts and struck at her breast to still her racing heart . . . even then, Daisy could see a small glint of calculation in the eye. To her surprise she found it endeared her to the woman. *Come*, she thought. *We're not so different under the skin after all!*

'Well now he'll have to marry you,' she noted complacently.

'Sir Lucius and Lady Lyndon-Fury won't hear of it. They'll pay me a handsome allowance – take care of the baby financially, too. They'll even agree to my living with Napier, but . . .'

'Living . . . in *sin*, you mean?' The voice dropped to a shocked whisper.

Daisy shrugged. 'Call it whatever you like, but . . .'

'Well, what would you call it?' she challenged, glancing nervously at the door.

'I'm not going to call it anything, because it's the last thing on earth I intend doing.'

'What then?' The worries swarmed about Mrs O'Lindon like wasps. 'Oh my dear, my dear! I think you should be guided by them, you know. They are powerful people and it wouldn't be right to antagonize them.'

'I'm going to camp on their front lawn. Not literally, of course.' She laughed. 'Their front lawn must be a couple of hundred acres. But I'll make them share the shame – if shame, indeed, it is.'

Her mother stared at her open-mouthed, first in one eye, then in the other. 'What are you saying, child? Of course it's a shame!' Then she smiled as realization dawned. 'Clever girl! To be sure, they'll never let it come to that. When they see how determined you are, they'll have to yield.' Again she conducted that rapid audit of her daughter's eyes. 'Where d'you get it, I wonder? Not from your father, that's certain. Nor from me, I'm sorry to say.'

'What?' Daisy was sincerely mystified.

'That indomitable . . . implacable . . . That *will* of yours. It frightens me to see it at times.' She smiled. 'And by God, it'll frighten them!'

Quietly Daisy told her, 'I don't think I'd marry Napier now, not even if he asked me.'

Her mother simply cackled at her cunning. 'That's it! That's it! Bring them to their knees!'

'No!' Daisy insisted. 'Isn't there too much of that already in this poor country? We spend too many hours down on our knees.'

Her mother laughed and said it was just the sort of thing her father would say; she seemed to want all her daughter's prickly awkwardness packed away in neat little boxes labelled 'second-hand'. Nothing would shake her good humour now and nothing would undo her conviction that Daisy was engaged in a diabolically cunning plan to force the Lyndon-Furys to relent. In the end Daisy shouted at her, 'Listen! I will *not* marry Napier. I'm going back to Keelity. And shall have that child. And every man in the county could beg to let them give it an honest name and I will not. Not before. Not after. I'll make my own way. And somehow – I don't know how, but I swear it before God and all His angels – somehow I'll see every Lyndon-Fury save one' – she patted her belly – 'wither in hell.'

The words went through her like a torchlight procession.

35

All that night Daisy woke and slept in fits and turns. She could not forget her words to her mother. At the time she had intended them as nothing more than a grand rhetorical flourish, torn from her by the hurt and anger of the moment – the *passing* moment, as she had thought. Now it seemed to refuse to pass.

The first time she awoke it was with only the vaguest feeling of dread. No, even 'dread' is too precise a word for that formless anxiety which stirred her from slumber. But as she tried to pin it down more exactly, to get her disquiet all nicely cut and dried, she became aware that something within her was resisting; something feared to know more exactly what it was that troubled her so.

The next time she awoke it was as if part of her had long since risen into consciousness and had been merely waiting for her eyes to open before pouncing. A voice – her own – said quite clearly in her mind, 'You must face it now.' No reason. No argument. The simple imperative echoed through the restless hollows inside her skull, driving out the last vestige of repose. She flung herself over on her other side, clamped the hem of her nightdress between her toes and pulled it down, curled herself in a ball, and shouted a silent, endlessly repeated 'No, no, no . . .' into her mind's ear to drown whatever intrusive revelation was hovering in the wings of her awareness.

Her baby started a swimming game. *That's it*, she thought. *That's why I can't sleep. Go on! Go on!* Exhaust yourself – then we can both rest.

The third time, she knew it was useless to resist any longer. In the still, frosty night she could hear the firemen shovelling to raise steam down in Dunleary coal harbour. Soon there'd be the tramp of boots along the road below as the casuals streamed out in search of a day's work . . . then the clatter of the first train . . . the hoot of the Kingstown ferry . . . no, there'd be little point now in trying to get back to sleep.

Where had her feet gone? She should have put on her sea-boot stockings. What good were they lying in the drawer over there? She sat up and pulled her knees to her chin, placing her feet in the remnant warmth of her body in the feather bed. At the same time she drew the quilt into a snuggly cowl around her head and shoulders. She used to do that as a child, when she heard the rain thrashing down outside. Wouldn't it be grand, she used to think, to be out there on the lawn, all snuggled up like that! The notion that such a downpour would saturate her bedding in moments had no place in so happy a fantasy. *Have I really changed since then?* she wondered in dour self-accusation. *Amn't I just as heedless of the real world now?*

But that was not the thought which had so disturbed her slumber. Now it came to her, clear as you'd want, and calm, too. *I meant what I said*, she admitted to herself. *Every blessed word.*

So that was it! She was facing it at last. Her oath of rage had not been torn from her in the quarrelsome heat of the moment; it had come welling up from somewhere deep within her, some dark and terrifying abyss of her spirit where, alone, such abiding hatred could survive. And yet, even while she put it to herself as a revealed fact – in the way a prosecutor might confront her with it in the box, she could hardly believe it.

For she could never consider herself a vindictive sort of woman. Just think of all the arguments and bitterness there had been between her and her mother. But did she harbour a grudge against that woman? True, there was a marked coolness between them now she was independent – why wouldn't there be. But hatred? She shook her head vehemently at the very thought. And what about all the people who'd played mean tricks on her down the years? Did she bear any malice for that?

What mean tricks?

She screwed up her face and waited for some memory to surface.

Well, the very fact that she couldn't think of one, not offhand like that, meant she wasn't a grudger, surely? People must have done things like that to her. Everyone got their share of it.

Her mind went back to those arguments with her mother, who was always fond of raking up tiny little incidents that you yourself had long forgotten. She'd roar at you a mile off for something you'd just done, and then, not content with that, she'd say something like, 'It was just the same when I asked you to . . .' do something or other. And she'd remember every little detail. And you knew exactly the same sort of thing had happened in reverse. She'd given her promise to you but hadn't kept it. But you couldn't remember because you were so busy getting on and enjoying the next day of your life. So didn't that just prove it! Her mother might be a grudger but that's one thing she, Daisy, surely was not.

She rose and went for a walk, out under the blear, cold pink of the pre-dawn sky. There was no more night in Dublin nowadays, not like you'd get it down in the country. Was that where she was destined to live now? An image of Stephen O'Lindon rose in her mind but she pushed it aside; she didn't want to go into all that now; it was too complicated. First of all she had to sort out this business of the Lyndon-Furys. Her outburst against Napier yesterday had certainly marked some kind of new departure in their . . . you couldn't call it love any more, not after that. Not after his last words to her, either.

Friendship, then?

What point was there in being mere friends after all they'd felt and done? It would be like those people who couldn't bear to bury a faithful old pet dog but had him stuffed and put in the hall.

She loved those houses, staring out over Dublin Bay, catching every sunrise. When she was little she'd always dreamed of living there one day. A house must overlook water. That was the thing. Her skin prickled as she realized she had just described the villa at Glaster. Well! She tossed her head angrily. It wasn't the only nice house along those shores. You could even get a site there and put up something much grander.

Again she thought of Stephen and again pushed him aside. Napier first. Love was over and done with. Friendship was a stuffed dog in the hall going black in patches. No, be serious. What could you call it? What did she really feel?

If Napier himself was to duck up now – just walking up the road from the station – what would she do? Throw her arms about him. Or cut the head out of him?

She stared into the hollow by the station entrance and her heart dropped a beat. It *was* Napier! Standing uncertainly at the portal as if unwilling to step out of the ring of gaslight into the surrounding dark. But there had been no train, surely? Or had she missed it? She closed her eyes and shook her head violently, telling herself it was just a figment of her tired brain. And when she opened them again, Napier was, indeed, gone.

And then she heard footsteps coming toward her, up the little rise. *His* footsteps. She'd know them anywhere. 'Hark! I hear footprints!' he'd said in that fog. Her heart began to race; the palms of her hands turned clammy in her gloves. Nearer and nearer he came; she could see him now – a dim silhouette against the pool of light below. Napier without a doubt.

Throw her arms about him? Cut the head out of him? She couldn't think. Her muscles froze. She just stood there, cast in stone, and waited.

As he drew nearer she could no longer look at him. She fixed her eyes on the paving stones beneath the nearest gaslamp, noting in exquisite detail each crack and imperfection, and waited for his feet to intrude. She thought she would die. She was struggling for breath and her heart was like some thirst-crazed creature that wanted to swallow before it had gulped the wherewithal.

A moment later she saw the first gleam of them in the penumbra beyond the lamp – well polished boots. New ones. Not his usual. Not the boots of an artist, at all.

'Does your mother know you're out?' he called jovially to her.

Not his usual voice, either.

As he drew closer he said, 'Are you all right, miss? Can I help?'

She just stood there, staring at the young stranger, and listening to someone, not herself, a bright young woman with a cheery voice, replying, 'Sure, I'm grand, thank you kindly. Was that the five-thirty?'

His brisk march slowed to a saunter. 'It was. And no one got off but meself except a milk churn. Are you expecting someone?'

'Half and half,' the unknown woman said.

'Well, the next will be there soon enough,' he told her comfortingly as he passed. Then, looking back over his shoulder, he called out, 'That'll be a grand day when the sun gets up.'

'It will, indeed,' she agreed warmly.

As his footfall dwindled into the dark beyond, Daisy leaned against the sea wall and took a deep breath – which then turned into the most monstrous yawn that almost burst her ribs apart. When at last she managed to breathe out, her heart had returned to something nearer normal, though it still gulped away. She even managed a shaky sort of a laugh.

And what would be the good, she asked herself, of thinking about Napier and getting her feelings about him all neatly pinned up and catalogued, if the *mere* sight of him was going to turn her upside down and leave her all of a quiver like that? For some odd reason, the question left her feeling both carefree and blithe. She turned and strode homewards, even skipping part of the way. And when she arrived she fried herself a gargantuan breakfast of liver, kidney, sausage, rashers, egg, and fried bread. But her frost-honed appetite withered in the aura of sizzling-hot lard and she only managed to get the plateful past her teeth by reminding herself that another was waiting to share it down there.

36

The train slipped out of Kingsbridge station and nosed onward into that Dublin–Kildare hinterland which, being far from any thoroughfare, is nameless to most who journey through it. 'Where it all began,' Stephen murmured as they picked up speed among the grimy tenements of Inchicore. Daisy, absentmindedly assuming he meant the railway itself, nodded, vaguely. Then she realized he was talking about his new business and smiled much more affirmatively. 'Sorry,' she said. 'I never got much sleep last night.'

'Nor me, neither,' he agreed. 'It's where to build the factory, you see. I can't make up my mind. What do you think yourself now?'

As on their previous journey, he was seated opposite her, facing the engine; this time they had only one other companion – a civil servant, or national-school inspector, or something in that line. He had an attaché case open on his knee and was running a fastidiously sharpened pencil up and down columns and lists, making ticks here and there. Daisy and Stephen felt quite alone.

'I thought that was all settled,' she replied. 'Tom Mangan's field, isn't it?'

But Stephen explained how Fitzpatrick's questions, reinforced by Mercier's at luncheon, had made him think about husbanding his precious capital and only spending it on what was absolutely necessary. Also, contrary to everything he had told her before, he now wanted to be much nearer the main road and the connection with the railhead at Simonstown. Until now he had said that, since all his timber would come up the Shannon by barge from Limerick, he could build well away from the main road, where land would be cheaper. 'What's happened to change your mind?' she asked.

He smiled enigmatically. 'One chair. That's all it took – one chair. I'm like a weathercock. I saw this chair in a shop on Ormonde Quay last night.

It gave me the fright of my life. You'd never believe wood might be bent into such a shape as that. And, of course, it can't. I was sure this fella had found some other way of doing it or beaten my patent.'

'Oh, no!' She leaned forward in alarm.

He grinned and held up a finger. 'Wait till I tell you. Hadn't the fella cut it into strips along the grain, and then bent the strips, and then glued it all back together again under heat and pressure, and then sanded and stained it till you'd search all Ireland to find the join. That's what your man told me in the shop. And it must be so, for without my machinery there's no other way.'

Even so, it seemed bad enough news to her. Stephen's apparent happiness was puzzling. It sounded as if this other carpenter had found a way of bending wood without the expense of all that elaborate machinery. 'What if this fella starts making boats the same way?' she asked.

He shook his head happily. 'The glue would part in the water.' Then he jabbed his upraised finger to emphasize his point: 'But *I* could bend up furniture from much thicker pieces. Where he makes seven cuts and seven gluings, I could manage with only three.'

'Is he a Dublin man?'

Stephen shook his head. 'Vienna, wherever that is. Beyond these islands, anyway.'

'Australia,' she told him. 'Or Austria. I always get them mixed up. Won't your man be only wild when he hears he's been sending to faraway places like that when he could have got the same only better here in Ireland!'

'With a wicker seat it was fourteen shillings, and padded and upholstered he wanted seventeen and fourpence, but I don't think that was his best price.'

'As much as that!' Her eyebrows shot up in avaricious glee. 'What's your best price, then? Or shouldn't I ask?'

'If I got the timber in at the right cost, I could do them padded at about four shillings apiece. Three for the wicker one. And getting the timber at the right cost is a simple matter of ordering in sufficient bulk – which comes back to not spending too much on putting up bricks and mortar, d'you see?'

She did.

'Especially,' he added casually, 'if the bricks and mortar are already there.'

'Where?' she asked, intrigued that he had thought it through in such detail – but then, he did nothing else all day, she remembered.

He licked his lips and studied her response closely as he told her. 'The old flax mill.'

She just stared at him.

'You know the one I mean now?' he pressed.

'I do. I haven't seen it but Napier mentioned it once. I thought he said it's now a whiskey distillery.'

'So it is. But they only use a quarter of the old place. They pulled the roof off the rest to cut the assessment, but the walls are sound as a bell still. A bit of oul' tin on the roof and some glass in the windows and a couple of new floors and 'twould be as good a place as your father's.'

'As good as *that*?' she asked sarcastically. 'Have you asked them yet, the Lyndon-Furys?'

'I'm only after getting the notion. Last night.' He smiled. 'About three o'clock.' Then, serious again: 'What d'you think yourself now, Miss O'Lindon?'

She shrugged awkwardly. 'I'd say that's entirely your decision, Mr O'Lindon. I don't see how I have any say in the matter.'

'There's a thing I meant to tell you now,' he went on. 'Just a hump and a skimp and a jump up the Flaxmills River, where it widens to form the old millpool, is the former overseer's lodging, which would be a house about the size of the villa at Glaster. The garden's gone wild and you need to fight your way to the door . . .'

She laughed. 'But with a bit of oul' tin on the roof and some glass . . .'

'Not at all,' he interrupted. 'That house was lived in until two years ago. Sean O'Keefe and his family had it until he went to America. And so what I was thinking was it would make a handy office if we turned the rest of the mills into a joinery and boatbuilders, d'you see. It would be well away from all the sawdust and shavings and the stink of the glue. Yet handy enough in the rain.'

'Then it would be better than my father's place,' she pointed out.

'Bedad,' he said. 'I was hoping you'd see it that way.'

She shook her head slowly and smiled at him. 'I don't know, Mr O'Lindon. Did you think all that out at three o'clock this morning, too?'

'Ah no.' He spoke as though modestly disclaiming such superhuman abilities. 'I'd say that was closer to dawn. A house should always be built by water, I thought. Didn't you once tell me that? Anyway . . .' He rubbed his hands briskly as if he could not wait to put them to work. 'That's the why and the wherefore of it all now.'

Lord Almighty, she thought, *would you listen to us!* She watched his lips move, she heard his words, understood them, gave out sensible replies . . . and all the while the real herself was sitting there wondering what it would be like to be kissed by those same lips. And the hands that helped shape his words and then conveyed them to her – what would they feel like in a caress?

And was himself wondering the same about her? Did he sit there, secretly yearning for the softness of her lips, the gentle touch of her fingers? How could she ever know? How would he know it of her?

Their behaviour reminded her of Swan yesterday, chattering brightly on when her very soul must have been torn apart, consumed with the knowledge that she needn't have yielded to Mercier – she could have crooked her finger at Napier, after all!

37

The town of Flaxmills stands at the junction of three roads, each one calling itself *the* road from Simonstown to Portumna. The thousand-odd citizens of Flaxmills enjoy the services of three general shops, two tailors, one bootmaker and saddler, three churches (or, as the Ordnance Survey prefers it, one church, Anglican, and two chapels, RC and Methodist), twenty public houses, and a barracks of the Royal Irish Constabulary. The twenty constables stationed there are just sufficient to ensure that the twenty public houses close at the appointed hour – even if they never actually shut. The barracks, also known as Fort Ireton, was originally a castle of the O'Carrolls, enlarged with corner towers and new breastworks during Cromwell's rampage.

The Flaxmills River, a tributary of the Shannon at Lough Cool, had always been navigable to smaller boats, at least as far as the ford around which the town originally sprang up (which was now drowned in a weir); so there had always been a fortification of some kind there. During the Napoleonic threat, around the turn of the century, the English realized that the broad and navigable Shannon and the huge esker of glacial sand and gravel that runs west–east across the middle of Ireland, from Galway to Dublin, would give the French an easy route for a back-door invasion. And Ireland itself would make a splendid base and a fertile recruiting ground. So where esker and river meet – at Banagher and Shannon Bridge – huge fortifications of earth and stone were hastily thrown up. Scarp and counterscarp, parapet and batis, glacis and faussebrassaye . . . the invading French would find their very language turned against them in one of the most lethal displays of military art ever put on public exhibition.

Then somebody remembered Flaxmills, a wicket gate in that huge back door. Fort Ireton would still secure the northern bank; but the old battery on the southern side was long ago incorporated into the mills. A new one was therefore constructed a half a mile downriver. And, as a final backstop, a Martello Tower – a giant chess-piece castle of dressed stone, beautiful in its simplicity – was sited on a bend of the river above the weir. Some forty years later, and almost half a century before Stephen brought Daisy to view the place, the river itself had been made navigable to ocean-going vessels.

On paper, then – specifically, on the little sketch map Stephen had drawn for her on the journey down – Flaxmills seemed like a town with all the advantages of ancient geography and recent history in its favour. It had more roads than it could possibly need and more river than it was currently using; and it was so absurdly overgarrisoned that even the most nervous entrepreneur must feel his investment safe. It should have been a bustling, thriving, jolly little town. The reality, however, was something of a shock.

It was, in fact, one of the drabbest, saddest towns Daisy had ever seen. True, she could hardly have picked a worse day. The sky was one uniform gray from horizon to horizon, and out of it there fell a steady, unremitting drizzle, of which the wind made so light a plaything that even a wide umbrella gave no shelter at all. Within seconds of stepping out of doors every surface – top, bottom, and sides – was drenched. Dismal gray cottages huddled cheek by jowl beneath decaying thatch that postponed rather than prevented the ingress of rain. The gravel of the streets, enriched down the years by the droppings of man, fowl, and beast, was now a dark, turgid loam that plucked at the feet as if begging the passer-by to stop and take root. A rich motley of weeds had already succumbed to the invitation – docks, thistles, nettles, cow parsley, and a universal carpeting of hairy bittercress. As in Dublin (and Cork and Ballybeyond) the local privates of the Idle Army leaned in doorways, staring incuriously at the drizzle and those mad enough to be out in it. 'Fierce,' they commented dourly. 'Shocking altogether.'

The lane that led up from the mills to the former overseer's house was metalled and dry – or, rather, it had drier patches amongst the puddles, which gave Stephen and Daisy somewhere to stand and swill the mire of the town from their boots. 'I'll say one thing,' Stephen commented, 'you'll never see it worse. So if you don't take agin' it today, won't you be happy enough for the year.'

'More than a year, I hope,' she asserted.

He hadn't exaggerated when he had told her you needed to fight your way to the house. Where the drive had once opened out onto an elegant carriage sweep around the formal circle of a flowerbed, there was now a jungle of briar, mountain ash, and hawthorn. Stephen or some other bold scout had come this way recently and hacked a passage to the door, but for which they would have abandoned their visit to a brighter day.

'Has all this grown since Sean O'Keefe left?' Daisy asked in amazement.

'Ah, no. They wouldn't give him right of way though the distillery, even the bit they weren't using. He came in the back way always, past the Martello Tower. You'll see it from upstairs.'

The house itself, visible only through squint-eyed glimpses from the heart of the volunteer jungle, seemed imposing and solid. Miraculously, all the glazing was intact. The door was not locked. Inside, it proved amazingly dry, for a dwelling that had had no tenant for the past two years. As they passed from room to room Daisy noticed that there were only three pails set out to catch drips – all working double-tides today. She checked the floors around them and noted with satisfaction that they were unstained; which meant that the pails had never overflowed; which meant that whatever they caught had time to evaporate before the next filling; which meant that the leaks in the roof were small. She did not work it out in such neatly logical steps, of course; no one in Ireland would need to do that.

One of the pails was two-thirds full; she opened the casement and tipped it away. The outer wall of the house on that side rose sheer from the river, overlooking the weir that terminated the navigable reach. 'Oh, but isn't that beautiful!' she cried. 'I love the sound of running water, almost as much as the sea.'

'You'll not miss it so much,' he replied.

Above the weir was a wide pool, the original head pound for the mills; and above that again, about a hundred yards beyond, was a dashing, rock-strewn, cataract of brown, peaty water, straight out of the Slieve Derg, and beetling over it, nestling in the bend, was the now romantic outline of the Martello Tower. Beyond and behind it stood something even more romantic to her – though she did not know it until he spoke its name: Sharavogue.

Even in its present ruined condition it was the crowning of the town. Part of her desired to live there now, regardless of its state. She could restore one room, surely? The rest of her mocked such pretensions.

She became aware that Stephen was staring at her, waiting for her to return to the here and now. 'Does anyone live up there?' she asked, nodding at the tower, for she did not want him to know what she had really been thinking.

'Oh God, they do.' He chuckled when he saw how crestfallen she was at the news. 'A thousand fat pigeons! 'Tis the biggest complaint in the entire district. They get fat on the farmers' grain and the Lyndon-Furys won't leave them be shot except in the way of sport. *His* sport, to be sure. And then he gives out at them because there's not enough barley for the malting!'

'Isn't that the way of it in this country,' she said bitterly. 'You have to run to stand still. If it's walking you're after, you must emigrate, so.'

She returned the pail to its place, where the drips beat a ringing tattoo in its empty maw. The ping-ping-ping! was just too widely spaced for a human to call it a rhythm.

'I never heard such po-litical sentiment outa you before,' he commented as he closed the window.

'It's different in Dublin,' she explained. 'When you see a brave sight of soldiers going by and the bands playing and the lord-lieutenant in his white plumes, well, it's like some sort of a pageant for the populace, with everybody smiling and waving. But in the country . . . I mean, the RIC in their uniforms, and the way they look at you – it's not the same at all, so it isn't. Ireland's always different from Dublin, anyway.'

'Is that it,' he remarked, in a tone that suggested he might have quite a different explanation for her new-minted antagonism for the powers that be. 'I never heard you talk like that at the villa.'

'I think I'll make this my bedroom,' she replied. 'And parlour. The two in one, why not. It will save on the firing. Lord, I'll live in God's pocket here! Where's your lodgings? Can I see it from here?' She crossed to the window and peered out intently.

Grinning at her bewilderment, he tapped at the next pane down and pointed off at an acute diagonal. 'If we cut down a tree or two and you leaned out as far as you could, you might just get a glimpse of it.'

'The distillery?'

He nodded. 'I'll shake down some straw in one of the rooms.'

'Oh, you can't!' she protested.

'Anyway, I'll not be in Flaxmills for the next month or so.'

Her heart faltered. 'But why not?'

'Because I'll be over in Parsonstown mostly. That's a thing I meant to tell you. I was working in Coolderg Castle once when the Earl of Rosse and his son, or one of them, were visiting. And they were talking about Trapper's pet scheme for a railway between Simonstown and Flaxmills and on to a new harbour to be built at Glenisk on Lough Cool . . .'

'Ah yes. I remember being told – it's an obsession with him, isn't it.'

'Anyway, the son seemed to know a lot about steam and mechanics and suchlike. The Honourable Charles Parsons. So I wrote to him last week with a copy of the patent and asked him who he thought would be best in the Midlands to make it. Of course, I never thought he'd volunteer himself! But they have a grand workshop there, from making all the telescopes and things, you see.'

During this explanation Daisy's unhappiness at his forthcoming absence turned to joy. She reached out a finger and touched him nervously, as if he were suddenly too exalted for such an intimacy. 'You and your friend Lord Rosse, eh!'

He nodded. 'If it does me no good, 'twill do me no harm. I'll be over here two or three times a week, anyway, because I want to see how the man I've picked as overseer can manage on his own.'

'Do I know him?'

He shook his head. 'But you can give me your opinion of him when the month is up. Would you ever cook him his dinner each day? And sit and talk with him, and make up your mind. His name's Shaughnessy.' He pronounced it the Midlands way – Shocknissy – so that it was a moment or two before she recognized it to be the name she knew as Shonnessy. 'Peter Shaughnessy. He's a Catholic but he's a good man for all that.'

'Do the Lyndon-Furys know?' she asked at once.

'What's it to do with them?' he replied over his shoulder as they made for the stairs to the attic.

'Nothing. But that won't stop them from trying to interfere. They've never let a Catholic out of those gates with wages in his pockets. They'll say you've let them down.'

At the stairhead he turned and held out a hand to assist her up the last two risers; the gesture carried a sort of mock gallantry that was nonetheless seriously intended. 'You wouldn't be . . . what'll I say? You wouldn't be in danger of promoting the whole tribe of Lyndon-Furys to be the arch-divils of Keelity, now would you? Because there's plenty I'd rank beside them.'

He kept a grasp of her hand, holding it high like a dancer in an old-fashioned minuet. Some intuition told her that if she did not do something he would slowly pull her to him and she'd end up in his arms. Nothing in his words or tone suggested it, but this intuition had a source beyond such simple clues. Panic gripped her. She wriggled free of his grip and walked over to one of the windows. 'There's something I must tell you,' she said flatly.

'What's that?' He came to her side and scratched at the dust on the pane. 'The sun's breaking through.'

She remained silent.

'What?' he prompted.

Courage failed her. 'I'm going to need half a ton of soap while I clean this house,' she said.

'You'll stay off your knees and you'll keep your hands dry,' he told her. 'I have Shaughnessy's mother engaged for all that. And Molly Flynn to see to the scullery.'

'Are you mad!' she exclaimed. 'Why waste money on their wages when there's a perfectly good pair of hands here?' She held them out in case he doubted her.

Once more he took them firmly in his own and, staring evenly into her eyes, said, in the quietest voice, little above a whisper, 'You know why full well.'

She thought of bluffing it out but one look into those deepset, intelligent eyes convinced her of the futility of that. 'You know!' she said aghast.

He nodded.

She frowned. 'But how?'

He pulled a rueful face to prepare her for something she might not enjoy hearing. 'Didn't I think it within five minutes of taking you up on the road that day?'

She shook her head. 'I can't believe that, Mr O'Lindon.'

He went on speaking as if she had not challenged him. 'On my way in to Simonstown didn't I pass her ladyship's carriage coming out, and herself with a face like thunder. Then half an hour later, on my way back out, when I picked up yourself and you told me your tale, I put two and two together.'

'And got five!'

He smiled, 'Not all at once. But I thought here's a colleen too spirited to come down here like a whipped bitch. A fine, fightin' sort of a lass, indeed. And the bloom on the skin of you, and the light in the eye of you . . . well, the notion struck me you were fightin' for two. But I wasn't sure till I worked at the villa.'

'But how could you know? How could you be sure?'

'Because there's a closeness I feel with you that I feel for no other.'

'And even so . . . even knowing that . . . you still . . . ? I mean, if what you claim is true, you already knew all this about me when you made your suggestion that I should . . .' She motioned vaguely with her eyes at the house all about them.

'Sure, 'twas more than a suggestion,' he said. 'You may call it a proposal if you will.' He raised her right hand to his lips and let the other one go.

She lifted it to his cheek. 'Oh . . . Mr O'Lindon!'

'Only if you will, mind. It's your privilege to take it any way you wish.'

He spoke calmly enough but only her own charged emotions had prevented her from realizing what enormous tension was in him. She could feel it in his finger, in the rigidity of his stance, in the anguish in his gaze. 'I don't know . . .' she stammered. 'I don't . . .'

'Love me?' he suggested.

'I wasn't going to say that.'

'I have enough for the both of us,' he assured her. 'If you turn from me now and go your ways, I'm not saying I wouldn't go on with my plans. But it would be a bitterness in my heart to be without you. I'd grieve for you, so I would.' He smiled wanly. 'There now. It wasn't you had to tell me something. It was me had to tell you – before you wore your fingers to the bone on scrubbing soap.'

'Oh, Mr O'Lindon.' She smiled back in the same way. 'It's not often I find myself at a loss for words.'

He let go her hand and turned on his heel to lead the way back below. 'You have a month to think it over anyway. I mean a month almost free of me. For yourself, to be sure, you have all the time in the world.'

'Have I!' she answered sarcastically.

'You have, of course.' He turned and assured her with his earnest eyes. 'Don't be thinking now that I've come out with this because I imagine you've little choice. For my part, if you were to tell me you *want* the child born out of wedlock and you'll only marry me after . . . well, 'twould make not *that* much difference to me.' He snapped his fingers.

At last she found cause for laughter. 'But why should I wish to do that?' she asked.

'Ah,' he replied enigmatically. 'Isn't that one of them things to be thinking about.'

38

Daisy soon realized why Stephen had chosen Peter Shaughnessy as his right-hand man, despite the criticisms he would have to face from his fellow Protestants that he had not chosen one of his own. Shaughnessy was a bits-and-pieces man, a double-scrutiny man, a worrier. 'Measure twice, cut once,' was his watchword. However, that was not her first impression of the man at all; indeed, for several days she had dismissed him as something of a dreamer.

At that time the work consisted entirely of restoring the roof and putting in a new floor where the original second floor had been; they had decided to omit the original first floor so as to allow enough vertical space in the workshops for manhandling long lengths of timber. Daisy found several opportunities each day to go down there with a message or a request; and each time, it so happened, she found Shaughnessy standing quietly at the hub of all that activity, seemingly lost in a dream. True, the progress was amazing, but she assumed that it was because the others were all such skilled craftsmen that they could manage without the directions of their nominal overseer. Certainly they were hard at work from twilight to twilight; no one ever seemed to be standing around waiting for one of the others to finish his particular task.

And then it dawned on her that the reason for this smooth dovetailing of labour lay in Shaughnessy's apparent idleness. Hour by hour, he could calculate exactly what each of the tradesmen should be doing and how that work would marry with the efforts of all the others; and it was precisely because those others were all such competent tradesmen that he could calculate to the minute.

When she saw Stephen again, at the end of his first week in Parsonstown, she told him of a cowboy she had seen doing tricks with a lariat at a circus in Dublin once – how he'd been able to make the rope jump this way and that without apparently changing the movement of his hand in the least degree. 'Shaughnessy's like that,' she observed. 'You'd think he was doing nothing most of the time and really he's doing the work of eight in his head.'

Stephen was pleased she'd had the wit to see it; he was less pleased at the amount of work – physical work – that Daisy herself was doing. The house shone like a herring's eye. The smell of dust had fled before the reek of carbolic and beeswax, 'emulsified in a lather of elbow grease,' as she proudly declared. Not a cobweb was to be seen and papers were spread in the room that was eventually to be hers, where half the ceiling was already whitened with distemper. He minced no words in telling her off. Where would be the gain to her if, thanks to these unnecessary exertions, she were to lose her baby?

At once her hackles went up. What was it to him? By what right did he tell her what to do and what not to do about *her* child? Did he imagine that his proposal – which she hadn't even accepted yet – now gave him some claim of ownership over her? In that case, what would he be like if she accepted? She wouldn't dare put her nose out of doors without asking his leave. However, she was becoming familiar enough with herself and the present disorder of her emotions to know what her spirit was really doing when it went in for this kind of bluster – it was seeking to avoid an uncomfortable truth at the heart of it all; so she bit off her tongue in the nick of time and yielded the point by her silence. Whatever it was that she might be avoiding, she did not go hunting for it when he had gone.

Their parting was cool but not frosty. Yet there was a certain contented gleam in his eye, which puzzled her at first; later it struck her that a friendship – and whatever else might be between them, she could not question their friendship – which could accept such coolness without risking a complete break must actually be quite strong – far stronger than the brief time of their acquaintance might suggest.

The grand simplicities of last year – indeed, of only a few months earlier – were nowhere to be found. Then all she had needed to whisper to herself was, 'I love Napier,' and all her emotions fell into harmony and sang the same anthem of wonder and adoration. But with Stephen, if that was, indeed, where her future lay, it would never be so simple. And that was odd because, on the face of it, he was a far simpler man than Napier, with a straightforward aim in life and obvious means to achieve it.

She tried to think about – in a way, to prepare herself for – the intricate labyrinth of conflicting feelings that life with Stephen might involve, but something in her rebelled at the effort; something hankered still for the sheer grandeur, the overwhelmingness of her first love.

She was still in that unsatisfactory state a month later when Madeleine called by. She admired the house and said nothing about the potholes in the drive, nor the even deeper holes where the treestumps had been winched out of the carriage sweep. She patted Daisy's stomach and raised a significant eyebrow at the bulge, thus becoming the first person to make an open comment to her on what all the world could now see. And then, when they were alone in Daisy's room, she said, 'Well, you'll be dying to hear all about Napier, I'm sure.'

'Indeed I would not,' she asserted stoutly. 'Where is he, anyway?'

'Wait till I tell you. He's gone back to London!' She paused for this dramatic news to take effect.

Daisy withheld her anger for the moment.

'And it's my belief,' Madeleine went on, 'that it's the plainest message he could send to you.'

Daisy tossed her curls contemptuously. 'And is that the truth! Then I'd as liefer get one out the corner of his mouth, for I might understand that better. Plain message, indeed! What does he know of me these days, anyway?' After a pause she added, 'What part of London did you say?'

Madeleine smiled sweetly. 'He knows of you what everyone tells him. Sure, isn't the whole of County Keelity talking about the bold Daisy O'Lindon and what she's after doing with Stephen O'Lindon? So there's the truth doubled for you. The servants at the castle prattle of nothing else, so there it's doubled again. And you may be sure my mother retails every last morsel in her letters to him – so he'll surely know eight times as much about you as you know yourself.'

Daisy could not help a smile at her way of putting it, which sounded like exaggeration but was probably an understatement. In the bars and shebeens of Keelity she was no doubt to have twins three months apart, fathered by the two men in it.

'He's got digs with a Mrs Fortis in Margaretta Terrace in Chelsea,' Madeleine added.

'Oh, but that's . . .' Daisy stopped when she saw the other's smile. She already knew. And she was right: It *was* a kind of message from Napier.

'Why are you telling me this?' Daisy asked.

Madeleine closed her eyes for a moment, a prelude to dropping her banter and speaking in all seriousness. 'Because I think you're about to make a tragic error, my dear,' she said at last. 'I've no doubt Mr O'Lindon is a splendid man and would make you a model husband . . .'

'In the name of God!' Daisy declared. 'The world has us married and the man himself hasn't yet put the question!'

Madeleine's eyebrows shot up at this unexpected nugget. 'Oh really?' she asked – in a tone so like Napier's that it gave Daisy's heart a wrench to hear it, slipping under a guard she had not realized was there.

'Well . . .' Daisy climbed off the high horse of her assertion. 'Not in so many words. Not going down on one knee, if you like.'

'Ah!' The curiosity gave way to understanding. 'Then he's not just a splendid man and model husband, he's also more astute than I'd given him credit for. But –' she soaped her hands and set the discovery aside – 'it makes not a pick of difference in the end. That lump on you is Napier's and the heart that's beating for it is still Napier's, too, I'm thinking.'

'Is he still getting his allowance?' Daisy asked – or, rather, she heard her voice asking. In her mind's eye she could see the house in Chelsea, hear his key in its door, smell his turps and linseed oil up in the studio, feel the caress of his voice on her like velvet . . . and there was no doubting that she, or part of her, was still his – carelessly, thoughtlessly his, with no regard to the sensible calculations her life now demanded of her. Not to mention that other life it now sheltered.

'He is,' Madeleine assured her. 'And to answer your next question, yes, I believe they'd continue with it even if you joined him there – even if he married you.'

'*If* he married me?' Daisy seized on the ambiguity like a sort of lifeline.

'Which you know he would, of course.'

'Oh would he, now! Sure, I'd like to see the evidence for that. Hadn't he all the opportunity he could wish for last autumn? And scant use he made of it.'

Madeleine smiled. 'Ah, but now he knows it would be with our mother's blessing.' The moment the words were out she knew it was the worst thing she could possibly have said – and the fact that it was the truth only made matters worse.

She saw the steely temper in Daisy's eye and mentally kicked herself hard enough to break a shin. For a moment she thought of blustering her way into unsaying it but realized that would not do; the only way was to brazen it out, or to debase it with the sort of 'good common sense' that had killed off so many of her own strong feelings both for and against the men who had so far engaged her own heart. 'You may sneer at that, my dear,' she added in the pontifical sort of tone that always infuriated her. 'But such things are important in life. I've no doubt Napier has often spoken dismissively of Mama, hinting that she holds no influence over him now he's such a big, bold, broth of a boy. Most men do, in my experience. But don't be taken in by it, will you.' She held up a knowing finger in the way that always drove her into an utter wax when her mother and other women practised it on her. 'A man who marries with his mama's approval is a thousand times more tractable than one who holds a nightly inquest with her in his head – and all over you.'

'Have you quite finished?' Daisy asked coldly.

Madeleine heaved a mental sigh of relief; at least some of the damage of her thoughtless remark had been undone and the contumely diverted upon herself. She tried to recruit a little smile from Daisy. 'The truth is, my dear, if you really must know, I desperately want you as my sister-in-law. It's all pure selfishness in the end.'

And Daisy did, indeed, smile slightly. 'All you want is a pied-à-terre in London.

'Paris, actually.' She bit her lip like a naughty schoolgirl. 'Also, at the risk of making you puke, I've missed you. Your friendship – I've missed it.' Although sheer flattery had prompted the words she suddenly realized, in the middle of speaking them, that they were, in fact, the plain truth; and that same impulse to truth now prompted her to add, 'I hope we might still be friends even if you go your own thoughtless way and marry O'Lindon instead.'

'But of course!' Daisy assured her.

The words brought none of the pleasure that might have been expected, from the fervour of Madeleine's expression of her hopes. 'It sounds as if that's what you've already decided,' she said glumly.

Daisy, looking Madeleine square in the eye, said calmly, 'You may tell Napier in your next letter that if he comes within a dozen miles of me, I'll make him smell Hell.'

39

At the end of April, 1886, there was huge excitement all the way from Parsonstown to Flaxmills. Stephen O'Lindon's wonderful new machine was to be carried down the road and installed at the new (or old-made-new) factory. It was a fine day, God be praised, and Bailey Bros' huge steam threshing engine turned up precisely on time for once, at the gates of Parsonstown Castle. The 'plank-bender,' or 'plank-binnder' in the local pronunciation, was already secured on a stone-haulier's cart and ready to go. At the moment it resembled nothing so much as a cat's-cradle of iron festooned with bunting and wrapped in a banner bearing the incongruous legend: *Welcome to His Majesty!* It was the only banner the Hon Charles Parsons had been able to find at short notice – and was so ancient that no one could any longer remember which particular 'his-majesty' it had welcomed. 'What matter?' he commented. 'Isn't the machine itself majestic enough? What do *you* say, Bailey?'

'Oh God, your honour, 'tis a firm and ugly contraption,' the man said admiringly.

And indeed it was: a fourteen-foot cube whose edges were defined by a framework of black-enamelled cast iron, inside which was an array of burnished metal rods and swash plates and gleaming bars with deep, square-cut threads spiralling the full length of them. There was a heart-in-mouth moment when the steam engine was backed through the gateway until its funnel almost touched the arch and the cart was levered toward it. Parsons ran his eye over the frame of the bender and nervously compared its dimensions with those of the arch. 'We may have made a slight miscalculation on our dimensions, old chap,' he muttered to Stephen. 'Tell Bailey to inch her out as slowly as he can.'

With their hearts thudding away like two rabbits in a sack, Stephen and Daisy watched the outer corners of the frame approach the stone. ' 'Twill never go,' he kept saying. ' 'Twill surely hit that stone.' But Parsons, who was on a stepladder at the back of the frame and had his eye trained along the edges in question, kept waving the engine forward, forward . . .

When the leading corners were no more than an inch from the inner edge of the arch and it seemed inevitable that one or both of them would strike the stone, Bailey stopped and raised an eyebrow at Stephen. He, in turn, looked at Parsons, who once again waved them onward. Bailey's hand went to the steam throttle and eased it off a couple of turns. Steam hissed and groaned in the cylinder. The piston moved to the end of its stroke – where a leaky stuffing box evacuated the condensate onto the road like a bull with a loose bowel. The crowd cried out and leaped aside, instantly returning their eyes to the top of the arch – anxious not to miss a moment of the forthcoming humiliation, the story of which had already half-compiled itself in their minds, long before they saw the castle gates that morning.

The gravel cracked under the wheels as the cart moved almost imperceptibly. Another turn, another groan, another second of bated breath. And then, by some miracle, an inch or so of the frame was to be seen against a background of stone rather than sky – and still Parsons's hand dared them forward. 'Lucky we didn't give her that third lick of paint after all!' he quipped. Stephen hastily looked beneath the wheels to see could they gain a thou' or two there, but every last grain of loose chippings had already been swept out of the path.

Bailey, knowing that the rear wheels of the cart were an inch smaller than the front – so that the highest part of the frame had already passed unscathed – opened the throttle with a flourish and emerged into Oxmantown Mall piping on his whistle like a demented screech owl. And there, while they paused to mop off the sweat and let their pulse subside, Stephen helped Daisy up into what was normally the drover's seat of the cart; there he sat himself beside her and fussed with her shawl. The baby had lately made up for its earlier refusal to show so that she was now enormous, which caused plenty of headshaking amongst the bystanders and many a *sotto-voce* opinion that 'anywan belly-up like that had no call to go flaunting her shame at the populace'. And would you look at Stephen O'Lindon tending her like the fatted calf! (The Bible was not greatly studied among them). And him in cahoots with the Honourable Char-less, too! Lord 'a Mercy, what was the world coming to altogether!

And then they were off – at a pace that would take them till nightfall, and that with no allowance for mishap, to reach Flaxmills. Stephen turned and gave one last grateful wave to his Honourable co-worker of the past month. 'A fierce man altogether,' he commented as he resettled himself and checked on her shawl yet again. 'He'd charm honey from the bees,' Daisy agreed. She waited for him to say, yet again, that she shouldn't have come, for they had argued over nothing else all yesterday while he had been at the factory, preparing the site for the new machine. But now he said nothing. Perhaps his awareness of the crowd's opinion touched some streak of perversity within him and made him proud of her for being there, proud of that independence in her spirit.

The crowds followed them out as far as Riverstown, a mile or two from the Duke of Cumberland's statue in the square that bears his name. Like Nelson on his column in Trafalgar Square, though not half so lofty, the duke provided the point from which all local measurements were taken. And Riverstown was at the outer limits of the universe for most of them; one or two might have been beyond it, seeking hire, or winnings at some point-to-point, but for the rest the world ended there – by habit if by no deeper necessity. And by habit most of them turned at the Little Brosna, whose meandering waters give the hamlet its name, and went back to their work as tailors, victuallers, lawyers . . . and all the other trades that keep a garrison town afloat. Just a few intrepid souls, who would as liefer step out briskly on a fine April morn as spend yet another day propping up the duke's column, crossed into the terra incognita of County Keelity.

At Simonstown the silver band came out to fête them on their way. There was a great deal of merriment at the legend on the banner, which people now took to refer to the 'plank-binnder' itself – thus making it seem as if Stephen O'Lindon had subtly filched something from the oppressor over the water. And men who had never touched a willing forelock to another soul now bowed and scraped before the machine and laughed at the chance to avail of the insult. Even Sergeant McNair, stern disciplinarian of the RIC, smiled at the incongruity of it all. Daisy saw him and shook her head in wonder. 'How would any stranger ever understand us?' she asked.

40

The lure of the mayfly was too much for Mercier. Unwilling to leave his young wife alone in the city where she had lately enjoyed so much freedom, and where many of those who shared her enjoyment of it were still at large, he dragged Swan along with him. Then, being anxious not to leave her at a loose end in a place where she knew no one – a situation she was past-mistress at remedying – he settled on the Star of the Shannon Hôtel in Flaxmills, where she would have her sensible young friend Miss O'Lindon to keep an eye on her.

When it transpired that the sensible young Miss O'Lindon was monumentally *enceinte* – and mysteriously so, considering her rather svelte figure only a few months earlier – he hardly knew what to say or do. But the mayfly is the mayfly, so he put the best gloss of a smile he could upon it and vanished into the predawn drizzle each day, returning at dusk with enough trout to feed the town. Lough Cool was not one of the fashionable lakes of the Shannon during the season and Mercier intended doing his bit to keep it that way; it saddened him to realize how he'd have to keep his boasting in check when he returned to Dublin, but discretion was a full keep-net, and that was cause enough for him. 'Fishing on Lough Cool?' he practised saying. 'Oh, not bad, you know. Not at all bad.' His accent kept veering into mainland English; the words did not muster comfortably with an Irish lilt. 'Bedad, we could hardly dip the oar for fear of braining a fish!' That'd be more like it, now. But the really funny thing was that when the Englishman said the fishing wasn't bad and the Irishman said you could walk dry-shod over the water on fishes' backs – they meant precisely the same thing.

'Is that the Star Hôtel?' Swan asked Daisy on their first morning together. 'I've slept better under the stars themselves. Mr Shaughnessy, when you're building a floor, does it take a special sort of a skill to make it a foot lower in the middle than all round the edges or can any passing ape do it?'

The foreman came out of his reverie and stared in alarm at the floor on which they were standing.

'No,' Swan assured him. 'Down at the hôtel.'

He grinned as comprehension dawned. 'Ah, well now, the man who built that place, Dessy Hogan, he's dead now, God rest him, he had the notion, d'ye see, to jut the bedrooms out over the walls below. And to save on the timber he told Mikey Finnegan, who owned it then, that if he put all the heavy furniture on the bit that jutted out, it would spring up the rest of the floor. The canting-lever principle he said it was, which he'd read of at the mechanics in Simonstown. Well, they never did put in the heavy furniture because they couldn't get it up the stairs.'

'And is it those mouldering heaps of bog oak in the passageway below?' Swan asked.

'It is, indeed, ma'am. So what you have there, d'ye see, is the canting without the lever. But it has its advantages, mind. When it does be raining, doesn't it carry the water well clear of the bed.'

'You needn't tell me,' Swan assured him. 'We had to move the bed twice last night. And then the landlord took pity on us and lent us an umbrella.'

Shaughnessy sucked a philosophical tooth. 'All his wealth is in that thatch,' he concluded solemnly.

'Like mine,' Daisy added lugubriously as they strolled back out again.

The drizzle had passed over and a fitful sun broke out between threats of showers, few of which materialized. They decided to stroll down the towpath on the northern bank of the river.

'I'm sure I'm keeping you from all sorts of important work,' Swan sighed unguiltily.

'Oh yes!' Daisy laughed. 'If Stephen catches me at anything, any little thing, it's more than my life is worth. He'll have a fit when he hears I went for a walk! Honestly! It's not an illness. If I'd wanted it to be treated as an illness, I'd have married Napier and lived at the castle and had the vapours and smelling salts – and the servants fetching and carrying for me all day long.' She shivered as at a fate narrowly escaped.

'Well, I wasn't going to talk about it,' Swan replied diffidently.

'Which?' Daisy asked with roguish smile. 'Napier and Stephen . . . or . . .' She placed a hand on the mound of her belly.

'That.' Swan nodded in the general direction of her midriff. 'It's fairly obvious Napier's not going to marry you. Or doesn't he know?'

'He knows. And it's me who's not marrying him.'

Swan was aghast. 'Truly?' Then her face cracked in a smile. 'Mother of God, but there's a magnificence in that!'

'In what?'

'You know fine well. You coming back here, camping in their ear, parading Napier's shame – isn't that the way of it?'

Daisy shrugged awkwardly. Now there was no Napier to fight over, she wanted to be friends – true friends – with Swan. At that moment she longed to tell her she was right, to marvel that Swan had seen it so quickly, to point out how similar they were in so many ways. And yet something held her back.

No matter. Swan took her silence for acquiescence. 'We've both had a narrow escape,' she said firmly. 'Or didn't you know? There was a time when I could have crooked one finger and . . . ah well! A narrow escape.'

They paused at the middle of the bridge and stared upriver, over the weir and pool to the dashing cataract and the Martello Tower crowning the bluff. 'Oh, it could be such a pretty town,' Swan cried out in dismay.

'What is wrong with us? Think what they'd make of this landscape in England. And look what we've done with it.' She waved a hand over the drab higgledy-piggledy of cabins, mean houses, and half-derelict factories.

'The money that made England so beautiful should have stayed this side of the water and done the same service here,' Daisy suggested. 'I suppose Mercier thinks I'm a scandal.'

They resumed their stroll.

'Which you are, indeed,' Swan rejoined. 'Sure, it's no fit way to take revenge. I wish Mr O'Lindon was here. I'd like to know why he hasn't taken you by the scruff of your neck and . . .'

'He'll be back tomorrow,' Daisy assured her, 'with, let us hope, a nice fat order book.' After a pause she added, 'I wish he was here, too.'

'You are going to marry him, I hope?' Swan asked. 'Or someone. Anyone. Before *that* happens.' This time she pointed more confidently at Daisy's belly.

Daisy nodded but did not actually say yes. 'The thing is, I believe I'd have married him long since, but for something he said to me when he proposed. Well, he didn't actually propose, but . . . oh dear!' And she went on to describe as best she could what Stephen had suggested that afternoon.

'Ah! So he jumped to the same conclusion as me. But surely he doesn't approve? Not if he really loves you. It seems an extraordinary thing for a man who loves you to suggest.'

Daisy nodded again, unable to disagree. 'But then he is an extraordinary man, you know. You might not think so on a slight acquaintance, but he is. D'you know what I almost said just now? When you pointed out how drab this town is? I almost said that Stephen will change it all one day. And the reason I held my tongue is not that I *don't* believe it. He will. I don't know where he gets it from. And he has no envy of any man. It's not that which drives him. And yet, I tell you . . .'

Swan touched her arm gently. 'I believe you. You needn't go on.'

Daisy smiled. 'You're only humouring me.'

'I am not. In fact, Mercier says the same as you. He meets a lot of people, you know, who assume a grand air and would have you believe they have the back-door key to the Bank of England. He says Mr O'Lindon's the exact opposite. He could end up owning half Ireland and strangers would still walk up to him and say, "Hey misther – where's the quare fella?" So I believe you.'

Her Dublin-Liberties impersonation was so acute that Daisy had to laugh, though she did not like what Swan had said. 'He's not *shabby*, you know,' she pointed out. 'And when you'd see him in his own factory, well, you'd never doubt he's the quare fella.'

'Sure, I was only exagerraaatin',' Swan responded, still in character. 'Anyway, we've strayed from the point. Why would he have made such a suggestion to you?'

They stepped off the road through a little rusty gate beyond which a damp track of clay led down to the towpath proper. They had to lift their skirts from the mud. Two Board of Works men who were prodding the bed of the river with a long pole eyed them brazenly but they lowered their hems again and stared them out; only when the men resumed their work did the two women continue with their promenade. 'The barefaced insolence of some people these days,' Swan commented. 'I don't know where this country's going.'

'Two-horses Flynn and Bell-the-cat Dolan,' Daisy said drily.

'You know them?'

'I'm getting to know everyone here. Two greater rebels never supped porter, nor so much of it. They rent a few acres and call themselves farmers. They've fought more skirmishes with the English without stirring from the fire than any man in Ireland. Two-horses was with Skin-the-goat and the Invincibles in Phoenix Park when they shot Cavendish and Burke, or so he'd wish you to believe.' She raised her voice and called out cheerily, 'Good morning, Mr Flynn, Mr Dolan. If you're fishing for kangaroos, it's a kindness to tell you you've some way yet to go.'

Dolan's lopsided grin told them that the real tale of it was even better. The pair of them were fishing for half a crate of poteen they'd been forced to drop off the bridge above last night just prior to an encounter with a gentleman in blue serge. But that divil got the worst of it. He must have a head on him this morning thicker than if he'd swallowed all six bottles himself.

When they were a little way down the towpath Swan commented that the town was remarkably quiet, considering it had been the scene of such a villainous assault on a limb of the law.

'The assault was entirely verbal,' Daisy assured her. 'And it probably consisted of the words: "Good night, yer honour. Sure that's a grand moon." With a muttered curse to follow half an hour later. Oh, they're the bold brave lads – those two!'

A little way down the towpath they passed a small, crudely whitewashed memorial to someone who had drowned at that spot over forty years earlier, itself now drowned in weeds. Swan crossed herself absentmindedly – which answered a question Daisy had asked herself at their chance meeting in Dublin. She said nothing.

'Mr O'Lindon,' Swan reminded her. 'And Napier's baby.'

'Oh yes.' Daisy sighed and returned to the theme with reluctance. '*Why* did Stephen make such an offer? It's so hard to read his intentions. Did he feel that, by his offering to marry me at once, I might think he was trying to usurp Napier's baby?'

'Don't be absurd!' Swan exploded. 'I shouldn't think it even crossed his mind.'

'Well, it crossed mine,' Daisy replied simply.

Swan had no answer to that.

Daisy went on. 'The thing about Stephen is he'll never tell you what he thinks you ought to do. And I'm not used to that. I don't think any woman is. I mean, haven't you grown up surrounded by men . . . and women, too . . . but chiefly men, who pass round the advice like snuff at a wake? I admit I don't pay a blind bit of notice to it, but that's not the point. It's what I'm used to. So I can't understand a man who only ever says, "It's up to you, colleen. It's your decision." It's like going on dancing after the music has stopped.'

Swan shook her head. 'So – what is your decision?'

Daisy's only response was a trapped sort of shrug. 'I'm not the sort who bears a grudge,' she said. 'Honestly I'm not. And yet I'd kill Napier if he were standing here now. I'd cut the head out of him with my own bare hands.'

The path deviated around a turning circle for barges. Swan noticed that it contained half a dozen lesser circles, rippling outward over the smooth water, where the trout were going mad for the fly of the month that was in it. She half-closed her eyes to reduce the scene to its simplest tones. In her mind she began to paint it.

'What d'you say?' Daisy asked.

Swan, emerging from her reverie, misheard the words as, 'What did you say?' And, unaware of having spoken, made up the first thing that came to her: 'I said never marry an artist. And never regret the decision, either.' Their earlier conversation came back to her very clearly then. 'Actually,' she went on, 'the real question you now have to ask yourself is what it's going to be like – being married to a man who knows and understands you so frighteningly well.'

'D'you think he does? Stephen, you mean?'

'Of course I mean Stephen . . . Mr O'Lindon!' she almost bawled. 'You may complain that he doesn't go marching up and down in buskins, paraaading his good advice for you to ignore. But he knows full well – you're the trout that's fished with a tickle. The hook and line to hold you hasn't yet been made. And he takes one look at you and immediately *knows* that!' She shivered theatrically. 'To live with such a man will take a rare sort of wife, that's all I can say.'

'Why?'

'God, woman, have you learnt nothing but a, b, and c? The entire secret of success in marriage . . . well, take my marriage now. I know what's going on in my head and I know what's going on in Mercier's head. And he knows what's going on in his head, and he knows what's going on in mine.

And that's four things to juggle, not two, because, to be honest, what I think is going on in his head bears no likeness at all to what is really fuming and bubbling away in there . . .'

Daisy chuckled. 'Fuming and bubbling? Mercier?'

Swan nodded with absolute assurance. 'You only get a glimpse of it now and then, but it's enough to tell me I haven't the first idea about the man. Or any man, come to that. And now and then I'll catch him looking at me and I know he's reached the identical conclusion concerning me.'

'But that's terrible! You mean, you're living at cross-purposes most of the time.'

'Of course. That's the price you have to pay for being able to keep some part of yourself private.' She tapped her forehead. 'In here.'

As they sauntered on downstream, with a brief peep of the sun on their backs, Daisy shook her head in bewilderment; it was as if Swan were some traveller from a far-off land, telling of the strange customs there. And Swan, sensing this, played up to it. 'That's the cause of all those eejit games married people play,' she went on. 'Like, we can be dining out at friends', Mercier and I. And he'll say something, about art, maybe, on which topic he knows somewhat less than a newborn babe – for which I'm heartily glad most of the time. Anyway, he'll come out with some opinion that he knows full well will put me in a fury. Unfortunately, to the rest of the company it will sound like a perfectly ordinary opinion expressed in a mild and pleasant manner. And I know that. I know that if I get up on my high horse and tell him what I think of it, which, as I say, he already knows or he wouldn't be saying it, *I'm* the one who'll sound like an argumentative little shrew. And they'll all be going away shaking their heads and saying how they pity the poor man being married to a termagant like me. So I have to smile sweetly and look as if I agree. And that only doubles the fury on me.' She laughed and added, 'Still, I do exactly the same with him over banking and business – on which topic I know nothing. And he just has to grin and bear it.' Her laughter grew as she nudged her friend and cajoled: 'And just think, Daise – if you marry O'Lindon, you'll be missing all that fun!'

'Thanks be to God!' Daisy answered stoutly. 'But you've made up my mind for me. The moment Stephen gets back I'll accept his proposal.'

'If that's what it was.'

'Or I'll propose to him if it wasn't. You are right, aren't you. He *is* the man for me.'

Swan smiled wickedly. 'I never said so. I hope you'll remember that in years to come, my dear. I never actually said so.'

41

The hours that Stephen had spent in soliciting orders were tallied in the dark rings beneath his eyes. Daisy had never seen him so exhausted, not even in the first week of the building of His Majesty (as the 'plank-binnder' was now universally known); then he had gone thirty-six hours without sleep and only agreed to stop when Parsons had threatened to withdraw from the enterprise entirely. She would have known nothing of his return if it had not been her habit to draw back her curtains and open a window each night before settling to sleep, no matter what the weather. On that particular night, which was fine and cool after a day of rain, she had run her custodial eye over the factory, as usual, and had just managed to glimpse a faintly guttering light at the window of the room where Stephen usually slept.

Happy that he was back, angry that he had not come directly to the house, she threw on her dressing gown, took up the lantern, and stormed down to the factory – at least, storming was her intention, though what transpired was more of a waddle. But all her loving scolding died in her throat at the sight of him. She caught him in the act of leaning over the nightlight to blow it out. At first she did not recognize him; indeed, she thought it was some ancient tramp who had crept in there to die. To be sure, it was mostly the stark underlighting that rendered him so ghoulish; the moment he drew back and smiled a welcome at her he became recognizably himself again. But it was a self so drawn by exhaustion that the sight of him still held her rooted where she stood. 'Did you eat?' she asked.

'I'm kill't entirely.' He lay back on his mattress and rubbed his eyes.

'You haven't eaten a pick, I'm sure.' She bustled angrily to his side and set the lantern down.

Guiltily he plucked the blanket around him – which alerted her into whipping it off him as far as his waist. 'You haven't even undressed!' she cried. 'And look at the state of you! Did you swim up the river or what? I could raise cress in those clothes. Get out, now! Get up with you!' She began smacking his arms and shoulders while he chortled and cringed to avoid her.

'It's not funny, Stephen,' she told him, managing to contain her own laughter for the moment. 'You'll only take a chill and what good'll that do us? Get up now! You'll come up to the house and get out of those sodden rags and put some warm broth inside you.'

'Oh, woman,' he groaned, curling himself into a ball. 'That's a woeful steam out of you.'

'Don't you talk to me about steam,' she flared. 'Look at you! Open your eyes and look if it's steam you want!'

He did as she commanded. 'Bedad!' he said.

'And there's another thing,' she went on, feeling the blankets, 'you'll not be coming back to this swamp. You'll sleep tonight where it's dry and warm, my lad.'

That threat brought him wide awake. 'What are you saying?' he asked quietly. They both knew there was only one dry, warm bed in that house.

As well as she could, on her knees beside him and with that great lump in her belly, she leaned over and kissed him full on the lips. 'I'm giving you that answer you wanted,' she murmured.

He just lay there, eyes closed, scarcely breathing; he might have been praying.

'Of course, you may have forgotten the question . . .' she added light-heartedly as she eased herself upright again.

His hand groped for hers and squeezed it. His eyelids, though closed, blinked several times and she saw a tear start out upon his cheek. 'Oh, Stephen,' she whispered, suddenly close to tears herself.

He opened his eyes, smiled awkwardly, blinked several times more, sniffed glutinously, and said, 'I'm tired.'

'I know. I know. Come now.'

Side by side, their arms so tight about each other you wouldn't know which was supporting whom, they walked up to the house in the most easeful silence they had ever known. At the doorway, feeling the moment should be marked by some declaration, he paused and said, 'I will honour you, my love. And I will honour you with days of glory.'

Ten minutes later, dry and fed, he fell asleep in her arms, the moment his head touched her pillow.

She lay there, cradling his fatigued body to her and thinking there could surely be no happier woman in all the world at that particular moment. 'I love you,' she murmured to him, brushing his brow with the words, 'and I love you and I love you . . .' She promised wonders to make him happy. They would have the best home a family could ever want. She'd work beside him in the business, never sparing herself, and together they would make such a success of it that . . . she faltered. How could you measure a success so unimaginably vast?

The image of Coolderg Castle floated into her mind but her imagination shied away from so exact a vow. '*Like that*, anyway,' she promised vaguely.

At last she dared let herself think of Napier – and was surprised to discover that no feeling for him now remained. Neither love nor hate. And that was the thought which brought her sleep at last: She, who had feared to find some remnant of love for the father of the child within her, was pleased instead to discover no hate for him.

But she was not the first woman who ever mistook her own emotional exhaustion for something more permanent.

42

No man had greater powers of recovery than Stephen. When Daisy awoke next morning he was already up and gone. For an hour or so, as she busied herself happily about the house, she assumed he was down at the factory. But then, when Shaughnessy came up for a jar of porter to reward a bargee who'd just delivered some timber, it turned out that Stephen had simply handed over a list of the orders he had drummed up in Dublin and Belfast and ridden on.

'But where?' Daisy asked.

'Killaloe, ma'am.' Shaughnessy's smile knew it all.

Her eyes narrowed, challenging him to say more.

'To see Canon Wilmot, ma'am.'

Understanding began to dawn. It was confirmed by the foreman's next words: 'The registrar for this diocese, ma'am.' At last the grin split his face. 'I think there's a special licence in it somewhere.'

She smiled, too. 'Did himself tell you to wait an hour before you informed me?'

He shook his head. 'Himself did bid me say not a word. But I was thinking what the shock of it might do.' His gaze strayed near her belly.

'Then you said nothing, so,' she promised him. 'But I'm thankful for your consideration. I'll be duly amaaazed, you may rest assured, Mr Shaughnessy.'

Three days later, when Stephen at last sprang his 'surprise,' she was too filled with consternation to leave much room for amazement or any other response. She knew nothing of the process of labour and, in her desire to play the whole thing down, both as a matter of health and of her own reputation, she had done nothing to remedy her ignorance. But it didn't take much common sense to realize that the strange movements and discomforts and outright stabbing pains from her loins and back were the prelude to the grand climax.

Even then, the first thought that popped into her mind was not of water and towels and couches and Bridey Hogan, the Flaxmills midwife; it was of a bright, lazy summer's afternoon out on the mountainy road above Rathfarnham where a giddy young girl, thinking herself head over heels in love, couldn't get enough of her man. That was the day all this began, she was sure of it. And yet now it hardly seemed to relate to herself at all; it might have been something she heard about in whispers in some long-forgotten gossip.

The same glazing of unreality tinted all the other events of that day. Her body must have given out the usual tangible warnings but as far as she was concerned they were masked in the even more usual calls of nature. So, although she knew the baby was getting ready to part with her, she had no idea how imminent it was when she let Stephen help her up into the gig for the brief drive up the hill to the church at the top.

He saw her wince at one of the spasms and asked anxiously if she was all right. She merely nodded and gave him a tight-lipped smile. She knew how important it was to him – and, indeed, to herself, too, now she had set her mind to it – to get the child born in wedlock.

He persisted: 'Will I ride up and bring the vicar down to you?'

'For the love of God, will you ever stop! I've a little twinge or two but it's nothing I've not felt this month or more.'

Only partly reassured, he called out to Shaughnessy as they passed: 'Would you ever go over to Bridey Hogan and ask her to come up to the church? Tell her it's only a precaution and she may return here with us.'

For half the drive up the hill Daisy remonstrated with him over the needless cost if it were a false alarm; for the rest of the way she bottled up her cries at the pains that silenced all talk of 'false' alarms.

The church was surprisingly full, considering the haste in which the ceremony had been arranged. Most of the local O'Lindons were there except for Stephen's sister Maureen, who was herself too far gone with child to attend; Swan and Mercier were there, to be sure; and so was Daisy's Aunt Kathleen and Uncle Brendan.

Her aunt's broad smile vanished when she saw how flushed and drawn her niece appeared. The mother of five, herself, she had enough of an instinct about it to need no second glance. She stepped out into the aisle and took Daisy's other arm. 'Are we in time?' she asked heavily. Then to Stephen: 'Why in the name of God didn't you bring us all down to her?'

Daisy leaped to his defence. 'I wouldn't hear of it.'

Her aunt's eyes raked the ceiling. ' 'Clare to God, you're each as bad as the other. How close are your pains?'

'Sure they're not at all . . .' The assurance was nipped by another hefty twinge.

'I sent for Bridey Hogan,' Stephen said.

'Then you're not a complete eejit.' Aunt Kathleen turned to the Rev. Twomey. 'Do the least that's needful, vicar, and as fast as may be.'

He nodded grimly and launched them at once, rattling along like a country train. But for Daisy that final stroll up the aisle had been the last straw. She stood at Stephen's side, racked in throbs of pain that were now continuous; her only relief was the faintness that also passed over her in waves and which brought partial oblivion.

Her responses were barely audible but she managed to make them all; it seemed that some part of her was only waiting to hear the pronouncement '. . . man and wife,' for no sooner were the words out than she squatted on her haunches and moaned like a beast.

The womenfolk crowded around her and Aunt Kathleen took charge at once. She sent the vicar off to get some smelling salts from his wife – though half a dozen ladies present could probably have furnished the article; and she told Stephen to go out and hurry that Bridey Hogan along. Then, while the men shuffled out, she and several other females brought spare choirboys' cassocks from the vestry and made an impromptu birthing bed in front of the altar, in the transept where Daisy had fallen. She lay there, eyes clenched tight, fighting the worst pain she had ever felt in her life – and wondering why it did not make her cry out, as many a lesser pain had done. A fleeting thought dipped into her mind: This pain was too important to banish with a yell.

An image of Stephen swam before her but she knew it was not real for he was somehow beneath her and she was cradling his head in her arms. It was a memory, she realized; she had held him thus only . . . how many million years ago? So soft his skin was, and yet so firm! His muscles were like those of the figleafed gods at the Academy School. The lambent colour of his candle-lit flesh was all about her; the rounded mightiness of it; the way it dimpled between one muscle and the next. She wanted to shrink until she was small enough to cocoon herself in those dimples and be safe for ever and ever . . .

And all while she dreamed, the women fussed around her. By the time they had finished, the midwife herself had arrived.

'I can't set foot in there, sir,' she declared, eyeing the vestry door as if it were the entrance to hell itself – which, as far as her own immortal soul was concerned, it was.

'For God's sake, woman,' Stephen yelled at her. 'My wife may be dying beyond!'

Uncle Brendan gripped his arm and shook it. 'Aisy does it, boys,' he warned. 'Where will shoutin' get us, only nowhere.' He nodded at Stephen's father who persuaded him to keep out of it for the moment and led him a short way off, toward the church gate. Mercier fell in beside them.

Several of the men argued with the midwife but it was – understandably enough – a situation that had never arisen before; all she knew was that a Roman Catholic entered a Protestant church on pain of mortal sin. Tom Walshe, the sexton and Flaxmills's oldest inhabitant, reminded her he'd caught her in there a time or two as a child, playing behind the altar with Peter Shaughnessy. So any impairment of her immortal soul was already accomplished. She blushed and said she'd had absolution for those times. Uncle Brendan asked her, reasonably enough, he thought, why couldn't she go in now and get absolution once again. 'Sure, what good's the confessional if you can't even do that?' he asked. But she was adamant: if they wanted her services, they were to throw Mrs O'Lindon on a hurdle and bring her out there. Wasn't it a mild day, and fresh air never harmed a soul yet.

Mercier said that surely the ban only applied when there was a service in progress. Hadn't St Pat's in Dublin employed a Roman Catholic sculptor last year to restore some of the monuments, and all he'd done was step outside during the actual services. Mrs Hogan said you'd never know what them Dublin jackeens'd get up to next, but that wasn't her understanding of the matter.

Someone sent for the priest to settle the issue but he was out giving the last rites to a farmer at the far end of the parish.

Stephen muttered to Mercier to go to the midwife and offer her five pounds.

'Guineas,' Mercier suggested. 'Make it more of a medical fee than a bribe, eh?'

Stephen shrugged helplessly. 'Anything. Anything. Just persuade her to go in to Daisy. Oh, dear God, I can't think this is real.'

Mercier did his best but Bridey Hogan had made too public a declaration of her faith in that enemy camp to swallow it at any price, pounds or guineas. The argument went back and forth but reached no different conclusion.

Someone suggested Elizabeth Carney, who used to be the midwife before Bridey, and she was a Protestant; but everyone knew why she was no longer in that calling – and, indeed, Stephen himself had seen her dead drunk on her own threshold on his way up to the church an hour ago. He looked at his watch. Only an hour! He felt as if he'd aged ten years since leaving the house below. In his impotent rage he seized the branch of a yew and shook it for all he was worth; a shower of dried leaves was his only reward.

The parish priest himself, Father Hennessy, arrived at that moment. He waited just beyond the church gate while they explained the dilemma; before they had done, Aunt Kathleen came out garlanded in smiles to say all was well and that Stephen now had a lusty baby daughter to worry over, too. They had to restrain him from rushing within at once.

'So,' the priest said happily, 'no harm done.' And he turned on his heel to leave.

Stephen ran after him. 'What would you have said, Father?' he asked. 'Would you have let her go in to my wife?'

The man turned and looked him up and down; he had witnessed too much anguish in his long life of service to be moved greatly by what he now saw in Stephen's face. In calmer circumstances he might have given a calmer – and theologically more correct – reply. But Stephen's vehement question and the ring of hostile Protestant faces beyond him, had the very opposite effect. 'How the hell do I know,' he snapped.

'You must!' Stephen insisted.

'Easy, man!' Mercier touched his arm, but Stephen shook him off angrily.

'Why?' Father Hennessy asked coldly, unaccustomed to being addressed in such a peremptory manner. 'The situation is unlikely to repeat itself during my lifetime. Or do you intend making a habit of it?'

How Stephen managed to keep his fists to himself was only a miracle. He spun round and strode away. But he'd hardly gone two paces before his anger and frustration seethed up in a red mist before his eyes. He wheeled about once again. 'And *you*!' He stabbed an insolent finger at the cleric. 'Let your people know that none of them need ever apply to me for work again. They'll get the same tender consideration you gave my wife.'

At a funereal pace Father Hennessy closed the distance between them; he was quite expressionless. Stephen clenched his fists and willed himself not to strike the odious monster who would have let Daisy die rather than yield a principle; in truth, the ferocity of his own anger frightened him.

'Do you suppose I *want* any of my people working for you and the likes of you?' the priest asked calmly. 'Didn't I warn Peter Shaughnessy? Be not deceived, I told him. Under the skin they're as alike as nails in a box. "Sure, but he's a daycent man, Father," says he. "Listen," says I, "you may walk the length and breadth of Ireland in amity with that man – with one and all of them – and at the end of it what will you find? Eviction, deportation, the order of the boot. That's all the promise they'll ever hold for you." That's what I told him.' He shook his head, more in sorrow than in anger. 'And hadn't I the right of it!'

Stephen, seeing how badly his blind rage had wrong-footed him, curbed himself as best he could. 'Oh, is it promises now, Father?' he sneered. 'Will you tell me this then – what is the promise of eternal life to Bridey Hogan if it's gained at the cost of another Christian's death?'

'And who has died?' came the sharp rejoinder; some of the man's magisterial aplomb deserted him.

'*I* have,' Stephen said at once, not intending to say such a thing at all. He was as surprised as Father Hennessy to hear the assertion; and yet there was something within him that surged up in wholehearted agreement as he added, in a voice so calm it was almost inaudible. 'A plague on you all!'

And now it was the priest who turned and strode angrily away.

43

Bad news travels fastest. By the time the wedding party arrived back at the house, Peter Shaughnessy and the three other Roman Catholic craftsmen had packed up and gone. 'Eejits!' Stephen cursed them. But mostly his anger was turned inward – that he had lost his self-control like that. He knew as well as the next man how thin was the ice in all dealings across the religious divide.

'Sure we're better off without them,' Billy Kennedy (who now had hopes of being made foreman) chirped. 'I wouldn't say a word against them mind. Grand lads, the lot of them, and they can't help what they're taught before they have minds to reason . . .'

'Shut up,' Stephen told him.

He went up to the house and let Daisy know what had happened, but she was too exhausted – and too happy at her safe delivery – to take much of it in. He gazed down at her fondly, and at the swaddled child beside her, and his heart overflowed with love. How could it be? How could two such bundles of mortal clay be more precious than all the world put together? With infinite tenderness he eased aside the baby's shawl and startled himself at the sight of her again. 'So much hair!' he murmured.

'It won't last, they say.'

'Did you feed her?'

'I tried. They never take much the first day. Like chickens.'

He chuckled and clenched his eyes and felt the water start out beneath his lids.

'What did I say?' she asked.

He took his head. 'That practical woman inside you.' He stooped and planted a kiss on the shawl, then on her brow. 'What'll you call her?'

Daisy merely smiled.

He kissed her again and left them to sleep.

Mrs Shaughnessy and Molly Flynn stood at the kitchen door, the one grim, the other fearful. 'How ruined will you be wanting the fowl, Mr O'Lindon, sir?' the cook asked. 'If they stand another ten minutes, they'll not be fit for a beggar.'

'You may serve it now, Mrs Shaughnessy. I don't know who'll have the appetite for it but we can't see it wasted.'

As it turned out, the two birds, both prime eight-pound capons, were cooked to perfection. The aroma off them, and the rashers, and the plump pork sausages, and the new potatoes, and the tender greens, revived everyone's appetites; the carcases were picked to the bone and the dishes wiped clean with trenchers of fresh bread. Mrs Shaughnessy paused in her clearing away. 'And that's the last of my time here, Mr O'Lindon, sir,' she said quietly. 'I'm sure you'll know why.'

Stephen, fresh from the futility of a public argument in the street above, said he'd come and discuss the matter with her in the kitchen. There he did his best to persuade her to stay. She agreed it would break her heart and Molly's to go, that Miss O'Lindon – Mrs O'Lindon, as now was – had been a grand woman to work for, that she and Molly had never, personally, found themselves so well suited . . .

She was only half-way through the panegyric when Molly Flynn, herself, put in her penn'orth: 'Please, Mrs Shaughnessy, ma'am, 'tis all well and good you handing in your notice, but I must stay here.'

'Oh must you, indeed? And what's Father Hennessy to say to that?'

Molly tossed her head. 'He may tell me he's to pay for my grandfather's physic. And he may promise to keep a great lump like me in shoeleather. And then I'll depart, and gladly.'

Stephen saw it was a timely reminder to the older woman of her own family's finances, with Peter now out of work. 'Well,' he said, ' 'tis your affair entirely, Mrs Shaughnessy. Mrs O'Lindon and I would be even sorrier to lose you than you say you'd be to go. But if that girl is intent on staying, hadn't someone better bide with her to keep her on the straight and narrow in this house of heathens?'

His experience taught him better than to stay and argue the point to its conclusion; he left the yeast of his suggestion to rise on its own.

For days after that the cook said no more than that she was 'tinkin' it over'. The town was riven in two by what had happened at the church that day. To Swan and Mercier, sophistical Dubliners, it was like every peasant farce that ever graced the capital's stage, though they contained their merriment in the company of their two friends, to whom it was, of course, a far more serious matter. Indeed, it could well be that their very survival in their fragile new business was now at stake.

When the baby – who still had no name – was three days old, Mr Woods, land agent to the Coolderg estate, called at the factory and had a long talk with Stephen.

'What did he want?' Daisy asked when he came up for his dinner.

'Sure, I don't know,' he replied. 'That man could talk a linnet out of a bush. There was one time there when he seemed like he was after warning me not to poach Protestants from the distillery. And the next minute I'd have his heartfelt assurance that if I meant what I'd said and would never go back to hiring Catholics on an equal footing but only when no decent Protestant was handy – the way it is with the Coolderg estate itself – then . . .'

He hesitated.

'Then what?'

'I don't know. There was a lot of fierce grand words in it, but nothing you could take to a bank.'

Daisy was silent.

'What's your opinion?' he asked.

She gave him a wan smile to soften the blow. 'I think you must go and make your peace with Father Hennessy, my dear. Couldn't you say . . .'

'That man's a worse bigot than any of the Lyndon-Furys even.'

'But wouldn't that make it easier on you?'

'I don't see how.'

'It means you needn't be sincere. If a man's after being unreasonable beyond all bounds, doesn't that free you to meet him by any means you have? All you need think about is that, without Peter Shaughnessy, we haven't much chance. You can't be out on the highways and byways, looking for orders, and at the same time back in the factory, running it properly. And he *does* run it properly.'

Swan and Mercier urged the identical course upon him. He was actually pulling on his best boots to go and eat humble pie at the presbytery when word came to him of events that were to make all apology unnecessary.

The previous day there had been a funeral up at the Protestant church. The deceased, Dinny Lynes, was a small farmer on some five acres, just outside the town. His youngest son, James, then thirteen, was captain of the town's junior football team and very popular with all his fellows, no matter what their religion. The rest of the team had decided to go up to the church and wait outside in the yard, to offer their condolences between the service and the interment; the Protestants among them naturally went inside, the Catholics waited silently at the door.

Whether a garbled account of these events reached Father Hennessy, or whether he decided that this demonstration was a public flouting of his own authority, coming so soon after the events that had set all Flaxmills by the ears, was never known for sure. But he decided to make an example of the two worst offenders (in his eyes), Sean Rafferty and Declan Finnegan, his own two altar boys. Some traitor got word to Declan Finnegan, who ran off across the fields, but the priest caught Sean Rafferty in the school playground, where he proceeded to make a prime example of him. He caught him by the ear and began kicking his shins and calves and ankles and backside, indifferently, as the hapless youth twisted this way and that in his efforts to avoid the heavy hobnail boots.

Then to everyone's horror they saw blood gushing down the lad's neck and it transpired that half his ear had been torn away from his head. The priest stopped at once and, though clearly shaken at what he had done, put a bold face on it and promised to mete out the same chastisement to any other bold lad who dared flout his authority like that.

The master came out, said not a word to the priest – which was indication enough to all what *his* opinion was – and himself carried the unconscious lad down the hill to Doctor D'Arcy. The doctor took his scalpel, completed the amputation, and cauterized the wound. 'We could have stitched him up,' he confided later, 'but I don't believe those ears had been washed since Easter. It was pure septicæmia, waiting a chance to get in.'

That same evening Stephen went out on the bog with his father and two cousins, to cut turf that ought already to be in the second stacking. For refreshment they carried two whiskey bottles of cool buttermilk, stopped with rolled-up newspaper, which they poked into the cold, soft turf, just above the water line. Then they threw back the top layer of white turf onto last year's standing and gazed with satisfaction at the rich black bank that now lay exposed. 'Bedad, if that's not better still than last year,' his father said. He was the eternal optimist; this year's turf was always better than last. 'You cut, boy,' he added, putting the slane into Stephen's hand. The three younger men stared at each other in surprise; he had never before yielded the master's place to any man. 'What are you waiting for?' he asked. 'It won't go blacker than it is.'

Cut, twist, lift, flick . . . cut, twist, lift, flick . . .

Stephen, who had cut turf with the slane often enough when his father was not there, felt nonetheless self-conscious at the ease with which he settled to the rhythm; he almost felt he ought to bungle the odd one, as a kind of unspoken flattery to the old man. But it required too much effort, too much change in his routine, to do the thing badly, so in the end he contented himself with throwing an occasional sod high or low by a few inches and grunting an apology to his father, who, of course, was catching each one and laying it where the two cousins would load their barrows and trundle them away. His father made no reply. The one sod Stephen cut with extra care was the one against the bank, which would show for twelve months what sort of man had wielded the slane.

'Oh, for the love of God!' his father grumbled, making Stephen pause to see what he had done wrong. Then, in the corner of his eye, he saw that his father's displeasure had nothing to do with him.

'Sound-as-a-bell' Kelly was working his usual way up the line of families out on the bog that evening, carrying news, making comparisons, sneering, begging a chew of tobacco.

'The original hurler on the ditch,' Stephen replied sarcastically.

His father capped him: 'If he were even that! When has that man been on a ditch in his life? *Even* on a ditch?' He raised his voice. 'Good evening, Mr Kelly. Is your lumbago at you again?'

'Sound!' the man responded. 'Sound as a bell. And is that Nick-o'-time O'Lindon with the slane then?'

Stephen waved the implement at him in jocular threat, asking, 'Is that a slane, then? And I thought you'd surely recognize the jawbone of an ass.'

Imperturbably, Sound-as-a-bell inspected the cutting Stephen had done so far. 'Sound as a bell,' he opined amiably. 'The fella was well trained, Mr O'Lindon, but I daresay he's outrun his teacher.'

Stephen miscast a sod within inches of Sound-as-a-bell's knees. 'You must mind yourself when there's idiots at work, Mr Kelly,' he warned.

'Ah! There's one man here has ye all bet still,' the other replied.

'One day, sure, you'll roll up your sleeves and blind us.'

'Which would be a respite to those deafened by the boasting,' Mr O'Lindon put in.

'Deafening is it?' Sound-as-a-bell retorted. 'Wait till I tell ye. There's a deputation of parishioners gone to see Father Hennessy this minute seeking compensaaation for little Teacup Rafferty.'

'Isn't it quick you are with the nicknames!' one of the cousins said.

Sound-as-a-bell chuckled. 'It's not my name for the lad. I'm after hearing it in Corrigan's.' He grasped his own ear and, lifting a fastidious finger like the ladies in the fashions, tilted his own head in imitation of a cup. 'But wouldn't it suit him?'

'To a T!' Stephen commented drily.

Sound-as-a-bell dissolved in laughter and they could see him suddenly eager to go on down the line – and then back up again – repeating the new joke before anyone else could spoil it on him.

'Will they get compensation?' Stephen called after him.

He turned and shook his head sadly. 'It'll sooner rain Spanish ladies.'

They resumed their cutting and their own family crack. After an hour even that petered out and they continued in a silence that soon became hypnotic. Every now and then Stephen would come to with a jolt and realize he had cut two or three entire rows without knowing it – or, to be precise, while redesigning one small feature of His Majesty.

It happened several times. Once he wandered off, trying to think of girls' names for a baby. Another time, he mustered a dozen good reasons for Peter Shaughnessy to rejoin the business. Another time he remembered the time when they had found a half-pound of butter that had lain in the bog for over a thousand years, put there by some ancient pastoralist to whom all this was summer grazing and preserved by the acid water of the bog ever since – indeed, the same acid that preserved the bog itself from corruption.

Then slowly he became aware of a slight disturbance – not enough to call a commotion – a small break in the rhythm up on the bank at his left, where his father stood catching each sod. He had cut deep into the bank by now and was having to throw up to the height of his own shoulders, so all he could see of his father without stopping and craning up was his boots.

But surely those weren't the old one's boots?

He stopped and looked up at last – straight into the impassive face of Peter Shaughnessy, who said, 'Come on, come on! Or d'you want a real man down there to finish it off for you.'

Without hesitation Stephen reached up the handle of the slane and let Shaughnessy pull him up by it. Moments later he performed the service in reverse for Peter; a bank of good soft turf, two feet above the water, is not exactly something a full grown man likes to *leap* down upon.

Stephen glanced at his father, who, with equal speed, yielded his place as catcher – but not to become a mere barrow man. Sacrifice for the greater good has its limits, after all. 'I'll go and see what sort of a mess those two jackasses have made of it,' he murmured.

44

May turned into the sort of June that Ireland experiences only three or four times in a century. The days, as people said, were very fond of the sun; there was even work for water carriers. The only people with thriving gardens were those lucky enough to live near the river and to possess backs strong enough and pails whole enough for the labour. Nor was water all that was carried betimes. Even the O'Lindons' turf, late cut as it had been, was all safe home by the third week in June – the same week that saw the first delivery of bentwood furniture to Loomis's Showrooms in Sackville Street, Dublin, which was only *the* furniture emporium for the whole of Ireland. Stephen brought home bills marked at three and six months for more money than he had earned in the best year in his life. Strangely enough, the realisation did not seem to elate him; he turned quite pale after he had done the calculations. Daisy, watching him closely, suspected that, despite all his planning and scheming, he had not fully considered that side of it – actual cash coming in, *disposable* cash.

In the unaccustomed heat the flies were prolific and the trout went mad for them in the warmer waters. Sweltering at his desk in Dublin, Mercier, in turn, went mad for the trout; when the bank closed at noon on Saturday he had a cab waiting to whisk him up the quays to Kingsbridge, where Swan would already be on the 12.35 to Roscrea with all their 'Friday-to-Monday' things, plus the hamper, the rods, flies, and keep-net. By four they would be on Lough Cool, she reading a light novel and giving an occasional touch on the oars, he casting his line in repeated assaults on his patience and the fish.

On the last Sunday in June, Swan went to first Mass, the others to early Communion, and by half past nine they were wrangling their way aboard a small launch below the bridge. It was the abandoned property of a former master of the mills, now dead; Stephen had found it, 'fierce holed and shocking altogether,' and had practically stripped and replanked it as a test of His Majesty in the boat-building line. In fact, as he pointed out the moment they were all safely aboard, the full test was only now beginning, for, until that moment, she had floated unladen.

For the mile or so downstream to the lough they anxiously watched the clinkers for signs of defective caulking, but the only water that came inboard was a splash or two over her gunwales from the leaping fish and one alarmed duck they caught napping. They mainly drifted with the current; Stephen put up a small foresail to give them a little steerage but it was often slack, especially where woodland came down to the edge of the towpath and turned the river into an airless suntrap. When they reached the open waters of the lake there was more of a breeze. They put up the only other sail they had, a tattered spanker, which bounced them in fine style, slap-slapping over the wavelets, to Turk Island, one of half a dozen outcrops in Lough Cool and the only one to boast a stand of trees.

The baby objected to this more violent motion and began to grizzle. 'Poor thing,' Swan said, reaching forward and tucking her swaddling in more tightly. 'We'll soon be there.'

'Let her kick.' Daisy pulled away the swaddling again and took her stockings off, too. 'She's just hot.'

'She's fretting for lack of a name,' Stephen insisted, glowering heavily at his wife. 'The law will be onto us soon.'

'Yes, how long have you got legally?' Mercier asked, shading his eyes and scanning the lake to see where they were rising.

'Two months,' Daisy said.

'One month.' Stephen's answer was simultaneous.

'Something of that order, anyway,' Daisy acknowledged. 'I will name her, I promise.'

'When?' Now it was Swan who spoke at the same time as Stephen; they both laughed.

'I will,' Daisy repeated.

The baby kicked her liberated feet in the air, still fretting mildly. Swan tickled them. 'What do your parents think of her?' she asked Daisy. 'Oh! Hazzums mettums grannie, yet, eh?'

'Her grannie's like that one.' Daisy nodded at Stephen. 'Obsessed with names.'

'I spotted your father coming out of his bank last week,' Mercier told her.

'In handcuffs?' The moment the question was out Daisy bit her lip and smacked her own wrists. 'It's not a fit subject for joking. If you run into him again, you may tell him I'll be in Dublin soon. He'll know what I mean.'

Stephen chuckled. 'Be sure he has a good drop of the craythur in his hand before you tell him.'

'He was looking quite prosperous, in fact,' Mercier added. 'Linehan told me he was at the subscription concert with your mother.'

Daisy's eyes went wide at the news. 'Wonders'll never cease,' she exclaimed.

'Why?' Swan asked.

'The last time she went out anywhere with him was before I was born. They went to view the Panorama when it came to Dublin and she said three people walked up to him and served writs. She swore she'd never go out with him again.'

They all laughed. Even Daisy; what else could one do?

The nearest thing to a harbour on the island was a shallow beach of sand and clay, fringed by tall reeds. The men gallantly carried the women ashore and then Stephen went back for the baby. 'I'll tell you one thing, little girl,' he promised her loud enough for all to hear. 'Your mother won't set foot back in that boat today until she's fastened a name on you.'

'Isn't it lucky I brought her shawl,' Daisy commented airily to the few fleecy clouds in the sky. 'It could be a cold night before morning.'

Swan laughed. 'Listen to us! You know what we sound like, don't you.'

'What?' Stephen asked.

'Married couples!'

It required several trips to carry the hamper and the rugs and the crib and the parasols and the cushions up to the fringe of the little stand of trees – Norfolk pines that gave scant shade, or, rather, gave it in wayward patches that crept inexorably over the ground. As soon as she could seat herself comfortably, Daisy gave a breast to the baby and the grizzling stopped. 'That's all it was, see,' she said contentedly. Swan felt a pang of envy at that moment – though most of her other recent glimpses of Daisy and motherhood and its responsibilities had left her unmoved.

Daisy grinned at her. 'Penny for them?'

Mercier tugged at an earlobe, which he always did when mildly embarrassed. 'If you want to know,' Swan replied, 'I was thinking 'tis a quare thing altogether.' She nodded toward the suckling child. 'If you think about it – one human being making food of herself for another.'

'They say you can give goatsmilk in a bottle and it's better,' Stephen threw in. Then he caught Daisy's eye and added, 'Not that I know the first thing about it, mind.'

Swan continued, 'When you see a cow and a calf, you don't think twice about it. I mean, it looks completely natural. But when you see a woman suckling a baby . . . I don't know. It's not the same, somehow. It's a bit of a jolt. For me, anyway.'

'There!' Mercier pointed to the Clare shore of the lake and reached for his spy-glasses.

Stephen spoke out in jocular tone: 'And what would you say, Mrs Mercier, at the sight of a grown man holding a bit of a shtick, with a bit of oul' string on it, and a bit of bent metal on that, and a concoction of peacock feathers and button thread on that?'

'Well now . . .' Swan pretended to consider the question seriously.

'When I first saw it I'd say it was also a bit of a jolt. But now, God be praised, it's starting to look completely natural.'

Mercier consulted his watch and tutted in vexation as he stuffed it back in his waistcoat pocket. 'There won't be time to get over there and do anything useful before luncheon. Unless . . .' He sighed and waited for his hosts to complete his obvious suggestion.

Daisy drew breath to speak but Stephen halted her with a sly wink. 'I'll defend a good Irish breakfast against anything else in the world,' he said contentedly as he lay back and tipped his hat forward over his eyes. He settled himself, liberated a couple of waistcoat buttons, and patted his stomach. 'It sticks to your ribs, so it does.'

Mercier scratched pensively at his smooth-shaven chin. 'And by God you'd need it,' he said, 'with a breeze like this. A good stiff breeze – that'll hollow a man out in next to no time, I always find.'

Swan, precisely caught between amusement and peevishness at the way Stephen was teasing, plucked a long stalk of grass and began imitating a fly, crawling up his face. Several times he shooed it away before he opened his eyes and saw what it really was.

'D'you know what a man said to me about you in the hotel last night?' she asked at once.

'What?' Daisy asked.

'They said wasn't he the clever one altogether for to go and patent a machine to "binnd" – that's the way they say it round here, isn't it – to "binnd" the planking for boats and then to go and build furniture with it instead. It put everyone on the wrong foot, he said.'

'Oh yes!' Daisy exclaimed contemptuously. 'Now that Stephen's shown what can be done, every idler in the district wants to be in the bentwood-furniture business. They should be up at five in the morning like him, trying out some improvement on the machine.'

Swan, on the point of making some amused reply to this outburst, suddenly changed her mind; she eyed Daisy shrewdly for a moment and then looked away.

'I really did mean to build boats,' Stephen said. 'I only got the idea for furniture when I passed that shop in Dublin.'

'And saw the prices,' Daisy put in.

Mercier gave a single preparatory laugh. They all turned to him. 'That's something we were talking about in the bank last week – the real reason why companies succeed or fail in business. Like the canals, for instance. They imagined that their business was selling space on barges to people with goods to move.'

'And isn't it?' the two women asked, mystified.

Mercier, sitting on his haunches, nodded at Stephen. 'Ask him.'

Stephen grinned lazily, like a man suspecting, and thus evading, a trap.

'No,' he said. 'It's moving the goods itself is their business, not selling the space to do it in.'

Mercier laughed and clapped with delight.

Daisy apologized sarcastically for not realizing at once what a huge difference there was between the two.

Mercier became serious again. 'But there *is*, Mrs O'Lindon. It's the difference between going bankrupt and staying solvent. And it's because they can't see the difference that so many canal companies here and over the water are in trouble. But' – he lifted an admiring finger toward Stephen – 'he can see it at once. Just as he saw at once that the machine he patented for boat-building isn't for building boats at all. O'Lindon! When you've made your fortune, as you undoubtedly will, for God's sake don't leave it all with the Hibernian. Put some of it with us.'

Stephen laughed and sat up. 'Why? Would you mind it better?'

'Not at all,' was the jovial rejoinder. 'But don't you see, man – I could then tell my directors we have this valued depositor on the shores of Lough Cool who badly needs our advice and guidance. Then Swan and I could take a daycent Friday-to-Monday for a daycent spot of fishing.'

Stephen, who had collected a small handful of pebbles during this persiflage, began throwing them into the water, trying to make each one land precisely upon the spreading ring of the one previous.

'If you could give him advice and guidance on how to relax,' Daisy commented, 'you'd do him a kindness. I never saw him rest longer than that.'

Mercier saw his chance to pursue his other wish. He sprang to his feet and declared that he'd never been able to rest idly, either. 'How about a stroll round this island of yours, Mr Crusoe?' he said to Stephen. 'A good brisk constitutional, eh – now that's your only man for an appetite.'

Stephen rose willingly to it. 'And what does that make you?' he asked. 'My Man Friday-to-Monday, I suppose.'

Laughing, they went off to explore the rest of the island, which measured all of one furlong by a couple of rods, poles, or perches.

Swan reached for the hamper.

'Sure that can wait till they're back,' Daisy told her. 'You'll only expose it to the flies.'

The baby fell asleep, her head lolling back from Daisy's one free nipple, now all wrinkled and shrivelled. 'Oh, you young thief of the world!' she said. 'Now I've got one full and one empty. Marvellous!'

Swan reached for the child while Daisy adjusted her clothing. 'Put a napkin on your shoulder first,' she warned, 'or she'll surely vomit all down you.'

The baby brought up a great rasher of wind; they both cried, 'Good girl!'

Daisy laid all the cushions within reach against a small boulder and leaned against half of them, patting the space at her left for Swan to join her.

'The peace of it!' Daisy sighed after a while.

'Mmmm.' Swan agreed.

'Still . . .' Daisy's tone was dubious.

'What?'

'It's deceptive. With a good telescope, now, you could probably pick out a hundred Fenians and Land Leaguers – and common felons, too, come to that.'

Swan gave a brief, humourless laugh. 'Well, that puts the Land League in its place.'

'I don't mean they're the same as felons. I only mean the peace is deceptive. Anyway, I don't want to talk about that. Not today.'

'What then?' Swan shifted the baby onto her other shoulder and went on patting and stroking her back.

'What were you thinking about, just now, when the men were here?' Daisy asked.

'Lots of things.'

'But when you spoke about what some old toper had told you in the bar . . .'

'Old toper! It was actually Mr Woods, if you must know. Land agent to the Coolderg estate and sober as a judge.'

'Very well. But I said something and you . . .'

'You leaped like a tigress to his defence – Mr O'Lindon's defence.'

'Yes. And you were going to say something and then you thought better of it. What?'

Swan rubbed her cheek dreamily against the baby's neck. 'Are you sure you want to know?'

'I'd not ask else.'

'It might open an old wound.' She cleared her throat delicately. 'Napier.'

Daisy laughed mirthlessly. 'That's well healed by now.' She looked across at her baby. 'I have the best part of him now.'

Swan dandled the sleeping child for a while and then risked a glance in Daisy's direction. She found her sitting up, hugging her knees to her chin, smiling broadly, and staring away into the distance across the lake. That pang of jealousy returned, not for the baby now but for Daisy herself – the way she always got what she wanted. Napier had been quite interested in her, Swan, until Daisy came along; then he'd hardly give her the time of day. And by the time she'd heard he was free again, she was married to Mercier. Not that she didn't love the man; of course she did. But he was no Napier. And now, having bungled all that, Daisy had fallen on her feet again with Stephen. True, he hadn't Napier's dashing looks, but there was that power in him to melt your heart all the same, even more than Napier, once you got to know him. Napier was febrile, not exactly moody, but there was an uncertainty in him that was completely absent in Stephen. Napier was a born third son. Stephen was solid as the Rock of Cashel. And those watchful Protestant eyes that looked into your soul and missed nothing! Mercier was right.

Stephen would get everything he wanted in the end – and he'd give it to Daisy like a garland. Swan wondered if Daisy really appreciated what she'd got.

'So . . . what about Napier, then?' she asked lightly. 'D'you honestly feel absolutely nothing?'

Daisy remembered that first day they had met, at the 'alfresco banquet' on St Stephen's Green – Swan's pointed questions and her well-concealed anguish at Napier's new allegiance. She nodded. 'It's hard to believe, isn't it. Actually, it just makes me so distrustful of feelings altogether. If a boat was to put out from Coolderg boathouse . . .'

She fell silent, still staring away into the distance but now *at* something rather than just vaguely. Swan followed the line of her eyes, expecting to see a boat putting out as she had described it; but, seeing nothing, she turned back and asked, 'What?'

'I never realized it before but you can actually see Coolderg Castle from here. Just the tip of the main tower beyond the . . . d'you see the big beech tree with some leaves already going yellow?'

'Oh yes.' Swan saw it herself now. 'Anyway, if you saw Napier putting out in a boat . . . ?'

But Daisy's mind was now far away across the lake. 'I stood on that tower with Napier last Christmas,' she murmured. 'He showed me the extent of the estate. Even out to Flaxmills – which you can't see from there, of course – but you can see the big fir tree on the hill that's in the way.'

'Ah yes!' Swan's tone was sarcastic. 'Dear Napier pretends to be all very scornful of landlordism and the ascendancy and all that. But under the skin, you know . . .'

'Oh, but it wasn't like that. He was telling me the history of the place, really. How the Furys got it from my clan, the O'Lindons, by underhand means and then acquired a veneer of legitimacy by marrying . . . an O'Lindon girl. She was from Flaxmills. That's how it all came up. There's a stone with her name on it at the top of the castle. Anyway, I was about to say that if he landed on this island now, my heart wouldn't skip a single beat.'

'But would you ask him to join our picnic?'

'I would. Yet only a few weeks ago, I'd have filleted him with a hayknife. Feelings! You can't trust them.'

Swan gave out a sigh of something that sounded oddly like relief. Daisy glanced at her and asked, 'What's it to you, anyway?'

'Oh, only that Mercier's mentioned my acquaintance with Napier once or twice. I suspect he'd like to cultivate the Lyndon-Furys.' She giggled suddenly.

Daisy, thinking she was embarrassed, suggested: 'Only he's not too sure how the O'Lindons might take to such a friendship? Well, let me put your mind at . . .'

'No! It's not that. The trouble is, he's not sure whether, ten years from now, the O'Lindons won't be *more* worth cultivating than the Lyndon-Furys!'

Daisy drew a sharp breath. 'Swan! That's a disgraceful thing to impute to the man you've married.'

'I know.' Swan giggled even more, and added to it a bright red blush. 'However, what you're saying is that if I just *happened* to run across Napier in Dublin, say, and he just *happened* to start mingling in our circle, and that led to the odd fishing or hunting invitation for us, down to Coolderg . . . the O'Lindons wouldn't take umbrage and imagine we were deserting them. Is that the long and the short of it?'

45

Stephen shaded his eyes again and stared out across the lake toward the Clare shore. 'Are they still there?' Daisy asked with that kind of weary exasperation wives keep for husbands who cannot take a hint. 'Is it the boat you're worried over? Sure, Mercier can handle a boat.' He shook his head and lay back again beside her.

In fact, he had sought out the boat so as to distract himself from his thoughts. And what he had been thinking was that he and Daisy had been married the best part of a month now and they still weren't fully man and wife – naturally enough, in the circumstances, but she had dropped a remark or two, those latest days, about how well she had healed; and her caresses had grown more lingering . . .

'Or another way we could make them,' he said, picking up their earlier conversation, which had been about the factory, 'would be to binnd the backs in larger sections over a longer time.'

Daisy burst into laughter.

'What now?' he asked, mildly offended.

'I was just remembering something Napier once said about you.'

Her casual use of the name brought him up with a shock; since the day of her outburst against her former lover she had not once mentioned him – and now just to toss the word out like that! 'What?' he asked.

'He said if you ever had a nickname, it ought to be Another-way O'Lindon. He said you'd tell him about some problem in the villa – simply tell him, as if you were leaving him to decide what to do about it. Naturally, he hadn't the first idea about carpentry and such, so he asked for your suggestion. And you'd tell him, and it sounded fine, so he'd say, "Right-ho. Do it that way." And then you'd say, "Or another way . . ." Exactly like you did just now. Another-way O'Lindon. I quite like that.'

'You know what they *are* calling me? Nick-o-time O'Lindon. How do you "quite like" that?'

She half rose and flung herself across him, burying her head in his broad chest. 'I'm sorry,' she murmured. 'But you've only yourself to blame for giving me the choice like that. You should have been more of a . . . you should have been firmer with me. You should have said now-or-never.'

His excitement returned and he felt his heart quicken; for fear she might notice it, he moved her to a slightly safer distance upon his arm and asked her, 'D'you think of him much – Master Napier?'

She pinched him quite severely. 'Don't you ever call him master. That's one thing he'll never be to you again. Listen!' She rose on one elbow and spoke with solemn eagerness: 'One day, come Hell and all Connaught against us, it will be Napier Lyndon-Fury standing cap in hand before Stephen O'Lindon.'

Her quiet ferocity nipped the laughter in his throat. 'Is that what you really want?'

Looking deep into his eyes she saw that the question was by no means rhetorical: if she wanted it, he would give it her. Sobered by that prospect she forced herself to laugh and say it was only a cod and snuggle herself again into his embrace. 'I am not a vindictive woman,' she said – twice, for she liked the sound of it. 'Funnily enough,' she added, 'Swan's after asking the very same question. As if revenge was all my care!'

The baby gave out a strange sound, half yawn, half snicker. He sat up at once and rearranged the parasol to shield her face better. Before he lay down again he fondled the downy hair behind her ears. Watching him, Daisy marvelled. She did not know many husbands who'd be as tender with their own offspring as he was with . . . whatsername.

'She's a minx,' Stephen said.

Daisy half sat up, grinning. 'Why? What's she doing?'

'No. Swan. What would she be wanting to know – asking you such questions?'

Daisy laughed again and flung herself back upon the cushions. 'I'll give you one guess.'

'What?'

'Dear Stephen! Just because she's a friend, it doesn't mean we have to *trust* her – not to the very end of the line, anyway. Tell me now – what's the only thing that stirs that one to action?'

He made an awkward tilt of his head. 'There's a flightiness in her,' he offered.

'That's no answer at all. The one thing that moves her is . . . ambition. Social advancement. Swan's set her sights on an invitation to Coolderg

Castle. That's all!' Daisy saw Stephen's eyes stray in the direction of the old tower. 'That's why she asked me what I might feel about Napier – because she wouldn't want to foul her nest with us.'

'What did you tell her?' He plucked a stalk of grass and began reducing it to shreds.

'The same as I'll tell you. The truth. That bitterness and anger I had . . . you remember?'

He nodded ferociously and laughed. 'Oh God I do.'

'It's all gone. I told you – I'm not a vindictive woman. If he was to row his boat over here now and step ashore, my heart wouldn't skip one beat. Look, would you ever stop tormenting that grass and give a poor tormented girl a kiss instead?'

He dropped the grass as if it were suddenly hot and, with an embarrassed, lopsided smile, bent to please her.

'*That's* what makes my heart miss a beat these days,' she murmured when his lips at last left hers. 'Lord, this heat! Aren't you roasted in those clothes?' With a coy smile she loosened a few of his waistcoat buttons. 'I'm kill't entirely with it under this skirt. Will I take it off?'

His heart missed several beats at that. '*Here?*' he asked.

'Why not? Aren't we man and wife?'

He stared all about them, seeing no one nearer than a mile. 'Here?' He repeated the question but now in a more speculative tone, looking about for a likely place.

She stood up, lifting the rug with her, trying to jerk it from under him. 'Come on,' she chided. 'They'll be back in an hour. You bring some cushions.'

In a daze of ecstatic disbelief he picked an armful and followed her up among the pines, some ten or twelve paces from the baby.

'We hardly need the blanket here at all,' she said airily, bouncing a foot on the carpet of soft needles.

How could she be so matter of fact?

Deftly she spread the rug with a single flourish, patting the edge of it as she sank to her knees, smoothing away wrinkles that were not there. She must have unhooked the waistband of her skirt as she walked for by the time she lay down it was already half off. She smiled happily and stretched up her arms toward him.

'The baby,' he said.

Daisy laughed.

'Sure, she's sleeping rings round herself.'

He knelt at her side and unbuckled his belt. Then, too shy to continue, he lay beside her and let her fingers do the rest out of sight. 'I never . . .' he began to stammer.

'Whisht now!'

'I mean I may not be as good as . . .'

With a great gasp she pulled him onto her. 'Be quick!' she panted. 'Oh Stephen! Haven't we a lifetime for being good! Oh, my darling, darling man!'

An hour later, as naked as Adam and Eve in Eden, he lay beside her, running his fingertips idly up and down her belly and chest. She shook her head and sighed. 'Nothing left.'

'I never saw a naked woman before.'

'I'm not naked. I'm nude.' She thought about it. 'No! By all the holy – I *am* naked!' She laughed at the discovery. 'Are they still fishing?'

He raised his head and stared out among the pine-tree boles. 'No. They're half-way back.'

'God, I must dress!' Daisy tried to sit up in a panic but his strong hand and arm reached out and pinned her down. She struggled briefly and then relaxed. 'Keep it for when we're back home tonight?' she pleaded seductively.

'Name the child,' he commanded.

'Oh, and is that it?'

'It is. You'll not stir from that blanket till you name the child – and never mind if they come back and see us like this.'

'You wouldn't dare.'

Grimly he increased the pressure of his arm.

'Well, see if I care!' She scrabbled blindly about her for a cushion and slipped it behind her head. Then she began to sing: '*Is it true that the women are worse than the men . . . They were sent down to Hell and were threw out again?*'

'Lord save us!' he raged. 'Was ever woman born more stubborn than you? Why will you not name her?'

She giggled. 'Ask me nicely. Take away your threats. I'll never yield to a threat.'

With the weary exasperation that husbands reserve for a wife who must be humoured he removed his arm. 'Will you please, please, *please* name the child?'

'Is there another cushion there?'

'That's not a proper name.'

'Is there?' She lifted her head and let him place it behind her. 'Yes!' She settled herself contentedly into its softness. Now, peering out among the trees, she could just make out the tower of Coolderg Castle. As she stared at it the smile left her face, until at last she was quite solemn. There was a hardness in her voice, all the more marked to him – coming as it did after such a soft, gentle, playful time together – when she said, 'Yes, it will be the right thing to do. The right and fitting name.' She turned those flinty gray eyes upon him and said, 'This child's name is to be Caroline.' She gripped his wrist urgently, to stop him from saying a single word, either of approval or protest. 'Caroline *O'Lindon*. God send she'll never forget the blood that's in her veins.'

Part II

Home is the hunter

46

'Loonan tells me Clancy in jail.' Daisy read the scrawl along the side of an unprimed door. On a window frame nearby, also waiting for its first coat of primer, she read a less literate but more triumphal message: 'Africa War. English is gettin the worst of it. Two ridgements is missing.' Liam Egan edged past her with a shamefaced grin and put a layer of pink over both legends. 'They served their purpose, Mrs O'Lindon,' he said.

'Is it true?' She nodded at the message on the window.

'Faith, I hope it is.' He looked at her in surprise. 'Don't you?' Her public stand against the Boer War was well known locally.

A slight nod of her head conceded half his point. 'I'd be glad to see this war ended by political means, Mr Egan. But I can't forget there are five good lads from Flaxmills out there on the veldt somewhere, never mind the rest of Keelity. To end it by their deaths is sending the bill to the wrong address in my opinion.'

'Ah, you've a point there, right enough, ma'am.'

'Why was it written on the scantlings, anyway?'

'The Rule of Silence, ma'am.'

'Even in the joinery?'

'In every Lyndon-Fury establishment 'tis the same. Er . . . would there be any truth in what they're saying? Is Mr O'Lindon to buy out the whole business box and dice?' He nodded toward Stephen, who was out in the yard, deep in conversation with Mr Woods.

'There's only two people can tell you that, Mr Egan.' She cast her eyes in the same direction.

His grin was pure disbelief, adulterated only by his acceptance of her lie. Sure, why else would she be there. Didn't she have the last word on everything the O'Lindons did. When they bought Ber Grogan's old boathouse that wasn't worth ten pounds, and Ber said he wanted forty, and Stephen O'Lindon laughed and told him he'd have to think again, wasn't it herself who said, 'He will not!' And instead of reminding the woman who wore the trousers there, didn't himself then count out the money on the spot and get his luckpenny back with a smile. No, the truth was there was only *one* person in all the world who could say whether O'Lindon would take over the joinery or no, and she was in here with her eyes like needles, reading more than seditious messages scrawled on doors and windows.

'It's not a bad oul' place,' he ventured hopefully.

'It's a dreadful oul' place,' she snapped.

'It is, indeed, ma'am. And that's the truth. But it could be improved, d'you see.'

It began to rain while he spoke – a sudden, vicious downpour that hammered on the tin roof.

She stepped aside from the worst of the leaks. 'So could the whole of Ireland,' she replied grimly. 'All it would need is a million acres of thatch.' She went to the door. 'O'Lindon! Will you come in out of that or you'll find your death!'

Stephen and Woods came shambling to the door, still arguing some point. 'I'll see. I'll see,' Stephen was saying as they entered the marginally better shelter of the joinery. He went straight to Daisy.

'What possessed you?' she asked, furling his jacket back over his shoulders and trying to tug if off him. 'It's shrunk already.'

'It has not!' He laughed. 'That's good Donegal tweed. And sure it was only a shower.'

'Two days old,' she muttered as she got it off him at last. 'And look at it already. You'd think it was your grandfather's hand-me-down. You look as if you burst through a ditch backwards. Well? What does your man say?'

'Fair dues to him. He's doing his best by the Lyndon-Furys.'

They began to saunter up the shed, keeping out of earshot of the curious, all of whom knew that the real decision was about to be taken.

'In other words,' Daisy interpreted, 'he won't budge below eight hundred.'

'Not yet. He will, of course. We both know the banks won't even wait to get the six hundred we're offering. But I'm wondering.'

'What?'

He eyed her guardedly. 'When Ber Grogan asked three times what his old place was worth . . .'

Knowing where he was going, she didn't let him get there. 'Who can say what it was worth? It was worth more than forty to us.'

'We could have got the same amount of lakeshore from the Coolderg estate for twenty.'

'Not so convenient.'

'Every bit as convenient.'

She sighed with vexation. 'I told you at the time. We'll never go to the Coolderg estate for anything, not for one blade of grass. *They* must come to *us*.'

He indicated the joinery all about them. 'We're haggling with them now.'

'But they came to us. That makes all the difference. They can come to us bit by bit, piecemeal, with the whole estate . . .' She broke off. From the expression on his face she realized her words sounded more ambitious than oratorical. She giggled, making herself deliberately girlish again. 'Go on – don't mind me, now. You do what you know to be best.'

'I was just thinking.' He spoke offhandedly. 'Six hundred . . . eight hundred . . . that's not the real point. It's today's point, right enough, here and now. But, looking to the future, it's neither here nor there.' He waited to see would she challenge that.

'Go on,' she said quietly. His argument seemed to be that they could well afford it – but that wasn't like him at all.

He looked into her eyes and smiled. It always gave him a visceral sort of thrill to talk about their business with her. It wasn't that they were of the same mind – by no means! – but they never lost touch with each other's thinking. They knew how far they could push each other from a particular stance, though each of them used quite different means to do so.

He continued: 'Ask yourself, now – what *is* the future? Suppose for argument's sake we agree to the full eight hundred, how long is that going to last them? They're in this hole because Trapper's gone mad over building his pet railway. Is eight hundred going to bring him to his senses? Six hundred might. Six hundred would satisfy his creditors and leave him with nothing over. Eight hundred would give him a bit of cash to pick up the work where he dropped it and get his fingers burnt all over again. So I agree with you. We shouldn't go above our present offer – as long as we're clear why we're doing it. It's to save Trapper from himself and to save the estate for the Lyndon-Furys.'

She half turned from him, letting her eyes roam at will up and down the joinery. Her gloved hand rose to her face and she began stroking her lips with a peculiar movement; if she had been a man, you'd have said she was brushing her moustachioes horizontal, first the right, then the left, with a curiously sensuous motion. Stephen knew the gesture well; it meant she was torn between two equally desirable, or undesirable, courses.

'People have to look out for themselves in this world,' she said at last.

'Am I my brother's keeper?'

She screwed up her face, trying to remember. 'Was he a good man or a bad man who asked that? I forget.'

Stephen took out his watch, looked at it, put it away, and nodded at Mr Woods.

'Why didn't they ask Napier?' she went on angrily. 'He must be making a small fortune nowadays. Eight hundred pounds is one good portrait commission, that's all. If he won't help, why should we consider ourselves responsible?'

'Now you have me flummoxed,' he confessed. 'Are you for the six hundred or agin it?'

'You said yourself,' she pointed out angrily, 'six hundred could be the higher price – in the long run.'

'I did not!'

'As good as. You as good as said the other two hundred would be a sprat to catch a mackerel. So I'm for the eight hundred. But we can't give in just like that. They've got to give us something more.' She grinned. 'I have it! That stand of trees below the villa. There's good beech and Chilean pine and . . .'

'Ten pounds!' he protested. 'It's not worth ten pounds, what with the difficulty of working the site and haulage and . . . anyway, it'd spoil the view to cut them down.'

'View!' she cried scornfully. Then, quite unprompted, 'Anyway, Napier never goes near the place nowadays.'

He took her two hands in his and shook them gently. 'You're sure?' he asked. 'Eight hundred if they throw in that useless stand of timber?'

She looked away from him. 'Oh God, I wish you hadn't said any of this.'

His smile was oddly knowing. 'Why?'

'It's only because it's the Lyndon-Furys – and what are people going to say?'

'You've never troubled your head about that before.'

'I don't give a tinker's cuss what they say about my opinions or the way we choose to live or anything like that. But we've come all this way without ever touching the Lyndon-Furys.'

'It's been hard enough,' he said, 'when you consider how much of County Keelity they own still.'

She looked up at him and he saw the anguish in her eyes. 'It is *only* business, isn't it, my darling?' she asked. 'If this was the Wilson joinery at Ballinahoorig, and one of them had a pet scheme like Trapper and his railway, we'd still entice them into folly like this, wouldn't we? We're not just doing it because they're the Lyndon-Furys?'

'We'd do it to the Wilsons, too,' he assured her – and then added, '*If* they had something else we wanted . . . some other ripe apple to fall into our hands.'

'And do they – the Lyndon-Furys, I mean?'

'You know it yourself,' he told her evenly.

'But from *your* point of view? I mean, it must be *you* who wants it, not me.'

'Why not?'

She shook his hands in vexation. 'Please, darling, don't be awkward now. You know it's important to me – and you know why.'

But he did not yield at once. 'It's been fifteen years,' he reminded her.

'Please?' she insisted.

'Anyway,' he added ambiguously, 'I'm as much an O'Lindon as you.'

'Begod, that's true!' She brightened at once; not for a moment did it occur to her that the scars on the O'Lindon clan were many centuries old whereas hers were – as he had said – only fifteen years upon her. Celtic wounds, after all, take millennia to heal. 'We'll do it so,' she said firmly.

47

Caro sat in the gig doing her best to look demure. She was not quite sure what 'demure' meant, but all the best ladies' journals agreed that all the best ladies, even those as young as 'nearly sixteen' (Caro's gloss on 'just turned fifteen'), should look it. Partly it was a matter of wearing gloves – which, as Aunt Madeleine said – she wasn't a real aunt – should always be drawn onto the hands before you left your room, and 'never, pray never, upon the stair!' Also you had to fold your gloved hands like this in your lap, lightly clenched, all eight fingertips pointing obliquely up. They certainly looked most demure, her gloved hands – but what a fright people would get if they could see the skin underneath!

She had Mammy to thank for that. *Her* daughters weren't going to grow up into useless ladies – 'like me,' Aunt Madeleine would add with her 'sweet' smile; and then Mammy would say, 'You! You're the lighthouse on the bog, brilliant but *uuuseless*!' No, the O'Lindon children were going to be like their Daddy, who could turn his hand to everything, and like their Mammy, who was the same. And no matter how much their business prospered and how many factories they had and how many men they employed, they were going to go on having their own daily chores and living in that dank, poky house behind the distillery and she'd never have a boudoir of her own and she'd have to share with Dervla until she left home and it was just too *beastly*. Why couldn't they buy Sharavogue and restore it, instead of a mouldy old joinery?

Still, sitting in the gig and looking very demure in her new straw boater with the green and gold ribbon and her new white gloves was extremely pleasant. A demure lady didn't need to keep her eyes downcast all the time; she could look up now and then; not to gawp, but to pass a cool and measured survey across the panorama with her eyes of an arresting icy blue. Icy blue-green? Icy green? Icy greeny grey?

Why couldn't she have had grey eyes? Hazel was so ill-making.

Actually, there were probably more demure girls with hazel eyes than any other colour, so perhaps it wasn't too bad. What were girls with blue eyes? Pert! Yes! Gwen of the Grange had pale blue eyes and Sir Tristram told her she was altogether too pert for his liking. And what about girls with green eyes? There was a mystery about them. That book Aunt Swan had been reading, which vanished so strangely, there was a girl in that with green eyes – green eyes and flaming red hair; and she was 'no better than she ought to be,' which didn't make sense. And that left grey eyes. The only grey-eyed heroine she knew of was the Countess Olga in *The Castle of Nivers*. Perhaps you had to be foreign to have grey eyes. Except that Molly Flynn's were grey; she said she'd wept the colour from them long ago. And, come to think of it, Countess Olga had done her share of weeping, too. So that put grey eyes out of court altogether, thank you very much.

Talking of putting out eyes, Billy Walshe got a bit of flying metal in his eye down at Lynes's the farriers and Doctor D'Arcy took the whole eyeball out and washed it and put it back in its socket and Billy was ringing the bell in church on Sunday the same as ever. That's one thing she'd love to do – ring the church bell, like the other girls had boasted they'd been let do.

And then, by a kind of magic that was so common in Flaxmills that she took it quite for granted, she saw Billy Walshe himself coming down the street; the fact that she had seen him go up the street only half an hour earlier, when Mother and Dad had gone in to see Mr Woods, helped cushion the surprise, of course.

'The pond is dry and the frogs all gone,' he told her lugubriously. Then he nodded at a raincloud in the sky behind her. 'That'll come too late.'

'Are they all dead?' she asked, feeling more sympathy for him than for the nasty, cold, slimy creatures of which he was so inexplicably fond. What was it about boys that they revelled in things like that? Slugs and snails and puppy-dogs' tails!

He shook his head dubiously. 'I expect so. The nearest water is a mile off at the river.'

He had something of a froglike look himself, Caro thought. But Aunt Swan, who had seen him fishing for eels under the bridge, said he had an 'interesting' face, full of exaggerations, 'like the way I might make the first portrait sketch and later go back and tone it down and pull it all together. I wonder will Nature and time do the same for that young man?'

'Maybe they could all have hopped down to the river when the dew was on the grass,' she said. 'Did you find any corpses?'

It did vaguely cross her mind to wonder if talk of corpses was quite demure; however, it was surely more interesting than sitting in the gig, looking at eight obliquely upturned fingertips in white cotton gloves.

'Have you e'er an oul' umbarella?' he asked. 'You're about to need it, I'm thinking. Will I hold the horse for you?'

She scrabbled under the seat and found something that would do; beneath her breath she undemurely cursed Armstrong, who swore he'd come back out of the bar if it even looked like rain.

Suddenly it began to fall in earnest. She raised the umbrella but saw she couldn't possibly leave poor Walshe down there with nothing but an old cap between him and the elements. She threw a blanket across her seat and leaped down to shield the both of them.

It was a curious sensation. The downpour isolated them from the rest of the world, so it felt as if they stood in a little bubble of their own, on the edge of the times, neither in the town nor out of it.

'Your eye looks well enough now,' she told him. 'Is it true Dr D'Arcy took it right out of its socket?'

He tapped his exaggerated cheekbone. 'He put it just there,' he assured her portentously.

'And you can do anything now? Hang upside down? Swim?'

'Anything.'

'Ring the church bells, too?'

Something in her tone alerted him to her especial interest. 'Indeed,' he said.

'You are lucky. Does it need a lot of strength would you say, hauling on them ropes? *Those* ropes?'

'Ah, not really. You kind of work up to it. Simon Brennan and me, he rings the tenor, I ring the treble. They're the only two that's safe. The others are all jacked up and pegged off.' He eyed her closely, surprised to see that she was still interested. Another victim for him and Simon, possibly – and quite a catch, too: Mr O'Lindon's eldest daughter, no less. There was sunshine at the bottom of the town, so he'd have to be quick about it. 'Did you ever see it?'

'I did not.' She held her breath.

'Would you like to?'

'I would.' She was aware now that he actually wanted to show off to her his skills in the belfry, so she could maybe strike a bargain. 'But only if I could pull the rope myself.'

He licked his lips dubiously. None of the other girls had actually volunteered themselves like that; they'd all had to be cajoled into it.

'Just one or two pulls,' she added. 'I only want to see if it really needs all those tremenjus brains of yours to do it.'

He fingered the incipient stubble on his chin. 'It isn't brains so much as weight, d'you follow.'

'I'm as heavy as you.' She squared up to him, shoulder to shoulder.

He came to a decision. 'I think I have it. There's a flight of stone steps goes up to the bells, and don't they begin in the rope chamber itself. So if you stood on the landing, about eight steps up, and Simon and I got the big tenor going for you, and you were to catch it on the way up, then the weight of you would bring it down again. And then you could say to all the world you'd rung the big tenor at Flaxmills.'

Her eyes glowed at the prospect. 'Oh would you, Billy?' she asked eagerly. 'Would you let me do that this Sunday? Tomorrow, that is?'

He raised a warning finger. 'You'd have to hold on fast. She'd lift you twelve feet and more . . .'

'I'm not afraid of heights. My boudoir window, don't you know, is thirty feet above the river and it doesn't bother me.'

'It's not the height so much as the sudden jerk of it. You'd have to be ready for that and to hold on like the divil.'

'I will, I will,' she promised avidly.

The knife-edge of sunshine swept up the street, where the flagstones and mud it had been heating ten minutes earlier now began to steam. He gave a great sigh of satisfaction and shook the raindrops off the umbrella.

'What colour would you say my eyes are?' she asked suddenly.

He gave a guilty start. 'What colour . . .' he repeated vaguely. 'What?'

'My eyes. What colour are they? I was arguing with Molly Flynn.'

'Oh, your eyes!' He laughed as he handed her back the umbrella. 'Brown without a doubt.'

'Brown!' she echoed scornfully as she climbed back into the gig and took off the old blanket where the seat was dry. 'Brown!'

'They are,' he asserted in a wounded tone.

'Sure any eejit who didn't spend half his life communing with frogs could see they're hazel. The only question is are they flecked with green or grey or gold or what?'

He stared at her in consternation. Such a fuss over nothing! He saw his chance to win his best glass alley back off Simon Brennan receding. Girls were just completely *stuuupid*. 'I'll see you tomorrow, so,' he said jauntily.

'Maybe and maybe not.' She did not deign to look at him – even though she knew wild horses wouldn't keep her from the belfry.

Breege Horan had rung the bells, and so had Molly White and Fiona Harcourt. So now let them try boasting of it and making her feel small!

The following morning, when everybody gathered before matins for a bit of crack outside the vestry door, there was plenty to talk about, what with Stephen O'Lindon gladly confirming that he'd bought out the joinery from the Lyndon-Furys. No one would notice if a demure fifteen-year-old girl slipped away from her brothers and sister and vanished among the memorials for a minute or two – and no one did.

In the rope chamber Simon Brennan was pouring scorn on the very idea that the high and mighty Miss Caroline O'Lindon would be interested in their little game with the girls of the town – not that the girls knew the game at all, or those same wild horses wouldn't have got them *near* the place. A slightly sweating Billy Walshe was keeping up his end of the argument and assuring Simon she'd come, and that she wasn't so high and mighty not once you got to know her. 'And just remember,' he added, 'so there's no argument like last time: white is for Walshe and blue is for Brennan. It goes with our names, not against them. Any other colour is a draw.'

At that moment the door opened and the demurest girl they had ever bet on slipped between them. 'Let me try it down here,' she said, pushing Billy a little to one side. The sound of the bells inside was only deafening; she had to break the sentence and push the bits in between the clangour.

But he resisted and rolled his eyes as if she had just done something extremely dangerous. 'You have to do it the way I said,' he told her angrily, 'or you'll have us all kill't on the spot.'

'Sorry.' She stepped back meekly. He pointed to the steps, which ran a quarter circle round the chamber, ending in a landing right beside the rope for Simon Brennan's tenor bell. Chastened but still excited she tripped up the steps and waited on the landing.

'On three!' young Brennan cried, holding up three fingers briefly.

She nodded and watched him enviously; how easy he made it look! He could even keep the rhythm going with one hand.

'One!' He held up one finger.

Surely she didn't need to do all this flying-leap nonsense? He was keeping it going with a single pull just at the right time.

'Watch the rope!' he cried. 'Two.'

She abandoned her speculation and concentrated all her attention on the rope. The speed of it was dizzying, except at the beginning and the end of the stroke. She'd have to take it at the beginning. No shilly-shallying. Step out and grip it like the divil.

Her heart, already beating like a mad thing, began running wild. Everything in sight suddenly blurred and began flying around her – except the rope, God be praised. That was as clear as if it were set in crystal. It must be at the top of its stroke. Yes, it was going down. A straw-coloured blur in the gloom of the chamber. Get ready!

She felt herself falling outwards, toward the rope. No going back on the idea now. It froze once more so that in the brief instant before her hands clutched it she could see every fibre.

'Three!'

But she was already there, clasping the rope to her as if a thousand feet separated her from certain death below. Despite Billy's warning yesterday, the sudden jerk on her arms was almost too much. But she just managed to hold it, and, moments later, eyes tight clenched, she let out a great 'wheee!' of delight as she soared to the stars.

Between ten and seventeen feet below her, the two youths craned their necks and strained their eyes for a glimpse of her knickers.

'White!' Billy yelled in triumph. 'I want my glass alley back.'

Hoping against hope, Simon went on staring up beneath those flying skirts – so that she nearly brained him on her descent.

It was so exhilarating she held on for one more ride, but this time neither boy so much as glanced at her; their interest in her knickers had quite evaporated by then.

48

As ever, the mayfly brought Mercier and Swan to the teeming waters of Lough Cool – along with their family of Scotch elkhounds, which took the place of the children they now realized they were never going to beget. For some time past they had renewed an annual lease on Omdurman Villa near the northern end of the lake, the property of a Major Saunders, who had been posted to India for a longish tour; so they were actually to be seen in Keelity in December as often as in the maddest month of all. But May was Mercier's annual holiday, so they were there for what seemed to Swan an eternity; fortunately, he no longer required her to accompany him and ply the oars. She could get on her horse and go leaping the ditches, trailing a phalanx of baying elkhounds to Flaxmills, and there either call on Daisy or ride on to Coolderg and see Madeleine.

She enjoyed visiting Madeleine but she had to ration her visits – for Mercier's sake, not her own. Madeleine had caused a scandal by marrying Thomas Coutts, the footman. Sir Lucius had eventually swallowed his rage and offered the couple the old water-bailiff's lodge, down on the lake. Since all the fishing rights were set, it was no longer needed. Mercier always took his binoculars when he went out on the lake, so, if he saw his wife with Madeleine, he'd row over and join them for tea. The trouble was, Madeleine made cakes that only floated into your mouth, but Mercier *knew* it wasn't good for him to gorge like that; the doctor had almost given up; so Swan rationed her visits as the only way of rationing him.

On the first day of their holiday in 1901 it rained from dawn to dusk, and she was glad enough to stand in the porch of Omdurman Villa and throw bones and bits of sheep's heads for the hounds to fight over in their amiable way. The second day was nice and soft – and so was the going in the fields. She set off with her pack just before ten. It was always one of the crowning moments of her year – that first, wild, free chase through wood and field, with the hounds streaking beside her like Java rats, baying in tones you'd not otherwise hear this side of the grave.

Down at the Flaxmills wharf Peter Shaughnessy heard it, far off as yet – a long, eldritch howl that chilled the blood. '*Now* it's May,' he commented to Padraig Kennedy.

'Begod!' Kennedy nodded solemnly. 'Wouldn't you think it the Earl of Hell and all his pack!'

Five minutes later, breathless, she trotted over the bridge while all the stray dogs in town growled and bristled their manes – and kept a wary eye on the five nearest bolt holes.

As she went up through the distillery yard she met Caro, who just happened to be coming down on her cob Sukey, a dappled gray gelding, 'with enough cunning to frighten the colleen and enough heart not to hurt her,' as Miley Flanagan, the livery master, put it when he sold Stephen the creature. 'Good morning Aunt Swan,' she said casually.

Swan nodded warily. 'And when did you saddle her up?' she asked tendentiously. 'About five minutes ago?'

'If you're going to Aunt Madeleine's, Mother says I can come if you don't mind.'

'Ah!' Swan lifted her veil and mopped her glowing brow. 'Whoo! I'm as out of condition as' – she was about to say Mercier but changed it to, 'as I've ever been. I suppose that means this is one of her *busy* days.'

'Did you hear we'd bought the joinery?'

'Ah, yes.' Swan laughed. 'Then I can guess what she's busy doing. Those poor men.'

'At least they don't have to work in silence any more.' She paused. 'Can I?'

'Why not? By all means.' Between the three points of her heel, her ashplant, and one of the reins, she turned Jubilee in his own length. 'Someone else has been schooling this fella,' she said. 'He wouldn't do that last year.' She patted him affectionately on the neck. 'Who said you can't teach an old horse new tricks?'

Caro hung back. 'Just one thing,' she said hesitantly.

'Yes?'

'Mother also said I've got to take Dervla, if she wants to come.'

Swan's eyes raked the heavens. 'And she does want to come.'

'I said she could have my best tortoiseshell comb instead, but she wanted the mirror as well.'

'That's the O'Lindons for you!' She laughed. 'Oh, come on! It's not the end of the earth.'

'But she's such a namby-pamby. "I can't lepp that ditch . . . Is that a bull in that field? . . . *When* will we get there – I'm tired." She doesn't enjoy it at all. She only comes to torment us.'

'But she likes being at Aunt Madeleine's and building enchanted gardens, so why not, eh? And, in any case, if your mother says that's the condition . . .'

'Yes, but if *you* say you're not feeling quite up to it today . . .'

Jubilee pawed the ground impatiently.

'I quite agree,' Swan told him. 'There's your answer, miss. Both of you or neither. Go and saddle up her pony.'

Five minutes later they went up through the town; everyone came out and stood at their doors to watch them go by – mainly the elkhounds, of course, creatures that could lift their muzzles seven feet high and frighten the stars if you let them rest their forepaws on your shoulder.

'Good morning, Mr Brennan . . . good morning, Mrs Fogarty – how's Imelda's chest now . . . ?' Thus Swan renewed the perennial illusion that she was one of the locals and a popular one at that.

They turned in at the glebe and cantered up the long slope of the landmark hill, with its single Noble Fir, which Swan always called 'that pine tree,' which, in turn, had led Caro to lose a bet with Billy Walshe, who told her it was a fir. As always they reined in at its foot and stood a panting moment to survey the landscape before them – the rolling hills that led down over bog, pasture, eskers, and parkland to the lake.

'*Abies grandis*,' Caro said firmly, patting its deep-scored bark. 'They have a tree by the castle where you can punch the bark as hard as you like and you won't skin your knuckles and old Mr Horan can remember the day they planted it in eighteen twenty-three and it's named in honour of the Duke of Wellington, Wellingtonia.'

'It skinned my knuckles,' Dervla muttered.

'Anything would skin your knuckles.'

'I'll set those hounds on you if you don't shut up,' Swan said evenly. She inhaled deeply several times, until she felt an incipient giddiness. ' 'Clare to God, if you could bottle this air you'd make a fortune with it in Dublin. Sure, we've nothing, only soot and grime, to breathe up there these days.'

Caro glowered at her sister. How could anyone with a stupid face like that even want to show it in public? With her frizzy, mousey hair, and snaggle teeth, and great strawberries for cheeks, and bulging, watery eyes that couldn't look you in the face . . . if *she'd* had a face like that at thirteen, she'd have taken one look in the mirror and cast herself from her boudoir window. She was stubborn, too. There was nothing worse on the whole wide face of this beautiful earth than a stubborn, whingeing, uuuseless younger sister.

'What's that gash in the hillside?' Swan asked. 'Have they started a new quarry there or what?'

'That's the railway,' Caro told her.

'Trapper's railway,' Dervla said.

'All right, clever-boots. Everyone knows it's Trapper's railway.'

'Good Lord!' Swan poured an excess of joviality over the squabbling pair. 'Has he started all that again? Where did he get the money? Surely . . .' Her voice tailed off. 'Ah, I think I understand. Let's ride that way and watch them, shall we? I love watching a good Irish navvy. He's such a brute, and so strong.'

It struck Caro that Aunt Swan was making a joke of it – talking like a West Briton, as Mother would say – to distract her two courtesy nieces. Really, she *did* like looking at the navvies, because last year, before the work on Trapper's line gave out, she'd always ride out of the way to watch, and she'd always 'talk like a West Briton' to make it seem like a joke. But this year there was a new element in it; this year Caro became aware that Aunt Swan's curious interest in the navvies had its parallel in herself. For whenever the boys went dipping in the river, in the rocky pools under the Martello Tower, the place reserved for them by convention, she, Caro, would somehow find things to occupy her in her boudoir and she could lose ten or fifteen minutes watching the lads at their sporting and play. And if she heard a tread upon the stair, she'd fly to the far side of the room and dust away cobwebs that weren't there – which was like Aunt Swan's joking about it, really, if you thought about it – which she at once stopped doing.

The hounds – Favour, Justice, Wormwood, and Eglantine – began to give out that strange, jaw-shivering whine of theirs, looking up with great, soulful eyes. 'Babies!' Swan berated them and dug a light heel into Jubilee's side.

She led them down over the stony hill flank, over ancient paths through cutaway bog, to the lusher pastures of the castle estate. The entire area was intensively hunted by the Keelity pack, of which Trapper was the master, so there was no wire anywhere, not even round the pheasant covert – though God and all angels help the rider unwary enough to take a short cut through those alfresco temples of the second member of the local trinity: 'Huntin, Shootin, and Fishin.' But that knowledge did not stop Dervla from reining in at every ditch and peering anxiously among the hawthorn and woodbine for telltale strands of metal.

It put Caro in an apoplexy, of course, and she would deliberately face Sukey at any part of the ditch that her sister chose to inspect, no matter if there were more suitable places nearby. 'Out of the way, you eejit!' she would shriek and go thundering past in a shower of clods, brushing Dervla by a whisker.

Soon Dervla began to stop before the highest parts of the ditch, where the hawthorns had not been laid for years, or where rotted trees lurked hazardously in the tall grass beyond. But Sukey, who would 'lepp a barn did you but ask him right,' went at them all and would blunder through what he could not clear.

Swan was so deep in her own thoughts she did not notice this dangerous escalation of dare and daring. It was Trapper who put a stop to it. He had spotted them coming and rode out to meet them. He had no idea what emotional game the two sisters were playing; all he saw was a foolhardy girl, flying at the most unsuitable bits of the ditch and giving her horse a nasty gash or two in the process. He went for Caro until she almost cried, telling her she wasn't fit to ride a rocking horse and if he ever saw her treat a poor creature like that again he'd cut a blackthorn and put a few scratches in her hide to see how she liked it. And she was to get some Stockholm tar on those wounds the minute she reached her Aunt Madeleine's. It was always Aunt Madeleine's, never Uncle Thomas's.

Swan saw the tears begin to well. To prevent a catastrophe she broke in: 'It's as much your fault, Dervla, as Caro's. You've been provoking her to it, haven't you.'

Trapper, still angry, turned to her. 'If you knew it, you should have stopped them,' he said.

'I didn't,' Swan told him equably – for she wanted information from him without his realizing it, so she refused to take umbrage at his tone. 'I'm guessing. But I know those two. Salome and Jezebel, they should have been named. Shouldn't you!'

The sisters exchanged glances and, slightly against their wills, smiled sheepishly. 'That's better,' Swan said. 'Now let's have no more of this nonsense. Sweetness and light, eh? Sugar and spice and all things nice!'

'Nyaaa!' Caro turned to her sister and simpered.

Dervla poked out her tongue and blushed.

And yet, for some curious reason, they both felt suddenly very warm toward each other, so that when Caro said, 'Come on – race you to the cutting!' they were off in a giggling horde of two and when they both went for the same sensible gap, Caro gathered Sukey and let Dervla fly it ahead of her.

'Oh, they're a handful!' Swan said, following them with an affectionate gaze. 'It's a stormy time, all pimples and rivalry. I remember it well.'

' 'Twas but yesterday,' Trapper responded gallantly. He could not take his eyes off the elkhounds.

'Thank God it wasn't,' she asserted in more robust tones. 'Well, Trapper, so you've started your line again.'

'I have.' They set off at a slow canter in the wake of the two girls. 'I think we'll break the back of it this time. I say, those hounds of yours have all the instincts of a true sporting dog. They're gaze hounds, aren't they?'

Swan laughed. 'I have no idea. What is a gaze hound?'

'Hunts by sight for preference, though they can hunt by scent. Look at that fella there. He's found.' He raised his voice and shouted at Favour. 'Give tongue, sir. Give tongue!'

Favour ignored him.

'The other thing about hounds is that they never for one moment imagine you could possibly be talking to them,' Swan commented.

They trotted through last year's cutting and rode on over the embankment to where the navvies were pushing onward through the next ridge of the esker. He let her go ahead so that he could admire her figure, which was still as supple and trim as when she'd been Caro's age – not spoiled by brats, of course. If she really was barren, then by thunder, she'd be a good filly for a ride on the back-stretch, he thought. Normally, Trapper wouldn't have turned his head to look at a woman. She'd need to get herself directly in his path, like that, and swing her body with unconscious enticement, too. Even then, his religion could easily recall him to his proper duties. At that moment, for instance, Favour belatedly obeyed his command and gave tongue at some fresh scent; then all the nymphs in Ireland could have disported themselves before him in a state of nature and he wouldn't have noticed.

'By thunder, Swan!' he exclaimed. 'If you'd leave those fellows with me when you go back to Dublin, I'd have them fit for Diana by July.'

'Who's Diana?' she asked.

He glowered at her, thinking she was teasing – and thinking it a joke in the poorest taste.

'Oh, *that* Diana,' she went on – confirming his suspicions.

But he wouldn't fall out with her, not now this exciting idea had arisen. 'Say?' he asked. 'I could get a couple of stags sent up. Old Burdett's got a good herd at Charleville. He'd part with a couple if he could join the chase. Fourteen-pointers, eh! What sport!'

'No Stockholm tar for them!' Swan commented.

'What?' He frowned. 'Oh. I see. Ha ha! No, you miss the point, old girl. Your stag's a true gentleman. It's a natural death for him, going down under an avalanche of hounds. It's like a fulfilment, d'you see. So . . . what d'you say? I promise you sport such as you've never seen.'

Swan dipped her head in acknowledgement of the offer. Her smile suggested that she might, on mature consideration, be quite interested. And, she reflected, it would mean she and Mercier could pass the whole summer at home without tripping over those four huge, panting corpses and mopping up great pools of saliva – not to mention those vats of purulent offal, and walking round the garden with a coalshovel full of stinking turd, looking for shrubs it wouldn't kill. Oh yes! She was certainly going to agree – but not quite yet. She still wanted to discover . . . certain things.

They caught up with the two girls and reined in. The navvies were immediately licked to death by the hounds, the passport to whose affection was a reek like a gluepot.

'You're sinking a pretty penny here, Trapper,' Swan commented.

'We'll get it all back. Tenfold! Did Mercier glance at the prospectus I sent him?'

'He did, but I don't think he shares your optimism. You know what bankers are.'

Trapper nodded dourly. 'But we'll manage it, with or without their help, never fear. They're the ones who'll be sorry. Mercier, too – him especially.'

Swan pricked up her ears. 'Why especially?'

His smile showed he was really joking, only it was the sort of joke that revealed an important truth, too. 'When the fortunes of the estate are restored, what d'you think will be the first thing I'll purchase back?'

'The joinery?' Swan suggested – though she'd have fallen from her horse if he'd said yes.

'That millstone? No! The fishing rights, woman. No one will fish Lough Cool without coming cap-in-hand to me!' He laughed. 'You tell Mercier to think again, eh?'

Swan nodded and let her eye rove over the cutting. It must be a sign of age, she thought, for she hardly looked at the navvies now; she was much too keen on getting the truth out of Trapper, without his realizing it, of course. 'You must have got a good price for the joinery,' she mused aloud.

'Not bad,' he answered modestly. 'We handled ourselves well, I believe.' He raised his voice to make sure the youngsters heard. 'Old O'Lindon seems to have the district mesmerized. They were all sure he'd pick the place up for a song. But we held out for our price and, by heavens, he knuckled under. He knew he'd met his match, d'ye see.'

She risked a direct question. 'Was there much of a difference between the price and the offer?'

In his triumphant mood he almost told her – which was not really what she wanted to know. But he hung back at the last, shaking his head as if to say she should know him better than that. 'But I'll tell you one thing,' he added. 'The price they offered wouldn't have allowed for any of *this*.' And he waved expansively at the men and machinery all about them.

'Goodness me!' Swan hoped there was enough light of admiration in her eye. Secretly she was exultant, never for a moment having imagined he would let it slip as simply as that.

'Why was he talking about Dad like that?' Caro asked as they rode away on the final leg of their journey to Madeleine's.

'Because he wants you to carry it home and tell him.'

'As if I would!' Caro responded scornfully.

Aunt Swan surprised her. 'Oh, but I think you should. I think your father would be delighted to hear it.'

'Why?' Dervla asked.

'And your mother. Because they're going to have the last laugh, that's why.'

'Oh if only people could be *nice* to one another,' Dervla exclaimed. 'Instead of laughing behind each other's backs and being mean over money. I *hate* it.'

Caro, whose thoughts had been on similar lines, decided not to voice them. The world in which her parents lived was obviously a lot more complicated than she had ever imagined.

'I must tell Madeleine,' Swan said, mostly to herself.

49

Dervla took the tray out into Aunt Madeleine's garden. Upon it lay a fragment of a broken mirror, some dried moss, a classical portico from an old dollshouse, everlasting flowers, a rustic bridge made of glued twigs, and a swan cast in lead, most of it still painted white, except for the beak, which was black and red; there were also little jamjars filled with seashells, bits of coral, white sand, and a tin full of translucent quartz chips. She placed everything in order on the rough old table in the summerhouse, which was fashioned from a vertical slice through the heart of an old beech trunk. She set the tray before her and began by placing the broken mirror upon it – which instantly turned into a lake, upon whose shores she set about building her enchanted garden.

Caro hovered nearby, torn between the magical world of the child and the mysterious world of the grown-up. 'Will I get some of that variegated Anonymous?' she asked her sister. They both knew its real name was Euonymous, but Uncle Tom had once called it Anonymous, not for a joke, so now they never showed him up, not in his own garden.

'If you like,' Dervla replied neutrally. She'd rushed into effusive forgiveness and sisterly love with Caro once too often to risk it again.

'Come and have a look at Tom's latest,' Madeleine was meanwhile saying as she led her visitor toward the studio.

Swan's heart fell; this was the penance for Madeleine's sparkling company and those wicked cakes. She would be expected to say how much she admired Tom's paintings – a never-ending collection of waterfowl, foxes, beetles, primroses . . . anything that took his fancy, for a never-to-be-published *Irish Artist's Bestiary and Herbarium*. Napier thought very highly of Tom as an artist, ever since he had come across one of his sketchbooks in the servants' hall; indeed, the rest of the family were convinced it was Napier who had first given the fellow ideas above his station. And it served him right, they'd add with glee – for he now had to buy sufficient of the oaf's childish rubbish to let him keep Madeleine in modest style; for the income from her legacy, the principal of which was entailed to her children, was not enough to keep them, even in their present humble manner in a rent-free cottage.

'They're lovely,' she said with outward conviction. 'So fresh. Such crude energy.'

'That's what Napier says,' Madeleine told her.

'Not a universal taste, mind – but then, what original artist ever was? Is he still in bed?'

'Good heavens, no!' Madeleine was affronted. 'He was up and out before dawn. He's found a family of otters up near the mouth of the Flaxmills. Mercier will probably run across him – I assume he's on the lake?'

'Where else!'

'Good. I've made some cakes.'

They drifted back to the verandah; the day was warm enough to sit just out of doors. 'You really shouldn't,' Swan replied. 'I'm not just saying that. You honestly shouldn't. Or *he* honestly shouldn't. Only put out a few, eh?'

'My dear! That would go against all the grain of my upbringing.' Madeleine was jokingly haughty. 'We must maintain some standards.'

'Please?' Swan begged. 'I do worry about him sometimes, you know.'

Madeleine smiled with genuine sympathy. 'I was only joking. I promise he'll have no more than two. I'll sting his fingers with your ashplant if he goes for more. He doesn't *look* fat, you know.'

'It isn't that. It's just . . .' She shrugged uncomprehendingly and patted her own midriff. 'It upsets him in some way. He can't tolerate cream or butter or fried food or sweets of any kind. He knows it – and yet he simply can't stop himself reaching for them.'

'Like Cornel and the bottle. Poor Swan, I know what it's like.'

She had been about to suggest a quick peep at her own babies: Theresa, six months old and fast asleep in her cot at the moment, and Young Tommy, two and a half, and about due to wake up from his morning nap. But she remembered Swan's childlessness and thought better of it. They settled into the creaky cane chairs on the verandah with a mutually reassuring sigh, indicating they both deserved this moment of idleness, even if it were to last all morning.

'I forgot to offer you tea,' Madeleine said guiltily.

Swan shook her head and gazed out over the lake.

'It'd be no trouble.'

Another shake of the head.

'Then tell me all about Dublin. Or Flaxmills, even. I've not been there in ages. How's Daise? She's been very busy, I hear, even for her.'

'Very!' Swan said with a significant emphasis.

'Oh?' Madeleine raised her eyebrows at once.

'I thought you could tell *me* all about it – buying the joinery, and so on.'

'My dear! I'm hardly considered a Lyndon-Fury these days. I knew about it, of course, but my scullery maid – if I had one – could tell you more details than me. What have you heard?'

'Then you didn't know that Trapper's started the railway again?'

That jerked Madeleine bolt upright. 'Never!'

Swan nodded confirmation.

'Are you absolutely sure? It's not just some gossip you've . . . ?'

'We met the man himself on our way here. Proud as a peacock. He insisted we ride out of our way to see it. All those beastly, brutish labourers.' She shuddered. 'I should think by the end of this week or early next you'll see them come bursting through . . .' She stood up and craned her neck. 'No. Not from here. But you'll certainly see it from your bedroom window. The last ridge of the esker.'

Madeleine had meanwhile half-collapsed in her chair. 'He's mad,' she said, almost to herself, shaking her head.

'But harmless, surely?' Swan suggested.

Madeleine just went on shaking her head. 'It's because of this rivalry with Portumna and the Clanricardes. They're going to have a railway, so Glenisk and the Lyndon-Furys must have one, too. Glenisk! Who's ever going to go there except a handful of fishermen and wildfowlers?'

'It has a harbour?' Swan offered. 'I must confess, I've never actually been there.'

'Exactly! Nobody has. Nobody in their right mind, anyway. The so-called harbour is a muddy drain where you could tie up three rowboats if the Shannon's not too low. And what else is there? Four bars and a blacksmith. And two brothers who make hurleys when they're not in jail for making poteen.' She sank her head in her hands. 'Why does he persist in it? He promised – after he ran out of money the last time – he promised that was the end of it.'

Swan cleared her throat delicately. 'Rivalry with the Clanricardes? D'you think that's it?'

'Of course. What else?'

'Not rivalry with Stephen O'Lindon?'

Madeleine thought it over and then responded with a light laugh. 'I honestly don't think Trapper's sufficiently intelligent for that. God knows, I take little enough interest in the outside world, myself. I don't give a rap for politics and I'm quite indifferent to all those old friends who simply don't notice me if we pass in the street, but . . .'

'Honestly?'

'Oh yes. They cut me stone dead.'

'I didn't mean that. I meant do you honestly not mind?'

Madeleine smiled tolerantly. 'Mind? My wedding day really was the happiest day of my life. How many women can say *that*, three years after the event! Dublin may be exciting but I tell you – the unutterable tedium of life in provincial society has to be experienced to be believed.'

'Really?' Swan was intrigued. 'But I thought it was one long round of calls and picnics and balls and hunting . . .'

'Hunting! Dear Swan – after you've drawn your thousandth covert and broken up your two-hundredth fox, you do just begin to wonder where the magic went! And as for the rest – well, all the fun you can have is so "dangerous" to a girl. It's all right for the men, but a girl ends up with a bad mate to avoid a worse fate. A good man is hard got, believe me. You were lucky to have one dancing in attendance at the right time. You don't know what it's like for the rest of us.'

Swan, trying not to preen herself too blatantly, settled back in her chair and smiled across the lake. There were several anglers in view, none of them Mercier. 'And so was Daise,' she mused. 'D'you ever wonder what everything would be like now if she'd married Napier instead? I mean, it's amazing to think – what is she? Or *was* she? The daughter of a perennially failing petty manufacturer. An artist's model! Little better than . . . well, no better than she ought to be.'

'Oh? I never heard *that* about her,' Madeleine interjected.

Behind a rose trellis Caro noted once again the appearance of that meaningless phrase – and spoken about her mother, too.

In a more wary tone Madeleine added, 'I don't suppose those youngsters can hear us?' She pitched her voice slightly higher and said, 'Caro?'

The girl did not budge.

'Caro? Would you ever go and see has Young Tommy suffocated in his cot?'

Dervla looked inquiringly at her sister, who shook her head vehemently and motioned her to silence.

Madeleine became easier again. 'Probably be all right if we keep our voices down. You were saying – no better than she ought to be?'

'I didn't mean it, not literally, not about her. I just meant it's what most people think about artist's models. I'm sure that's why your father wouldn't countenance the marriage. The Catholic business was just a red herring. After all, he hasn't cut you for marrying Coutts, and his mother's Catholic, isn't she?'

'Girls don't count. Not when there are three males to carry on the blood line.' Madeleine chuckled. 'Not that *our* three have covered themselves in glory at stud! Only one known offspring in wedlock – and not in Napier's wedlock, either!'

'Ssssh!' Swan looked about them as if she herself were guilty.

And Caro watched and wondered and thought to herself, *No, surely not Aunt Swan?*

Madeleine bit her lip but continued to smile.

'Anyway,' Swan went on, 'what I was about to say was – suppose Napier *had* married Daise, just think how different everything would have been! Stephen O'Lindon wouldn't now be employing half of Flaxmills. And there'd have been no . . .'

'Oh come,' Madeleine interrupted. 'Don't you think O'Lindon would have made his mark anyway?'

Swan shook her head and eyed the other speculatively.

'You can tell me,' Madeleine encouraged her. 'It'll all go in one ear and out the other anyway.'

'Is it generally known how the O'Lindons started?'

Madeleine shrugged. 'I always assumed her father primed the pump for them. He's a manufacturer himself, isn't he?'

'Ha ha,' was all Swan said to that. 'No, they took out a mortgage.'

'The O'Lindons! Go into debt?'

Swan imitated Mercier. 'We only call it debt when it turns sour. While it's sweet we call it investment.'

'Anyway, a mortgage on what? Surely they hadn't . . .'

'On a farm and a fair few acres O'Lindon owned.'

Madeleine shook her head. 'Sorry! That won't wash. O'Lindon never owned any land, much less a farm and a fair few acres.'

Swan nodded confidently. 'You know that. And Mercier discovered it pretty smartly when we first started coming down here. But the Hibernian Bank still doesn't realize it. They held deeds to four ruined walls that you can't see for brambles and a handful of acres of cutaway bog that would just about support a couple of goats – and on *that* they lent eight hundred pounds! And I'll tell you something else for nothing: It wasn't O'Lindon did the talking.'

'You don't mean she lied?'

'Not at all. But hasn't she a way with the truth? Dearest friend and all as she is to both of us, *she* could sell geese as swans.'

Madeleine sighed, agreeing yet not wishing to be drawn. 'Napier will never marry, you know,' she said, staring out over the lake. 'Not while Daise is alive. He's turned into such a romantic.'

She glanced at Swan and was surprised at the anger and the bitterness she saw in those normally amused eyes.

Swan, realizing she had given something of herself away, turned it to cynicism with the comment: 'A profitable romanticism, I'd say.'

Madeleine shrugged the remark aside. 'D'you ever see him in Dublin? He never comes down here – for obvious reasons.'

'A couple of times a year, perhaps. He comes over the water mainly to see Dairmid Trench. He usually dines with us. But Mercier's uneasy about him. I think he suspects there was once something doing between Napier and me.'

'And was there.'

Swan smiled and ran her tongue archly over her lip. 'Now that'd be telling.'

Caro absorbed this ambiguous reply with interest. The impossible was turning into the merely improbable.

Madeleine laughed. 'Then I take it there wasn't or you'd certainly tell.'

Swan pouted and lost interest in the subject – or, rather, she remembered the one subject she wanted above all others to explore. 'About what we were saying earlier,' she went on. 'Selling the joinery – and Trapper now having the money to restart his railway . . .'

'Yes?'

'Doesn't it seem a bit odd?'

'In what way?'

Dervla left her enchanted garden and came to her sister's side. 'Shouldn't eavesdrop!' she whispered vehemently.

If Caro had had a weapon of some kind, she'd have killed her there and then. But, as things were, what could she do? If she tried reasoning with the little idiot, she'd miss something important. If she pinched her, the howls would end everything – and the subsequent explanations would bring down the wrath of heaven upon her in the form of two irate aunts-by-courtesy. So she did the only possible thing: she matured by a couple of years in as many seconds. And that, in turn, enabled her to smile lovingly at Dervla, slip an arm about her shoulder, hug her to her side, and, with a barely audible *sssh*!, managed to seduce her into maturing a little, too.

'Well,' Swan was saying, 'during our last few visits all the talk was of how Trapper would have to climb down and settle for much less than he wanted. Every figure under the sun was bandied about, of course. He wanted ten thousand . . . five thousand . . . he'd settle for a hundred, he was so desperate – all the usual mythmaking that goes on in this country. But they were all agreed that if the O'Lindons held out, the banks would force your bro' to sell – and all they'd be interested in, of course, was in recovering the debt.'

Madeleine stared at her aghast. 'I hope you're not about to confess that the O'Lindons tried to wheedle the information out of you?'

Swan was equally scandalized. 'Of course not. Never a breath of it. They're scrupulous in that way – and in any case, Mercier wouldn't divulge a word.' She gave a couple of grim laughs. 'Mind you, everyone else in the whole of County Keelity was buttering us up like mad, hoping for a little whisper in the ear. But forget all that! The O'Lindons could work it out for themselves, even without knowing the exact sum involved. She's got a pretty shrewd head for business by now. She'd have known to the nearest fifty or so how long a leash *any* bank would have allowed Trapper on the mortgage of the joinery.'

'And with everything else already entailed or promised up to the eyeballs!' Madeleine commented dourly.

'Quite! So she must have known it was around five or six hundred. And yet, having hung on and hung on for months, hoping Trapper would be forced to sell, they suddenly give in and pay out enough to allow him to start up his railway again. That's what I meant. Now doesn't it strike you as *odd*?'

'Why d'you keep saying *she*? He's nobody's fool, either.'

Swan dipped her head in acknowledgement of the error. 'Slip of the tongue. I meant they, of course.'

Madeleine pursed her lips in a smile of accusing disbelief. 'Slip of the tongue, my foot!'

Swan made several awkward gestures, as if this were the last thing she had wished to happen. 'It sounds *awful* to say it, I know, and I'll be struck dead by lightning on the way back, but do you think it at all possible that . . . oh dear! I can foresee a time when Trapper again runs out of money. Even if he finishes the railway – you said yourself – it'll never even start repaying the outlay. So what'll be sold off next? The distillery's closed. Trapper could sell the bricks and mortar, I suppose. But who to? I'll give you one guess! The joinery's already his. Then there'd be nothing left in Flaxmills. Stephen O'Lindon would own the town. And what would Trapper sell next?'

Madeleine shrugged. 'A farm or two, I suppose.'

Swan nodded and gazed out over the lake, as if that concluded her inquiry. But then an afterthought seemed to strike her. 'And when several farms have gone? When there aren't enough rents to pay for the upkeep of the castle? And the hunt? It must all cost a pretty penny.'

'And you think . . .' Madeleine could not put it into words. 'No!'

'You're probably right.' Swan nodded reassuringly.

Madeleine laughed. 'You've been reading too many romances. Good heavens – it was all so long ago.'

'Fifteen years.'

The figure caught Caro's attention. She held her breath.

'What *are* they going on and on about?' Dervla asked in a plaintive whisper.

Caro didn't even hear her.

Madeleine was saying, 'And Daise isn't the one to harbour a grudge like that. And devote the rest of her life to a long-drawn-out revenge. It's only bitter, disappointed failures who have the *time* for such nonsense. Anyway, she could never have kept it a secret so long.'

'Perhaps she didn't,' Swan suggested. 'Perhaps she told us, right at the very beginning.'

Madeleine just went on smiling and shaking her head.

'Then ask yourself this,' Swan concluded: 'What names did she give Napier's daughter?'

Dervla lost the last shreds of her patience. 'I'm going back to my garden,' she said, struggling to be free.

Caro gave her one final hug and let her go. 'Yes,' she said, sauntering after her. 'They're just a couple of gossipy old ladies.'

And who was Napier's daughter? she wondered, casting around among the girls of her own age in the district. If 'it all happened fifteen years ago' – whatever *it* was – she must be around that age by now. And what names *did* Mammy give her? Or *suggest* for her, Aunt Swan must mean. It was all too confusing.

And yet the annoying thing about it was this vague feeling, hovering somewhere in the back of her mind, that it just needed one more little bit of an explanation and it would all become clear.

50

Only little Sheridan was excused, on the grounds that a five-year-old boy might do more damage than his help, or the good of his soul, was worth. The remaining O'Lindon children set to with the usual mixture of reluctance and gusto, for this particular chore came round once, and sometimes twice, every year: the removal of the bog from the least accessible and most dangerous windows in the sheer wall above the Flaxmills River. For Finnbar it was the first time, which brought complaints from Dervla that she had started helping when she was only seven, so why had Finnbar been excused until he was nine?

'Because he's a boy,' Daisy told her wearily, 'and boys are eejits in the house. Tuck your shirt in, Stevie.'

'It is in,' he said without looking.

'I am not an eejit in the house,' Finnbar complained.

'It's only half in.'

'It wasn't *me* who spilled ink on the windowsill,' Finnbar added.

'Informer!' shouted Caro, who was leaning outside her window, cleaning the farthest panes. 'Go and get some more water. This is filthy.'

'I've only just brought it.'

'It's still filthy. There's half the Bog of Allen on this side.'

'I don't see why we can't let the rain do it.'

'Go and get some more water and stop giving out.'

'Who spilled ink on the windowsill?' Daisy poked her question into a gap in the nonstop argument that passed for conversation among her brood.

'I did,' Caro confessed. 'And I got it all up and it didn't leave a stain.'

Finnbar cleared his throat with meaningful menace.

'If you don't fetch more water, I'll throw this bucket over you.'

'Tuck your shirt in, Stevie. I won't tell you again – and you've missed a great patch in the middle of that pane.'

'The bit of the shirt that's out is wet,' Stevie replied with gentle patience. 'If I tuck it in, I'll get a chill on my kidneys and probably die, I should think. And what dirt d'you mean?'

Caro stepped between them, walked up to Stevie's window, wiped the offending dirt off the inside of the pane, and returned to her own station.

'Oh *that* dirt!' he said at once. 'I hadn't done the inside, yet.'

'I don't know why we bother with them,' Caro commented wearily to her mother. 'We'd do it in half the time if they just fetched the water for us.' She raised her voice and added, '*Without* slopping it all over the place!' to Finnbar, who was just entering with the next pailful.

In the corner of her eye Daisy saw Stevie tweak his shirt out an extra inch or two. She turned and stared at him. He grinned back at her in the way he knew she could never resist – and, sure enough, a moment later, despite all her attempts at self-control, she broke into a smile.

But she turned it to her advantage in the battle of wills that now raged between them. As she walked slowly toward him, her smile developed a glint of menace. When she was right beside him she put her mouth to his ear and murmured, 'If that shirt-tail isn't tucked away within five seconds, I'll show you what a wet shirt *really* looks and feels like.' She held her sponge over his head. A drop or two fell but he did not flinch.

He counted out five two-second seconds and only then tucked it away. 'If I take a chill and die,' he said stiffly, 'everyone will know who to blame.'

Daisy returned to her window and for a blissful five genuine seconds, a kind of peace reigned.

'I still don't see why I had to start cleaning windows when I was seven and Finnbar was excused until he's nine,' Dervla started all over again.

'If you say it once more,' Daisy told her, 'I'll make you scratch where you don't itch.'

Finnbar sat on the window sill, grinning happily and swinging his legs.

'And if you dent that paintwork, I'll eat you,' Daisy told him. 'Jesus, Mary, and Joseph! We do this every year. You know it's going to happen. You know nothing short of a broken leg will excuse you. Why can't you accept it with good grace and just get on with it? You're all noise and no wool, as the divil said when he shaved the pig.'

'Bell-the-cat Dolan has carved an effigy of Charles Stuart Parnell out of wood,' Stevie said.

'What good does that be doing him?' Daisy asked. 'Sure, 'twould only frighten off the thrushes that eat the snails.'

'Slugs and snails and puppy-dogs' tails,' Dervla chanted.

Stevie ignored her. 'And he has another one of the archbishop,' he said. 'And the people drawing home the turf, don't they all be croosting a sod or two at one or other of them. And when they're gone by, Dolan's wife does come out and does be gathering it up. They have a grand little heap o' turf out the back, all kindly donated by the passing carriage trade.'

'They'll soon stop,' Daisy assured him, 'once that tale gets around.'

'They don't, it seems. They all know it by now. 'Tis like a local sport – to see who can knock the spots off Parnell or the archbishop first.'

'Trapper said he can knock spots off of Aunt Swan's dogs,' Caro said.

'Hounds!' her brothers corrected her in contemptuous unison.

It pained Daisy to hear her children – and everyone else in the country, come to that – call him Trapper. To her way of thinking, such affectionate usage belonged to the engaging sort of rogue who slept drunk beneath the ditches and was always up before the RM for some petty misdemeanour or other – not to the heir of the district's leading landowner. But there was nothing she could do about it. The tide was too strong.

'Has he finished his railway yet?' she asked. The question was automatic, to show how little interest she took in any affairs of the Lyndon-Furys. In fact, she knew to an inch how far the line had progressed – or, rather, the roadbed that would one day support the line, for not a yard of metal had yet been laid. She knew already that only yesterday the final stretch of the embankment had been laid into the terminus at Glenisk.

'They finished it,' all four children replied.

'Daddy told you at supper last night,' Caro reminded her.

'They're having a grand luncheon at Glenisk today,' Stevie added. 'With champagne!'

'Did they get the pigs out the ticket office and the fowls from the waiting room?' Daisy asked scornfully.

The station buildings had been completed about five years ago and had acquired those rent-paying tenants in the meanwhile.

Finnbar put in: 'Daddy says 'tis the only line in the world where all the bed is finished before a single rail is laid. Why do they call it a bed?'

His mother laughed. 'Because when it's really finished they'll have feather mattresses and canopies of silk all the way from Simonstown to Glenisk. And that, I may say, is as likely as metal, given the present price of steel. If they'd laid the rails at the same time as the bed, sure, they'd have rusted to wire by now. What's he doing with Aunt Swan's hounds? I never thought that was serious.'

'Caro and me saw them following a drag in the park last week,' Dervla piped up. 'Didn't we, Caro?'

Her elder sister confirmed it with a nod. 'And one of them rioted after a hare instead and didn't he just get a slice of the ashplant from Trapper!'

Daisy shook her head in vexation. 'Well, it just shows where idleness and frivolity can lead. I can't understand your Aunt Swan permitting it.'

But she could, of course. One evening spent in Omdurman Villa, tripping over those four vast hounds and pretending not to notice the offensive smells they vented every other minute, helped her understand why Swan would yield them up to a willing keeper for however long he remained willing.

'I know why,' Caro said slyly. 'It's because when Trapper asked her for the lend of the hounds – not the first time but when he came back and really persuaded her – he said she'd bring them back to Dublin with a fine haunch of venison and what a tale *that'd* make when she served it up to her grand Dublin ladies and gentlemen!'

Daisy laughed. There were times when Trapper's cunning almost redeemed the man.

When they had finished washing the windows, Daisy and Caro stayed on to give them their final polish. 'We could have done it quicker ourselves,' Caro repeated her earlier assertion.

'It's good for their souls.' Daisy paraphrased hers. When Caro made no further comment, Daisy turned to see what might be distracting her – and found her staring out of the window.

Was it the boys swimming again, Daisy wondered? Caro was starting to notice such things. She left off her own polishing and went to join the girl.

But no lean, pale, muscular bodies were disporting themselves in the pool below the tower today. 'Penny for them?' she asked.

'I was just looking at Sharavogue. Why didn't they sell us that instead of the joinery? What use is that old pile of stone to them?'

'What use was the joinery – the way they managed it! They got rid of the bigger millstone, that's all. Anyway, Sharavogue wouldn't have fetched enough.'

'How much would it cost?'

Such intense eyes the girl had, Daisy thought! She'd break hearts one day without even knowing it – and soon enough, too. 'More money than *you've* got in the bank,' she said.

'But not more than you and Daddy have.'

Daisy dipped her head in concession. 'I'm not saying we won't buy it.'

Caro turned with such hope in her eyes that Daisy felt constrained to add, 'When the time is right.'

'Nyaa! Why isn't it right now?'

Daisy stared at her in perplexity. She knew a mother should make no favourites among her children and yet she could not deny that Caro was very special to her. She loved them all, of course. She wanted what any mother would want for her children: to grow up strong and sound in mind and body; to be proud of their family and name; to be independent; to make something of themselves when the time came. But for Caro she wanted more. It was not that she wished to bind the girl to her apron springs; but she wanted her to become a true friend and confidante as well as a 'mere' daughter.

'Why not now?' Caro pressed, seeing her Mammy in a rare quandary.

Daisy sighed. 'I wonder . . . are you old enough?'

Caro desperately sought some way to demonstrate her maturity. She almost blurted out that she had rung the great tenor bell of Flaxmills but felt somehow that was not enough. Then she knew what would do the trick. 'Can I ask you a question and you won't be angry?' she said.

'What?' Daisy eyed her warily.

Caro licked her lips. 'It's about Aunt Swan and Napier Lyndon-Fury.'

Daisy felt the blood drain from her cheeks. She laughed to divert the girl's attention and told her to go on.

'Did they . . . was there ever . . . oh dear!' She closed her eyes, swallowed hard, and blurted out, 'Did she ever carry his child?'

'Dear God!' Daisy sat down with a thump and fanned her face with her polishing duster. 'And what do you know about the carrying of children, may I ask?'

'What you told me – and some of the girls at school.'

'In other words, everything!' Daisy gave a weak laugh; her brain was racing ahead, trying to imagine what garbled story the girl had heard, or overheard, and how she might gloss it best.

Caro, delighted at her mother's good humour when she might just as easily have descended like a hundred of bricks, preened herself and said, 'Just about everything, I suppose. Was there any sparking between Aunt Swan and himself?'

'Well, I think there might have been. But what makes you ask?'

Caro stared guiltily out of the window. 'I wasn't eavesdropping, but sure I couldn't help overhearing. It was just things she and Aunt Madeleine were saying.'

'It's what they call "picking up bacon rinds"! You learn the size of it, but you miss all the meat. Well, I'll tell you this – I'm sure your Aunt Swan never carried any child of Napier Lyndon-Fury's.'

'But someone did. That's what they were talking about.'

Daisy shrugged noncommittally. 'Accidents can happen, of course – which is why we women have to be so careful how far we let our feelings carry us. But, as I say, I'm sure Aunt Swan never got so swept away. You know we were all students together, she, Mr Lyndon-Fury, and I?'

Caro nodded. 'And she was his belle?'

Daisy laughed. 'Every girl was his belle. Oh, he was such a handsome divil! And, between you and me and the four kingdoms of Ireland, he was a bit of a rogue to boot. But sure it means nothing at that age. Calf love. It was before I met your father, of course. After that there was no choice in it.'

Caro smiled contentedly and let her eyes stray back to the far horizon, to Sharavogue.

Daisy laid a hand gently on her arm. 'The reason I asked if you're old enough . . . I mean, there are things I'd like to tell you. And discuss with you. Things I'd welcome your opinion on – you know what I mean. But I'd have to be sure you wouldn't go telling it to others out of school.'

'Sure I wouldn't!' Caro protested.

'Not even to your bestest-bestest friend?'

She shook her head solemnly.

Daisy smiled. 'Then let's make a start with something small.' She nodded her head in the direction of Sharavogue. 'You'd really like to live there?'

'And have my own boudoir!' The girl gasped and held her breath.

'Well, let's just say you may not have too long to wait.'

Too overcome to speak, Caro flung her arms about her Mammy and clung to her, shivering for joy.

51

When it became known that this year, for the first time ever, Mrs O'Lindon would be attending the Coolderg Castle garden party – in her capacity as a committee member of the Church of Ireland Protestant Girls' Rescue Mission, of course – the tongues ran wild. It wasn't simply that she had never done such a thing before, and everybody knew why, it was that she should have chosen this year of all years to break with her own tradition.

For the tongues were also running wild about the fortunes of the Lyndon-Furys. True, the writing had been there on the wall for a long time. There was the generally threadbare clothing which the family seemed to be trying to make fashionable . . . the quarters that went by with the servants' wages delayed or only part-paid . . . the broken lead in the roof valleys that was no longer patched . . . the discounts Mr Woods offered for rents paid in advance . . . the wayleaves on Trapper's line on which no rent had ever been forthcoming . . . when you drew back and looked at it, sure the signs were as plain as the Bog of Allen Lighthouse.

And yet, on the other hand, when you looked at some of the other 'grand families' around, there was nothing so particular about the Lyndon-Furys that you'd kick yourself for not noticing. What with a disastrous quarter-century in agriculture, the depredations of the Land League, the millions of pounds' worth of investment the Fenians had frightened off, and the general way in which anyone with a scrap of sense was extracting every penny from the country while the going was fair, and lodging it safely abroad . . . well, the Lyndon-Furys were in goodly company.

There were even some who'd tell you that their air of genteel poverty was all one big act. Sure, hadn't everyone a threadbare suit and a set of frayed celluloid cuffs and boots that had shown better toes, never mind toecaps, to the world, which they wore to assessments and meetings with the Revenue? And wouldn't it be nicely expedient to all them foreign baboons for the world to think them poor – when that same world wanted an abatement of rent, a new roof, a deeper well, a secure haggard, a stone floor . . . and all the other 'landlord improvements'? No, me boyos, the Lyndon-Furys were as smart as fresh lime, squeezing every last drop of Irish blood and sweat and carting it by the gold ingot to their manor in England.

Only the news that Mrs O'Lindon was at last to attend the great garden party made the boyos pause and think there may be something in this show of poverty after all. Hadn't she been seen pacing out the walls of the distillery a year before the collapse of *that* business – and invigilating every slate on it with her byenoc'lars. And hadn't Molly Flynn, back in 1896, five years before the purchase of the joinery, found a feint-ruled exercise book with all the calculations pertaining to the same. Sure that one could catch the whiff of a court sale before the bailiff to enforce it was born. All the extra servants who were drafted in from the villages to assist at the great occasion were jocosely warned by their friends to keep an eye skinned on herself – Mrs O'Lindon; and if she took out a surveyor's tape, they were to make particular note of her target so they could get in a bid of their own. She was a clever one, that Daisy O'Lindon – no doubt of it. Oh, she'd herd mice at a crossroads.

Stephen brought all this gossip home, usually to their bed between prayers and sleep – just to share her amusement. But at last even he was infected by it and felt he had to ask her why she had changed her mind.

'Because I was wrong never to go,' she replied simply.

He lay back and linked fingers behind his head. 'I have to believe that,' he said, 'for I never heard you use those words before.'

'I have,' she protested. 'I'm often wrong.'

'When?'

'What does it matter now. Often. But I never thought it might hurt Caro, d'you see.'

He considered the matter and replied, 'I do not.'

'Ah, some good-natured friend will surely retail a pack of lies and sedition to her – and if I'm seen to be out of concert with the Lyndon-Furys, it will only add colour to the scandal.'

'So now you'll turn up and hobnob with one and all – as if nothing had ever gone amiss between ye?'

'Not for my own sake,' was the virtuous reply. After a brooding silence she went on, 'D'you think I'm wrong? I could always take a chill or something.'

'I was after recalling something your father said last Christmas,' he replied. 'He said if you ask Daisy why she does a thing and she can't tell you, or she just says it's because she wants to, that's grand. You need have no qualms about it. But if she gives you a good reason, you should begin to worry. And if she gives you a damn good reason, take heed for your hair and start digging trenches.'

'Blather!' she cried scornfully. 'I'll tell you a good old Dublin word for the likes of him that a lady shouldn't use, but it's spelled g, o, b, s, h, i, t, e. And that's what he is.'

'You don't think it's true?'

'It's true of someone, I'm sure – whoever he and his cronies were discussing in the bar when one of them came out with it. And it wasn't my father, for he hasn't the wit.'

A day or so later she returned to the topic – again during those few assured moments of privacy they enjoyed before dropping off to sleep. 'I was wondering,' she said, 'would I tell Caro the truth about the way it was?'

'To what end?' he asked.

'To spike anyone's else musket. She's given me a quare look lately. I think someone may have passed a remark or two already.'

He stared at the ceiling a while.

'Well?' she prompted.

'There's a thing I meant to say now. What colour' – he cleared his throat delicately – 'would Caro's, you know, underthings . . . what colour would they be?'

She stared at him in astonishment. 'What in the name of God . . .'

'Just tell me. You'll see why. Would they be white?'

'Of course. How else would I know if that bag of idleness over the bridge has washed them clean?'

'Well, Peter Shaughnessy was after telling me he overheard Billy Walshe and Simon Brennan telling the lads in the hurling team what colour all the girls' underthings are in Flaxmills. Molly White and Breege Horan and Fiona Harcourt . . . and our Caro. They knew them all.'

'Sure they're boasting. How would they know a thing like that – unless they stood outside Mrs Mulcahy's and took a note of what was on the line and what household sent them down. And even then they couldn't, because she never puts the intimate washing out in the garden, only in the old pheasant run.'

'All the same . . .' He shook his head dubiously.

'Of course they're boasting,' she asserted with even stronger scorn. 'Look at their fathers – aren't they the hurlers on the ditch, the pair of them? They'd tell you how to build a clock but they couldn't foot turf if they hadn't their neighbours for a pattern. As if our Caro would do anything to give those two jackeens the sight of her knickers!'

Stephen knew her well enough by now to know that when she protested at such length and with such vehemence, her assurance was something less than copper-fastened; she would, in her own time and manner, now raise the business with Caro. He, too, thought it most probable that the lads were boasting of an invented achievement, but a more uncomfortable explanation could not be ruled out.

As for telling the girl the truth about her parentage, he found himself precisely torn between agreeing to and forbidding it. He had, indeed, considered the idea already for he knew as well as Daisy how tongues can wag.

'You didn't answer my question,' Daisy prompted.

'There's no doubting she'll learn the truth one day,' he agreed. 'But sure, haven't we always known that?'

'Have we? We never talked of it.'

'I think of that phrase we say every Sunday: "Not with our lips but in our lives." There's a lot to be said for that. Let the lips of the world say what they like about her parentage, we'll show her the truth of it in our lives – that she's *our* daughter, born in lawful wedlock' – he raised his eyes in tribute to that skin-of-their-teeth achievement – 'and we're as proud of her as any two parents could be.'

Daisy felt the pressure of tears behind her eyelids. She slipped her arms about his neck and whispered, 'God help me, Stephen, I forget the goodness that's in you.'

'Blather!' he murmured happily, caressing her back through the thin flannel of her nightdress.

Soon he began to ease it up about her waist.

'Be careful now,' she cautioned with a beating heart. 'It's that dangerous time of the month.'

52

Swan came down for the Coolderg Castle garden party. Normally she would not have been seen dead at such affairs because, quite frankly, they were for the sort of people who were not completely acceptable socially – worthy people like doctors, vicars, local councillors, government officials, and the more substantial shopkeepers and tradesmen . . . even lawyers, provided their practice was not *too* criminal. In short, they were the sort of people to whom local society owed the debt of recognition rather than the accolade of acceptance. Recognition required no more than a garden party; acceptance would imply a seat at the dinner table, which would be going altogether too far.

And since Swan had flexed the muscles of Mercier's bank rather heavily to get her feet beneath the ancient oak dinner table at Coolderg, she would not normally have tarnished her status by appearing at so lowly a function as a garden party. But the moment Madeleine told her that Daisy was to be there, she decided it was something that wild elkhounds would not keep her from attending. Unfortunately, the bank was undergoing its annual audit and Mercier could not get away. Swan came down alone on the Thursday before the party, which was on the last Saturday in June, to give herself two good nights' sleep before the fun.

She had only a daily maid and a living-out cook at Omdurman Villa, so she was quite isolated and alone at nights. Normally, with four huge hounds about the place, that would not have bothered her, but, since the creatures were being schooled by Trapper, she was a little more nervous than she might otherwise have been. On the first night she dined *en famille* with the O'Lindons; Daisy behaved throughout as if her previous non-attendance at the Coolderg garden parties had been the most trivial oversight – in other words, she would not be drawn on the topic in the slightest degree. On the Friday night Swan was to have dined with the Couttses, but Tom had rowed up the lake and left a message calling it off. Young Tommy, it seemed, had passed a terrible night, and, though he now seemed well on the mend, the rest of the family was exhausted.

So it was with some trepidation that she answered a knock at the door, just after nine that evening. In fact, she carried a poker concealed behind her back. She almost dropped it when she saw who her caller was.

'Napier!' She just stood and stared at him.

'Hello Swan. How are things?' He took a small pace across the threshold.

Still in a daze she stood back and let him pass. 'What are you doing down here?'

'Damned if I know!' He gave an ironic laugh. 'In fact, that's my . . . I was hoping I might . . . sort of talk it over with you and Mercier.'

'Go on through. Have you eaten? All I can offer is a bite of cold salmon or some beef sandwiches. The servants have all gone hours ago.'

He paused and patted his stomach, as if it might have devoured something without informing him. 'God, I *could*, too,' he said. 'Would you mind awfully? Beef, I think. We'll have a surfeit of salmon tomorrow.'

She laughed. 'You always had that way with you. I don't know what it is. The moment one sees you one wants to press food upon you, or sew on buttons or . . .' She did not elaborate a third possibility. 'In that case, you can join me in the kitchen. I'm singlehanded here. Mercier's in Dublin, by the way.' She revealed the poker at last, as if that proved it.

'Oh!' He stopped in his tracks and half turned to the front door again. 'Perhaps I ought to go, then.'

'For the love of God!' She brushed past him and went down the passageway to the kitchen. 'How long have we known each other? How long have I been married, come to that?'

'Exactly!' He followed her, soaping his hands, making a joke of it.

In the kitchen she laid down the poker and picked up the carving knife, which she pointed briefly at him, grinning in jocular triumph. As she started to carve the beef, however, she grew serious again. 'What did you want to talk about? Does Daisy know you've come down? You heard she's going to the garden party tomorrow, I suppose?'

He smiled bleakly. 'I didn't know it when I decided to pay this visit. I thought it'd be the one place where I'd be sure of *not* seeing her.'

'Oh, it is so *stupid*!' Swan exploded. 'How long has it been? Fifteen . . . sixteen years?'

'Fifteen years, two months, three days,' he replied lugubriously.

'Napier!' she scolded.

He chuckled. 'I only know because Maddy asked me the same question. She thought it disgraceful that I *couldn't* answer. So now I've shocked both of you.'

'It'd take a lot more than that to shock me,' Swan assured him. 'D'you want to know if I think you should stay indoors all day tomorrow? Or go back to London . . . actually, where *do* you live these days?'

She cut him two slices of bread, put the butter knife into his hand, and slapped the butter dish down in front of him before he said, 'Oh . . . yes . . . of course.' But when she saw how thick he spread it, she regretted her action.

'Paris,' he said. 'Fontainebleau in the summer.'

'Poor boy! I do feel for you.'

Deftly he anchored two rounds of beef in the butter, raked half the pickle jar over them, and clamped the top slice of bread over the lot as if it might otherwise take flight and escape him. 'If I'd known she was coming,

I'd have stayed a million miles away,' he admitted. 'But now I wonder if it wouldn't be for the best. I mean, it's absurd for us to go on avoiding each other after all this time. We've got to get back to behaving like two civilized human beings sooner or later.'

Swan retrieved the butter dish and spread the next two slices herself. She made no immediate reply but nodded encouragingly instead, wanting to hear more of his thoughts before she weighed in with her own.

'The thing is . . . hell hath no fury, and all that . . . no pun intended. Maddy can't tell me how Venus will take it. Or won't tell me.'

'Venus! I'd forgotten you called her that.' She grinned cattily. 'And if you do meet, I'd try to avoid it, actually.'

'Oh? Is she grown . . .'

'She's had five children, Napier. And they are a prosperous pair, the O'Lindons – exceedingly.'

He sighed. 'So I gather. Still, it's a shame to think of Daisy losing her figure.'

'Oh, I'd not say she's lost it,' Swan cut in hastily. 'But she'd take a bit longer in the mornings to *find* it than she used to. Put it like that.' She drew in her own stomach and wished she had not eased her corsets an hour or so earlier.

He noticed. 'No one could say that of you, Swan. You're still the sylph that drove us all wild in Dawson Street, so you are.'

'Ah, g'wan!' She spoke and laughed in the tones of the Dublin Liberties. 'Listen, I have some porter I keep for the gardener. Or I have a new supplier of poteen from across the water.'

'From England?' he asked incredulously.

'No!' She pointed westward. 'From County Clare.'

'Oh, that water.' He guffawed. 'You *are* going parochial.'

'Never mind that. The last lot we had, from Flaxmills . . . well, I never swallowed so much as a thimbleful and I'll swear I couldn't open my eyes for two days.'

'I'll try the new stuff, so.' He nodded his thanks. 'Is it good?'

'Twice through the still.' She set a small tot of the clear liquor before him and poured another for herself.

He downed it in one and gasped at its pleasing bite. 'Begod!' He smacked his lips and savoured it again. 'But that beats Banagher. That's better than the stuff we used to sell legally.' He put his empty glass before her. 'A bird never flew on one wing, they say.'

'You'll not walk on one leg if you have too much of this,' she warned, refilling his glass.

She took a careful sip of her own as she studied him, eating with gusto while his hands turned the sandwich this way and that, composing it as for a painting, finding its best aspects and most suitable lighting; he probably wasn't even aware he was doing it. How old would he be now? Mid-to late-forties, anyway. Yet there was hardly any sign of age on him. A little heavier under the eyes, perhaps. His crows' feet a little deeper. But his hair was as dark and luxuriant as ever. Not a wisp of gray in his beard – and beards were often the first to go that way.

What was that tale about a man who led a life of depravity but all the marks of it were to be seen in his portrait in the attic, not on his face? Did Napier lead a life of depravity, she wondered? He'd never married. The Parisian women would surely throw themselves at him, being so handsome and such good company, and so famous and all. How many, she mused? Or did he redirect all that sort of energy into his art? Great artists could do that. Perhaps the finest thing Daisy ever did was to leave him for Stephen. Every night, for just a few minutes, he'd set a light in the window of his soul to guide her back to him, shed a brief tear – and then he'd never need *look* at another woman. Which was the same as saying he'd be free of the whole silly business, free to get on with his art.

Which was he? The practised roué, or the dedicated artist? Looking at him you could never tell. Talking to him you could never tell. Well . . . maybe, talking. If you tried hard enough.

'What are your feelings about Daisy?' she asked. 'It's not that I'm prying – though I am, to be sure – but it could affect the way you'd be when you and she happened to bump into each other.'

He nodded at the justice of that. 'Well, I never married,' he offered, as if that said it all.

'Because no other women could ever hold a candle to her, in your eyes? Or because you lost faith in all of us?'

He tilted his head from side to side. 'Six of one, half a dozen of the other. I was very hurt for a long time, I have to say that. But either I'm past it all now or it's so deeply buried it amounts to the same thing.' He finished his second tot and edged the glass her way again.

'Eat that other sandwich,' she advised as she obliged him with a further pouring.

He obeyed, more from duty than hunger.

'Has there really been no one else since Daisy?' she went on. Then, making a jest of her curiosity, she added, 'Remembering the way you were *before* she came along!' She caressed her lips briefly with the tip of one finger, hinting that they shared in her recall; and, indeed, he had kissed her once – or, to be exact, several times – at the ball that ended their second year in the Academy School.

'Oh yes!' He suddenly realized how ungallant his tone must sound. 'Well, to be sure, I never forgot that night!'

'Liar!' She laughed. 'And you don't slide out of my question so easily.'

He shrugged. 'There have been one or two light-hearted *affaires*.'

'One or two?'

'Ten or twenty.'

'Or a hundred or two?'

His hands invoiced and delivered the concession. 'I said light-hearted,' he reminded her.

'Then you *did* lose faith in all women. That's how disillusioned men all behave.'

'All of those women were married, I hasten to add.' He spoke the words to his glass but fixed her with a sudden speculative stare as soon as he had finished.

She took a quick sip of her own and fanned her face. 'I'd forgotten how this stuff always brings me out in a flush,' she told him. 'I must look a sight.'

'For sore eyes.' He put his glass down and tilted back in his chair, locking his hands behind his head and staring pensively at the ceiling.

By God, he thinks he's got me, she thought. If Mercier were here, he'd be seething in silence to see furniture treated so.

If Mercier were here, none of this conversation would have taken place. She wouldn't be drinking poteen – which she didn't really like at all. And she would be pushing all these other thoughts and feelings back into limbo where they belonged. What if Napier asked her directly? Came straight out with it?

She decided not to decide anything.

'Do the O'Lindons worry your people?' she suddenly heard herself asking, much to her own surprise and certainly to his.

But in his case the surprise was pleasant. 'You're amazing, Swan,' he said.

She realized he meant it, too. If the words had been part of some campaign of flattery leading up to *the* question – the one she had decided not to decide just yet – they'd have been more polished, and he'd have followed them swiftly with the next salvo. Instead, he just sat there, smiling and shaking his head, handing her the initiative.

'In what way?' she asked.

He chuckled, as if her question were surely tendentious. 'Well, of course you know that's what I really wished to discuss – but I could never bring it up, not off my own bat, so to speak.'

She nodded sagely, as if he had seen right through her; but all she could think of to say was, 'Ah.' She took another sip. It wasn't such bad stuff, this County Clare poteen. It was a Protestant made it, the man who ferried it over said. A deacon of his church!

'I'd hate to strain any loyalties,' Napier added. 'But I've been hearing about their extraordinary progress – the O'Lindons – and it does appear to have some alarming aspects.'

'Quite,' Swan agreed.

'On the other hand . . . if any business around here is likely to fall on hard times, it's almost bound to have the name Lyndon-Fury – since we own the lot.'

'*Owned* the lot.' She watched her fingers move the glass with infinite care until it rested exactly, but exactly, upon a knot in the pine table top – as if she needed to demonstrate that the drink was taking no effect whatever.

'Yes.' He sighed. 'I suppose the old guard in Paris must feel the same about us – moving into their old studios in Montmartre – getting all the attention they used to get. It must look to them as if we're deliberately seeking to kill them off. Actually, we don't give a tinker's cuss what becomes of them. We have no feelings about them whatever. We just want our own ideas about art to take over.'

'Which, indeed, they are doing.'

The words were easy and automatic. Beneath their unruffled surface she was thinking that none of the Lyndon-Furys was a match for Daisy and Stephen. Trapper and Sir Lucius were imprisoned in an Ascendancy Ireland that was dead and gone, only they couldn't see it. Cornel was imprisoned in a bottle. And now Napier was showing his fatal flaw – that he could so easily see all sides to any question. It would make him hesitate for a fatal moment too long at a time of crisis.

Actually, Stephen was a bit like that; he needed Daisy's ruthless determination to carry him through those potentially fatal moments. What if Napier got the power of such a woman behind him?

God, but I'd make him see what side his bread was buttered!

The thought was out before its farcical character struck her, then she laughed.

'Ah, so you're only saying that,' he observed.

She floundered, trying to remember what words she had spoken. She abandoned the attempt when she realized that this was one of those rare moments in life when absolute frankness was in order. 'No,' she told him. 'I was just thinking how like Stephen O'Lindon you are. You both see all sides of every question. Daisy's the one who brings down the hammer.'

His eyes went vacant as he vanished into reverie. 'Yes,' he said at last. 'In the brief time were were together, she . . .' Another vacant moment concluded with the assertion, 'She was the one.' He stared at her with those dark, intense eyes. 'Can you keep a secret? If I asked you to keep it from Daisy, could you?'

She nodded, wondering why no words followed; the thought crossed her mind that he was practising some kind of hypnosis upon her. The thought followed it that it would just suit her to believe that. She closed her mind to the thought which came welling up in the wake of that.

'Trapper has asked me to join him in the projected railway.' He frowned. 'Have you got brothers or sisters?'

'Yes. A brother and two sisters.'

'Perhaps you know the sort of rivalry I'm talking about. I mean – for *Trapper* to ask *me* to join in his pet project!' His eyes said there were no words to describe it.

'You'll do no such thing?' she asked in a tone that expected his agreement – which came at once.

'Indeed! But that's not my point. What I'm saying is, it shows how desperate things are in general if he's prepared to swallow his pride and almost beg me like that.'

'Could you, in fact, afford to?' she asked before she could stop herself.

'Oh yes.' He became all nonchalant in a determined effort not to sound smug. 'I could probably buy out the whole family estate – and put it back on its feet. Become a model landlord . . .'

He hesitated, but she finished the thought for him: 'And give the O'Lindons a damn good run for their money!'

His smile was half boyish glee, half grown-up chagrin. 'That's the rub, old darling. I try to tell myself I'd be doing it for the family honour. But I know full well . . . I mean, all my life I've scoffed at that sort of thing. Our day is done – the big Anglo-Irish landlord. You've only got to look about you. I've always known it . . . felt it in my bones. Art was my way out. It's my religion now but in the beginning it was just a way out. And yet I'm' – he recruited her pardon like a naughty schoolboy – '*bloody* tempted to do it.'

'Take part in Trapper's railway?'

'No! Restore the fortunes of the old estate. Cock a snook at history.' He lowered his gaze. 'Except we know what I'd *really* be doing . . . who I'd really be cocking that snook at, don't we!' He laughed. 'Oh, Swan, I'm so glad I had this talk with you. I'm so glad you're the perceptive lass you are.'

'But I've said nothing!'

'You have. You speak with your eyes. I say things and I see you judging them without a word spoken. I've made up my mind – not a penny of mine is coming home here to County Keelity. The O'Lindons may inherit the earth and the fulness thereof. It's what history wants, anyway.'

Swan knew it was plain common sense and yet she felt the sharpest pang of disappointment at his conclusion. Also a certain measure of guilt that she might have helped him to it.

'And now,' he added, rubbing his hands gleefully, 'I can face a meeting with our Venus – oops, Daise – with perfect equanimity. I don't care what she feels or what she says or what she does. I can at last say I'm over . . . whatever it was.' He scratched his head as if he had forgotten something. 'Oh yes! We'll still keep it a secret though, won't we?'

She rose and came to him round the table. He grinned, watching her all the way, intrigued – for he had no inkling if her purpose – until she jerked his chair upright. Which brought it to rest some eighteen inches from the table. Which, in turn, gave her enough room to seat herself firmly in his lap and plant a fervent kiss on his astonished lips.

She broke from him long enough to murmur, 'It would be ever so much safer if it were a secret that could cut both ways, my old darling.'

And she returned her lips to his and raised his hand to her uncorseted bosom.

53

There would be bowling for a pig on the old yew walk, or you could fish for washers with a magnet in the walled garden, or take a lucky dip in the bran tub at the foot of the wall that Cromwell slighted in 1654. Actually, it wasn't bran but sawdust – 'O'Lindon sawdust,' as Seamus Boland remarked when he tipped the sack into the barrel. There was to be an archery range in the avenue of lime trees, where young men could half swoon over young women who, for all their skill with Cupid's bow, seemed to need an inordinate amount of tuition before they could loose an everyday arrow. There was a pony-jumping contest in the park for the under-fourteens (hands and age group). And the Simonstown Silver Band would be there to play the usual selections from Gilbert and Sullivan and Percy French beneath an awning beside the refreshment tent – which, unlike the musicians, was teetotal.

Sawdust was not the only O'Lindon contribution to that year's festivities at Coolderg Castle. Since Stephen had acquired the other joinery, his original factory down by the river had gone over exclusively to boatbuilding. There, His Majesty and a later version of the same machine (called, naturally, the Prince) turned out a steady run of clinker-built boats, from little one-man tubs to great pleasure launches. It so happened that the firm had recently completed an order for twenty small rowing boats for the Belfast municipality, to be hired by the half-hour on a lake in one of that city's parks. The O'Lindons diverted a dozen of them to the castle for the day of the garden party.

'Wasn't that very noble of you,' Swan said when she heard of it. She came over to Flaxmills for an early luncheon before going on with the O'Lindon party to the castle.

'It was Daisy's idea,' Stephen told her.

Swan had not even doubted it.

Dervla, Stevie, and Finnbar, who were taking part in the pony jumping, rode their own mounts over. They knew they were already disqualified from the turn-out prize, for their own father was the judge of that; but a rosette for a good round of jumps was all they really wanted. Caro and Sheridan – respectively too old and too young for such excitement – rode with the grown ups in an open landau.

'I say!' Swan ran an admiring eye over the line of it. 'This is something new.' One cotton-gloved finger tested the deep shine on the lacquer.

'Stephen built it himself,' Daisy said with nonchalant pride. 'Springs and everything.'

'No!' Swan turned her wide eyes upon him. 'I don't know why I'm surprised, actually. It has all the hallmarks of your handiwork. But where d'you find the *time?*'

Daisy answered for him. 'Hasn't he been up at five every morning since Christmas.'

'I wanted to see what sort of labour was in it,' he explained as they seated themselves and the ladies opened their parasols.

'Is this to be a new line for your joinery, then?'

He shook his head. 'It's too fretful altogether. You'd need twenty different machines.' He gave a nod to Peter Shaughnessy in the driving seat and off they went. Sheridan, happy as a sandboy at Peter's side, shouted a gleeful but redundant, 'Giddaaah!'

'Machines!' Swan said in disgust. 'When you can do beautiful work like this by hand, I'm surprised you can even think of horrid old machines.'

It was an ancient bone between them; he did not rise for yet another gnaw at it.

Daisy said, 'If you'd get up at five every morning and join him, you might soon develop a remarkable taste for a labour-saving machine or two.'

When they reached the Protestant church at the top of the hill, Peter let the horses amble to recover their wind; he gave the reins to Sheridan, Emperor of Rome, returning in triumph from the wars in Gaul . . . if only those grown-ups would stop chattering and laughing.

Caro remembered for the twentieth time to elevate her nose; noses were being carried quite high that summer; eyelids, on the other hand, were lowered until they obscured the entire upper half of one's field of vision. The new landau was simply marvellous but the occasion was marred by the presence of Sheridan. She had to accept the fact that her parents were a distressingly plebeian pair. Getting up at five in the morning and working away with fishglue and fretsaws! It was *too* bad. If they had the faintest idea of social grace, the 'right time' to buy Sharavogue had been several years ago; and if they'd only done it then, Sheridan would now have a nanny who'd be tending him this minute in a dogcart, well out of sight on the road behind.

'Will Aunt Madeleine's sister be there?' she asked Aunt Swan. She would have preferred to ask, 'Will Countess de Jompe be there?' but her mother's hoot of derision was still in her ear from last time: '*Counter jumper!* What sort of a name is that for a Christian, I ask you?'

'I expect so, darling. She never misses, does she. Not that I've been to one of these ghastly affairs before. But *noblesse oblige*, you know.'

'Didn't you ask Aunt Madeleine?'

'Ah . . . no. In fact, I didn't go to the Couttses last night. They sent word to say Young Tom was poorly.' She made a glum face and added in sepulchral tones, 'So I dined in lonely splendour. Not even the hounds to keep me company.'

Daisy pricked up her ears. Whenever Swan made a theatrical song and dance like that, there was more to it than she was telling.

Swan smiled indulgently at Caro. 'I know who you really want to see.'

Caro blushed. Actually, it wasn't true. That stupid pash for Patrick de Jompe was over and done with ages ago. It was Gwendolen, Patrick's younger sister, she really wanted to see. Gwendolen (never Gwen) was a girl of her own age who lived exactly the sort of life she, Caro, hankered after. She had her own lady's maid, her own boudoir, her own dress allowance – all the things the O'Lindons could easily afford if only they weren't so . . . plebeian. Gwendolen had the run of the castle, naturally, so she'd be able to sweep Caro past the footman, the one with the sour face that they always put at the door to keep back 'the great unwashed,' as her ladyship called her outdoor guests. And once inside they could race up to her boudoir in the tower and comb each other's hair and discuss the knights who were erranting all over the place with their favours, Gwendolen's and Caro's, tied to their helmets or lances or wherever knights errant put such things. And forget the whole stupid garden party and its oafish, rural amusements.

Caro was sunk so deep in this pleasurable reverie that she missed most of the conversation on the way over. It was her father who brought her back to a sense of the present by standing up and deliberately trying to rock the carriage – which equally deliberately, it seemed, resisted his efforts. 'Not bad, eh?' he commented to Swan. 'I'd say I learned more about suspension and springs than ever I did about coachbuilding.'

'Oh, God, Swan,' Daisy leaped in to confirm it. 'He had this thing off its wheels a score of times, and shook the bones out of us while he got it right to his liking.'

Swan laughed. 'I had no idea all this was going on. I mean, I've been coming down fairly regularly and you've said not a word.'

Daisy smiled at Stephen. 'Sure he'd never say a word until he was sure. His Majesty was built in his head two years before he spoke of it to a living soul.'

They swept in past the gate lodge onto the potholed terrain of the castle drive. Stephen resumed his seat. Carefully avoiding Daisy's eye he said, 'I was thinking of those motor-car contraptions. Building coachwork for those things might be a better notion altogether. I was looking at one in Simonstown this week, a Reynold, I think it said.'

'Renault?' Swan asked; she spelled it out and then pronounced it in the proper French manner.

'Sure that was it.'

Swan bit her lip and looked uncertainly at Daisy, who asked her was anything wrong.

'I wonder?' was the ambiguous answer. Last night, before he left Omdurman Villa, Napier had told her he'd driven down in his new Renault, which he was going to race in Phoenix Park. He'd also asked her to warn Daisy that he'd be at the garden party – which she had decided to leave until it was too late to turn back. She stared from one to the other and, realizing this was as good an opportunity as any, she availed of it. Casually smoothing out her gloves – so as not to alert Caro to the fact that her words were in any way remarkable – she said lightly, 'The youngest of the Lyndon-Fury brothers, Napier – who was at art school with me – he's bought a Renault. Perhaps he's come home?'

Not a muscle twitched in Stephen's face; Daisy turned and stared out over the park.

'He lives in Paris nowadays,' Swan added. 'He's quite a famous painter over there.'

Daisy continued staring out across the park, as if she wanted to be first to see the castle. 'You're very well informed,' she said in a tone one woman might use to tease another gently.

'Maddy told me.' Swan turned to Caro. 'That time you and me and Dervla rode over.'

Caro nodded but she knew it was a lie for she had overheard almost every word that passed between the two women on that occasion.

Daisy suspected it was a lie, too, but for the more general reason that she had known Swan and her little ways a long time now. She continued to pretend to take only the coolest interest in the news, though her heart was racing at the thought that she and Napier might bump into each other around any corner this afternoon. It was one thing to resume normal social relations with the Lyndon-Furys; it was quite another to start hobnobbing with Napier himself, all on the same day. She wondered if she were up to it quite.

'Maddy says he's enjoyed a great success lately,' Swan went on. 'Oodles of oof.' She made it sound like a quotation. 'She said he could buy out the Coolderg Estate ten times over.'

The look that passed across Stephen's face at this news astonished her.

Until that moment she had always assumed that the driving force behind their unspoken rivalry with the Lyndon-Furys was Daisy, and that her purpose was to avenge the slight Napier and his mother had done to her. But now, in that glimpse of hardness and fear in Stephen's eyes, she saw it might have roots more ancient and profound.

'Isn't that Aunt Madeleine going foreanenst us?' Caro asked. She instantly kicked herself at the provincialism. 'I mean in front of us? That's her governess cart, I'm sure.'

'I do believe you're right,' Swan said, already planning how to 'rig' Madeleine, as the racing fraternity says, into supporting her little white lies. To her relief, when they arrived at the start of the carriage sweep, Madeleine pulled her nag aside and headed directly for the stable yard, which was actually part of the home farm rather than of the castle proper.

But then, Stephen said, 'You may bring us to the stable, Peter.'

'Sound, boss,' Shaughnessy chirped.

'But why?' Caro whined, beating Daisy to it by a hair.

His smile craved their indulgence. 'Sure, we might get a sight of that oul' motor car again.'

'And leave us tramping through all those horseapples!' Daisy complained. 'No, thank you.'

Sheridan leaped down and ran toward the castle, shouting, 'I'm all right. I'm all right! I'll go and look for Finnbar.' For once nobody called abuse or reprimands after him for his recklessness.

'We're as good as there now,' Stephen said. 'If it's not to be seen, we'll turn directly about and go on to the castle door.'

The promise was scarce made before they heard Madeleine's excited shriek of, 'Napier! What are you doing at home? Nobody told me.'

Daisy felt the blood drain from her. She scrutinized Caro to see whether the girl had noticed; but she was watching her Aunt Swan, who had risen and half turned in her seat, gripping the top of the valance for dear life. What had the girl *really* overheard that day? Daisy wondered. How much did she understand about grown-ups and the secrets they keep from each other? Daisy remembered Stephen's worries about the girl and how those two young blackguards knew the colour of her knickers; this time the implicit fear did not seem so easily discountable.

Her thoughts rang in an empty skull. She could concentrate on nothing – not with Napier there.

Go on, she told herself. *Look at the fella!*

Her eyes remained fixed on Caro. And she could feel Stephen's gaze upon her. She almost burst out laughing when she realized what a tableau they must make to Napier or anyone else in the yard: Swan was staring at him and Madeleine; Caro was staring at Swan; there was herself staring at Caro; and Stephen was staring at her – a right-down regular *tableau vivant*!

The comedy of it enabled her to turn to Napier quite calmly at the last. Even so, her level tones surprised her when she said, 'Mr Lyndon-Fury!' as if the meeting were no more than a mildly pleasant surprise.

He swallowed heavily and bowed to her, hat in hand.

But now she had accidentally taken the initiative she was not going to yield it easily. 'It must be years,' she went on. 'I don't know whether you remember me? I used to be Daisy O'Lindon. Well, I still am, in a way. I'm sure you already know my husband, Stephen O'Lindon.'

'Indeed.' Napier was happier on this more familiar ground. 'Hello, O'Lindon. What a long time it's been.'

'Glad we are to see you here again.' Stephen stepped down and shook his hand, avoiding any title of address.

Napier glanced at Caro and Swan – Madeleine being about thirty yards behind him by now, handing her pony in charge of the groom. 'Swan?' he asked uncertainly. 'I didn't know you graced little affairs like this. How nice to see you again.'

'You too, old darling!' Swan laughed rather effusively.

Madeleine was now running up to her brother, rekindling all the surprise of her earlier greeting. 'I *knew* it was you,' she cried, flinging her arms about him. 'Just wait till I tell Thomas. He swore it wasn't.'

Napier frowned in bewilderment. 'Wasn't what?'

'Napier!' Swan interrupted anxiously. 'You haven't met this young lady yet, I think? Caroline, this is Aunt Madeleine's baby brother, Mr Napier Lyndon-Fury. Miss Caroline O'Lindon.'

'Forgive me, Miss O'Lindon!' Napier leaped between her parents and came to the foot of the landau steps, holding up a gallant hand.

Caro stared into his eyes and knew at once that he was the most handsome, godlike man she had ever met. When he grasped her fingers and raised them to his lips – without a trace of condescension as far as she could see – she thought she'd die. And yet, a sign of her growing womanhood, part of her remained aloof from this swirl of emotions . . . remembered that, according to Aunts Swan and Maddy (and notwithstanding her mother's denials), this man had a daughter somewhere whom her mother had named in some way to spite him . . . that her mother might have cause to harbour a grudge against him . . . that Uncle Mercier half-suspected there had once been 'something' between Aunt Swan and this demigod and that the woman herself did not deny it, even when Aunt Maddy had pressed her in the warmest, friendliest way.

God, weren't grown-ups the slimiest things! Look at them now – all smiling and badinage so you'd never suspect a thing between them! Butter wouldn't melt in their mouths.

Meanwhile the rest of her was feasting on his beauty, committing every line and feature to memory for later transubstantiation into the most *parfit gentil* knight, who could wear her favour anywhere and any way he liked.

Stephen had meanwhile walked over to a nearby stable, where he had caught a telltale glint of metal. 'Aha!' He turned and grinned at them. 'The famous Renault.' He spoke the name in perfect imitation of Swan's perfect French.

'Quite right.' Napier lifted his eyebrows in surprise. He still held Caro lightly by the hand, which seemed to justify his turning to her and asking if she had ever seen a motor car.

She told him there were two or three that passed through Flaxmills from time to time.

'Well come and look at mine,' he invited, leading her across the yard – which was, in fact, singularly free of horseapples for once.

'Yours?' Madeleine echoed in surprise. She giggled at the other two.

'You bear a most famous name, you know,' Napier was telling Caro, 'in the history of both our families.'

'Napier with a motor car!' Madeleine exclaimed.

'But surely you knew?' Swan asked urgently.

'Not I! That fella hasn't sent as much as a postcard to me in the last ten years.'

Napier, listening with half an ear to this exchange, faltered momentarily in his history of the first Caroline O'Lindon.

'But I'm sure it was you told me.' Swan realized that even if Madeleine caught the despair in her insistence, she could not now say, 'Silly me!' and fall into line. She sighed. 'Still . . . if you didn't know, it can't have been you. I wonder who it was?'

Napier cleared his throat meaningfully.

Swan was very quick. 'You?' She thumped the butt of her palm against her brow. 'Of course! When we met in Dublin! You're going to race in the Phoenix Park, aren't you.' She turned excitedly to Daisy. 'Did I mention that? He's going to race it in the Phoenix Park.'

'Yes. You said.' Daisy stared at the motor. 'It looks beautiful, Mr Lyndon-Fury.'

'Goes beautifully, too, Mrs O'Lindon. Would you care for a spin round the park?' He stared around and generalized the invitation. 'Anybody?' His eyes came to rest on Stephen.

'Ah, you take the ladies, Lyndon-Fury. You and I can give her a proper trial later.'

'You're on!' Napier's eyes glowed. 'God, I never thought you'd be such a connoisseur.' His eyes invited Madeleine to step aboard but his hands made no supporting gesture.

She took the hint. 'Wild dogs wouldn't get me in one of those things,' she protested.

Swan, who, but for Madeleine's pointed refusal, might have accepted, took the hint as well.

Caro was just about to step aboard when her father's hand closed about her arm. 'I want you,' he said, 'to help me. I'm to judge the ponies for my sins and I know as much about them as Lord Nelson's bad eye. I want a real connoisseur at my side, d'ye see.'

Connoisseuse, Caro thought as, forlornly, she watched her mother climb into the car and sit in solo state behind the most handsomest man on earth.

'I'll be left go on the proper trial with you and Mr Lyndon-Fury, won't I?' she suggested to her father as Napier swung the motor into life.

When it started on the first swing he explained diffidently that it was only because the thing was already warm.

Stephen chuckled at Caro's intensity. 'That man' – he nodded toward Napier as the car pulled out into the yard – 'is so in love, I'd not doubt he'd give you a solo ride, too.'

'In love with who?' Caro asked sharply.

'With his motor car, to be sure. What else at his age?' He laughed again, but this time it was to mask his sudden thought that what the girl had called the *real* trial was actually now in progress.

54

Before they reached the end of the yard Daisy realized that sitting in a motor car, bumping over cobbles and potholes, was rather like sitting in a carriage bumping over cobbles and potholes – only noisier and smellier. 'All right?' Napier called over his shoulder. 'Just grand,' she assured him.

A wave of relief passed over her. Thank God this encounter had come at the very beginning of the afternoon! What a torment it would have been otherwise. And for what? She studied the back of his head, the set of his shoulders – which was all she could see of him. It was not a Napier she'd have recognized.

To be sure, no one would have worn such an outfit back in the eighties – what King Edward had mocked at as 'clothes to go rattin' in,' though even he himself now wore them down in the country. But it wasn't just the unfamiliar hacking jacket and cloth cap that made Napier so unrecognizable; it was, she realized, that she had hardly ever seen him from behind. In fact, she did not think of him in the round at all. Whenever she remembered him, which was surprisingly often for someone who had dropped out of her life more than fifteen years ago, it was always as in a portrait, either in profile or facing her.

In profile, his background was the Dublin Mountains, as she had seen him in those sly, melting glances she had loved to steal as they drove side by side along the mountainy road, her whole body glowing at the prospect or the memory of the pleasures they took there. And where was it now, all that turmoil of emotion, that passionate dedication of herself to him and him and only him? She surveyed her first love from this unfamiliar angle and delicately probed herself for some remnant of it – quite prepared to flee and deny its very existence if she found anything at all. But there was nothing.

Emboldened, she next tried to provoke herself. If no ember glowed, might there still not be one small spark beneath the ashes that she could fan to life again? She began to trawl for memories, things she might have suppressed as being too painful to carry down those years. The sun was splitting the trees as it had done so often in that summer of 'Eighty-five; the smell off the hayfields as the swathturners clattered their way up and down the sward was a powerful spur. But no twinge of those feelings remained. Honestly, she told herself, there was nothing.

It surprised her even more to find there was no remnant of her hatred for him, either. But then, perhaps the one had fed off the other, so that neither could survive the withering of its opposite.

Again she was overwhelmed with relief. This day, which had seemed to halt in dread the moment Swan let out her little trickle of poisonous surprise, was turning into one of the best ever. And yet she was woman enough to regret the necessity of her relief; she would have liked to find some small residue of those feelings, which had once seemed so eternal, so all-consuming. She wouldn't have wanted to find anything large enough to threaten her, of course – just a little warmth that could be safely cradled, to be starved or fed at whim, and let out for a romp once in a long, long while. She was Irish enough to want all things and all manner of things to be both true and possible.

'I was hiding there,' he said, 'in the stables.' He let the motor die to a tick-over on a long, gentle downhill so that he did not need to raise his voice. 'I was in a blue funk about meeting you again.'

Daisy was on the point of confessing much the same but a surge of pride prevented her. 'God, Napier, it was all so long ago,' she said instead.

He moved the gearstick into neutral and let the motor idle to a standstill. 'You're not really interested in this thing, are you,' he commented. 'Would you care for a walk?' He smiled wanly. 'Lay the ghost for good and all?'

'I ought to go and say hello to your mother. This is really very rude of me.'

He turned from her and stared out over the park. 'Remember that tree, the fallen one? That Christmas? With snow all around?'

'And me going blue in the face telling you we could live very well without a penny out of this place – and you in a blue funk about *that*, too.' Her own vehemence surprised her, coming so soon after her fruitless search for the stump of a feeling about him. She laughed to soften her outburst. 'Don't mind me, me oul' darlin'. I've had to grow hard in business. Work hard, grow hard.'

He chuckled. 'At school they always said work hard, play hard.'

'There's little time for play,' she told him. 'One day, perhaps.'

He was still staring at the tree. 'When that old oak fell,' he said, 'my mother told them to leave it. She thought it would whiten and look quite romantic.'

'And so it has.'

His finger picked out other giants, also left to rot where wind and time had felled them. 'And what of them? There comes a moment where romance shades into neglect. Incidentally, talking of trees, why did you buy that stand of pine below the villa?'

She shrugged. 'No particular reason.'

'It seemed such an odd thing to do.'

'It was on the spur of the moment. We'd haggled for weeks over the price of the joinery and we just wanted to be done with it – but not to give in, d'you see. So I suggested, "Throw in those trees and we'll shake hands on it." A kind of luckpenny, that was all.'

'You wouldn't cut them down, though, would you?'

She glanced at him with interest. 'Would you mind? You're hardly ever here.'

'I believe I might come back in the summers, you know. Paris is dreadful in August – and not much better in July, either. I thought I might open up the villa – now the old associations are . . . just history.' He smiled shyly at her. 'I'll buy them back, if you like, rather than see them cut down.'

'I won't cut them,' she promised. 'I mean *we* won't cut them.'

He eased himself from the car and opened her door to hand her down. 'A little stroll won't hurt, eh? Your man was very good to allow this. I envy him his confidence.'

A wounding comparison rose to her lips but she killed it there. In its place she committed herself to a leap in the dark: 'Didn't Swan tell you there'd be no harm in it?'

'When we met in Dublin . . .'

'No. Last night, When you met in Dublin she wouldn't have known I'd be coming here this year. Even *I* didn't know it.'

After a pause he said, 'She *told* you about last night?'

Daisy laughed, mainly to hide her triumph. 'She and I are very old friends by now, Napier, my dear.' She took his arm, partly to increase her own self-assurance that this man exercised no power over her, partly to add to his discomfiture. She felt him grow satisfactorily tense.

'Even so . . .' He let out a voiceless *whoo!* 'She's very free with her reputation. I had no idea Mercier had stayed behind in Dublin, or I assure you I wouldn't have called on her at all.'

The combination of his unease and this wholly unprovoked protestation opened up a new vista for Daisy. From Swan's earlier lies, and the way Napier had so swiftly stepped in to her rescue, she was sure that the pair of them had met last night; and Madeleine's remarks could only mean that she and Thomas had spied Napier rowing or sailing up the lake – so that fixed the place of the meeting, too. But that anything else might have occurred between them had not so much as crossed her mind until now. It was, she found, a little frightening; her mouth went dry and her heartbeat turned all weak and uneven.

However, her response to that sort of fear or threat was always some kind of attacking – or at least forward – movement, either in earnest or in jest. 'Faith, you're a wild goose for too long!' she chided. 'Have you forgotten – you can't stir a foot in Ireland without you'll be watched by a fox – and him as likely to stand on two feet as four.'

To give the poor man time to think over the implications of that, she told him the story (true, as it happened) of how she'd bought some curtain material in Dublin only two weeks earlier and the woman behind the counter had remarked that it would go well with the cushions she'd bought in Simonstown in January – and it turned out that the draper who'd sold her those cushions was that woman's brother.

Naturally, the tale only served to increase his alarm. 'I hope word of it doesn't get back to Mercier, that's all,' he said. 'He'd have every right to horsewhip me. It's not as if I'm an intimate friend of the family.'

'Only of Swan, eh?' She gave his arm a conspiratorial squeeze.

His response to that, or, rather, his lack of it, for he froze into a kind of apoplectic terror, confirmed the suspicions he had moments earlier aroused. Her own purpose achieved, she immediately started pointing him toward the numerous avenues of escape that he was too frightened to see for himself. 'Go on, Napier! You just enjoy the *idea* that you have a bit of a reputation. You're as harmless as china teeth, I'll bet. Anyway, I thought you dined with them often in Dublin. That's the impression Swan likes to give.' She laughed. 'She even asked *me* if I minded!'

'Of course she did.' Napier gladly hauled this conversational lifebelt around him. 'The last thing in the world she'd ever want to do is offend you.'

'Why didn't you ever come down here?' she asked. 'Not even to see Caro?'

His only response was a single, mirthless laugh.

'What's that mean?' she pressed him.

'You obviously recovered from it all very swiftly.'

'Perhaps because I wasn't aware I had any other choice.' She thought that, down the years, she had felt every possible emotion for this man, from the extremes of love to the depths of hate; but now she realized she was wrong. The one thing she had never felt was repugnance. But she felt it now.

He couldn't even say a conventional word of praise about their daughter! He'd put the child in her belly, deserted her – as good as – and left her with all the care and heartache of rearing the girl . . . and now he couldn't even say well done, what a grand girl she'd turned into . . . the things that would trot off *anyone's* tongue. People should be punished for being so crass.

Her anger dwindled and died. Sure, it would be like punishing a teething baby for crying. That's all he was – an emotional baby. He'd never grow tall enough to see over the ditch of his own childish feelings. Hadn't he just proved it?

'There! There!' she murmured.

He gave another single laugh. 'You're right, Venus. I behaved pretty badly. And after you left me, I was worse.'

Perhaps artists needed to remain like children? They needed to maintain that steady stream of pure, raw emotion, untinged by adult wisdom and compromise. She thought of saying as much, and then realized how patronizing it would sound. Then the further qualification occurred to her: Only an adult would think it patronizing; an artist might actually take it as a high compliment!

While she dithered between sharing and not-sharing the insight he resolved the matter by saying, 'D'you know, I *still* sometimes wonder what I'm going to do when I grow up?'

Their stroll had carried them as far as the fallen tree. By unspoken agreement they halted there and turned to face the castle. The strains of 'The Mountains of Mourne' carried to them over the rolling parkland; ladies in summer frocks and gentlemen in blazers and white flannels made startled specks of colour on the ancient and usually tranquil scene. Daisy felt a sudden intimation of the passage of time, not of the hours of this day but of the years of her life. So little done, so much yet to achieve! Was it because of his last remark? Or could it be the sudden juxtaposition of this summer scene with the snows of that long-gone Christmas, when her dreams and prospects had lain in a different life, almost in another world?

It was suddenly too cosmic for her to grasp. She gave an involuntary shiver – which, of course, he did not notice. Moments later all that remained of her intimation was the mild panic it had stirred.

'You never married,' she commented lightly.

At precisely the same moment he said, 'Didn't Caroline turn out a grand young lass!'

Laughing, she took his arm again and nudged him back toward the motor. 'Better late than never,' she commented. 'Tell me now, how does a rich and fashionable painter fight his way through the thickets of proud mamas, all eager to thrust their marriageable daughters upon him?'

'Seriously, Venus, she's a credit to you – and Mr O'Lindon, too, of course. But especially . . .'

'Yes, yes! How d'you stay out of their clutches? All those pretty young spinsters!'

'I ask to paint them nude. That stops them!'

She knew he meant it as a joke, to close the subject as swiftly as possible, yet she could not help blurting out, 'Ah! So the news has reached Paris, too!'

'What news?'

'That you *never* marry *any* girl you've painted in the nude.'

She heard her own bitterness in her mind's ear even before the words were out. She struggled to prevent them but felt powerless against the flood tide of a resentment that seemed to have come from nowhere. 'Take me back,' she said angrily. 'We should never have come out here. We've nothing to say to each other any more.'

55

Lady Lyndon-Fury pounced upon Daisy and carried her off the moment Napier set her down at the turning to the stable yard. Unlike her son she came out with all the things that would trip off anyone's tongue – how pleasant it was to see the O'Lindon family here in such force . . . what a charming young lady Caroline had proved to be . . . such a shame they'd drifted out of touch, especially living so close. She spoke as if it had all been the merest accident and utterly baffling to her.

'Well . . .' Daisy was slightly bemused. 'We haven't been entirely out of touch, you know. I see quite a lot of Madeleine. And we saw a great deal of Trapper earlier this year.'

The woman's apparent good humour vanished and her lips compressed to a thin, grim line. 'Yes,' she said. 'I hadn't forgotten.'

'Napier looks well,' Daisy went on.

'Hmmm.'

'Paris seems to suit him.'

'Ah.'

'Or the life of an artist does.'

This time there was no response at all.

'And I gather he's thriving very well, too. You must be proud of him.'

'Are you doing this deliberately?' her ladyship asked icily.

'Doing what?' Daisy asked in surprise.

'Everything in your power to provoke me, I'd say.'

'Lady Lyndon-Fury!' Daisy laughed tendentiously. 'I'm sure I have no idea what you may mean.'

'Paris suits him, does it? The life of an artist is just the ticket for him, eh? And what a small fortune he's making at it! Sure we both know what you're doing, Mrs O'Lindon. You're saying how right you were all those years ago. You were right, right, right and we were wrong, wrong, wrong.'

'I'm sorry it seems like that to you . . .' Daisy began.

'Pshaw! You're as sorry as the cat that got the cream. Why did you deign to visit us today? Did Napier write to tell you he was coming?'

Daisy's eyes raked the heavens for support – and then saw something that made her freeze with alarm. Not quite in the corner of her eye, but not so directly as to allow her to be certain of it, she thought she had glimpsed two young female heads up on the battlements. And though both had been wearing dunce caps, or long, pointed hats with bits of tulle fluttering from them in the breeze, she was fairly certain that one of them had been Caro. But the moment she turned her eyes fully upon the tower they ducked out of sight.

'Forgive me, Lady Lyndon-Fury,' she exclaimed, cutting across whatever the other was saying – to which she had not listened at all. 'I think my daughter and your granddaughter have gone for a skit and a laugh up there on the top of the tower.' She turned on her heel and stalked away, hastening to the castle keep as fast as would attract no attention.

The sour-faced footman took a step forward to interpose himself between her and the door; then he saw her face, hesitated, and decided that discretion was the more rewarding part of valour. Daisy, seeing she had won anyway, was magnanimous enough to say, as she passed him, 'My daughter and Miss Gwendolen are up on the roof of the tower.'

As she vanished indoors he scanned the battlements, saw nothing, and thanked his stars he was safely down here rather than up there with those poor girls.

The first flight of stairs up through the Georgian wing posed no difficulty; but the next, up the steeply winding circular case of the ancient tower, knocked some of the urgency out of her. She paused for breath at the next landing and came out into the passageway.

Nothing had changed. In fifteen years they had not relimed any of the walls, moved the cobwebs, smoked out the bats. Hunting people are the slovens of the universe, she thought. She had seen the inside of enough country houses by now, most of them at auction, to be sure of the verdict. 'The slovens of the universe!' she said aloud, wishing Lady Lyndon-Fury were there to hear her.

Then she realized that this was the level of Napier's old bedroom and of the room she and Madeleine had slept in. In fact, the door to his room was no more than a dozen paces to her left. Still panting slightly she walked toward it, startled by the reverberant rustling of her dress as magnified by the curved ceiling overhead. She put her hand to the latch, raised it with infinite caution, pushed the door three inches ajar – and lost her nerve. Or her curiosity. God rot the lot of them, she thought.

Leaving it ajar she turned on her heel and went back along the passage. Something still prevented her from continuing her ascent, though her wind was quite recovered by now. She opened the door at the farther end and peered into the Georgian part of the house – along the passage that had led to her bedroom. That, too, had hardly changed, though it was now furnished with three pails and a chamberpot set to catch the drips from the leaking roof. The chamberpot had a broken handle – what was vulgarly called 'a t'ummer' because you had to hold it by your thumb.

A gust of a draught came from nowhere and slammed the door behind her. A chill ran up her spine as she remembered the 'ghost' she had seen – or, rather, Napier trying to scare her. She turned and opened the door again, half expecting to find him behind it, playing the same sort of prank. But the passage was empty, of course; the same puff of wind, she noticed, had slammed his bedroom door, too.

Now she felt capable of completing the ascent.

56

'The slovens of the universe!' said a voice outside the door. Swan looked at Napier and turned pale. *Daisy!* She mimed the word plainly enough for him to lip-read. He nodded, put a finger to his lips, and held his breath. Like rabbits in a snakepit, they stood and watched the door. Napier could not have lifted a feather to save his life; Swan felt the stomach fall out of her. When the latch began to rise she had to fight an impulse to scream. She stared wildly about her for some convincing evidence that she was not really here, that this was not Napier's bedroom, that he was a mirage, that this eejit, eejit folly had not happened.

Well, to be sure, it *hadn't* happened – yet. They'd only just come into the room half a minute ago. They hadn't so much as touched each other. But for all the good *that* would do, they might as well be paradise-naked and riding the beast with two backs at full gallop, once Daisy got sight of them.

It took three centuries for the latch to rise to the top of its keep – and three more for the door to open as many inches.

Swan closed her eyes. This was what death felt like. At the very least she was going to retch, '*Ave Maria, plenia gratia* . . .' she prayed under her breath. Her fingertips tugged at her buttons for beads.

There was a rustle of a dress outside . . .

A dwindling rustle . . .

'*Oh Holy Mother, I'll never fall from grace again! Get me out of this and I'll not let him lay a finger on me!*

There was the click of a latch at the far end of the passage.

Napier danced a silent jig on the carpet – or one that would have been silent if the floor had not been so old.

'Are you mad or what?' she risked hissing at him as she went to shut the door.

He put a finger to the crook of her elbow and shook his head. Then, taking more care with the floorboards, he tiptoed to the casement and threw it open. The sudden inrush of air slammed the door; like an echo they heard the farther door slam, as well.

Swan almost collapsed with relief – until she saw him raise a cautionary finger and point toward the passageway without. A moment later she heard the distant latch open once again and all her terror rekindled. Napier, who had meanwhile crossed to his own door, put his eye to the keyhole and peered down the passage. Moments later he straightened and gave her an exhausted smile. 'Safe,' he said quietly. 'But we'd better keep our voices down.'

'Never mind voices!' She pushed past him. 'I'm going down.'

'In God's name!' He grabbed at her but she eluded him and went outside. A couple of paces down the corridor she stopped, clasped her hands behind her, and stared up at a painting: a man in a starched ruff, glowering at the world through half an inch of soot. 'Is this that ancestor you were telling me about?' she asked airily, making no attempt to keep her voice down. 'Why don't you clean him up, poor chap?' She strained her ears toward the spiral staircase but no sound came from it. Had Daisy gone beyond earshot or was she eavesdropping just out of sight?

Napier came to her side. 'We simply can't talk out here,' he whispered vehemently.

'We can and we shall,' she whispered back. 'I must have been mad.' She raised her voice. 'Let's go back downstairs. It's too murky to see anything here.'

'We can't talk about what *I* want to talk about.' His whisper was growing louder.

She rounded on him. 'I know what you want to talk about! And I can end it all in one word: *No!* Never again. That's never going to happen again.'

'It certainly is not,' he assured her in an angry hiss. 'Not if you go and blurt it out to all the world. Why did you have to tell Daisy of all people?'

She stared at him blankly, thinking it an ill-considered joke. '*Tell* Daisy?' she echoed. 'But I've done no such thing.'

'Well, she says you did.'

Swan glanced about them and then returned to his bedroom, grabbing him by the arm and dragging him with her – not that he was unwilling to go. Once inside, she shut the door and threw the bolt. 'Now say that again.'

He folded his arms and stared her full in the face. 'When I took her for a drive, not half an hour ago, she was able to tell me that I visited you last night at Omdurman Villa.'

'She was fishing! Just because of a tiny slip I made in the carriage. God, and I'll bet you blabbed it all out.'

'I did not,' he protested. 'I tried to turn it aside. I pretended I thought she was talking about when I dined with you and Mercier in Dublin, but she interrupted me and said no, no, she meant last night. And I still pretended I had no idea what she was talking about. And then she told me.'

'What?'

'That you had confessed it all to her. She said you and she are very old friends and never keep any secrets from each other. She said you'd told her we'd been intimate.'

'Napier – I simply don't believe you. She actually said that?'

He shrugged. 'Not quite in those words. But she dropped some heavy innuendo about it. I said that although I dined with you several times a year in Dublin, I wouldn't say I was intimate with you and Mercier. And she gave a dirty sort of chuckle and said just with Swan, eh? And nudged me with her elbow.'

Swan collapsed into a chair, which swayed alarmingly beneath her.

'Whoops!' he told her. 'That's just for hanging trousers on, old thing.'

She inserted a fingernail between her front teeth and gnawed at it. 'My God, Napier! I swear I didn't tell her. You'll just have to believe me. The question is, who did?' After a moment's thought she slumped her shoulders and said, 'No, that's not the question at all. Any one of two dozen people could have seen you coming up the lake – and put two and two together. Especially as it was dark when you went back. Did you have a lantern?'

He shook his head.

'There you are then. It wouldn't take much in the way of malevolence to jump to the right conclusion. And believe me, malevolence in these parts is like snuff at a wake. No – the real question is: Why should she lie about *me?* Why should she tell you *I* told her? I never did her the slightest harm.' She grinned suddenly. 'D'you think she's jealous? Yes! That's it! Napier!' She turned a gleeful smile on him. 'Our Daise is still lighting a candle for you? What d'you think of that?'

Beneath the cloak of this playful badinage she felt her heart turning to stone. Daisy O'Lindon would pay dearly for this day's work. The time and the manner of it she knew not, but she would make her pay.

57

The tower of Coolderg Castle had battlements in the Hibernian style, with two steps up and two steps down to each castellation. In the centre of each is a hole through which a lucky attacker with a well placed arrow could certainly make an unlucky defender's eyes water. No one has ever demonstrated the slightest military advantage in the arrangement but it undoubtedly gives the Irish castle a more pleasing and romantic appearance than does the stolid, gaptooth finish that is favoured elsewhere in Europe. It was a meet trysting place for two girls in love with all things medieval – as long as they did not look behind them.

The roof of the tower ought to have been a flat sheet of jointed lead over dressed flagstones, as, indeed, it had been until around 1720. But the lead had punctured over the preceding centuries and the owners of the day had done no more than their successors to keep out the rain; so the barrel-vaulted roof below had finally collapsed, killing several dozen pigeons, who were then the only inhabitants of the top-floor bedroom. It had been replaced by a modern pitched roof of timber and blue slate whose ridge was level with the sentry walkway that formed the inside base of the castellations.

This made it invisible from outside and preserved the appearance of a flat-roofed tower, but it unfortunately created a deep valley inside the east and west walls, into which those who missed their footing on the eroded walkway would inevitably fall. And to judge by the variety of patches and cracks in the slate, it was no rare occurrence. That was the danger which had led Daisy to climb the tower.

Gwendolen, standing on the east side and therefore above one of those valleys, was mindful of the uneven stone beneath her feet; she pressed herself tight against a castellation and, peeping around its upper riser, drew a longbow at the throng below.

'Who are you going to kill?' Caro asked.

'Not the fair Sir Napier,' Gwendolen promised archly.

'Ha ha! I only ask because we don't want to waste our arrows on the same target, silly.' She was secure behind the stout chimney that was disguised as the centre castellation on that same side.

'Heavens, it's Uncle Cornel,' Gwendolen exclaimed. 'We don't need to waste anything on him.' She forgot her bow and laughed. 'Can you see him? He's behind yon tent where the band is. I mean the troubadours. Are.'

'Oh yes.' Caro saw the familiar pudgy figure in a suit of white linen. 'What's he doing?'

'I'll give you one guess. Uncle Trapper said that if he'd buried a flask of whiskey every five yards along the line of the railway, Uncle Cornel would have dug the way for him single-handed. Mustn't it be terrible to have your whole life spoiled by a single need like that.'

'There's that utter varlet Billy Walshe. In front of the band. I'm certainly going to kill him. He thinks he's so clever. Him and that Simon Brennan.' She loosed off half a dozen arrows in swift succession.

'Steady the Buffs!' Gwendolen cautioned.

'They're worth every one,' Caro said darkly. 'The coxcombs!'

Gwendolen was impressed. 'Prithee, what slight have they done thee, fair damozel?' she asked.

Caro looked all about them and then, keeping below the battlements, scurried to her friend's side; there she rose and whispered the awfulness into her ear. Gwendolen laughed, blushed, bit her lip, and stared angrily at the two youths, who were wandering off toward the pig bowling, insensible of the fact that Caro's deadly aim had turned them into pincushions. 'Worse than varlets,' she said. 'They're caitiffs!'

'And just for a bet!' Caro added in disgust. 'Breege Horan told me. They did it to her, too. And Fiona Harcourt and Molly White. Just for a *bet*.' She gave out a savage sigh at that ultimate iniquity. 'Still, they'll have to bet on something else now because we're telling all the Protestant girls.'

'What about the Catholics?'

'Sure they only have the one bell, and it's an old crone who rings it who's about a hundred years old I'd think.'

Gwendolen chuckled. 'I wonder does she trick the young lads so she can see the colour of their unmentionables?'

Caro laughed so much she almost fell onto the roof. Gwendolen busied herself dispatching half a dozen more of the investing army to their Maker. 'I suppose,' she remarked casually, 'you really have more right to defend your honour here from this tower than me. I wonder is there a castle somewhere in Austria or Bohemia where *I'd* have the right?'

'We lost our right in Cromwell's time,' Caro said glumly.

'Who's Cromwell?'

Caro stared at her in astonishment; babies in Ireland learned the name with their mothers' milk.

'This is 1348, remember,' Gwendolen chided. 'Cromwell hasn't even been born yet.'

'Oh yes!' Daisy gave a skip or two of joy. 'Yes! So this is still an O'Lindon tower and I'm defending my honour here by right. Oh, no.' She slumped again. 'In 1348 this was still part of Ely O'Carroll. Oh God, isn't history a beast! I hate it! I hate it!'

'All right then.' Gwendolen tried to soothe her. 'Let's say it's 1642 or whenever Cromwell was here. And this is still the O'Lindon stronghold and we . . .'

'But that's not medieval,' Caro objected.

'It is *here*,' Gwendolen assured her. 'We're the last two fair damozels in Ireland and we're pledged to keep the torch of chivalry burning here at Coolderg or suffer death in the attempt. A fate worse than death, even – whatever that is. And those are Cromwell's Roundheads down there, raping and looting and pillaging . . . actually, what's the difference between raping and looting and pillaging?'

'Pillaging is like taking little things and looting is taking more valuable things and raping is taking the most valuable of all. That's what Sister Ignatius told Philomena Quirke, who told it to me.'

For a while they stared at the crowd, who were raping and looting and pillaging nothing more valuable than sandwiches and lemonade.

'If that was really an army of Roundheads,' Gwendolen said in a hushed voice, 'and we were really a handful here, under siege, just imagine how frightened we'd be!'

Caro nodded. 'Especially when you remember what the real Roundheads did to the O'Lindons.'

'What?'

'Did they never tell you? They pushed dozens of us to our deaths over these battlements.' She shrank against the stone as she spoke.

'God have mercy!' Gwendolen peeped over the edge. The hundred and three feet between her eyes and the flagstones below suddenly seemed a hundred and three times more terrifying than before. 'All that way!'

'It wasn't on this side,' Caro went on. 'You know where the ballroom leads into the main guard – that big stone arch? That used to be the main door to the tower, and they fell just in front of that because all that Georgian wing didn't exist then. The last ones fell on top of the ones who went before and they weren't quite dead, but Cromwell buried them all, dead or alive, in a pit of lime by the yew walk. And you can hear them screaming still. Uncle Cornel told me once when he was at Aunt Maddy's, that he was alone in the castle one night when everyone else was at the hunt ball and he'd heard them screaming like the damned in their chains.'

Gwendolen gave a snort of a laugh. 'I should think he hears something like that every night of his life.' She gave a jerk of her head toward the gap of the castellation. 'I'll look over if you will.'

Gingerly they squeezed into the same narrow space and inched their eyes toward its outer rim.

'*How I Kissed The Blarney Stone*, by Eileen D'Over,' Gwendolen said. 'I leaned over, see? That's one of Uncle Cornel's. He's always giving out stupid jokes like that. You'd want double pay to laugh at them.'

'Jesus!' Caro exclaimed in horror. 'That's my mother with your gran. Duck for Christ's sake or she'll see us!' She herself was already crouching in the lee of the stone. 'Oh God, oh God, please make it so she never saw us. If Thou wilt grant this prayer, I'll never swear again.'

After a longish pause Gwendolen risked a peep. 'She's gone,' she declared. 'Grandmama's there but your mother's gone.'

'Oh God, she saw us! She's on her way up here, I know it!'

The spiral staircase, the only means of reaching the roof, and of leaving it alive, ended in a kind of stone sentry box on the farther, south-west, corner of the tower. They raced to it as fast as their terror and the crumbling walkway permitted. They immediately threw open the door and held their breath. There was the unmistakable sound of someone ascending – someone wearing a long, swishing dress.

'She'll kill us on the spot!' Caro whimpered.

'If we stand one each side this door and tight to the wall,' Gwendolen suggested, 'she'll have to come out and turn. And whichever she sees first, the other would have a chance to escape.' Nobly she added, 'And I'll make a noise, because she won't be so hard on me.'

For an age they stood one each side of the box and waited. Then Gwendolen went again to the door and listened. 'No one,' she reported. 'It mustn't have been her, or she wasn't coming here. It was one of the maids going to the bedrooms. Wait till I slip below and see.'

Boldly she plucked up her skirts and took the steps two at a time. Caro realized she ought to follow, for if there really were nobody on the staircase, this was her chance to escape. Perhaps her only chance. Yet still she hesitated.

Then she heard Gwendolen coming back – and playing a typical Gwendolen prank, too: coming up with a measured tread, and making her skirts swish, and pretending to wheeze.

Caro stood four-square in the open door, her arms folded, a supercilious smile on her lips. When light from the slit window into the staircase cast the faint image of Gwendolen's shadow on the farthest visible step, Caro called, 'Ha ha, very funny, I don't think! Even my Mammy's not as wheezy as that!'

'I'll . . . give you . . . funny . . . when . . .' The sentence was not completed but Caro felt her insides tumble and her hair start to fall out. The voice was undoubtedly her Mammy's.

'Is it my turn to ride in Mr Lyndon-Fury's car?' she asked in a straying treble piping she hardly recognized. 'Gwendolen and me were down in the room below and we heard a monstrous fierce banging on the slates so we . . .' Her voice tailed off as her mother came into view.

She was smiling!

'It's all right, dear,' she gasped. 'God, you'd think with the number of stairs I climb at home . . . I'm ashamed.'

'You're not cross?' Caro asked, still unable to believe it.

'I was when I started out.' She force-inhaled several lungsful and then tripped lightly up the final half-winding. 'Whooo! That's better.' She turned her face to the breeze and, unbuttoning the top half of her blouse, used it as a bellows to cool herself. 'You wait till *you* get to be a hundred,' she warned.

Caro, unable to believe her good fortune, laughed immoderately – until Daisy told her it wasn't that funny. 'Well,' she went on, 'here we are at last, eh?' She squeezed past her daughter and went cautiously around the walkway, beyond the chimney, to where the girls had been standing. 'Last time I was here the fashion in dresses made this almost impossible. You wouldn't know how lucky ye are with the simple things we wear now.'

Intrigued, Caro followed in her wake. 'I didn't know you were ever up here before. When was that?'

'Oh,' Daisy said vaguely, 'before you were thought of. Before you were born. Napier Lyndon-Fury brought me up here to show me the view. In our art-student days, you know.' Her eyes strayed over the distant parkland. 'Nothing's changed except a few more trees are down – and none set to replace them, of course.' She turned and smiled at the girl to show that her next remarks were entirely jocular and not in any way to be taken seriously. 'Look long and hard at all that, Caro – at the dead limbs nobody lops, at the thistles left to blow, at the fallen oaks, bleaching and gathering moss. And here, too, about us: the cracked slates they mend with jackdaws' nests and answer with a pail below, the weeds among the chimneypots, the slime below the chutes upon the walls . . .' She faltered, aware that the banter had gone out of her tone and that bitterness had taken its place. She forced herself to laugh. 'Pay no heed to me. All I'm saying is that nothing lasts. One day even the English will be gone.'

It was such a wayward sentiment that Caro was nonplussed.

'Six generations. That's as long as they've been here,' Daisy murmured, more to herself than her daughter.

'The English?' Caro asked.

'No.' Daisy smiled fondly. Then her eye was caught by the chimney beyond. 'Did you ever look at the big stone in the base of that?' she asked. 'Come here till I show you.'

She ushered her daughter before her until they could squat one each side of the large dressed stone that formed the foundation of the chimney. Her fingers traced out the monogram Napier had shown her all those years ago. 'You'd have seen it better when the light was aslant the face of it, but there it is: *CO'L*, with the *O* to encircle it like the risen sun. Caroline O'Lindon, and the date *1689*, *Anno Domini*. How any Lyndon-Fury can sleep sound in his bed with the weight of that poised above is only a marvel, I'm sure.'

Caro stared at the great stone. The size of it! And the weight of it! *History!* she thought. She forced a small laugh and asked her mother if she were serious.

Daisy shrugged noncommittally. 'Of course not. But it's gas to think of what was and what wasn't and what might have been . . . and might be again . . .' Her voice wandered off among the moods and tenses. 'But if it's serious talk you're wanting, my lass, there *is* a thing I meant to ask you those days that went past now. There's probably a completely innocent explanation but I'd like to hear it from your own lips. Someone told me the other day they'd overheard Billy Walshe and Simon Brennan making the most outrageous boasts about several local girls; including you.' She darted a quick glance at her daughter and was surprised to see her ears turning the colour of a beetroot.

A moment later Caro was outdoing Gwendolen, with her skirts above her knees and taking the steps three at a time.

Daisy rested her face against the cool stone of the box and closed her eyes. 'Oh dear,' she said. 'Oh, my God! What on earth do we do now?'

58

Napier pushed the pride of the Renault stable to its limit on the uneven driveway and the wheel-scarred lanes around the demesne. Talk was impossible beyond the cave-man level of 'forty, by Jove!' or 'eighteen hundred rpm!' As they re-entered the park, jolting over the ruts created by the ill-hung gate, Stephen shouted, 'How slow will she go without refusing?'

Napier throttled back. 'D'you mean in bottom gear?' he asked. 'She'll go slower than an average saunter. It's called stalling, by the way, not refusing.'

'In top gear,' Stephen told him.

Napier, showing off, kept her dangerously near the speed where she might put a con-rod out through the side of the crank case. 'Slow enough to suit anybody's maiden aunt,' he commented.

'You have it there, right enough. ' Stephen nodded sagely.

Napier realized that, whatever his companion was deriving from this jaunt, it had little to do with the mindless pleasures of speed and power. 'Anything else you'd like to try?' he asked.

Stephen eyed him speculatively. 'If I could see her over the sawyer's pit behind the stables?'

Napier laughed. 'I knew it'd be something I'd never have guessed in a million years.'

'Sure, I'd like to learn what's in the making of one of these things.'

He got grease on his hat from the transmission; he tore his sleeve on a bolt holding the exhaust tube; he skinned his knuckles trying to see how much lash there was in the engine mounting; but he emerged from the pit with the germ of a new business fermenting in his brain.

Napier, who had studied him closely throughout the inspection, asked, 'Will I be pitted against an O'Lindon racer at Phoenix Park next year?'

Stephen grinned. 'A racer with O'Lindon coachwork, maybe.' His tone conceded the possibility. 'But that would be only for the advertising that's in it.'

'Rather like lending the rowing boats for today's party, in fact!'

'That sort of thing. The real business wouldn't lie in races, I'm sure. I'll tell you one great thing I've learned today: This motoring game – it's a rich man's diversion now. That you couldn't argue with. But it can't remain so.'

'Really?'

Stephen shook his head. 'There's too much utility in it. You'd sit on carpet tacks to get about the country at that speed.'

Napier sucked a dubious tooth. 'She cost the best part of two hundred, you know.'

Stephen merely grinned.

'Well,' Napier said thoughtfully, 'no one can accuse you of lacking commercial judgement, I'll say that. Here – we'd better introduce you to some soap and a needle and thread before Dai . . . Mrs O'Lindon sees you.'

Stephen glanced briefly at the top of the tower. Napier followed his gaze and asked, 'What?'

'I thought I spied her up there when we drove off, talking to Caro.'

'Really?' Napier asked sceptically. 'What a strange place to be, on an occasion like this.'

Stephen sniffed.

After a pause Napier went on, 'Isn't it odd – we've not met since . . . well, for fifteen years. Can you believe it? It doesn't seem that long.'

'It does and it doesn't,' Stephen replied.

Napier chuckled. 'There are one or two things I'd forgotten about Ireland: "It is and it isn't . . . I might and then again I mightn't . . . Whatever you think yourself, now . . ." It's a grand place for echoes, so it is.'

They wandered up through the walled garden. Neither thought it odd that the one topic that was uppermost in both their minds was the very last that either would broach – even though Daisy and Caro had just been mentioned.

'Ye had grand weather for it,' Stephen said, 'considering what ye might have been dealt instead.'

'God be praised.' Napier amused himself with his rural parody.

They came to the shed where the gardener washed his pots and greenhouse utensils; today the ladies had commandeered it for boiling the water for the tea, which was served in a tent nearby. They gave the men a small bowl, some soap, and a towel, and watched with amusement while Stephen sponged off the worst of his sins. To mend his torn sleeve he took a bit of gummed paper and stuck it down on the inside. 'Sure, a dab of the dark-blue ink on the gap and you'd never know it wasn't whole.' He surveyed the half-mend with pride.

The tea ladies exchanged glances but said nothing.

They sauntered back outside in search of the blue-black ink.

'What's next on the agenda?' Napier asked.

'Find Daisy and Caro, I suppose.'

'No, I meant the O'Lindon agenda. 'What's the next step in your unstoppable progress? Are you seriously thinking of coachbuilding for motor cars?'

Stephen scratched his head diffidently. 'I'm seriously thinking of looking into it. But then . . . I don't know what it's like in painting, but in any kind of business you have to be thinking all the time of getting out. And of sitting tight. And of expanding.'

'Getting out!' Napier echoed in surprise. 'That sounds drastic.'

'I mean getting out of one line and into another. There's a lunatic in Wexford says he can build boats in concrete. Working boats. People laugh but there used to be lunatics who said iron and steel would float. A thing like that could ruin us. You have to be ready for any sort of a change all the time, d'you see.'

'Talking of lunatics – you wouldn't be thinking of going into railways, I imagine?' Napier asked with a grin.

'By God, I would not.' They wandered through the conservatory and on into the castle. 'The banks will get their fingers burnt there,' Stephen added.

'There'll be ink of some colour in my mother's writing desk.' Napier rolled up the lid. A bottle of Stephenson's blue-black stood upon the blotter. 'Someone saw us coming,' he commented.

While Stephen dipped the pen and drew it back and forth across the gap in his 'mend,' Napier went on: 'The trouble is the banks *don't* get their fingers burnt. While the borrower still owns one string of pearls or one acre of land, they'll collar it.'

Stephen smiled, mostly to himself. 'They'll only lend you money you can prove you don't need to borrow,' he murmured. 'Daisy told me that – the same day she left – the villa.'

There was silence.

Stephen glanced up and quizzed him with his eyebrows.

Napier said, 'It worked out for the best – all things considered. It could have been a disaster.'

Stephen held up his sleeve with pride. 'If I do more, the paper will tear.'

'She has an eye like a travelling rat for business,' Napier added. 'She saw that I could live by my painting long before it dawned on me. She knew nothing about art, mind. But that's the extraordinary thing: People who are good at business don't necessarily know anything about it. They just know whether it will succeed or fail. It's magic, really.'

Stephen flapped his arm gingerly as they went back toward the conservatory, to hasten the drying without risking the gummed paper.

'When I make a painting,' Napier continued, 'the last thing I think of is whether it will sell. I paint it the way I know it *must* be. It would have driven her mad – and then she'd have driven me mad.'

Stephen smiled. 'That's another thing she's good at.'

'Ah, but you'd be a match for her. You're a match for each other – a perfect match, in fact.'

They saw Daisy herself in a temporary parting in the crowd and turned toward her. 'Listen till I tell you,' Napier said, as if their impending encounter with Daisy now forced him to come rather hurriedly to the point. 'If you *are* thinking of going into coachbuilding for motor cars, and if a bit of working capital from a very sleepy sleeping partner wouldn't come amiss . . .' He tapped the side of his nose. 'Bob's your uncle.'

'What in the name of God have you done to that sleeve?' Daisy cried out when they were still ten paces away. Her gaze shredded the gummed paper as Stephen – all injured innocence – raised his arm for inspection.

'Lord 'a mercy,' she exclaimed. 'And how did you get ink all over your shirtsleeve?' She turned to Napier – and from the smile on her face you'd think there was never a cross word between them. 'Would you ever give him the lend of one of yours, my dear? He can't walk around like that.'

'I have the very thing.' Napier turned to go. 'You stay there, old fellow. I'll go and get it.' After a pace or two he called over his shoulder, 'Then I must take young Stevie for that spin I promised him.'

'Well?' Daisy asked when he'd gone.

'I tore it on a bolt sticking out proud under his motor . . .'

'No!' She cut across his explanation. 'Never mind all that now. What were you *talking* about? Did he say anything about me? We fell out, you know, when he took me for that jaunt.'

'He said nothing as to that. It's a grand experience, driving around in a car.'

'But what did you talk *about?* My God, I'd rather break rocks for ha'pence.'

'We talked about business, mostly. Motor cars. Railways. Different ways of building boats . . .'

She gave out a strangulated gasp. 'There's a million things in this world I'll never understand – and they all either shave or they grow beards. You were gone with him nearly an hour. Did you learn nothing at all?'

'Sure I learned plenty. There was a grand old painting of . . .'

'Never mind the old paintings. Didn't he . . . ?

'Just hold your horses and listen, will you. There used to be a grand old painting of naked men hunting a boar. D'you remember it? Over the fireplace in the drawing room. You could hide a regiment behind it – a grand thing altogether.'

'I do.' Daisy smiled as the memory returned.

'Well it's gone. And there were two big silver plant pots – chiffoniers, was it they called them? Used to stand each side the oul' lady's writing desk. And they're gone, too.'

Daisy face cracked in a broad smile. 'What else?' she asked eagerly.

'I couldn't say. That was all I could name, now. But I'll tell you this for a penny: that room has a lot more of emptiness in it than when I was last there.'

She nodded with satisfaction and then asked what he'd been doing in there.

He held up his sleeve and said, 'Ink.'

'Well, I declare!' She sighed and returned to her earlier preoccupation. 'Did he not mention me at all?'

'He said you had an eye . . .' Stephen hesitated and then changed his mind. 'A good eye for a painting. Or good judgement or something. He said you realized he could live by his work long before he did.'

The news intrigued her. 'Did he sound as if he regretted it?'

Stephen laughed. 'Not a bit. He said it was the closest shave since they brought out the patent razor.'

'G'wan!' She pouted. 'Did he say anything about Caro?'

'Not a word. He said she'd turned out grand or something. Was that you and her on the top of the tower?'

She nodded glumly.

'Is it something the matter?' he asked.

Reluctantly she told him.

59

Doctor Morgan came out upon the stairhead, where four anxious eyes watched for his slightest hint. He smiled and nodded. Daisy and Stephen let out one combined gasp of relief and went back into the parlour, where the doctor soon joined them. 'Intact,' he said. 'Whatever they did, it wasn't . . . what we might have feared.'

'A drop of Bushmills, Doctor.' Stephen pressed the glass into his hand.

He supped gratefully and breathed out dragon's breath.

'Still,' Daisy sighed, 'there's no smoke without fire – and that lass's cheeks certainly caught fire when I asked her. The question is, what do we do now? If she's not been interfered with, we might do more harm than good by making a great song and dance.'

'That's the way of it right enough.' The doctor nodded solemnly and savoured his whiskey again. 'And I can't advise ye there for I'm sure there's no medical reason to prefer one course over another.'

When he had drained his glass and gone, Stephen said, 'It's not your way to let sleeping dogs lie.'

She nodded at the truth of that. 'When I was in Dublin yesterday I talked it over with my parents. And my father asked me if I remembered an incident at Killiney Spike when I was about nine. And apparently there was this man who went about there exposing himself to females and it upset me and the polis wanted me to go into court against him and my father put his foot down. He said if they'd made a great spleen about it, I might have had neurasthenia or something all my life. And the fact that I can't remember a ha'penny part of it shows he's right, doesn't it.'

'I suppose it must.' Stephen gnawed at his lip. 'Still, we can't simply leave it there. I agree we shouldn't bother Caro any more, but we'll have to have it out with those boys. They can't go about boasting the things they're boasting and no one does a thing about it. I'll have a word with Canon Lucey.'

'Sure he'll know what's to be done,' Daisy agreed. It was like wandering around for hours with some litter in your hand and at last finding a basket.

Unfortunately for the Protestants of Flaxmills, Canon Lucey only thought he knew what ought to be done. Like many a sleuth before him, he became so immersed in the crime that he quite lost touch with its context. Otherwise he'd never have gone as far as he did.

During matins the following Sunday, when the banns had been read and next week's preacher had been announced and the world had been told that the parish magazine would not now be ready until next week, he concluded with the words: 'And now – an occasion of joy in heaven, for if a lost sheep is returned to the fold, is not the Shepherd more joyful at it than at the nine-and-ninety that never strayed? And today we have not one but two lost sheep come to the altar of repentance. For the past year they have faithfully rung the bell that summons us all to our worship in this place. Even now they sit in the choir like the two cherubs we took them for. Yet, tender though they be in years, they have strayed most grievously from the paths of righteousness. Simon Brennan and Billy Walshe – stand up.'

The miserable lads not only rose in their stalls, they came down the choir and stood at the transept, immediately in front of the canon and, like him, faced the astounded congregation. His visage was serene with the knowledge that the Lord's work was here well done; they had the stunned and disbelieving gaze of creatures on the scaffold.

With episcopal aplomb the canon placed a hand on each of their heads and continued: 'It is not the practice of our church to engage in public confession – except for our General Confession, of course, which we have already made together. Yet canon law does not forbid the practice – from which fact we must conclude that there may be rare occasions when it is, precisely, called for. Verily, I believe this is one such. I have assured these two young sinners that if they will truly repent of their folly and make a clean breast of it before you all – which I do to prevent the spread of scurrilous rumours and innuendoes of a kind I know to be already current among you – then no more will be said of the matter. They will be cleansed of their impurity in the Blood of the Lamb and taken back into our fold as stainless as mortal man or woman may ever be. Begin!'

He took a hank of hair in each hand and twisted it until they winced. But he relaxed again as, in a unison whose raggedness would have made the choirmaster wince had the words been sung, they gabbled:

'We are very sorry for what we done. Did. We only did – done – it for a bet and with no deeper wickedness intended nor even thought of. We now realize how foul and shameful it was to use God's House and the summons to Divine Worship for such nef-air-ious purpose and wish the young ladies concerned to know that no personal disrespeck was intinded them.'

Simon Brennan added, 'Amen.'

Billy Walshe, the ordeal over, stared gratefully out into the sea of faces, and it suddenly dawned on him that no one out there had the faintest notion of what they had been talking about. Now that he was in good grace once more, not only with Canon Lucey but also with Your Man Above, all his cockiness returned and he improvised a helpful explanation. 'Sure 'twas only the *colours* we were after looking for, d'ye see? If they was white, I won – *w* for white and *w* for Walshe, like – and if they was blue, Brennan won.'

'Thank you, Walshe,' the canon interrupted. 'You may spare us the particulars.'

Simon Brennan thought his fellow sinner had made a hames of his supplementary explanation – leaving out the most important bit. Canon or no canon, he blurted out, 'Sure how else could we tell the colour but by sending them up on the rope?'

With weary asperity the vicar resumed his grip upon their locks and twisted them back toward the choir. The moment their backs were turned, there was a fit of apparent praying as heads bowed into hands. Hands clenched temples and pressure-bled them white. White handkerchiefs were fished from pockets and handbags to be stuffed into mouths, padded over noses, scoured around eyes. And eyes met in mute prayer for someone, anyone, to restore the solemnity that was in it no longer. And when it came to the hymn:

> Jesu, where'er Thy people meet
> There they behold Thy mercy seat . . .

it was only that Charles Edwards, the organist, had the presence of mind to pull out grand swell, tremolo, diapason, double octave and play *fff* that saved the day.

60

The stags were a brace of magnificent 14-pointers, just as Trapper had day-dreamed them when he first put the idea to Swan. He released them into the park during the week after the garden party, and they bounded away at once to the crest of the nearest ridge. The sun was just rising and a thin mist veiled the hollows and dells. The two splendid creatures stood there and gazed about them, breathing gilded steam upon the silvery air, posing as if they knew just how regal they must appear with the sun caressing their flanks and antlers.

'By Harry!' Trapper murmured in an ecstasy. Already his mind's eye could see them toppling beneath an avalanche of elkhound.

He had got some old skins from the Burdetts, from the same herd at Charleville, and for the next few weeks he drag-hunted his pack over the estate farms with the four big elkhounds. He avoided the park itself, for the stags were roaming free throughout the length and breadth of it, becoming familiar with the terrain and establishing their territory. Fellow members of the Keelity Hunt rode with Trapper on those occasions, mainly for the pleasure that was in it, for with a drag hunt you are at least sure of a good chase over ditch and field. Also, to be sure, they wished to accustom their mounts to the huge hounds, which would otherwise have thrown them into a terror on the great day.

Despite the lack of gore, they had grand sport of it, and they made a stirring spectacle – a couple of dozen well-fed gentlemen in pink and their buxom, well-fettled women, any of whom could fly a horse over any ditch in Ireland – and all streaming across the countryside in the wake of those hounds of Hell, whose sepulchral baying seemed to rise out of the very bowels of the earth. In passing, they made a goodly mess of a fair few acres of malting barley, which was then coming into the peak of its ripeness. And, as with everything else where money and the Lyndon-Furys mingled, compensation was slow to come and niggardly when it finally did arrive.

For Two-horses Flynn it was the last straw. For years he had waged a running battle with the castle over the five acres he farmed down on the shore of Lough Cool. When his father, God rest him, had bought the place back in the 1870s, the Lyndon-Furys had retained the sporting rights. It had seemed reasonable enough at the time. The five acres had formed the southern end of the demesne – a finger of land jutting out into the lough. The only sporting rights they had talked about was shooting overflying wildfowl and fishing one particular reach that was good for the trout. It never occurred to the Flynns that they'd be up before the justice for snaring rabbits on their own land – but they were, many a time, and fined five shillings for it, too.

When Trapper decided that the hounds needed training in water – for a stag might easily seek his escape across the lough – he dragged the skin down to the shore, across the narrow strip of water to Flynn's, on over his five acres, and then out into the lough proper, where he had a boatman tow a raft with an old set of antlers on it to let the hounds hunt by gaze. Two dozen riders milling about on callow land that never really dried out soon reduced it to a mire. Flynn took one look at the aftermath, put on his Sunday suit, and went directly to Crombie and Crombie, Solicitors-at-Law, in Simonstown.

It was a bombshell, for even in Ireland, where neighbours will sue for a blade of grass, a man would think twice before starting an action against the Deputy Lord Lieutenant of the county, the biggest landlord, the owner of all sporting rights for miles, the local JP, and the Lord of Lower Egypt – especially if those august personages were all one and the same man. But that is what Two-horses Flynn instructed Crombie and Crombie to do on his behalf.

At first they said he hadn't a chance, but when he told them it had been a deliberate drag hunt rather than the chance pursuit of a wild animal that had happened to cross his land, they changed their tune. It seemed highly doubtful to them that sporting rights could include the right to drag a lure across a man's land and then follow it with horse and hound.

Trapper's solicitors were of the same mind, too. Without even seeking counsel's opinion, they advised him to pay up. He offered five pounds; Flynn demanded fifty; they settled at eleven pounds, thirteen shillings, and fourpence – or what Flynn called 'a nice round sum'. He had given up social drinking in order to meet his solicitor's expected bill, so he was now able to go back to his regular fifteen pints a night; it cured the tremor in his hand and eye at once – which proved, he said, the value of good drinking to a man and the evils of abstinence. In the pleasant haze that now reclaimed his waking hours he forgot his triumph as swiftly as he squandered its proceeds.

Trapper, however, did not.

Flynn left a gate open one night, or so the constabulary concluded, and two of his cattle strayed half way to Borrisokane; they cost a guinea to get back out of pound.

Then a spark from his chimney, or so the constabulary concluded, fired his rick and consumed all his straw for that winter.

Then his best-laying goose lost a foot in a rabbit snare. It was no use Flynn protesting he never set snares. There were a couple of dozen convictions to the contrary. But he knew damn well he never set *that* snare – inside his own haggard of all places.

People told him they were sorry for his troubles but among themselves they said it just proved that you couldn't use the law against the law.

Nobody pointed out that the Lyndon-Furys weren't exactly the law.

His troubles abated as the last Saturday in September, the day of the great stag hunt, drew on and Trapper's every waking hour was devoted to the perfecting of his pack. Even the laying of metals along the line to Glenisk could not distract the mighty hunter.

'Where did he get the money from?' Daisy asked Stephen when news of it reached her – which was about seven minutes after the first consignment arrived at the railhead in Simonstown.

Like her he had no idea.

'Napier?' she speculated. 'But he told me he wouldn't put a penny into anything connected with Coolderg.'

Stephen darted a surprised glance at her. 'Did you ask him?'

She nodded. 'Why not? How else could I find out, as Simon Brennan said about the knickers? He must have got it from the bank.' But she found it hard to believe – and even harder to let be.

'Mercier's behind it personally,' she said another time. 'They wouldn't advance another farthing without he said yes. I wonder has Trapper some kind of a half-nelson on Mercier?'

Stephen pooh-poohed the idea; Mercier was as straight as the military road.

'Or Swan?' Daisy mused. She noticed he did not protest her stainlessness. 'D'you think Trapper discovered what was going on between her and Napier and threatened . . .'

He laughed at her intensity. 'We don't know anything at all was going on between those two.'

'We do. He told me.'

'Sure, men like to brag. And everyone likes to put two and two together and make a hundred. Look what we all made out of a bet on blue or white!'

'But . . . say whatever else you like about Napier, he is a gentleman, Stephen. He might brag about the conquest of a parlourmaid – and even then only to another gentleman – but not of a lady like Swan.'

Stephen turned to the window and gave a friendly nod to a passing cloud. 'Isn't it only marvellous?' he asked it. 'Let her get a sniff the Sharavogue is on the market – and she'd tell you how to build a gentleman!'

She threw an arm around him from behind and, taking him unawares, wrestled him to the ground. 'I've a half-nelson on *you*,' she whispered vehemently in his ear. 'And now you'll say you're sorry for all your mockery.'

He put on the quavering tones of a stage yokel. 'Begorrah, Mrs O'Lindon, ma'am, have mercy! Only name your price and when the banks are open tomorrow, ye'll have it in full.'

'Say you're sorry,' she insisted, giving his neck an experimental tweak.

'Lord 'a mercy! Ye'll cut the head ou'a me!'

'Say it!'

At that moment Caro walked in. She was in her riding habit. She stared down at them with lordly disdain. 'As the man said, is it a private fight or can anyone have a go?'

They straightened up with tolerant sheepishness. 'You're supposed to knock,' Daisy told her with little heat.

'I only wanted to ask if you'd cap me for the staghunt tomorrow? It's a pound. Only if you won't, I can mend my gloves and do without the new muff and take it out of my dress allowance.'

'Would you listen to the girl!' Daisy mocked, giving out exaggerated groans as she rose and dusted her dress down. 'Was there ever such nobility before? You may mend the gloves in any case,' she added more severely. 'Will Aunt Swan be there?'

'Of course she will.' Caro was astonished that the question should even arise. 'She's honorary Master of the Coolderg Elkhounds for the day and Trapper's her whipper-in.'

Daisy glanced in triumph at Stephen, as if this news proved something conclusively.

'Well?' Caro prompted.

Her father nodded amiably. 'Of course.'

'Thank you, thank you!' she skipped to him and kissed him warmly on the neck. 'Oh, and Aunt Swan says could we kindly collect Uncle Mercier from Simonstown as he's not been well lately and it would be an hour's wait for Farrell's car to bring him here. He'll be on the four-thirty.'

'And what will herself be doing then?' Daisy asked sarcastically. 'Don't bother telling me.' She looked at Stephen and shrugged. 'I suppose we'll have to.'

He gave her a provoking smile. 'I suppose *you'll* have to. But wouldn't it be a grand chance to sound him out on the commercial prospects for County Keelity in general?' He licked his lips and added, 'And harbours and railways in particular?'

61

Daisy passed him just as she left the town on her way to collect Mercier at the station. 'Mr Flynn,' she called out, reining in her rather mettlesome horse with difficulty. 'May I lighten your way for you?' He turned and stared blankly at her; she guessed he was fluthered and regretted her charity. 'Bedad, ma'am, I'll thank you. Is it Simonstown you'll be making for?'

'It is, indeed. Jump in. I can't hold this fella – he's two days in his stall.'

Flynn leaned toward the gig and let his feet catch up before he lurched into the seat beside her. 'May the saints preserve you, ma'am. You're a star.'

'You'd not have got far on those legs,' she told him drily as she unleashed the horse and gave him his head for the next furlong or so.

'Isn't that the truth now. I want you to know, you never spoke a truer word, Mrs O'Lindon, ma'am. Sure, I don't know what's come over them. They haven't the head for the porter and the malt that once they had.'

'And whose fault is that?' she asked in jesting belligerence. 'You've had the spoiling of them these forty years and more. You should never have given up for Lent.'

'Lent, is it? Sure it wasn't Lent at all. It was when I thought the lawyers would scalp me. Begod, that's a grand young gelding, so he is. Did ye get him off Miley Flanagan?'

Daisy confirmed the guess. 'Last spring. He's not an aisy man to try beating to a bargain, but I did well enough, I'm thinking. What's wrong with that mare of yours?' She realized he was not quite so drunk as his gait had made him seem. Just a bit hearty, as they say.

'Bell-the-cat has the lend of her for his harvest. I've little enough to gather since England's glory went trampling down my fields.'

Daisy thought of telling him he'd had little enough there even before that most profitable day. 'A mean lot,' she agreed lightly. 'Sure, they'd take the *turf* – let alone the bread – out of a man's mouth.'

He chuckled. 'They would. Many a true word, ma'am. Of course,' he remarked with casual boldness, 'you'd be knowing as much about them as anyone – though you weren't born in Keelity.'

'I suppose I might,' she agreed, as if she'd never bothered to consider the point. 'Ah, but they're a band with one tune. There's little enough to know about them.'

'They've ruined me,' he said lugubriously. 'And I don't mind who hears me say it.'

'Only me and the wind,' she assured him. 'Still, as the fella said, there's always someone worse off than yourself.'

'I'd like to meet them, so,' he whined. 'I'd like to shake them by the hand.'

'The ones I feel sorry for – I'm not making light of your own troubles now, you understand – but the ones I pity more are those who have their farms gashed with two lines of bright steel. For of one thing you'll be sure – they'll never see a penny piece in payment for the wayleaves they granted.'

'Isn't that the truth of it.' He sucked a sad tooth and shook his head at the dolefulness of life and the perfidy of Albion – and the general unchangeability of everything. 'I went to law against the devil – and the courthouse in hell.'

She had expected more fire from Two-horses Flynn, the only small man who ever stood up to the might of the Lyndon-Furys; perhaps that one excursion into bravery had exhausted his resilience.

'If the farm was mine, now,' she said, 'I know how I'd make sure of my payment. I could think of a hundred and one uses for bars of steel that some obliging stranger left lying around *my* land without buying my leave.'

He chuckled but his fuddled imagination wasn't up to a suggestion or two of his own. She went on to supply them: 'I saw Fergal McKee the other day. He'd burst a hole in the side of the old Charter School to keep his cattle in there. And he was casting a new lintel over the hole, using a few strands of sheep wire for the reinforcing. Faith, he might as well use embroidery thread. Wouldn't a length of leftover steel have served your man better?'

Flynn chuckled at the bravado of the suggestion.

She tightened the noose a little. 'And you yourself now. Wouldn't half a dozen lengths of scrap steel make a grand utilitarian bridge when the flooding turns your farm into an island.'

His eyes went dreamy at the thought of such a luxury. 'I've no rails on my land, though,' he pointed out.

'But Dolan has. Wouldn't he be grateful enough for the lend of your mare to share his good fortune with you?' She laughed. 'Ah, but where's the point. It's all a castle in Spain. We're not like that in Keelity. We're not a vindictive crowd, sure we aren't. We'll content ourselves with talk of retaliation but we're too soft-hearted and daycent to do a damn thing about it – pardon my French.'

'You think so, ma'am?' He appeared stung, as if he supposed she were referring specifically to him.

'I do, Mr Flynn,' she said sadly. 'The English will stay and the rails will stay.'

He was silent a while but she could see the knuckles whiten on the hand that gripped the rail before them. 'I never supposed I'd hear you speak in such terms, Mrs O'Lindon, ma'am,' he said at length.

'Because I'm a Protestant?' she asked with brutal directness. 'D'you think we're all tarred with the same brush? What was Wolfe Tone, then? He never said the Rosary in his life. Mind you,' she slipped in, 'I don't suppose I've said a word this evening that hasn't already crossed the minds of many a farmer between Simonstown and Glenisk. Or what's your opinion now?'

'Sure the whole country's only seething with it, ma'am,' he reassured her – reassuring himself privately meanwhile that he was merely anticipating his own efforts at fomenting such discontent, and only by a week or two, at that.

62

Daisy halted the gig at Simonstown station – exactly where Lady Lyndon-Fury's carriage had stood, so many years ago. The coincidence did not strike her until she gazed about herself; the memory brought a faint smile to her lips. It was late September now and the leaves on the limes were turning to russet and gold. The alternative name for lime was linden – another coincidence for you.

She wondered if she'd gone at it a bit strong with Flynn. The trouble was these country people had such an all-or-nothing attitude to life – they were either roaring drunkards or confirmed teetotallers, blasphemers or saints, bone idlers or work-to-the-boners. Your middling sort of men must all have emigrated. Still, if Dolan prised up a rail or two, and held the line to ransom, Trapper would have to get out of his hunting pink and take account of the real world for once. The wayleaves would cost him the best part of a thousand pounds but a downpayment of about half that sum would keep the farmers happy for a year or two. And hey presto! – as if by magic – there would be the O'Lindons with five-hundred and fifty in ready money with the smell of roses on it; and all they'd want in return was the freehold of Sharavogue and a fair few acres around and about.

Even now, having turned the idea over in her mind for almost two months, it still produced a slight shock to think of herself as the mistress of a fine house like that. Caro would certainly be pleased; and Daisy herself was glad she'd taken the girl into her confidence from the beginning. She wanted her trust and friendship more than anything else in the world. Sometimes it made her ache to think how much she loved that girl.

Not that she loved the other children less, mind; but it was a different sort of love. She wondered would they be surprised at her apparently abrupt change of mind about living in a grand place like Sharavogue? Probably not. It had always astonished her to see how readily children accepted almost any large decision their parents made on their behalf. They would brawl like divils over some minor command like, 'You'll wear that blue ribbon or you won't go out at all.' But tell them, 'We're moving to Scotland tomorrow,' and all they'd say was, 'Will we take the cats and the dog with us, too?'

The fact that she herself had once exhibited the same unquestioning acceptance hardly helped her to understand it in her children. Just look at the way she'd got on the train for Simonstown that fateful day, full of high spirits at the thought of becoming a maid to a 'real lady' – who had turned out to be Madeleine of all people! If she'd had one small pick of common sense, she'd have laughed her mother out of Ireland at the very idea. But then look what would have happened to her. She'd have stayed in Dublin and done the sensible thing. She'd have married a civil servant or a bank clerk and lived all year for the garden party at the viceregal lodge. She'd have given little suppers for Castle Catholics and all the other petty hangers-on. And she'd have wasted her life darning socks and turning the sheets sides-to-middle. So perhaps there was some hidden purpose in it all. And children should go on accepting their parents' larger decisions in the same unquestioning spirit, no matter how absurd, because who could tell where it might lead.

Actually, she reflected, moving to Sharavogue was not a simple matter of carrying their furniture another half mile up the hill. It was the start of a move into a different sort of world altogether – the ambiguous world of the landlord, the Anglo-Irish, and the full-blooded West Briton. It was going to be like riding three horses at once.

In fact, through her various committees and charities, she'd been making tentative steps in that direction for weeks now. It had begun at a charity concert at Belivor Castle, back in the summer, when she'd met Eve Bassington. It wasn't anything the woman said so much as her whole attitude. Daisy knew no more about the Irish upper classes than she had been able to glean from novels. She thought of them as essentially English but with a sort of soft spot for Ireland. Yet there was Mrs Bassington, talking to her, Daisy, without a trace of condescension, seeking her opinion on this and that – and listening as if the answer were important to her.

And then Miss Sheridan had squeezed herself apologetically between them and listened avidly, too. Miss Sheridan was from an old Keelity family but her branch of it had lived in England for the past hundred years and become thoroughly anglicized; she had lately taken a house at Killaloe, at the foot of Lough Derg, and was 'rediscovering her family's roots' with a thoroughness that could only be called Anglo-Saxon. Napier said she'd come to Ireland in order to write something misty and Celtic. In accents that would have blended well into a Surrey garden (but nowhere else), she had declared that what was so *mahv'lous* about Ireland was 'the delightful eopenness of lended socahty heah!' What she meant, of course, was that people like Eve Bassington would both entertain and listen to people like Daisy O'Lindon.

Daisy, who until then would have put the Bassingtons and the Sheridans in the same camp, saw Eve Bassington glaring at Miss Sheridan with ill-disguised venom. At that moment it had dawned on her that Anglo-Irish society did *not* conform to the English pattren at all.

She began to regret her wilful refusal to take up the occasional invitations that had come her way. And that regret, in turn, had led to Sharavogue, so modestly grand, so quietly elegant on its commanding eminence above the town. For how could she take up invitations unless she could return them? And how could she return them without a place like that?

Her mind skated idly over these and other recent developments as she waited for the train from Roscrea. At last it came rattling up the Cut and braked with a screech just inches from the buffer, where it stood in clouds of steam that hung about the platform, refusing to dissipate in the dank autumnal air.

By coincidence Mercier's compartment came to a halt directly opposite her. She expected him to be leaning out of the window, looking up and down the platform for Swan; he always said that no matter how tired he was, the ride up the branch line to Simonstown would put fresh heart into any man. Today, however, it seemed that the magic had not worked. He just sat there with his head bowed, pinching the bridge of his nose between finger and thumb and rubbing it with mechanical tenderness.

He can't be praying, she thought as she yoo-hooed and waved to catch his attention.

The moment he saw her he took a grip on his fatigue and sprang down upon the platform. He was carrying nothing but an attaché case, a heavy overcoat, and a long Trinity scarf, which he wrapped around him before it could trip him up. Waving back to her – including an extra one to show how delighted he was – he clamped the case awkwardly between his knees while he shrugged himself into his overcoat. He seemed to think this required some explanation when he at last joined her in the station approach. 'Now they can conduct the heat of the steam into the carriages,' he said, 'they've gone mad altogether. I couldn't turn the regulator down at all. Nothing the matter with Swan, I hope?'

'She's gone hunting mad,' Daisy told him.

'But nothing *new*?' He grinned dourly. Some of his energy deserted him as soon as he was seated beside her. 'God, but I'm tired, Daise. This has been one almighty week, I want to tell you.'

'But you still have them bet?' she teased. 'They haven't found you out yet?' She clucked the horse into life; the outward ride had settled the fella and his start was smooth.

'They weren't too pleased about . . . well, some of my decisions,' he admitted. Then, no doubt feeling that this cast him in altogether too dubious a light, he added, '*One* of my decisions, actually.'

'The man who never made a mistake never made anything,' she assured him. 'Is it a matter of opinion or a matter of time?'

'Dear God!' He chuckled and shook his head. 'You can always put your finger on the wart! It's a matter of time, since you ask.' After a pause he added, 'And soon.' After a further pause. 'I don't see any reason why I shouldn't tell you. It was my decision to renew Trapper's bill at six months. Is the railway truly going to open next week? Lord, I hope so!'

'Oh it will indeed,' she assured him stoutly. 'Every last bolt is tightened and the inspector's hammer has rung the whole Hallelujah Chorus out of it. There's nothing to stop him now only the stag hunt this Saturday – tomorrow, that is.'

'That's what worried my directors most, you know. I shouldn't have told them. I should have said they were still waiting for a split pea for the guard's whistle to come from England or something. They'd have believed *that*! But what they couldn't swallow was that a man should bankrupt himself . . .' He paused, laughed awkwardly, and added, 'Well, in a manner of speaking – you know what I mean. They couldn't understand that a man would pour so much of his available wealth into such a venture and then put off the opening of it in order to hunt a stag!'

'Isn't there a hunting man among them?' she asked. 'Do they live in Ireland at all, at all?'

Her ebullience seemed to renew his spirit for he brightened and said, 'Perhaps they may one day appreciate there are some things about our country ways that are quite beyond them.'

' "Our" country ways?' Daisy echoed. 'You feel you're a County Keelity man now, eh?'

'It's where I wish to be buried – in the fullness of time, pray God.' He stared about them in the gathering twilight and smiled with approval at the passing countryside.

Daisy, following his eye, said, 'O'Lindon Country.'

He chuckled. 'The once-and-*future* O'Lindon Country, you might say. I hear the present bearers of that ancient cognomen are beginning to "go about"?'

'The lighter the news, the faster it spreads. How did it get to you?'

'Eve Bassington is a cousin of one of our directors.'

Daisy realized that Stephen's name must have come up in conversation at the bank – and at a fairly high level, too; she would dearly have loved to know the context.

'How d'you find her?' Mercier went on.

Daisy described the incident with Miss Sheridan and her later meeting at Macken's Hôtel. 'I'm used to Catholics lumping all us Protestants in with the Anglo-Irish,' she said, 'though I don't suppose there are too many in Flaxmills who'd think that way now. But aren't I just as bad – lumping all the Anglo-Irish in with the West Brits?'

He stared at her in surprise. She asked why.

'I thought your interest in politics began and ended with the Boer War.'

'Sure one thing leads to another,' she told him. Then, after a silence, she added, 'No, it goes deeper than that. When I was young and foolish, I used to despise all those merchants and tradespeople who dabbled in politics. They just want their snout in the trough, I thought.'

'And weren't you right?'

'Yes and no. I resisted all that myself. I wasn't going to let our success go rushing to our heads. No armies of servants and gold plate and fine carriages and such.'

'Well, you certainly managed . . .'

'No but wait till I tell you. It doesn't work in the end. You can only hold out so long. There comes a point where it's downright irresponsible – to our children, to our workers, to our*selves* even – to stay aloof from . . . the way the world works.'

'Aha.'

'I don't like it, though,' she went on vehemently. 'Don't ever tell Stephen this because I don't think he'd understand and it would hurt him. And anyway, I don't mean it the way it sounds. But when Napier and I were engaged I kept urging him to give up his allowance and stand or fall by his art. Live by it, and damn the poverty! I wouldn't have cared how poor we were. I'd have gone out and scrubbed floors. I'd have scraped up the soap off the launching ramps in the shipyards. I'd have scoured the markets at eleven each night for the scrag ends . . .'

'You had it all planned.'

'I have it all planned *still*, Mercier. The foolish, headstrong colleen who couldn't wait to shrug the yoke of the Lyndon-Furys off our backs never died.' She tapped her breastbone. 'I contend with her in here every day of my life. There was an excitement about those days that has gone from me. But where? That's what I can't understand.'

'It's called "getting old".'

She gave a single, dry laugh. 'That's another thing I was never going to do.'

He chuckled. 'You speak as if there are no compensations.'

'Compensations!' She snorted. 'I'll tell you what compensation is. If you see a man with one short leg, you'll notice the other is always a bit longer. That's by way of compensation!'

'Dear me! And I supposed *I* was the one with the black dog on my back. I spent most of the journey down wondering why we bother to go on at all, but you've quite cheered me up.'

She recalled that she herself had said to Flynn – not two hours ago, and almost at this very point along the road – that there was always someone worse off than oneself. She laughed and said, 'There you are, then!' After a while she added, 'Don't be thinking I still wish to run off with Napier now. That wasn't my point at all. It was the utter simplicity of that way of life, you see. That's what I meant.'

'What about the Lyndon-Furys then?' he asked casually.

'What d'you mean, "what about them"?'

'You once told Swan . . .'

Knowing what he was going to say, Daisy interrupted: 'That's another part of growing up. Sure I bear them no grudge at all now. Live and let live, I say. The way it's all turned out – wasn't it for the best in the end?'

He shrugged noncommittally. 'The "end" is not yet known to us. Still, as the family's principal banker, I'm relieved to hear it. You and Stephen are reaching a position where you could make life pretty uncomfortable for them if you chose.'

His frankness, which was so uncharacteristic of him, astounded her. Did it mean that the Lyndon-Furys' affairs were far worse than even gossip presumed? She realized he might retreat into his customary diplomatic shell if she pressed him directly, so she trailed a small red herring instead. 'Her ladyship has no time for me at all,' she told him. 'I can't think why. I never did her the slightest harm. But when we met at the garden party she ate me a mile off – up and down the banks.'

He absorbed the comment in silence.

'Can you think why?' she asked. 'Has she ever said anything to you?'

His answer came with customary reluctance. 'I don't think she took too kindly to your naming Caro, Caroline. It seemed to her like . . .' He hesitated.

'A declaration of war?' Daisy suggested.

'No. I was going to say "an impertinence," actually.'

He saw Daisy's knuckles straining the fine leather of her gloves. He could feel the anger radiating from her. And 'black dog' resettled upon his spirit; for, though she spoke not a word, she nonetheless answered the question he had wished to ask her for years past – ever since he'd known her, in fact. All her protestations that she bore no grudge and would live and let live were as nothing when set beside that simple visceral reaction.

His despondency was as much for Daisy as for himself and his bank's considerable investment in the Lyndon-Fury estate. She was such an extraordinary young woman – so gifted, passionate, deep, devious . . . And yet she was so utterly unaware of the power of those gifts, and the true nature of those passions. Could she not see that they might easily conspire to destroy her?

63

The sun was well up by the time the Coolderg Elkhounds, a one-day, bobbery pack under their master, Mrs Mercier, took to the field. It was Saturday, the 28th of September 1901 – a day none of them was likely ever to forget. Excitement was high as they trotted down the drive from the stables to the front of the castle; the hounds, sensing that something more than the usual drag was afoot, whimpered continually and gave vent to an occasional howl that hinted at an intolerable rapture. At the castle itself they had to pause for the photographer from the *Keelity Vindicator* to expose his plates, which took no more than ten minutes, though it seemed a lifetime. An officious little man with a cork foot, he bustled round like a pendulum that had lost its clock, blowing a referee's whistle and wondering why the hounds merely stared at him for a couple of seconds and then went on with whatever they were doing before. Only Trapper with his whip was able to move them – more or less – to where they were wanted.

But at last the stirrup cups were quaffed, the exposed plates resheathed and stacked back in their tin box, and Swan, with an inquiring lift of the eyebrow at her whipper-in, led the way down over the haha and into the park.

The hunt had put Daisy in a quandary. Wild elkhounds would not have driven her onto the actual greensward of the Coolderg demesne, but the chase would be a spectacle the country would talk about for years, so nothing would keep her from observing it, either. She decided to sit in her carriage just outside the eastern wall, where the home-farm gate would give a view of most of the central portion of the park. There the music of the hounds would tell her whether to drive round to the northern end, near the Coutts's cottage and Glenisk, or southward to the villa and Two-horses Flynn's few acres, for a closer view. She wanted Stephen to come with her but he was to meet her father in Dublin to discuss the purchase of the freehold on the japanning works, where Stephen wanted to site the coach-building enterprise – or perhaps another joinery; he still hadn't made up his mind on that. At any rate, he told her with martyred dedication that he had no time for such frivolity as the stag hunt – and she told him with equally martyred devotion that she'd come to Dublin with him 'if he liked'.

Smiling at the memory, she sat in lonely state by the Coolderg home farm and waited for sight or sound of the hunt.

Augusta Lyndon-Fury was out that morning, too. Her lumbago had prevented her from riding for some years past. But, like Daisy – though she would have detested the comparison – nothing would keep her from today's grand spectacle. She followed as closely as she could in a light governess cart drawn by a frisky little pony, which at least gave her the freedom of the rabbit-cropped turf and the grass that had been cut for hay; a heavier carriage would have confined her to the main drive and the back lane to Madeleine's cottage.

The going was soft and she followed the hunt a little to one side, to avoid the poached ground in the immediate wake of the field. Even so her little cart rattled like a kettledrum as she strove to keep up. At every knoll she reined in to enjoy the scene in tranquility. What a noble sight they made, trotting over the park in the crisp September sun! The only thing that marred it was the inclusion of the wretched O'Lindon girl. Caroline, indeed! Her blood seethed every time she thought of it.

Caro almost came to grief at their first canter. She was so busy surveying the distant slopes that she missed a fallen tree, well camouflaged by moss and the last white beards of unchecked thistle. Her cob Sukey, who had carried a succession of incompetent drunks in his time, was well used to fending for himself and making his own decisions about when to jump and when to go round; he almost threw Caro off at this first 'fence,' which was fortunately no more than two feet high at that point. With a superhuman thrust at her stirrup, which caused the tendon in her knee to crack audibly, she regained her seat just before Sukey gathered himself on landing; so she was ready for the rebound, if only just.

'Well ridden, young miss,' Marcus Talbot cried appreciatively, and there were other grunts of approval, too.

Caro gave him a grateful smile and threatened herself with all sorts of horrors if she wasn't more careful in future.

'I've seen them up there near St John's graveyard a time or two, around this hour of the day.' Trapper pointed his whip in the general direction. 'It's as good a place as any to draw first.'

'We'll make for it, so,' Swan agreed. She put the horn to her lips and winded it – something she had been practising for weeks past.

Trapper cracked his whip and the hounds came to heel seeking their new direction from him.

64

The baying of the hounds was all the signal they needed. 'Right, lads,' cried Bell-the-cat Dolan. 'Lift her good and aisy. We'd not wish to be damaging private property, now, would we!' A great guffaw of laughter greeted this suggestion as a dozen backs bent to the task. Six picks, four nailbars, and two crows prised up the first rail of the day. Two-horses Flynn was already unscrewing the bolts on the fishplate that secured its mate.

'By Christ but there's weight in that!' Podge McManus cried out when they came to lift it down the slight embankment to the waiting horse. 'She'll never carry two of these.'

'Sure, she'll only have to drag it,' Dolan explained. 'And it's not above a mile she has to go.'

'But look at the country, man,' Seamus McGee put in. 'She'll be in it to her hocks before she's gone a quarter the distance.'

'Going the distance, is it?' Flynn asked scornfully, for the mare was his. 'I want to tell ye – she'd fly the Grand National itself with those two rails for ballast.'

But when they had both rails secured to the adapted harness and saw how it creaked and sagged, every man there knew the creature wouldn't go ten paces dragging such a weight. 'Holy Mary,' cried Declan Martin. 'Who'd'a thought such handicap could be got into two bars of iron?'

'Anyone would who helped lay the line,' Tom Byrne commented.

They all turned to him. 'And was it yourself was in that gang?' several of them asked.

He said it was.

They asked why he hadn't sung out before and he replied that no one had asked him and if they'd been in their fields like Christians instead of popping Guinness corks in Doyle's bar, they'd have seen him plain enough.

They considered that point too irrelevant to require an answer, but they asked him how the rail had been carried to where it was needed.

'It's only amazing,' he assured them. 'For the minute a pair of rails is in place – and never mind minute – the very *second* the rail is set down and bolted tight, you may push a truck along it with one hand. And if the truck has more rail on board, you make take that down and extend the line further.' He added that before any of them would see the bottom of his glass, the line would be a mile off.

It began to dawn on them that there was more to stealing a railway line than twelve broad shoulders and one good mare. Tom Byrne then informed them that the truck which had carried these very rails was in a siding at Flaxmills Road, not three miles distant.

They brought the rails back to the top of the embankment, hobbled the mare to graze, and set off for Kelleher's Bar – which is what Flaxmills Road was called before the coming of the railway.

65

The first stag caught the scent of the hounds shortly after they left the castle grounds, for the breeze was off the lough and he was in the northeast corner of the demesne, a couple of miles away; the scent he caught was what they had emitted on leaving the stables, of course.

For the moment he was not especially worried. He had scented and heard them for weeks past and they had always gone off in some other direction. He was even blasé enough to trot a little distance upwind, to the ridge of the intervening hill, to see what might be happening today. But there was nothing in sight.

He grazed for a while and then ambled still farther upwind, moving steadily downhill from the eastern wall of the demesne, against which he might otherwise be trapped. He could hear them now, not continuously, but the occasional eldritch howl of excitement and the even more occasional winding of the horn.

So today *was* different. On all previous occasions their racket steadily dwindled away to silence; but this morning it was growing louder by the minute. Now he began to feel the first stirrings of alarm. His tail twitched nervously and his head went up high.

Caro it was who saw him. 'View!' she shouted in high excitement. 'View hulloo!'

'Where away?' called Trapper, but her outheld crop answered him at once. He spurred his horse to pass out the hounds and turn them onto the new line of their quarry.

The scent was so fresh they were reluctant to be lifted but he managed it at last. By then the stag was crashing out through the far side of the poplars and racing back downwind as fast as his leaps would carry him. Trapper brought the pack round the copse, where they picked up the even fresher scent at once, setting up an excited baying as they set off in hot pursuit. The humans hung back a second or two, awestruck at the incredible beauty of the stag as he sprang away up the distant slope. Then they, too, were after him in full cry.

Lady Lyndon-Fury reached the hilltop at last and saw that the country before her was impossible even to her light equipage. However, she also saw that the stag was heading for the eastern wall, so she turned about and made for the lane up to the home farm. From there a narrow track ran along the hillside just inside the boundary wall, leading to the graveyard; from anywhere along it she would have a splendid view of all that happened. She flicked her whip at the pony and got him up to a sprightly pace.

'He's making for the old graveyard,' cried Trapper. 'Clever beast.'

'Why?' Swan asked.

He jerked his head back toward the rest of the hunt. 'Can you imagine this lot milling around among the gravestones there?'

The moment Daisy saw the line the stag was taking, she set off from the home farm, going northward to try and intercept it at the Lyndon-Fury graveyard; she was halfway there before Lady Lyndon-Fury came within view of the home farm, so neither woman had any idea how near the other was.

Even without the ruined chapel and the rusted iron gate Daisy would have known where the graveyard lay. The capstones at that point were flat and dressed smooth, sloping a few degrees toward the outer road, whereas everywhere else the wall was crowned with random rubble laid on edge. As soon as she arrived there, she eased her carriage down over the bank at the roadside and drew in under the trees at its fringe. It took a bit of doing but at last she got the wheel of it within an inch or so of the wall, so that she might use its mudguard as a vantage from which to peep over. *God, Stephen'll wring my neck*, she thought when she saw how her weight bore down its elegant curve; but the excitement of the day put her conscience on the long finger.

She had arrived not a moment too soon. As she raised her head gently above the capstone, feeling like a sniper spying over his parapet, she saw the stag not fifty yards away, just beyond the graveyard railings. Fortunately, he had his back turned to her at that moment and was peering anxiously down the slope for a sight of the hunt, which was now in full cry, just beyond the ridge. Daisy wedged one foot between a couple of stones, to relieve her weight on the mudguard, and settled to watch the fun; never for one moment had she imagined she might come as close to the kill as this – for the creature would certainly be trapped here if he dithered much longer.

The stag obviously heard something to Daisy's left, back in the direction of the home farm. Taking care not to move her head, she swivelled her eyes as far as she could in that same direction and saw, to her annoyance, that Lady Lyndon-Fury was driving a ridiculous little governess cart as fast as it would go up the track toward them. She wanted to shriek at the woman, to tell her she was about to spoil everything.

The stag, taking fright, leaped the railings into the graveyard and then, casting wildly about, saw the large, flat-topped tomb that marked the grave of Hugh Lyndon-Fury. It was less than ten paces from where Daisy stood and just a yard from the wall. It was also far too high for any stag to reach in a single bound, unless driven to it by fear of imminent death – as this particular monarch of Coolderg now proved. She heard him grunt in what sounded curiously like surprise as he achieved the lichen-slippery roof of the monument. There he paused a fraction of a second to gather himself for a further leap onto the boundary wall itself.

In that fraction of a second, between the spindly gracefulness of his legs, Daisy saw Lady Lyndon-Fury's pony rear in surprise, turn on a sixpence, and bolt off down the hill. Slowly, as in a dream, the dark shape of her ladyship's body fell in its wake, hit the ground, and lay still.

'Mercy!' Daisy cried aloud.

The stag darted a startled glance her way but was already committed to the second stage of his leap. From the flat top of the wall, and with no check in his momentum, he launched himself horizontally forward between two of the trees and landed near the top of the bank that levelled the road. A further bound brought him to the opposite ditch and from there he was away like the ghost of a cat, across the pasture, up the hill, until he was lost in the wilderness of the Slieve Derg mountains.

Reluctantly Daisy turned her eyes from him to see whether Lady Lyndon-Fury was stirring again. But the dark shape in the long grass lay ominously still.

She surveyed the wall, wondering could she take the path of the stag in reverse; but the overhang on the monument was too wide and the drop too great to allow it. She leaped down into the soft leafmould beneath the trees and ran back to the rusted gate by the roofless chapel. It was narrow and low; a tall, broad-shouldered man would have to stoop and go through sideways. A small boy, by contrast, could easily have got over between the top of the gate and the vault of the arch. But for Daisy there was no way through. It was locked, and probably had been so for decades to judge by the rust on its hinges. She grasped it firmly and shook it in her frustration.

A large flake of rust bounced off her glove and shattered on the stone at her feet. She gave it another hard shake, experimental this time. More rust fell, now on the inside. The withered pin of the upper hinge, which had originally been mortared between two large, dressed stones in the jamb of the arch, moved easily in its decayed socket. She took a new grip on the gate, with her hands as near that hinge as possible, and shook it with all her might.

It proved absurdly easy. As soon as the rusted pin had a quarter of an inch of play, the weight of her onslaught snapped it in two – so that she almost pulled the whole thing outward and on top of her. As it was, she yanked it far enough, once the top hinge broke, to free the latch. Then the wrecked gate swung awkwardly on its lower hinge and let her in.

She ran at once to where her ladyship lay. By now the hunt was in view, half a mile down the slope. The four hounds were less than a furlong away.

At least the woman was breathing, Daisy noted with relief; and there was no sign of blood, nor had she fallen in an unnaturally twisted position. Indeed, she looked for all the world as if she had simply decided to lie down and take a nap. Gingerly Daisy pinched her cheeks and started calling her name.

She glanced up to see how near the others were. The pony had halted a hundred yards away and now stood, between the shafts still, with a kind of guilty, sheepish look on its face, tossing its head every so often. The hounds rioted off their line and milled around the two women, filling the air with the stink of their throats and saliva. It was Favour's lick that first roused Lady Lyndon-Fury. The others joined in.

'Go 'way! G'wan outa that!' Daisy shooed them off furiously.

They licked her too, with their impartial devotion – until Trapper's voice recalled them to their purpose, whereupon they slunk off in search of the abandoned line.

'Try not to move,' Daisy told her ladyship. 'You took a tumble, that's all.'

'You!' The woman's voice was a phlegm-laden wheeze.

'Trapper'll be here in a shake. He'll tend to you.'

Lady Lyndon-Fury struggled to sit up but a pain somewhere in her body made her cry out in agony. 'What have you done to me?' she yelled.

Trapper arrived at that moment, leaping out of the saddle even before his horse could halt. 'Mama!' He ran the last two paces and fell to his knees at her side.

'The stag lepped onto that big tomb and then cleared the wall,' Daisy told him. 'The pony took shy and bolted. It frightened me out of a year's growth, too.'

Trapper nodded as he put rough knuckles to his mother's brow. 'Are you hurt at all?' he asked. 'Can you feel your toes?'

'What's *she* doing here?' was the only reply. 'Wasn't the daughter enough to bear?'

Daisy rose and started to walk away, but Trapper called after her, 'Mrs O'Lindon, don't mind her. I'd be glad if you'd stay.' His eye took in the broken gate and he added, 'Have you your carriage nearby?'

'Beyond,' she told him. 'I'll stay of course.'

He nodded and turned back to his mother.

The rest of the hunt had meanwhile come to a respectful halt a hundred yards or so away – except for one of the riders, who went to collect the pony and cart and bring them back to the track. Caro spurred forward to join her mother. Daisy reached up and gave her a pat on the knee. 'You've lost your first stag, I'm afraid, darling. He's in Tipperary by now.'

'What happened to her ladyship?' the girl asked.

'Nothing. Just winded, I think.' Daisy saw the cart lurch as it was dragged back up the slope. 'And she's broken a wheel by the look of it. I suppose I'll have to take her back to the castle.' She sighed at the prospect.

Trapper had meanwhile established that his mother could move both feet and all her fingers; the woman herself swore she was suffering nothing more than pins and needles. The moment he had helped her to rise she slapped his hands away and said she was perfectly capable of walking unaided. 'And would you take those hounds and go on after the other fellow or you'll lose him, too,' she snapped. 'Where's my cart?'

'It's broken,' he told her. 'You're going back with Mrs O'Lindon.'

'I will not! And would you take your hands off me! Send for another carriage and be off with you. What are all those people gawping at? Send them away!'

' 'Twould take half an hour to get another carriage here. Look at you! You're shivering to death.'

'I will not go with that woman.' She stood her ground and stared angrily at her son.

'Just go, Trapper,' Daisy told him. 'I'll manage her well enough.'

The woman rounded on her. 'Don't you *dare* tell my son what to do. Manage *me* indeed!'

'Go on!' Daisy ignored her. 'She'll sing this tune as long as you're here. Send someone for the doctor now and I'll get word to you when we're back at the castle.'

'Trapper?' his mother began to plead.

He looked uncertainly from one to the other.

'It's the only way,' Daisy said.

Reluctantly he nodded and turned his horse back toward the hunt.

'Trapper?' his mother wailed.

'Will I stay and help?' Caro asked.

'Bless you, darling, no,' Daisy replied. 'You go on and get your money's-worth.'

'Traitor!' Lady Lyndon-Fury called after her retreating son. A moment later she was alone with the woman she hated most in all the world.

66

For a while they stood in silence, three or four paces apart, watching the hunt retrace its steps down the hill. 'Now you have an audience of one,' Daisy said quietly. 'Will you come and let me bring you home?'

'I'll die first,' she replied, but that cutting edge of absolute assurance had gone out of her voice.

'I suppose you think that's an unlikely event,' Daisy said.

'What d'you mean?' The woman's glance was an odd mixture of anger and anxiety.

'It's my belief you've broken something and you're too stubborn to admit it.'

'I have not!' she declared with all her former vigour.

'Prove it, then. Show me you can walk.'

'Don't you come near me!'

'Show me then and I won't.'

Daisy knew she had won when the woman's first steps were in the direction of the broken gate; but she also knew she was right when she saw the pain in her expression. Lady Lyndon-Fury had something more serious than pins and needles.

Daisy went ahead of her and pushed the gate as wide open as it would go. The woman's face as she hobbled through the gap was beaded with perspiration.

'Dear God!' Daisy shouted angrily. 'If you aren't the stubbornest old she-goat in all the world! Would you put your arm around my shoulder now and let me support you!'

All the fight seemed to have gone out of her ladyship. She leaned against the wall and panted, 'Would you ever bring the carriage here to me? I do seem to feel a little twinge in my hip.'

'I would if I could,' Daisy assured her in a gentler tone. 'But look at the ruts – not to mention that low branch. Put your arm round my shoulder now. Which side does it pain you?'

She patted her left hip, the one against the wall. Daisy went behind her and squeezed in on that side, getting her head under the woman's arm. 'Now!' she said jovially. 'Pretend I'm Mary Queen of Scots and you're taking me to execution. Wouldn't that put some spring in your stride?'

Her ladyship gave a sour laugh. 'You needn't think you . . .' she began but the pain overcame her as they moved off.

'I don't like this one bit more than you do,' Daisy told her.

'If you . . . really think I'd die . . . out here,' the other grunted between spasms of agony, 'why don't you leave me? Isn't it just . . . what you . . . want?'

'What a disgraceful thing to say!' Daisy exploded. 'If you were a child of mine, I'd fill your mouth with soapflakes for that, so I would.'

'It's true though, isn't it.'

'It is not! Lord a'mighty! What ever makes you think that of me?'

Lady Lyndon-Fury said nothing and Daisy did not press the question. They grunted and swayed their way to the carriage, where, with no small difficulty and a great deal more pain, she got the woman into the seat.

'Would you lie down?' Daisy asked her.

'No, I'd be sick. If I had a cushion here, I could half-lean . . . yes, like that.'

Fortunately, Daisy had brought a good supply of warm rugs and she soon had the invalid as snug as possible in the circumstances. To be near at hand in case she were needed Daisy drove from the well of the carriage, standing up and controlling her horse as much by calls as with the reins. Lady Lyndon-Fury, her eyes hooded with the torment from her hip, watched her with a kind of grudging admiration as she sought a gentle passage back onto the highway and, once there, steered adroitly around the worst of the potholes.

'Of course,' she sneered, 'it wouldn't suit you at all, would it.'

Daisy made no reply.

'To have me just drop down and die out here. No, that wouldn't do.'

'You're just a silly woman,' Daisy told her calmly. 'I wish you could hear what an eejit you sound.'

'I saw it in your eyes the very first time we met, when I turned you off at Simonstown.'

'That was never you! I felt some respect for the woman who did that. So it couldn't have been you.'

'Oh, you're so clever with the words, aren't you, Mrs O'Lindon! But you don't deceive me. I know what you've been wanting, ever since that day.'

'If I cross your palm with silver, will you tell me?' Daisy almost laughed out loud, it was so absurd. Why did she bother to answer the woman at all? Only because that one would take silence for admission.

'The ruin of our family.'

Daisy raised her face to the heavens and laughed. 'The ruin of your family!' she echoed scornfully. 'Lady Lyndon-Fury, *dear* Lady Lyndon-Fury, I would no more plot the ruin of your family than I'd send the birds to bring me rain from the clouds - and for the very same reason. Lord, you people do give yourself airs!'

'Methinks the lady doth protest too much,' the other said drily.

Daisy shook her head sadly. 'You really do imagine you're important enough for me to waste my life away on such plottings and machinations. You can't be right in the head - that's all I can suppose.'

'I pity your husband.'

'Snap,' Daisy said blithely.

'And I pity that poor daughter of yours - Caroline. Lord, such airs and graces!'

Daisy dropped the reins and turned to give the woman a stinging slap on the cheek. 'You're a foul-mouthed old bitch!' she shouted.

The blow was hard enough to sting her own hand, even through the glove. But Lady Lyndon-Fury did not flinch at all. She merely gave a smile of triumph and said, 'So that's it! Caroline! Now we know!'

67

Mercier had a line out for a pike that he suspected of decimating the trout in this reach of the lough; he was also casting, rather forlornly, for the remaining specimens of that tribe, just below the spit of land belonging to Two-horses Flynn. The gentle southern breeze was carrying him slowly up the lough. If it took him as far as the Coutts's before one o'clock, he promised himself, he'd bring his sandwiches and beer ashore and eat with them.

By eleven o'clock he was adding the further promise that if the declining wind hadn't brought him that far north by then, he'd jolly well help it out with the pocket kerchief of a sail he was carrying.

From time to time he heard the distant excitement of the hunt, though the adverse wind attenuated it to the very limit of his hearing. He thought of Swan and what an intoxication it was to her. And he tried not to think of Daisy O'Lindon and what he had seen the other evening – all that anger and resentment, hidden even from herself because it was too strong to acknowledge. If she had to live with it out in the open, it'd tear her apart; but what might it do to her all pent-up like that?

Swan was the same, mind. Perhaps all women were, under the skin – creatures possessed by passions they dare not acknowledge. The O'Lindons were among their dearest friends, yet Swan was as envious of them, or of Daisy, as if they were arch rivals – especially now it was clear that Daisy was starting to 'go about' in society and mingle with important people. You could point out till you were blue in the face how hard they'd worked for it all, and she'd grant Stephen his rewards ungrudgingly; yet she behaved as if Daisy had broken some natural law, or as if God had unfairly suspended some universal principle that would otherwise have kept that particular woman 'in her place'. But if you put it to Swan that she was jealous, pure and simple, she'd laugh as if you were mad and say nothing could delight her more than to see Daisy starting to accept her social responsibilities at last.

All this kowtowing to Trapper and aping the ways of the hunting gentry was part of it, of course. She wasn't truly a hunting person. Look at the way she used to mock them not so long ago. She said if you walked into a strange house and it was full of dog hairs, mud, and the smell of sodden clothing – and had more than half a dozen buckets set to catch the leaks – you could offer a hundred to one it was a hunting household. But now they were the salt of the earth to her. She was a quare one to explain at times.

He remembered how she had angled for months for an invitation to dine at Coolderg Castle. And for what? Shepherd's pie and rhubarb tart – that's what it had been! Served on a bed of icicles. She'd thought it a deliberate insult until Napier told her she'd been lucky not to have got given salt cod and boxty. But it made no difference in the end. The class of the Ascendancy still held her imagination in thrall. She was the real stuff of which Castle Catholics are made.

Wait now! That was going a bit hard on the oul' girl. Look at the other side of it. Didn't her small failings make her all the more endearing in her way – the fact that she could see what gobshites they were, and *still* be dewy eyed about them?

And gobshites was the only name for them, those Lyndon-Furys. County sheriffs, justices of the peace, masters of foxhounds, guardians of the Poor Law – they practically had the power of life and death . . .

A bite!

He gave the line a gentle tug. You could never tell with pike. No gentleman, he! You'd think you were hauling in a waterlogged branch or an old boot.

It was a waterlogged branch! He threw it away in disgust, rebaited the hook, and cast the line again.

Where was he? Yes, they practically held powers of life and death, yet their agent was in the bank every other month looking for new bills and extensions on the old ones. And if you demurred, you'd be invited to a buffet or two at the castle next time you were down; more food on icicles. And if you granted it, they'd bow gracefully from a great height when they passed you in the street. And pass you they would. *Glances* on icicles, then!

The granting of bills and extensions was uncomfortably close to the nightmare of the week now past. Lord, but he'd scraped through the audit by the skin of his teeth. He must have been mad to listen to Swan. Not that it was fair to blame her; the final decision had been his. Still, if the railway failed, that would be the end of the Lyndon-Furys and *finis* for him and Swan, too.

He corrected the thought: If it failed swiftly.

If it failed slowly, over ten years, say, the directors would get used to it. The Simonstown–Glenisk Line would merge into the general background of failed Lyndon-Fury enterprises – the joinery, the distillery, the plantations up in the mountains . . .

But if it failed swiftly – well, they really were on a doubtful branch over a ravine full of crocodiles. He shuddered and forced his thoughts back onto more general matters.

Would the bank ever really foreclose on them, he wondered – on anyone like the Lyndon-Furys? God knows there were enough of them, up and down the country! All teetering on the verge of collapse – half their estates bought out by the Land Commission and the rest in pawn to the banks. But would the banks foreclose? In any rational country they'd have to, but Ireland somehow didn't work like that. Here the directors would say they're good Protestants and they've been with the bank for generations so we'll give them a little more time. And there'd be enough 'little more times' to see any man safely into his box.

Now that was a definite bite!

Despairing of any sport from the ungentlemanly pike he hauled in on the line. There was *some* resistance – enough to halt the drift of the boat and pull it feebly upwind again. And then the creature was swinging inboard, where it lay in the bilge, faintly stirring. Ten pounds? Perhaps twelve. Quite a fellow, anyway.

Funny to see a fish with such wicked teeth taking its own death so unresistingly. What could you do with them? You couldn't eat them. Europeans did, but then they ate horses, too. He pulled out one of the brass rowlocks, intending to stun it – for it was too large to finish off over the toe of his boat, as he would a trout. Then it occurred to him he might get it stuffed. Perhaps even give it to the stuffed animals museum in Merrion Square? 'Presented to the Museum by J.L. Mercier, Esq of . . .' No, best not say where of. Or whereof! Give the imagination a chance to roam. Can't you see him now – J.L. Mercier, Esquire? A squire on a thousand acres of rough shootin' in Connaught. Neighbour of Yeats's over the water. Often he'd row over for a convivial evening together – or is it curraghs they have there?

Anyway, you could see him standing there on the hillside, J.L. Mercier, Esq. Gun broken over his arm, two Irish setters fussing at his feet, while his raptor's eye quarters the heather for . . . what would it be? Capercaillie or something, or was that only in Scotland? Anyway, he was an Irish gentleman to his very fingertips. Foreigners might think him English but another Irishman would know better.

Yes, he'd get the thing stuffed and he'd present it to the museum.

Next moment he was startled out of his wits by a violent crashing and grunting among the reeds to his right. In his pleasurable musings he had allowed the boat to drift rather close inshore. A moment later he found himself almost face to face with a full-grown, fourteen-point stag – who was every bit as startled at the confrontation.

It lasted less than a second and then the creature was back among the rushes, discernible only by his antlers, which were proud above the fronds, and by an occasional and ever-less frequent flash of his red coat among the green and beige. But in that moment when J.L. Mercier, Esq., had stared into the large, dark eyes of the creature, he had glimpsed the controlled terror of the hunted; and in that same instant he had discovered in himself more of the hunter than he had ever suspected was there. He felt no emotion toward the stag, beyond a sudden and intense desire to see it chased to a standstill and then killed. He wanted a part in its death. He suddenly felt his isolation from those who had driven it here; he wanted to join them, to be in the ring.

There was no fishing worthy the name today, anyway. Even the petty triumph of catching that old pike at last had suddenly dwindled to nothing. He swiftly wound all his tackle inboard and, fitting oars to rowlocks, threatened to break them in his efforts to follow the stag.

Even then it crossed his mind that, if the creature took to the waters, he might yet play the crucial part in the kill.

68

Why do moths immolate themselves in candle flames? Why do hares on the very point of escape turn and virtually hurl themselves into the jaws of the pursuing hound? And most especially, why did that stag, having outrun his pursuers, and with the whole Kingdom of Munster beckoning across a narrow tongue of marsh, choose instead to launch himself into Lough Cool, beneath whose waters all his advantages sank like stone? Trapper's scream of triumph at the sight of the magnificent animal, now reduced to plunging and lumbering through the water, must have curdled his blood and put the power of desperation into him.

'There's Mercier!' Swan cried. 'Mercier! Yoohoo! Can you head him off?'

She need not have bothered. Her husband was already testing the oars, the rowlocks, and the gunwale to their limits in his efforts to join the hunt.

Trapper offered more practical advice: 'Try and get round the fella. Bring him back up the lough – level with the shore, if you like. He'll come out when he's tired. We'll withdraw and stay quiet.' He looked ominously at the hounds.

Mercier eased oar. 'What?'

Trapper repeated the bare elements of his message: 'Go beyond! Drive north . . .'

Mercier understood and resumed his task with double the frenzy.

The stag might have seemed a clumsy mover when viewed from the land; Mercier, in a boat built more for stability than speed, was soon of a different opinion. He felt quite done-in before he had closed even half the gap between them. His muscles had not been so tested since those awful days at school, when hearty sportsmen had cursed and menaced him through mud, mist, rain, and the last shreds of his stamina. Yet now, as then, powerful forces sustained him and saw him through; then it had been hatred of his tormentors and a determination not to give them the satisfaction of seeing him yield; now it was the blood-lust of the hunt together with the realization that the entire success of Swan's Great Day depended on him and him alone.

He paused long enough to rip off his overcoat and jacket and then resumed his efforts with liberated vigour. The years flew off him as his muscles found an exhilaration they had not known since his youth.

His course took him behind his quarry, on a diagonal line that would let him head the creature off toward the north, back into the Coolderg demesne. There was therefore a minute or so during which he could not see the stag, except in snatched glances over his shoulder. It gratified him to note that the animal was also tiring; it was certainly swimming more slowly now, for, even though his own efforts had come off their peak, he was still gaining on it, slowly but satisfactorily.

The caution that had made him such a good banker - and which he had so uncharacteristically shelved in his recent dealings with the Lyndon-Furys - now warned him against drawing too close. If a wounded stag was a dangerous beast, as all the world knew, then so was one at the end of its tether. And those mighty antlers were no less imposing at water level than they had been when towering above him on dry ground. One casual flick and they'd cut the eye out of you at least.

As his diagonal carried him beyond and away from the stag he saw that it, too, was turning - away from him, of course. He laughed aloud, thinking how exactly like a sheepdog and one errant sheep they must seem. He had often watched them from this very boat, over on the Clare side of the lough; it never ceased to amaze him how the dog could guess where the sheep was going and then move so as to halve the angle between that and where the dog wanted it to go - then a new guess, a new move, and a further halving of the angle, until it was on the right line. Such a smooth curve they made on the hillsides. But if the dog guessed wrong, the sheep would turn abruptly, perhaps even double back, and all the good momentum would be lost.

An instinct unconsciously gained during those observations now came to Mercier's aid. He glanced at the shore. Swan alone remained mounted, watching his every move; the rest were all out of sight and, as far as he could tell, Trapper was managing to keep the hounds quiet, too. So far, so good.

Mercier edged a little deeper out into the lough. The stag veered even more toward the north. Another outward move, and now the creature was swimming due north, parallel to the shore. If you knew what you were about, and kept your head, it was as easy as eating whipped cream. His heartbeat slowed to something you could begin to think of counting without giving yourself a heart attack. The sweat poured off him but the gentle southerly breeze carried it away in grateful draughts of coolness. He could keep this up for ever, which was more than could be said of the stag; any moment now its aching muscles would tell it to head back to shore. Mercier edged closer and narrowed the gap, in case it tried to break out into the lough instead.

What actually happened was that a trout leaped from the water not a yard in front of the stag. In its panic the animal turned abruptly westward, toward the middle of the lough, now quite heedless of the pursuing boat. Mercier, who did not check on the creature with every single stroke gave three strong pulls before Swan's horn alerted him to the change. By then he was almost upon the beast.

Now *he* panicked. Realizing that another superhuman effort to get around the far side of the stag would be beyond him, he dropped one oar, raised the other, and brought it down smack on the water just in front of the animal's face. Like a horse put to a jump on the wrong foot, the stag turned the wrong way – toward the boat. A moment later its horns locked with the prow and its head went under. Panic turned to blind desperation. In its efforts to free itself it threatened to overturn the boat entirely. Mercier leaned over to help it extricate itself. His hastily rolled-up shirt sleeve unrolled, got soaked, and wrapped itself cloyingly round one of the fourteen points. The rest was inevitable.

The police surgeon said that the thrashing of those mighty antlers as the stag broke the surface at last had snapped Mercier's neck in a trice. He wouldn't have known what happened. There was hardly any water in his lungs, he certainly didn't drown.

69

In normal circumstances Mercier's tragic death and the subsequent funeral would have kept the pints flowing in every bar in Keelity for weeks. But when the government inspector rode out the following morning to certificate the new line to Glenisk, the very name of Mercier was pushed out of sight and over the horizon. From Francie O'Kelly's farm, a mile outside Simonstown, to a piece of cutaway bog just north of the Coolderg demesne, not a single, solitary rail remained. The sleepers were there, the carriers, the fishplates, the nuts, the bolts – all where the mischieeevious Little People had discarded them; but of the rails themselves, not a glimmer, not a hide nor hair of them, not a whisper (though some there were who said that if you listened carefully, you might hear the tinkling sound of distant laughter).

Trapper was, naturally, beside himself with rage. He stormed up the line visiting the farms on either side and threatening blue murder – indeed, a whole rainbow of murders – if the metals weren't replaced as swiftly as they had been removed.

Francie O'Kelly stood beside his newly-turned dung heap and said he didn't know what His Honour was talking about but he was sorry for his troubles, now.

William Condron said he'd been in Parsonstown all yesterday and could name a hundred men who saw him there. Privately he wondered if it was true that the bog would preserve that class of steel and not eat it away on him.

Fergal McKee gave an experimental tap or two at the wooden shuttering around the lintel he cast last night to replace the thing he'd previously made with chicken wire. In his opinion it was a terrible crime for any man to have done and he couldn't name one in those parts who'd be mean enough to do it; they must be across the water, safely back in County Clare – and that was where His Honour had best be seeking them.

Dermod Quirke was at his spring ploughing – two seasons early for once.

Mick Fogarty had discovered a blockage in an old shore that drained his haggard.

And 'clare to God! Was that Rory O'Hanrahan with fresh scaffolding and building boards up around that old barn of his at last?

Such industry! What had come over the place, altogether?

Now some of those men were tenants of the Coolderg estate. Wouldn't you think a good landlord would be only gratified to see so much unaccustomed dedication to the land and buildings – instead of ranting and roaring over the countryside and giving people up and down the banks like that?

The constabulary poked and pried and dug in the fields and turned over a few dung heaps – and, to the enormous surprise of the owners of those locations, they did discover the odd rail or two; but the rest might as well have been in the middle of the Atlantic Ocean for all the luck they had in retrieving them.

And so, too, might Trapper's credit.

70

Mercier's family certainly expected him to be buried in the plot next to his parents in Glasnevin; but Mercier himself had directed otherwise, and that could not be argued with. And so he was laid to rest on the following Tuesday in the Church of Ireland burial ground at Glenisk, whose wall was lapped by the waters of his beloved Lough Cool. At their full winter height they reached the very footing of the wall; even today, after a dryish summer, they were a mere stone's throw away.

It was the first day of October, bright and mild, with an autumnal sun filtering down through leaves on the turn to gold. Not a breath of wind disturbed their delicate placing in the lattice of the trees. Swan, who had wept every grain of salt from her eyes the past two days, kept a brave hold on herself throughout the ceremony. When it came to the actual interment, when the coffin vanished into the maw of the grave, she closed her eyes and shivered. But when she opened them again they happened, by chance, to fix on a certain spot on the lough. And at that precise place and moment a fish – a trout, she assumed – leaped out of the water, looked at her with its beady eye, and fell back among its own widening ripples.

She smiled at the happy coincidence.

Those around the grave – and they numbered a hundred or more – were surprised. Napier, across the cloven earth from her, raised an inquiring eyebrow. She darted her eyes beyond him, toward the ever-widening circles on the water. He turned, saw it, and smiled, too.

So, indeed, did a few others who followed the gesture and took in the scene; but many did not – Daisy among them. In years to come they were to remember that shocking moment – when Mercier's coffin vanished into the earth and his wife smiled at Napier Lyndon-Fury, who immediately smiled back.

When the first rattle of clay hit the lid of the coffin, there came the murmur of quiet conversations.

'He'll be sadly missed here,' Stephen whispered to Trapper, who had gravitated to his side; Daisy was a few paces away, standing by Madeleine, with whom Swan had been staying since the accident.

'More than I can tell you,' Trapper replied heavily.

By unspoken agreement the two men shuffled slowly to the back of the crowd, where the minister's voice barely carried and they could talk in low tones. 'I was sorry about your trouble, too,' Stephen said. 'A bad business altogether.'

'The ruin of me,' Trapper confided.

'Ah, it may not be so black. Tell me one thing, now. I know we've been at each other's throats in the past – commercially, I mean. Personally, I never bore you the slightest hard feeling.'

'Nor I you, I do assure you,' Trapper returned awkwardly.

'But Mrs O'Lindon was saying only last night, when we first heard of this business with the rails . . . she said such lawlessness must be driven out before it ruins us all. What's to stop any man with a grievance against me from firing my lumberyard?'

'That's very true.'

'She says we should offer a fifty-pound reward for information leading to the conviction of whoever did it – the ringleader, you know. Myself now, I'm for it, but I said I'd seek your opinion first.'

Trapper, like many men who fancy themselves strong and hard, was touched to the point of tears at this. He tried to express his gratitude but the words could not squeeze past the lump in his throat. He pulled out a large silk handkerchief, none too clean, and blew his nose hard into it. The trumpeting caught Swan's attention and she turned, smiled sympathetically at him, and gave a grateful little nod at his public display of distress. He took off his hat again and gave a stiff little bow.

'I'll post the notices, so,' Stephen said.

'You're a white man, O'Lindon. Always knew it.'

'How has your father received the news?'

'Taken to his bed. Says he'll never rise again. Between you and me, I think he may be right.' He drew very close to Stephen's ear and murmured so that even he could barely make out the words: 'Also between you and me – and I mean strictly between us – I happen to know who the ringleader was, and I'll not let it go with him. I'll give him a shirt full of sore bones.'

Stephen turned to him, raised an eyebrow, and mimed the word, 'Who?'

Trapper winked and shook his head. 'Never mind. I'll know his shadow when I see it.'

The funeral tea was held in the hall and main guard at Coolderg Castle.

Stephen noted that two more pictures had gone since the day of the garden party; even people who had seen the inside of the place only once or twice before were aware of the gaps, of the incompleteness of the collection.

Madeleine, who by her own choice had not visited the castle for years, was shocked. 'The place is flying out the windows,' she said to Daisy as they stood before the gap that had once held the great bear hunt by Rubens.

'Sure that one went years ago. Didn't Swan ever tell you?'

Madeleine shook her head and went on staring at the weeping wall.

Daisy chuckled. 'She probably never noticed. She had stars in her eyes every time she came here.'

Madeleine gazed coolly at her. 'More than one could say of *you*, my dear.'

Daisy chose to take it as a compliment. 'Indeed,' she agreed heartily. Then, changing tack abruptly, 'Did you see her smile at Napier when the coffin was lowered? What was all that about at all?'

'Yes.' Madeleine bit her lip. 'It did seem a bit . . . you know. Did she ever do a line with Napier? He never said.'

'She was always the flirt,' Daisy allowed. 'She'd court a haggard full of sparrows for want of a man. And have you noticed her skin lately? I never saw her looking so' – she lingered on the word – 'blooming.'

Madeleine smiled – and immediately struggled not to. 'You don't think . . . ?'

Daisy raised a laconic eyebrow and shrugged. Then, turning back to the space where the painting wasn't any longer, she added idly, 'I suppose there's nothing to stop them selling off everything bit by bit. They've a long way to go yet before they reach the level of you and me.'

Watching her, Madeleine felt a shiver pass up and down her spine. But was it, she wondered, at Daisy's total inability to see herself as she truly was? Or could it be something more precise than that? Did Daisy quite genuinely and honestly believe that the O'Lindons and the Couttses lived on something resembling a par?

The blindness of people in general never ceased to astound her. The trouble was, you had to lose, or give up, almost everything you possessed – and marry a good and wise and modest person like Thomas Coutts – in order to regain your own vision.

71

Trapper knew that Two-horses Flynn continued to take rabbits, despite his several convictions for poaching. Last time the RM had warned him that the next conviction would earn him a spell 'up the Cut' – not his words, of course, but the local euphemism for going to jail. Far from deterring Flynn, the warning had simply made him more cautious. 'There's no sleeping it out with *me*,' he boasted in his favourite bars. 'They'll have to stir themselves nice and early to make good that oul' threat.'

Trapper took the man at his word. A day or so after Mercier's funeral, and less than a week after the Little People put their spell on the line, he was out at Flynn's well before dawn, wrapped up warm in an old coachman's coat, fortified with a nip of good brandy, and cradling his trusty double-barrelled shotgun across his knees. He had chosen a place where a gap in the wall gave rabbits easy passage between the two properties. If he were Flynn, that is where he would set his traps – and remove them before sun-up, too.

He chose well, for he had not been there ten minutes before he heard the sudden snap of the iron jaws and the terrified shriek of an animal in pain. A rabbit, beyond doubt, a large buck by the sound of him. Flynn's tigeen was half a mile away, but he'd surely hear the commotion, Trapper thought. Twenty minutes later he heard the man himself approaching. What annoyed Trapper most of all was that the trap had been laid on the Coolderg side of the wall; the fellow wasn't even poaching his own land! Still, it provided all the more excuse for blasting away.

Trapper had chosen a range that would give Flynn a nasty peppering – maybe blind him in one eye with luck – but not one that would risk his life. It would be enough of a warning to him, and everyone else, that nobody insulted and stole from the Lyndon-Furys with impunity. A week from now, in dribs and drabs, lengths of rail would mysteriously begin to reappear, littering the line on each farmer's land. Those farms where the track remained bare would start to feel only too conspicuous; then a shotgun cartridge sent through the mail would be enough to restore the entire line and finish the rebellion.

Trapper smiled to himself. The RIC and the judiciary were all very well in their way. But for seven hundred years the English had been teaching the populace that it was both honourable and patriotic to break the law; they had it blunted as a weapon of 'natural' justice, which now lay, instead, in the arsonist's torch, the hamstringer's knife, the shotgun's warning fusillade, the bullet in the mails.

The first light of false dawn laid a faint and bleary finger of pink upon the skyline as Trapper raised the shotgun to his shoulder. The illumination was just sufficient to show the movement of the man as he came to the gap in the wall. The rabbit was still screaming.

Perhaps its racket drowned out Trapper's warning cry of 'Poacher! Halt or I fire!' Flynn certainly took no evasive action.

Trapper aimed off about fifteen degrees and let him have one barrel.

For a moment there was utter silence. Then the rabbit started screaming again. Of Flynn there was no sign.

Trapper leaped to his feet and finished the creature off with the toe of his boot, throwing it well into the Coolderg demesne before turning his mind to the hunt for Flynn. The man would surely have made for the lough shore, he reasoned.

But then, from a hundred yards off in the opposite direction – towards the muddy creek between Flynn's peninsula and the rest of the country –

came a taunting laugh. 'You missed me, your honour, sir. Missed by a mile!'

It wasn't true, in fact. Five or six pellets had found their mark and were causing Two-horses slight discomfort, but he wasn't going to give Trapper Lyndon-Fury the satisfaction of knowing it. As soon as he had delivered his taunt he turned and set off like the wind for the open country beyond the creek. When he reached the edge, he paused long enough to be sure of pursuit; then, picking his way with an assurance that would (and often did) carry him safely through the mire, even when blind drunk, he hopped and lepped to safety.

Trapper had less luck. Halfway over the creek he slithered in the ooze, caught his ankle in an old waterlogged tree trunk that lay half in and half out of the mud, and pitched headlong. The gun went skittering before him and lodged in the branches of the fallen tree. Cursing like a demon he tried to rise but all he did was slither into deeper water. He gathered his legs beneath him for a spring back to the firmer shallows, only to feel the bottom yield at the pressure. Then his boots sank into a fathomless space that was filled with something of the consistency of half-melted butter. After that, every struggle seemed to suck him deeper into the cloying mass.

'Flynn, damn your eyes!' he cried out. 'Come and help me, confound you.'

Flynn paused in his flight and listened.

'I'm stuck,' came the distant cry.

Smiling to himself he crept back as silent as a shade; it could be a trap, of course.

'Over here!' The cry was more plaintive now. It was certainly from a direction that lent colour to the claim.

He sought the protection of a stout sally and called out, 'Has yer honour any sort of a landmark at all?'

'Can't see a bloody thing. I was tripped up by some kind of waterlogged tree on its side.'

That as good as confirmed it. 'Would your honour have the goodness and patience to wait till I fetch a lantern and a curt of rope?' he asked.

'Devil take you!' Trapper called back. 'I'll freeze to death while you're gone. Just find an old branch or something and throw it me. I'm damned sure I could get myself out if only . . . Flynn?' He heard the sounds of the man's departure, which Flynn no longer bothered to conceal. 'God's curse on you!' he called after him bitterly.

'And the divil bless your honour, too!' was the murmured reply.

Flynn took his time about it – enough, indeed, to brew a cup of tea. He poured it lovingly and helped it stand up with a hint of something stronger. He drained the dark, aromatic mixture with relish and set off in search of rope and lantern.

It was a good half hour before he arrived back at the creek. By now the true dawn was almost strong enough to render the lantern superfluous; but it would help, he thought, to bring out the finer details of Lyndon-Fury's countenance. He wanted to see that anguish – to have something to treasure during the long winter evenings ahead.

'Christ but you took your time,' Trapper cried malevolently as he saw the approaching lantern.

'Sure there's nothing worse than a piece of rope that'd part company with itself at the first pull.'

'Throw it here, man, and stop your blather.' Trapper held out an impatient hand.

Flynn spotted the gun, incongruously cradled in the bough of the tree. 'Jesus, Mary, and Joseph!' he cackled. 'Isn't that a sight for two sore eyes!'

He broke the gun and took out the cartridge, which he popped in his pocket with a grin. 'I'll save yer honour the postage, so,' he explained cheerily.

'Fuck you, Flynn! I'll see the colour of your brains if I have to use the butt. And you needn't think this is the end of the affair, either. I'll hound you and your cronies to the gates of hell until you put back my rails. A dying dog wouldn't change places with you before I'm done – so you may wipe that stupid grin off your face this instant. And *give me that fucking rope*!' He held out his hand with the assurance of one whose word was law.

The grin, stupid or not, vanished from the other's lips. Trapper's words had painted a sudden picture of his life over the next weeks or months. His every move would be watched, his every petty trespass stamped upon with all the majesty of the law. *Their* law. Let his horse shy at an oul' sack blowing in the ditch and he'd be up in court for reckless driving. Let the wind knock the legs from under him and he'd get three days for drunk and disorderly.

Blind rage possessed him, helped, no doubt, by the poteen. He'd never be free of their persecution. And who was it said that while one Irishman remained unfree, Ireland herself was still in chains. A new and terrifying corollary struck him: When one Irishman liberated himself from his particular bondage, he struck a blow for the whole nation. He turned and stared at the gun.

No! screamed every cautious fibre in his body.

Yes! urged an anger that had fattened down the centuries of persecution and injustice.

Slowly his fingers snaked into the pocket where they had popped the cartridge only moments earlier.

The fatal wound was convenient to Trapper's left eye – and, quite consistent with the explanation devised by Sergeant McNair of the RIC. Trapper, who, as all the world knew, was his own gamekeeper, had caught

Flynn poaching rabbits and had given him a mild taste of one of the barrels. Flynn, of course, said he was out pulling thorns into the gaps where the cattle might stray – before dawn, indeed! But it was obvious he'd been poaching. The dead rabbit with its leg all torn proved it. And the muddy footprints beyond the creek showed which way the ragged rascal had run, and how Trapper had followed him – with the gun unbroken and the fatal cartridge still loaded. Once he blundered into that fallen tree in the dark, the rest had been virtually inevitable.

By the time the sergeant had it all neatly pieced together, it was so seamless and convincing that Flynn had to remind himself that *he* was the real hero of the action.

72

Swan, in deepest black from head to foot, glanced at Napier and inclined her head toward the door that led to the spiral staircase. Daisy, who had been watching the pair of them like a travelling rat ever since she had intercepted that enigmatic smile between them at Mercier's funeral, averted her eyes conspicuously, pretending to listen to Madeleine with the most intense interest.

'When I went home last week,' Madeleine was saying, 'I wondered how long it would be before I was back here in the castle again. Years, I thought. I'd never have believed we'd all be back in exactly one week. And for exactly the same reason. God works in mysterious ways, all right.'

'Yes! Isn't it,' Daisy sighed.

Swan left the main guard by the spiral stair; nothing odd in that, mind – the cloakroom set aside for the ladies was up there. But then Napier went up the main stair, the one that led out of the ballroom. True, he was carrying a tray on which stood a bottle of soda water and some petits fours. True, his mother was up there in her bedroom, prostrate at the double blow of Trapper's death and the stroke Sir Lucius had suffered on hearing of it. Nonetheless, it was an odd coincidence.

Madeleine smiled wanly. 'What are you really thinking about, Daise?' she asked.

'Sorry!' Daisy inhaled sharply and gave a single, self-deprecatory laugh. 'You know me. You know the way I am. I can't help thinking . . . there'll be estate duties now. And was the railway secured on Trapper's own surety or as a general charge on Coolderg? It sounds dreadful, I know, but someone must take care of these things.'

'Cornel, you mean,' Madeleine replied bleakly. 'He's about as much use as . . . the Pope's balls.' She wiped away another tear and explained to a shocked Daisy: 'One of Trapper's favourites. *En famille*, of course.'

'Of course,' Daisy gasped.

'I never even liked him much,' Madeleine went on. 'I don't know why I feel so weepy. It must be, you know, coming on top of Mercier's death. Both so sudden and so violent.'

Caro came up, but not to join them. 'Excuse me, Aunt Maddy,' she said. 'Mammy?'

Daisy slipped an arm about her and gave her a hug. 'What is it, precious?'

Caro, embarrassed at so public a display of affection, said, 'I'm feeling a bit queasy, you know. D'you think Gwendolen and I might slip outside for a few minutes?'

'Of course, dear.' Daisy ritualistically felt the girl's brow but drew no conclusion from it. 'Gwendolen must ask Aunt Rosina, of course.'

'She's already said yes.' Caro skipped away, but after only a pace or two she turned and, as if it were the merest afterthought, added, 'Or up the tower, perhaps?'

'No,' Daisy said at once. 'It's too dangerous up there.'

'Oh!' Caro started to whine, caught the glint in her mother's eye, and thought better of it. 'Very well, then. We shan't go out at all.'

'What a quick cure!' Daisy exclaimed.

'You were very categorical,' Madeleine remarked when the girl had gone.

Daisy glanced furtively about them, preparing the other for the revelation to follow. 'You don't know who I saw going up there just now!' Then she told her.

Madeleine nodded and bit her lip thoughtfully.

'You don't leap to your brother's defence,' Daisy commented.

'There's something I didn't tell you,' Madeleine replied. 'Back in August, the end of August, the garden party – remember? Well, the night before, I saw Napier rowing up the lake in the general direction of Omdurman Villa. The following morning, Thomas was out at the crack of dawn, as usual, and saw him rowing back.'

Daisy stared at her in astonishment. 'And you didn't put two and two together?'

'I didn't know there were two and two to *be* put together. I forgot to mention it to Tom and he said nothing to me until last week, after I passed on your comment about how "blooming" Swan looks these days.'

Daisy made a little round 'o' of a smile and nodded.

'What d'you think?' Madeleine asked. 'D'you suppose she's breaking the news of it to Napier now?'

73

Swan stared out over the park, which was damp and autumnal; she shivered. 'I don't feel safe up here,' she said. Napier chuckled. 'I'm sure the builders would be pained to hear you say that.' She turned to face him, not sharing his amusement. 'The O'Lindons?' she remarked. 'On the contrary, I'm sure they'd be delighted.'

He put his arms about her and drew her into his embrace.

'Oh, Napier,' she murmured. 'Everything's going so . . . *pfft*!'

'Have you and Venus fallen out?' he asked.

'I think you could stop calling her *that*, don't you? It's hardly appropriate any longer.'

'Oh, well, I wouldn't say that,' he teased.

She butted his shoulder with her forehead, not entirely playfully. 'She and I haven't exactly fallen out,' Swan replied. 'But I don't want to talk about her. Oh God, my darling, I wanted you last night. Couldn't you possibly come to me? The nights are long now. It's not as if you'd have to . . .'

'How can I?' His tone was placatory – conveying that he was as distressed by it as she. 'If I go up the lough, Maddy will see me. And if I go round by land . . .'

'Even after dark?'

'Coutts will, anyway. Or some poacher. I only need to be spied once rowing north without a light and the whole county will know why.'

'Don't be absurd. Lots of people go out without lights.'

'Yes, but only for quite ordinary criminal purposes. Not confessional business. Talking of the confessional, did you hear the one about the young man who wanted to find a willing wench, and so he . . .'

'Christ, Napier!' she exploded, shrugging herself violently out of his embrace. 'Can't you be serious ever? Trapper used to go out without a lantern – and no one ever thought he was sniffing around some widow across the lough.'

Napier sighed. 'Can't you see the difference? He had the estate to protect. He enjoyed being his own gamekeeper. Hunting humans was his favourite sport. I don't know why he didn't sharpen his teeth and wear a bone through his nose.'

Far across the park Swan saw one of the stags – the one from the lake or the one that had fled to the mountains? Trapper would have known at once. Did they have some kind of instinct that told them it would be safe to come back here now? 'Yes,' she said, turning to Napier, 'Trapper did at least try to protect this estate. Who'll do it now, I wonder?'

He nodded unhappily but volunteered nothing.

'That's a fair raft of empty bottles in the back courtyard,' she went on.

'From Mercier's wake, surely?'

She shook her head.

'God!' Napier's fist crashed against one of the battlements. 'The doctor told him the next drop would kill him . . .'

'And it didn't,' she pointed out. 'So why should he believe anything that man says?'

'He has no liver left to speak of. How can he go on?'

'I think he'd die if he stopped now. But never mind him. Have you thought of what it might mean to you?'

He glanced balefully at the sky. 'Indeed, and I have. I've thought of nothing else since . . . you know. If Cornel kicks the bucket – or barrel, in his case – I suppose I'd have to come back.'

'Hah!' Her single mirthless laugh, a laugh of scorn, startled the rooks in the nearby trees, who flew up in a black rash against the gray sky.

'What?' he asked in surprise.

'Come back?' she echoed in even deeper scorn. 'What d'you suppose there'd be to come back to?'

He waved a hand vaguely across the landscape.

She turned from him again and, grasping the upper step of the nearest battlement, shook it – shaking only herself. The words came out in angry shudders in between: 'God send me strength.'

'I wish you'd speak plainly,' he told her, growing angry himself now.

She counted down her passion, drew a deep breath, and faced him calmly. She stared into his eyes, trying to see if he was being deliberately obtuse, and decided he was not. 'It's true,' she said sadly, 'you *are* a different breed, you West Britons.'

He groaned. 'Please,' he said sarcastically. 'I can take most things from a woman, but not that. I thought you were going to speak plain?'

'Very well. If you want it plain, I'll tell you. If you leave this place to Cornel's mismanagement, the only way you'll ever come back here is as a grace-and-favour pensioner of Daisy O'Lindon. There now! Is that plain enough for you?'

He threw back his head and roared with laughter. 'Is that it?' he asked. 'Dear God, how little you know her!'

Swan stood her ground quite calmly. 'How little one of us knows her. That's certain.'

'You have fallen out with her!' He was still smiling.

'I have not. We are still the warmest of friends.'

'But?' he prompted. 'There must be a "but" in it somewhere.'

'Well . . .' A slight awkwardness crept into Swan's manner. Then, all in one rush, she blurted out, 'I don't think she should have such a free run at it. That's all.'

'Free run? What free run? You're talking in riddles again.'

'Since the day your mother spurned her at Simonstown station – oh yes, I've heard all about that, and from her own lips, too. A grand joke she makes of it. A great bit of after-dinner crack. Well, she can move her lips whatever way she wants but she can't change the light in her eyes. And I tell you, since that day only one ambition has consumed Daisy O'Lindon: to see the Lyndon-Furys ruined and herself back here as mistress of Coolderg.'

Napier no longer laughed. Not that he took her at all seriously, but he was seriously concerned at her mental condition. 'Go on,' he said.

'Oh God, Napier, I wish I could open your eyes to it. You're the only one who can do anything.'

'Yes, yes,' he said. 'Go on.'

'Trapper would have handed the whole thing to her on a silver salver . . .'

'Electro-plate,' he corrected, trying to lighten her mood a little. 'We're down to the electro-plate by now.'

She groaned and clenched her teeth. 'And you'd give it to her for a joke, I'm sure.'

'It'd be a wonderful one, too. Was there ever such a white elephant as this? Whom the Gods will destroy they first make owners of Coolderg Castle.'

'Well then . . . there's no point in saying anything more, is there.' She shrugged and turned her back on him again.

He stepped gingerly to her and put his arms around her from behind. Expecting resistance and being gratified to feel none, he rested his chin lightly on her shoulder. She leaned back into him and murmured, 'I'm going to have a baby.'

Smooth as silk he turned and kissed her on the ear – and went on kissing her there for some time, in silence. *If brains made as much noise as machines*, she thought, *I'd be deafened by now*!'

'Will you marry me?' he murmured at last.

'No,' she replied.

74

November turned dry and cold with a series of sharp frosts that brought down the leaves in a rush, despite the lack of gales that year. One Sunday afternoon the lads in Glenisk, having nothing better to do after Mass, took a jar of poteen down to the defunct railway station and placed it securely upon the only piece of rolling stock the company still possessed – the flatbed truck from which the last of the rails had been laid. Then they hitched a rope to its coupling and hauled it between them up the only remaining bit of the line, a three-mile stretch across the bog and the northern tip of the Coolderg demesne. It took them the best part of two hours, for it was slightly uphill all the way; but, by the same token, once they reached the end of the line, they would, they reckoned, have a grand, long, gentle downhill ride with nothing to do but sing, and pass the jar, and feel the wind as it winnowed their hair.

The jar was passed a good few times before they finished the uphill part of their labours. The volume and wildness of their songs drew Swan's attention as she was riding Jubilee over to the Couttses.

'You'd never believe it,' she told Madeleine later. 'They were as fluthered as you'd wish for and still be able to stand – and not all of them could do that. And they went ranting and roaring down the line to Glenisk, splitting the whole country with their song.'

'And how did they stop?' Madeleine asked. 'Is there a brake on that thing?'

'There is, but they were too drunk to wind it. No, they stopped with an almighty clang on the buffers. Actually, it didn't look as if they were going very fast but all I can say is thank God the lough is high and there was water just beyond the wall!'

'Did they go in?' Madeleine laughed at the picture it conjured up.

'The wagon didn't but they did. Like a shot off a shovel.'

As their laughter died, Swan became aware of something rustling beneath the cushion in the small of her back. It was a magazine. She pulled it out, more to stop its noise than from curiosity. But the moment she saw the title her eyes went wide. '*The Tatler*!' she exclaimed. 'Maddy! What's come over you at all at all? Fie!'

Madeleine pulled a face. 'I tried to hide it when I heard you at the gate.'

Swan started turning the pages with interest. 'I tried everywhere for a copy last week in Dublin but they'd sold out. And of course in Keelity they haven't even heard of *The Girl of the Period* yet. It's not bad, is it! Did you see that? A hundred and thirteen gatecrashers at the Duchess of St Alban's ball! Isn't that typical of the English – they counted them! I think I might subscribe. Everyone was talking about it in Dublin. How did *you* get hold of a copy?'

Madeleine gave a haughty sniff. 'If I may say so, Mrs Mercier, I resent this tone of incredulity at the thought that I might . . .'

'Ah, gwan ou'a that!' Swan mocked.

Madeleine broke down and laughed. 'Caro left it, if you must know.'

'Ah!' Swan's tone implied she had at last heard something believable.

'But wait till I tell you,' the other went on. 'It wasn't Caro who bought it.'

'Daisy!' The smile vanished from Swan's face.

Madeleine pouted. 'How did you know?'

'No one will believe me about her – at least, none of you Lyndon-Furys will. Napier's the same. You see her there, scrubbing her own front door step and with her hands all wrinkled from the washing soda, and you think she's like those Scotch Presbyterians who'll work themselves into their graves and leave a fortune.'

Madeleine nodded uncomfortably. 'I must admit I have always thought that of her. But then . . . Sharavogue and so on, you know . . .'

Swan leaned forward with interest. 'I know about Sharavogue. Tell me about the "and so on". I *don't* know.'

'Oh, the O'Lindons have been hiring servants like Old King Cole. They even have a butler now.'

Swan's eyes mimed an inexpressible surprise as she leaned forward to hear more.

'They moved in last week. While you were in Dublin. They've spent an utter fortune getting the place ready. It even has a bath with piped hot and cold water and piped drainage, too. And Stephen got them to build that in only two days. They can't pull the wool over his eyes, you see, because they all know he could do it himself. And better.'

'You mean to say he *didn't* do it all himself?' Swan asked sarcastically.

'Not him! He's too busy at that new factory of his in Dublin, for building the coachwork for cars. It's where her father used to have his biscuit-tin factory or whatever it was. Did he not call to see you? Perhaps he didn't know you were in Dublin too. Tell me how it went?'

'God, the money just sticks to them!' Swan exclaimed.

'Haven't they worked for it,' Madeleine protested.

'Yes and no.' Swan had the air of a woman with a secret to impart.

'If it's scurrilous, I don't wish to hear,' Madeleine warned her.

She smiled. 'Not a bit. It's the plain, unvarnished truth. They started on borrowed money. In fact, Mercier and I met them the very day they got the loan.'

'You don't need to tell *me* about borrowed money. Nor any Lyndon-Fury. At least the O'Lindons made it work for them.'

'Ah, but what was it secured on? Mercier couldn't *believe* it when he found out. Didn't they borrow a thousand pounds on the strength of a house that had crumbled to its foundations and a few acres of furze and cutaway bog that wouldn't keep an ass in provender. But that was Fitzpatrick at the Hibernian Bank, God rest him. She had him there!' She crooked her little finger till the sinews stood out.

'Not . . . you don't mean she and he . . . ?' Madeleine pretended she could not frame the indelicate thought. Actually, she was remembering that Swan had told her this tale before, some years ago. How it must have rankled with her! The venom was still one hundred and twenty proof.

Swan laughed. 'Oh no! It worked with Napier all right, but Fitzpatrick was never that much of an eejit. No, she put the stardust in his eyes, the way she managed her father's business and got it going great guns again.'

'Bully for her, then!' Madeleine smiled. 'You wouldn't be just a teeny bit jealous, Swan?'

'You may think what you like,' Swan said huffily. 'But don't say I didn't tell you.'

'You didn't.' Madeleine smiled sweetly. 'About Dublin? Twice I've asked you.'

Swan made it an excuse for laughter and for getting back into a more friendly mood. 'It was all quite straightforward – as anyone who knew Mercier would have predicted. He never talked about death much but he'd prepared for it down to the last little detail. I sold the residue of the lease – for more than we gave, in fact.'

'My!' It amused Madeleine to see how alike Swan and Daisy were at times. That little show of modest pride was exactly what Daisy would have managed if the tale had been hers.

'Mercier always said it would happen. Once all that Fenian violence died down, you wouldn't know the country for the prosperity that would come pouring down out of the skies.'

'And your furniture?'

'All rented. That's all gone back. I had the divil of an argument with the quare fella about one or two little scratches, which I hadn't even noticed. Honestly, they were so small. But I wore him down in the end. And so, in short' – she smiled wanly to show she'd rather it were otherwise – 'dear, darling Mercier's left me really rather well off.'

Madeleine tilted her head sympathetically and gave an equally wan smile.

'And that's not all.' Swan's tongue lingered on her lip; a new merriment in her eyes invoiced the rest. 'I'm going to have his child.'

'Oh, Swan! How absolutely marvellous! When?' You'd have sworn that the thought Swan might be 'in an interesting condition' had never even crossed Madeleine's mind.

'Next March, as far as the doctor can tell.' Swan saw some well-bred arithmetic going on behind Madeleine's smile.

'Oh, I'm so pleased for you.' The smile did not even flicker when the nine-month count-back from next March brought it smack into the period when she had seen Napier rowing alone up the lough to Swan, who had also been alone (or at least without her husband) that night.

'It won't surprise you to know we'd been trying for years and had almost given up hope.'

'Fifteen years!' Madeleine managed to say it without *too* much incredulity.

'Yes,' Swan agreed awkwardly. She realized that Madeleine had her doubts and that only something fairly drastic would overcome them. She prepared to blush. 'As a matter of fact – don't ever tell this to a soul – but we went to see a doctor in London, all very anonymous and dreadfully shame-making. But he told us to, you know, "do" it *every day* for six months.'

'Swan!' Madeleine breathed in sharply and fanned her face with a limp hand.

'Sorry!' Now Swan blushed, bit her lip, lowered her gaze. 'I don't know what made me say that. Deplorable. Do forgive me.' She looked up miserably. 'I'll go if you like.'

Madeleine would never have believed her surprised outburst could have such an effect; now, of course, she felt awful about it. 'Swan!' she laughed cajolingly. 'Don't be silly! It was just a bit of a surprise, that's all. I mean, it's not a topic we've ever . . .' She paused and broke into an impish grin. 'Did you say *every* day?'

Swan smiled shyly and nodded. Her spirit danced for joy; it had worked. 'We were both absolutely sick of it after only three weeks,' she confessed. 'But we persevered, manfully – womanfully, too – and . . .' She patted her midriff.

'Did Mercier know before he died?' Madeleine, now regretting her foul and unworthy suspicions about Swan and her brother, was eager to make it all up to her.

Swan nodded but did not actually say so – not that she believed in ghosts, but one never knew. 'Anyway,' she went on, 'that's not all I have to confess.'

'Goodness!' Madeleine laughed apprehensively and held her hands near her ears. 'Go on. I'm ready this time.'

'No!' Swan reached over and pulled the nearer arm down. 'Nothing more like that, I promise you. The thing is, Napier has asked me to marry him.'

'Ah.'

'You don't seem too surprised.' Swan frowned. 'Has he spoken of it to you?'

'My dear, I'm the very last person he'd discuss such a thing with. But I *have* observed the odd lingering glance between you, you know.' She almost mentioned the smile at the funeral but decided that might be too near the bone.

'Oh, and we thought we'd been so discreet.'

'You've accepted him, of course?'

Swan shook her head. 'Not yet. Perhaps not ever. I just don't know.' She stared away out through the window, where the westering sun was gilding the hithering-thithering ripples on the lake. 'I must go soon or I'll miss evensong. The odd thing is, Mercier and I talked about it only a month or so before he died.'

'About you marrying Napier if you were widowed?' Madeleine asked incredulously.

Swan nodded. 'Not just out of the blue. We'd been to a funeral. Old Mr Fitzpatrick's, in fact – the Hibernian Bank manager I was telling you about. Anyway, Mercier said he hoped I'd marry again if I wanted to – not let his memory stand in the way. And I said the same to him, of course. And then he gave that little chuckle of his and asked who I'd choose. And for some reason, I said Napier.'

'For "some" reason?' Madeleine echoed sceptically.

'Really his was the only name I could think of. Still unmarried, I mean. Also . . . well, perhaps you don't know it – if he never spoke to you about that sort of thing – but he and I . . . well, it wasn't anything, really, when we were students at the Academy School together.'

Madeleine distinctly remembered that Daisy had once told her that Swan had been sweet on one of the other students there – one of the Joyces from Oughterard in Connemara. So which of them was telling the truth? If Swan had been keen on Napier and Daisy stole him from her, it would explain a great deal. 'I didn't know that,' she remarked. 'But then, as I said, we never talk about things like that. Very Irish! What did Mercier think of your choice?'

'Oh, he approved. He wanted to know why, of course. I didn't tell him there'd once been something between us. I said Napier was so different from him in every way, while still being a thoroughly daycent fellow. So there'd be no conflict of loyalties and no making of comparisons all the time. That satisfied him. Also, of course, Napier was still unmarried.'

'And is, it seems, likely to remain so! Why did you turn him down? You practically had Mercier's blessing on it.'

Swan shrugged awkwardly. 'I wouldn't say I actually turned him down. I just wanted time to think about it. Of course, the baby makes a difference.'

An irreverent thought struck Madeleine. Wide-eyed she asked, 'You won't leave the decision . . . you know . . . to the last possible moment?' Then she burst out laughing.

'Oh, ha ha!' Swan replied angrily. 'I *was* intending to ask you a serious question.'

Madeleine smacked her own wrist, but her eyes still bubbled with amusement.

'I was going to ask you what you think of it? Me marrying Napier. He is your brother, after all. What will people think?'

Madeleine sighed and forced herself to be serious again. 'My dear, you know what people will think. And even if they don't think it, they'll say it. Just take a leaf out of Daisy's book.'

'Oh, thank you very much! Very likely! What d'you mean, anyway?'

Madeleine smiled. 'We're so used to Daisy O'Lindon as we know her now – the woman she's become, I mean. We tend to forget what she was and what might so easily have become of her.'

'*I* don't.' Swan cut in vehemently.

'But people in general. An expectant girl without a wedding ring is supposed to crawl into the workhouse. After she's dropped the little parisheen, she's supposed to emerge into nothing better than obscurity. Certainly if she keeps the child she emigrates to America or somewhere. And even there she lives in dread that some kind soul from home, passing through, will tell the child the truth. But not our Daise. She stays put where everyone knows her story. She marries the brightest man in the county and . . . well, you know the rest. But can you think of a soul hereabouts – one single, solitary soul – who would *dare* breathe a word to Caro about all that?'

Looking rather thoughtful, Swan shook her head and murmured, 'No.'

75

Christmas that year fell on a Wednesday, and since Roman Catholics took St Stephen's Day off as well – or 'Boxing Day' as the heathen English call it, making a holiday out of a holy day – it meant there was a great big hole in the middle of the working week. It annoyed Daisy especially. 'The only ones who can't take a holiday,' she complained, 'are the masters. *We* have to pay *them* to stay at home in idleness.'

Stephen nodded philosophically and let his eye stray back to the *Freeman's Journal*. Daisy's Christmas tirade was not so bad as the midsummer one, when all the O'Lindon enterprises closed for a week and the workers took home a full two weeks' pay. 'Isn't it all allowed for, my love?' he said. 'When Tony Redfern down at the hardware tots up the bill to seven pound fifteen and fourpence, and then says, "Make it an even seven pound, Mr O'Lindon," sure hasn't he put twenty-five per cent *on* the price in the first place – to be able to knock off the ten. But, by all the holy, you'd think he was the Lord of Lower Egypt himself handing out the largesse with a wink and a smile. "Seeing as you're me best customer, Mr O'Lindon," says he.'

Daisy knew it very well, of course. But it was one thing to know it and quite another to see the money go out through the books and when she knew that the machines were standing idle.

And Stephen knew Daisy knew it. His simplistic lecture was a tease. 'Aren't I the same,' he went on, rubbing it in. 'I give the holiday money into their hands with a smile. "You're fierce good lads, altogether," says I. "You've deserved every penny and I'm here to see you get it." It's a kind of insurance, d'you see.'

'Would you hark at the man!' She begged the clock to contradict her. 'Are you thinking of going in for parliament next, or what?'

He chuckled and settled himself contentedly to his paper.

Daisy, about to throw more turf on the fire, caught herself in time and rang for a maid to come and do it. 'Seriously,' she said when the girl had gone, 'if they don't give us Home Rule, the Fenians will take it, and then where will we be?'

'Mmmm.' He glanced at her long enough to show that, contrary to appearances, he was listening – which was, indeed, half true.

'It'll be a poor lookout for the Protestants then,' she went on. 'Why can't the English understand it? They're such fools. And as for that crowd in Ulster . . . !'

'Indeed, indeed. They'd cut off their nose to spite their face.'

'No, that's the English. The Ulster Prod would cut off his face to spite his nose. There's no use looking to them for help.'

He lowered his paper at last. 'What's all this leading to, my love?' he asked. 'You're not seriously thinking about . . . parliament and that?'

She relaxed and smiled. 'No, but I had to get your attention somehow. Where it's leading is this: I think it's no good looking to anyone, anywhere, for help. We're just so much fluff in England's pockets, along with all the unpaid bills they stuff there. They'll brush us off and say good riddance. So we must look to ourselves alone. *Sinn Fein!*' She laughed.

'Begod, that's a new twist on it,' he commented.

'Seriously, though . . .'

'Ah, how I've come to dread those words!'

'Listen till I tell you. We've got to make sure that we can't be winkled out and pushed to one side. Whenever it happens – and God alone knows whether it'll be five years, or ten, or twenty, but whenever, we've got to be . . . we've got to make it so that if they cut us out, they'd be after cutting the heart from their own selves. We've got to *be* the heart of County Keelity.' She saw him smile at the grandiosity of her conclusion and so added, 'Or this part of it.'

'Ah!' His tone suggested he could accept that much.

She drew a deep breath and went on, 'The way the Lyndon-Furys did it was all wrong, in my view.'

He eyed her warily. 'Why talk in that tone, for God's sake? Aren't they still in Coolderg Castle? Don't they still set five thousand acres? Isn't old Sir Lucius still the Deputy Lord Lieutenant? Stroke or no stroke. Don't talk as if they're finished.'

'With Cornel inheriting, they surely are.'

'He's a born Lyndon-Fury. The responsibility may be the crowning of him.'

'Pigs may whistle but they've poor mouths for it!' She did not, however, pursue that line since it would inevitably have led to Napier. 'Well, I was only using them as an example. The way you'd get no work with them if you were Catholic. The way they'd snipe at the priest on the Board of Guardians. They way they'd invite Protestants to dine at their table and Catholics to join them after for coffee – the ones they couldn't afford to snub. The Penal Laws may be dead and gone, and they'd tell you they never enforced them anyway and they certainly don't want them back, but' – she tapped her forehead – 'up here it's never changed. There's no live-and-let-live up here. And to me that's a recipe for . . . that's like asking to be cast aside when the boot's on the other foot and the other foot is the one that's kicking the ball for a change.'

After a thoughtful moment he said, 'I'll tell you what has me worried.'

But Daisy had not quite finished. 'All I'm saying is that while the Lyndon-Furys are what they are – I mean, *you* may say they're spent but they're still the Lyndon-Furys of Coolderg – and as long as that goes on, *they* are what people will think of when they hear the name Protestant. Not Stephen O'Lindon – who never once turned away a good Catholic worker. Not Stephen O'Lindon, who does his marketing where the price and quality are best and never mind whether the man goes to Mass or takes communion. Not Stephen O'Lindon, who gave the biggest donation for the new altar in the Sacred Heart Convent – by God, it'd be a wonder if half the county doesn't suppose we're Catholic anyway!'

He did not smile at the thought. 'In a way,' he said, 'I'm after thinking the same. Only, not being a woman, I can't soar to the heights of rhetoric and persuasion like you . . .'

'Would you ever skip to the next chapter?' she asked. 'I read that one till the page wore out.'

'Seriously, though,' he said with a straight face, 'you know what we're like here in Ireland. I was after talking about it with Mercier's father only last week. He says all Celts are the same. It's worse in Scotland.'

'Everything's worse there. What in particular?'

'The way if a foreigner comes in and makes a fierce success of everything, we'll clap him on the back and swear he's the grandest fellow since Adam – and mean every word of it, by God. But let one of our own get a cut above the rest and God help him! The tongues will turn to razors. D'you know how I happened to be discussing it with old Mercier? He told me he'd heard we were bankrupt! And from two independent informants! And Hugh Deasy told me the other day that a little bird told him I'd sent twenty thousand pounds to America in a strong box under armed guard, to spit in the eye of the English Revenue.' He sighed at the absurdity of it all.

Daisy stared into the flames; the turf was too dry, it was burning too quickly. 'It's since we moved here to Sharavogue,' she said. 'That's what's started the envy. Now the whole world thinks we're as rich as Damer of Shronell.'

'That's the truth,' he agreed. 'While I wore moleskins and you scrubbed the doorstep, no matter how much profit we made, the tongues were dipped in honey.'

After a pause she said, 'Caroline.'

'I think so, too,' he agreed. 'Will I be the one to tell her?'

76

The St Stephen's Day hunt of the Keelity pack started sombrely enough. Everyone could remember a fair few chases on that particular fixture with Trapper as master; many, even among the ladies, would admit to a couple of dozen, if not more. He had been such an active master, such a stickler for every little detail; the unwary eye still expected to see him everywhere – over the brow of the next little rise, emerging from behind that well-loved and well-preserved piece of covert. His successor, Major Croome of Cloonulty, near Borrisokane, was a worthy man; but there'd only ever be one Trapper. As the Rev Tierney had put it in his funeral oration: 'The piper with his bellows may go home and blow the fire.'

Already the farmers around Coolderg were taking advantage of the new hand at the helm, precisely because they knew it was not at the helm but, more likely, trembling for the first whiskey of the day or already clutching it. When the hounds drew blank at Temple Well, the first covert of the day, they went on to Tully Wood between Bell-the-cat Dolan's and Gregory McHugh's – only to find the undergrowth all cut out of it, as if the place were being prepared for felling.

'What a thundering disgrace!' Swan said to Napier. 'Surely that woodland's not set to McHugh? What does Woods think he's at – allowing such a thing?'

'Mr Woods has gone,' Napier told her dryly.

'Gone?'

'He wasn't paid for the last six months. What other choice had he?'

Swan surveyed the carnage (or cleaning up, depending on your point of view). 'Well, someone must put a stop to all this.'

The remark raised several eyebrows in the immediate vicinity – and even more, later, when it was passed on in variously embroidered forms at dinner tables and At Homes up and down the county.

Napier, who was having trouble enough putting a stop to his mount's bad habits, paid her scant heed. He was annoyed with her anyway for insisting on riding despite her 'interesting' condition.

Major Croome, who did not know this part of the hunt's country too well, came over to ask Swan's advice. She, feeling greatly flattered, trotted off with the master to the next hilltop to point out a valley on the far side of the ex-railway line.

Caro saw her chance. The obligatory tributes to Trapper's memory had passed her by. The disappointment at Temple Well had not touched her. All she knew was that the most handsome man in the world, Napier Lyndon-Fury, had joined the hunt; the fact that he was one of the world's worst horsemen hardly dented her idolatry. If he fell, she'd be the first at his side, cradling his unconscious head in her lap, keeping him from choking on his tongue . . . and later, during his long (oh please let it be long!) recovery at Coolderg Castle, in that sumptuous four-poster bed, she'd nurse him back to full vigour and take care of his every need. Would he like egg custard? Mrs Rumbold had taught them how to make that, because, as she said, although they were all young ladies and would one day be the mistresses of households and never have to cook in the regular way of things, there'd be times when their husbands were poorly and they'd want to bring him a light and easy dish they'd prepared with their own fair hands. Oh, she hoped Napier would adore egg custard. (Her mother had taught her to cook about a million other things, to be sure, but Caro had forgotten them all on the day they moved to Sharavogue.)

With the firm pressure of her ashplant she made Sukey half-pass over to where Napier was checking his mount, and spurring it forward, and lifting its head, and shouting 'Damn you!' and 'Good fella!' all in the same moment. 'Uncle Napier,' she said. 'Come here till I show you something. Come on, Grayfellow.' She clucked him up.

The horse, which she had ridden many times, calmed down at the sound of her voice and followed eagerly. At the far corner of Tully Wood was a derelict cottage, more substantial than most, which had stood empty and roofless since the days of the Famine. In the lee of it, out of sight of those who might be amused at the spectacle of a grown man taking instruction in horsemanship from a girl of rising sixteen, she lengthened his stirrups, got his heels well down, took away his spurs, brought his hands together, told him she'd swaddle him if she saw daylight between his ribs and his elbows again, and generally gave him a pointer or two about making his life – and Grayfellow's – a bit less miserable.

As he watched her solemn little face invigilating his response to all these instructions, he was filled with an enormous sense of love and sadness toward her. *My daughter*, he thought. But she wasn't. She was Daisy's, every inch. She had the same intensity, the same bossiness, the same humour, the same ruthless determination. Look at her now! You'd think the heavens would open if he didn't ride this damned nag properly.

All of a sudden she was stricken with remorse. 'You don't mind my telling you . . . all this?' she asked.

'I thought you were going to say "telling you off"!'

She giggled. Even the way she tilted her head was just like Daisy.

'Of course I don't mind,' he assured her. 'I'm jolly grateful. Actually, to be quite honest, Little Face, I'd just about decided to call it a day. On the whole I think I prefer the *iron* horse. What about you?'

She remounted Sukey. Now *there* was a difference between her and her mother. Daisy rode like a tinker woman on her way to market; Caro became part of the horse the moment she was up.

'I never rode in one,' she said, 'except Daddy's, of course.' She didn't reproach him with having forgotten her on the day of the garden party.

'And what d'you think of it?'

She pulled a face, not wishing to be drawn into a comparison with his beautiful machine.

He smiled. 'Yes, it is rather a . . . what shall we say? Rather a *solid* affair. Not at all like your sprightly Renault. I say, would you care for a spin?'

The Stephen's Day meet suddenly seemed the dullest in the calendar, but she kept her elation well hidden. 'I'd better see you back to the stables, anyway,' she said. 'You're not safe to ride alone.'

They trotted back through the wood, only to find that the hunt had gone. Swan alone remained, riding up and down the fringe of the trees but not, for some curious reason, calling out their names. 'There you are!' she said crossly – as if she had been calling them for ages. 'I was beginning to worry.'

'Miss O'Lindon thought my horsemanship so defective as to be a menace to myself and others,' Napier explained. 'Very considerately she led me aside to correct my hundred most glaring faults.'

Swan relaxed and smiled at Caro. 'Yes, I was thinking of doing the same myself. Aren't you good!' She turned to Napier. 'D'you know, when this one was about twelve, Mercier and I brought her parents a present – an ornamental plate from Belleek. We didn't know that only the week before they'd bought the identical one – not that it mattered because they make a handsome pair. But didn't this little lady here slip away and hide the one they already had! She didn't need a glance from her mother – not a word spoken – she just slipped away and did it, didn't you, love? They don't make too many like that, now.'

Caro, a little overwhelmed at this, asked how she knew.

'Because I'm the world's most incurable busybody,' Swan replied. 'Are we going to rejoin the hunt or what? The poor Major! It looks as if we may draw blank everywhere today. The foxes' tribute to Trapper.'

Caro and Napier exchanged glances. 'Actually,' he said, 'my *glutea maxima* have taken all the pounding they can for one day. If I go to one more draw, I'll be on crutches for a month. So I was going to trot back home, and this young lady – who is every bit as thoughtful as you say – offered to keep me company and . . . put Humpty together again if he had a great fall.'

Swan turned to Caro, all solicitude suddenly. 'Oh darling, you are so kind! How like you that is. But there's no need. I can see this poor cripple home. You know how much you've . . .'

'I don't mind, Aunt Swan,' Caro broke in impetuously. 'Honestly. Uncle Napier's . . .'

'But you know how much you've been looking forward to this particular meet. Besides' – she flashed a coyly significant glance in Napier's direction – 'I do feel just a little delicate myself today.'

'But Uncle Napier's promised me a spin in the Renault. He said we'd go all the way around both loughs and be back in time for tea.'

Napier cleared his throat but she avoided his eye.

'Did you?' Swan asked him.

'You heard her yourself. Why don't you come along, too?'

Caro held her breath.

'I think not.' Swan spoke with icy slowness. 'And *both* loughs is out of the question.'

'Just Lough Cool then?' Napier offered Caro, who grinned happily back at him.

During their return to the castle Swan recovered all her good humour and was especially attentive to Caro. As they crossed the carriage sweep she slipped from Jubilee and said, 'Come on, darling. Uncle Napier can lead them down to the stables – time he made himself useful for a change. We'll go and find you something more suitable for a long, chilly drive in an open tourer. I think you must be stark, staring mad. Are you good at punctures, by the way?'

By the time Napier returned, Caro was kitted out as if the photographer from the motoring magazine were due at any minute. 'You may use my scarf and goggles, of course,' Swan told her. 'They're lying on the back seat, I think. Hurry up, Napier! She hasn't got all day.'

Napier changed in a flash; he didn't trust this sudden switch of mood in Swan at all. He had no idea what she might be up to, but she was surely up to something. Perhaps it went with her 'interesting condition'? Daisy had been even more unpredictable at that time, too, he recalled. The sudden way in which Swan had agreed to marry him was another case in point – especially when she had been so categorical in her refusal until then. How could anyone ever really understand them?

On his way back downstairs he met her on the first landing, 'sharing a joke with Caro,' as that new society magazine of Swan's would put it. He swept up the girl and took her to the stairhead – but there he changed his mind. 'I'll just have a quick word with your aunt,' he said. Then, speaking loudly behind his hand, like a comedian doing an on-stage aside, he added, 'You know what women are like once they reach "a certain age".'

'I heard that,' Swan called out from the passageway leading to the drawing room.

A moment later, after Napier had joined her and said something too quiet for Caro to hear, Swan replied, very loudly, 'Of course I don't mind. Don't be absurd!'

'Keep your voice down!' Napier told her, and then mumbled something else that Caro did not catch.

Knowing they were discussing her, and feeling dreadfully embarrassed by it all, she raced to the bottom of the stair to wait for him. She had forgotten the overhead grating – the hole through which the castle's defenders once rained down arrows and boiling oil on intruders below. And through it she clearly heard Aunt Swan say, 'But I *am* delighted, darling. It would be absurd for me to resent the fact that my husband-to-be is taking his own daughter out for a drive in his car! Now run along and enjoy a wonderful day together.'

77

Caro felt as if her mind were being attacked from many directions – as well as bursting from within. Reality itself grew thin and started to dissolve; the instant-by-instant rapport between her eyes and the old stone walls, the massive iron-grated door into the armoury, the worn flags beneath her feet, the December-dark vista into the ballroom beyond was shattered. She could still see each of them but they bore no fixed relationship to one another. For a while she was too stunned to do anything but stare at them, seeking to reassemble them into her familiar world once more, as if they were the building-brick toys of some gigantic child who had tumbled them and run away.

The first words that broke through her bewilderment were, *of course*. As with the elements of the scene around her, they, too, did not relate to anything. They were just words, as stones were just stones; but she held onto them for all that, trusting that they would also reassemble into something coherent, and soon.

Next she realized she was smiling. *His* daughter. *Of course*.

But there was no 'of course' about it. She thought of her daddy, or the man she had always called her daddy, and he *was* her father.

Uncle Napier was *another* father. *Of course*.

'Father' was just a word now. Old loves, old loyalties, old feelings were all creeping back out of the rubble, dusting themselves down, looking about, and saying, 'Nothing much has changed, really.'

At last she dared to tell herself: 'Napier is my father.' No point in calling him 'Uncle' any longer. But the 'father' that was Napier was nothing like the 'Daddy' that was, well, *Daddy*. Stephen. Mammy's husband.

The phrase *of course* began to puzzle her. Why, of all the frantic, riotous, explosive words that might have come crashing up to the surface at a time like that – why those two?

'Which century are you lost in, Little Face?'

Napier was standing in the ballroom, at the foot of the grand staircase, peering at her. Was that a worried frown? Too dark to see. 'Isn't it gloomy here,' she remarked. 'D'you believe in ghosts?'

He walked toward her, as far as the door beside the armoury. He gave only the briefest glance at the open grille above but it was enough to alert her to his suspicions. If he challenged her, would she admit it? No answer occurred to her. She might and she mightn't.

'I've actually heard them,' he told her solemnly. 'On this very spot, too.' He turned about and pointed to the threshold of the door into the ballroom, which had once been the main door into the castle. 'You know that a good number of your ancestors were rounded up by Cromwell's men . . .'

'Yes. Mammy told me that story.' She shuddered, glad to have some external emotion on which to fasten. 'Horrible!'

'Here's where they landed.' He tapped the vast limestone slab with his motoring boot and held out an arm to usher her outdoors. When he touched her there were no sparks, no jolt of electricity, no thunderclap from on high. She realized she was coping with the shock rather well. 'Mammy told me you said you'd heard them?' she prompted.

Extremely well, in fact.

'Oh, did she tell you that? I was exactly where we are now, just leaving the castle.' He opened the door and shooed her out. 'Then I closed the door behind me like this.' Its bottom stile grated in the gravel on the unswept threshold. 'Then I heard them inside there, just the other side of the door, howling like a thousand banshees.'

He paused, as if it might happen again now. The wind soughed in the bad fit of door to jamb; there was a faint, erratic piping through the keyhole. Caro looked up at him and laughed.

He smiled. 'I know what you're thinking, Little Face. Was I entirely sober? Well, it wasn't that. And it wasn't really the howling, either. That's not what frightened me – and I promise you, I was never more terrified in my life. It was the most . . . monstrous feeling of malevolence. The purest spite. The purest hatred you could ever imagine. The O'Lindons of those days, they must have been . . .' He shook his head, unable to find a strong enough word.

He was so intense about it, so convinced, that the hair prickled on her scalp. Transfixed now, she watched his every move.

He stretched out his arms and pushed against the door, as if desperate to keep it closed. 'It was a pressure of unutterable hatred and malice and hostility. Against *me*. I don't mind confessing it, I just turned and ran, and ran and ran . . .'

Suddenly Caro herself gave out a scream. 'I hear them!' she shrieked and took to her heels out through the ruined keep. But her screams turned to laughter and she cried, 'Race you to the car!'

She thought she'd beat him easily, seeing how uncomfortable and unfit he had looked on his horse. But to her surprise she heard his heavy footfall gaining on her as they raced down the gravel drive. Her laughter shaded back into screaming. Half way there he thundered past her and kept on running. When she arrived at the stable yard he was standing nonchalantly by his car with one foot up on the running board, like a big-game hunter with his 'bag'.

'At last!' he called out. 'I was just about to send out a search party.' But then his collapse into breathlessness gave him away.

Caro ran laughing to him and gave him a brief hug of happiness. 'Oh, Uncle Napier! I'm so glad we didn't stay with the hunt!'

He was much more fun as an uncle, she decided, than ever he would be as a father.

'You're a funny one,' he said, tousling her hair. 'This morning nothing would have kept you from riding to hounds.'

'*Can* we go round both lakes? Or isn't this old thing up to it?'

He laughed. 'Just for that, you can swing her. Put your thumb the same side as your fingers or it could backfire and break your wrist.'

She started it on the third swing, which Napier told her was pretty good.

She climbed in beside him, pulled on her cap and goggles, and tucked in the rug all round. Yes, she thought, she was being pretty good. Mrs Rumbold would be proud of her. *What Every Young Lady Should Know*: 'The stronger a lady's intimate feelings may be in the company of a gentleman, the more ardently will she strive to contain them and maintain her outward composure.'

Uncle Napier might suspect all he wanted; but never, not by the flicker of one eyelid, would she confirm it for him.

Swan watched them go. And to make quite sure of it she went up to the top of the tower and listened to the roar of the engine – Napier showing off – until it had faded into silence. She had already decided what must be done if the Coolderg estate was to be saved; the sight of the O'Lindon Stone sitting there so smugly, so irremovably, merely confirmed her in that resolve. Caroline O'Lindon, indeed! The impertinence of it – as Lady Lyndon-Fury so often said.

As for rescuing the estate and keeping it out of the clutches of Daisy O'Lindon, well, Napier still needed bringing round to it. But perhaps the events of the next day or so would awaken him to his responsibility.

She was now quite sure she'd be alone for several hours at least; her ladyship hardly left the old man's side these days. They were billeted far off in the south-corner-tower, where the ladies' maids had been lodged in the good old days. There they had made a bedroom on the ground floor for Sir Lucius. Swan went below to the guest bedroom. The dust that lay thick on every surface pleased her; it showed how right she had been to choose this room for her hiding place. Taking care not to disturb any of it she went to the far corner and opened the wardrobe. The creak of its hinge made her start guiltily. She froze and listened. The castle was so quiet she could hear the ticking of the grandfather clock on the stairs. She breathed again and crouched to search among some old blankets tossed loosely in the corner.

One bottle.

Two bottles.

Bushmills, three times distilled. His favourite. But would one bottle do the trick? Sure, couldn't she always come back for the second if it didn't.

She hefted the first – and, she hoped, only – bottle in her hand and went cautiously back to the passageway. Caution continued to rule her all the way down to the library, for she paused at every turn and scouted for the sight or sound of servants.

At last, unobserved and unhindered, Swan reached the library door, where she gave a hesitant knock.

'Come in,' Cornel cried gruffly, a bear with a sore head these last few days: ever since Dr Morgan's absolutely final edict of prohibition.

She entered with her hands behind her back. What a pathetic sight he was! Veins all over his face like marble, and puffy flesh beneath it; his eyes never stopped watering.

'Oh, you,' he said and turned morosely back to the window.

Her smile was merry, even mischievous. 'I've brought you a present, Cornel my dear,' she told him, holding forth the single bottle in triumph. 'A belated Christmas present. I think you deserve it.'

78

They stopped at Linford, a one-street village that called itself a town, on the shores of Lough Cool, directly opposite Coolderg Castle. 'A ham sandwich and a Guinness?' Napier suggested. 'Or would you prefer cheese? We could take it down to the harbour and kick our heels in the sunshine.' When Caro chose ham he laughed. 'You're a carnivore, too,' he said.

While he went into the pub, she strolled on down the narrow lane to the harbour, which was only fifty yards away. Did he mean she was a carnivore like him – or like her mother?

Her mother.

Yes – her mother – and Uncle Napier.

'Uncle' was a bit . . . she didn't want to think about all that. But then, want or not, she found her mind in the thick of it once more. All those thoughts hovering at the rim of her awareness. In a way, the thing that surprised her most was her lack of surprise. Was it numbness? Or . . . the thought intruded delicately . . . was it that some secret part of her had always . . . known it?

No. She certainly couldn't say that. Suspected it then?

Not even that was true – look how wildly wrong her guesses had been after overhearing Aunt Swan and Aunt Maddy, that time.

She felt a kind of desperation to explain her lack of surprise. At length it seemed possible, just possible, that something in her was ready to be told those things Aunt Swan had blurted out. And no sooner had *that* thought found grudging acceptance within her than she began to elaborate, to build upon it.

She hadn't exactly been ready to hear those particular truths (if truths they were), but *any* truths. Her awareness had not been of a mystery so much as of a vacuum inside her; and anything can fill a vacuum.

The focus of her thoughts now drifted away from herself toward her mother and Uncle . . . no, Napier. Plain Napier. What else could she call him? She saw the pair of them as in a fading photograph, stiffly posed, caught in discomfiture by the lens. In her mind's eye she tried to make them move. They must have danced, walked through the fields, strolled the streets of Dublin . . . She couldn't picture it.

She did not *want* to picture it.

And thus she absorbed another great truth about herself that day. She did not wish that newly revealed life of theirs to become a part of her own. She wanted to keep this revelation of Aunt Swan's as she would keep a precious gift – securely locked in its case and hidden away in a cupboard somewhere. She didn't want it in her daily life.

It was another way of saying that her life was hers and their life was theirs – and this, the moment that might so easily have drawn them all together, was, in fact, the moment when the great unravelling began. At last she understood that strange sense of almost guilty relief she had felt, and instantly suppressed, in those first dumbstruck moments. She, the growing girl, had been awaiting this release for some time past. In her heedless desire to be herself, she cared little what form it took nor whence it came. It had come, and that was that. Now she was a slipped greyhound.

When Napier joined her he was empty handed. 'They'll bring it down to us in a jiff,' he explained.

Daddy would have waited and brought it himself.

No, she mustn't start turning everything into a comparison. Daddy would have stayed in the bar for the crack that was in it. He'd have come away with more than sandwiches and stout; there'd have been handy gossip, too.

She had a fleeting intimation of the ways in which people like the Lyndon-Furys could become isolated and lose touch.

He sat on the wall beside her and opened his trench coat. 'Aren't you afraid of going brown in the sun?' he asked.

'Sure there's no power in it, not in *that* month.'

'When I was young, a brown skin meant you had consumption. People avoided the sun like the plague.'

'I thought people with consumption were pale as milk?'

'Yes, but the sun was the only cure, you see. If you had brown skin, people would nudge and point you out.'

The publican came down with their sandwiches and stout, a pint for him, a half for her. Napier gave him a shilling and told him to have one himself.

'And four of his cronies,' Caro muttered as the man departed. 'It can't have come to more than sevenpence halfpenny, d'you realize.'

He laughed. 'You *are* like your mother, you know. I'd love to have met your grandmother. A shopkeeper's daughter, wasn't she?'

She tried to think of something equally wounding to hint at in his family.

He, aware that she had taken the remark amiss, hid his silence in a large bite of ham.

She stared across the lough at the smudge of dirty gray stone that was Coolderg Castle. Was there anywhere you could escape seeing it, she wondered? Following her eyes he said, 'It's a funny thing, isn't it – the rise and fall of families. I don't suppose that'll be a Lyndon-Fury stronghold for very much longer.'

She stared at him in astonishment, wishing she had not just bitten off such a mouthful.

'Well, I'm certainly not going to live there,' he added. 'I spent too many years trying to escape it to want to go back.'

'Oh,' she said.

His gaze returned to the castle. 'And it was harder than you might imagine, too.'

'I'm sure,' she said.

'Did Aunt Swan ever tell you about those days? When we were all at the Academy School? She was part of it, you know. And your mother. Our friendship goes back to then.'

Caro shook her head and took a tentative sip of the dark liquid. It was awful, but, being a lady, she gave no hint of her distaste.

'Chuck it in the harbour if you don't like it,' he said. 'I'm sure he's got some red lemonade or something up there.'

'It's very nice,' Caro lied. 'I have drunk it before, you know.'

'Oh. Good.' He took a sip himself and went on, 'D'you still want to do both loughs?'

Caro thought it over. One mile of road was pretty much like another. From the point of view of comfort she ought to say no. On the other hand, two loughs was a better trophy than one – twice as better. 'I think so,' she replied. 'If you don't mind?'

'Your whim is my command, Little Face.' He broke into a smile. 'Actually, I want you to do me a favour, too – if you don't mind?'

'What?' She took another sip. It was starting to taste less dreadful.

He smiled at her directness, at the lack of any softening phrase, such as, 'If I can, I will.' With a self-deprecatory shrug he replied, 'I made such a tremenjus eejit of myself today, and you were so good at rescuing me, I was wondering if you'd continue to brush up my horsemanship? A lesson a week – that sort of thing.'

'I'd have to wear riding breeches,' she said at once.

He roared with laughter and then clapped his hand to his mouth. 'Sorry. Sorry.' He did not look in the least contrite. 'It's just that everything you do and say is so . . .' He shrugged.

'Like my mother?' she suggested wearily.

'Yes. I really am sorry.' He began to look it now. 'I can see how tiresome it must be for someone to keep saying it. I suppose when I know you better I'll see all the ways in which you're different.'

'As long as you do, then,' Caro warned him.

'I promise.'

They munched and supped in silence for a while before he went on, 'Not that you should object all that strenuously. She's one of the most admirable women I know. You could do a great deal worse than be like her.'

Caro took another bite, nodded, scuffed her heel against the dead water weeds clinging to the harbour wall. She might and then again she mightn't.

'Tell you what,' he said. 'I'll make a bargain with you. You know these Jodhpur-breeches that are all the rage nowadays? Where the gaiters and breeches are all in one? I'll buy you a pair of those if you'll tutor me.'

'Done!' She reached out a ham-greased hand and shook his firmly. 'Does that mean you're going to stay in Ireland for a bit? Mammy thought you'd go back to Paris quite soon.'

'No, I'll be staying for a bit. For quite a bit, perhaps. I don't think poor Cornel will make much of a fist of running the old place – otherwise, believe you me, I'd be off in a hack.' Some other point occurred to him. 'Have you ridden astride before then?'

She blushed and nodded. 'At Sharavogue, where no one can see.' Artlessly she parted her thighs and patted their insides, where her skirt fell into her lap. 'The pain here the first time was only *screw-shiatin*', as Mrs Shaughnessy says. But, oh, the control it lets you have over the horse! I could lepp a six-foot fence, which I'd go a mile to avoid side-saddle.'

'You could? Or you did?'

She grinned guiltily. 'I did. God, I nearly died at the size of it! Don't breathe a word to Mammy now.'

'I wouldn't think Daddy'd be too ecstatic about it either.'

But she squinted and tilted her head to one side. 'Ah well, I wouldn't say that, now. His point is you may take any reasonable risk if you're well prepared for it.'

'Wise man. Of course, we Irish are famous for the other thing – taking risks first and preparing for them afterwards.' He held out his hand for her empty plate and glass, only to find her doing the same to him.

She won but only as far as the inn door. When he came back out he said, 'We no longer keep the pig under the table, alas. If we did, certain places might be all the cleaner for it. D'you want to stretch your legs before we start off again?'

'I want to plant a sweet pea.' She giggled and looked at him. 'That's what Mammy does be saying.'

He chuckled but she saw a sadness in his eyes, too. 'I know,' he replied. 'I did be knowing your Mammy when she did be saying it.'

They found some bushes at the edge of town and went their ways. When she rejoined him on the road he was again staring across the lake at the Castle. 'Linford derives from O'Lindon's Ford, you know,' he said, not turning to her. 'This is actually where your people came from.'

'And yours,' she pointed out.

He smiled directly at her then. 'Isn't it all so complicated!'

'And ancient!'

'And stupid!'

They both laughed. She slipped her hand into his as they started walking back to Linford. 'If you escaped it successfully, Uncle Napier,' she asked, 'why are you talking of staying?'

He was silent a while and then, giving her hand a squeeze, said, 'Can you keep a secret, Little Face? Only for a few days, because it'll be in the *Irish Times* next week. Your Aunt Swan and I are going to be married.'

He felt no little jolt of surprise in the hand that held his – which was the confirmation he had been fishing for all this while. 'You don't seem too surprised?'

She pulled her hand from his and readjusted her cap. She did not replace it when she had done.

'I hope everyone else takes it as calmly,' he went on. 'We're worried it could cause a bit of a scandal – coming so soon after poor Mercier's death.'

A cloud that had obscured the sun moved away: Caro gave a little skip as they passed out into the sunshine again.

'Aunt Swan wants me to do up the villa there.' He pointed at the tiny spot of red brick on the farther shore. 'There'll be talk about that, too – overlooking the very spot where he died.' He laughed awkwardly. 'In for a penny, in for a pound, eh?'

'Didn't Daddy work on that villa once?' Caro asked. 'We were all out fishing with Uncle Mercier one day and he said something about making one of the newel posts in there.'

'That's right. So he did!' Napier spoke as if he had forgotten it.

'And Mammy was staying there then. That's where he met her.'

'Did he tell you that? You know it all, then. I'll bet he didn't tell you I was rather sweet on her then?'

She smiled at him. 'I think I guessed that.' She didn't add that it was only a few hours ago.

'I'm sure you did. Ah, but it came to nothing in the end. That's the way of it.' They had arrived back at the car. 'Beat your previous best,' he challenged. 'Start her in two.'

She did.

They drove round both the loughs at a spanking pace, and without a single puncture. It made sustained conversation impossible. Their intercourse was confined to exclamations of delight at the more picturesque discoveries, or of alarm at sudden hazards along the way. The number of hens, goats, pigs, and asses who seemed to think that the highways were for their leisure alone was only phenomenal. When they arrived back at the Coolderg stables Caro felt as if she had climbed a mountain.

This time he took her hand as they walked back to the castle.

'About this morning,' he said.

'Yes?' She held her breath. Would she or wouldn't she?

'What your Aunt Swan said?'

'Yes?'

'You did overhear it, didn't you.'

'Yes.'

He squeezed her hand and swallowed audibly. 'Does it make any difference?'

'No.'

She gave his hand an answering squeeze and, slipping away from him, ran to tell her Aunt Swan they *had* done both loughs after all.

79

Caro saw Swan on the second landing and called out to her. Her aunt called back over her shoulder, 'Be with you in a moment. I must just fetch a blanket for poor Cornel. He's not too bright, I fear.' She hastened on down the passage to the second guest bedroom.

Caro went back to the floor below, to the library, thinking she might help. She found Uncle Cornel in a heap on the floor, giggling – or was he weeping? He was bathed in sweat and trembling all over. The cause of his condition was obvious – an empty bottle of Bushmills lying on its side in the middle of the carpet; how could Aunt Swan have missed it? Anyway, a blanket was the last thing the man needed, sweating like that.

She raised his head and cradled him on her lap. He opened his eyes and stared blankly at her. For several seconds the brain cogs whirred and then his fact lit up with a smile that touched her heart. 'Caro!'

'Yes, Uncle Cornel.'

'Cornel,' he repeated. 'And Caro.'

'Yes, Uncle Cornel.'

'Caro!'

'Yes.'

'I love you.' He began to weep.

Moved almost to tears herself she quelled the remains of her distaste and hugged him to her. 'You'll be all right,' she promised. 'Aunt Swan's gone to . . . get something for you.'

'Swan!' His weeping turned easily to laughter. 'She's a pal.'

'Yes. Just relax. Don't try and talk.'

'A real pal. And you're a pal, Caro.' Tears welled in his eyes again. 'Caro.'

'Yes, Uncle Cornel. It's all right now.'

'Caro.'

'Yes. I'm here.' She looked around at a loss, not knowing what to do. Why was Aunt Swan taking so long? Should she hide the bottle?

'Caro.' The tears flowed in earnest again. 'I tried to kill you once.'

'Would you gwan out of that!' She hugged him tighter and shook his head. 'You knocked me down on your bicycle and I had a little graze on one elbow. Killed me, indeed!'

'You could have been . . . all . . . just lying there.'

'A little graze-een of a graze. The mercurichrome was worse than the hurt *you* did.'

'I love you, Swan.'

She laughed. 'Yes, yes.'

'You don' b'lieve me . . .' His words were so slurred he seemed to be talking in his sleep. She wished he were. 'I love you. Always loved you. You're a pal.'

Now it was her laughter that threatened to turn into tears. Where *was* Aunt Swan? 'Stop trying to talk,' she said, quite sharply.

She doubted he even heard her. He just went on muttering that he loved her. To shut him up she asked in an even more peremptory tone where he had managed to get the whiskey. She had to ask three times before he'd listen.

'*You* gave it me.' He giggled. 'B'lated Christmas present. I love you, Swan.'

Thank God Aunt Swan herself returned at that moment. She startled Caro, who had not heard her coming although the door was slightly ajar; but the girl's relief soon outweighed her surprise.

'Oh!' Swan surveyed the strange tableau that greeted her.

Caro pointed silently at the empty whiskey bottle; the child in her felt treacherous; the rising woman told her she was only being responsible and mature.

'Oh,' Swan said in a different tone, censorious and weary. '*How* did he smuggle that in here? I searched high and low when I brought him his luncheon.' She dropped the blanket upon him, as if he no longer deserved sympathetic nursing, and shouted in a tone usually reserved for the deaf or the senile: 'You're a thundering disgrace, you old reprobate!'

'He is quite poorly, all the same.' Caro offered timidly.

'My dear!' Swan smiled indulgently. 'It's a storm he's weathered a thousand times. Would you ever slip down and ask Napier to go for Doctor Morgan?'

80

Caro felt a certain responsibility toward Uncle Cornel after that – especially since Aunt Swan was being so unsympathetic.

It was odd, Caro thought, how so many things in her life were suddenly changing – especially after so many years in which it seemed nothing would ever change. Two weeks ago, Uncle Cornel wasn't even in the halfpenny place with her. She couldn't have mustered an opinion of any kind upon the man, except the general one – that he was hearty before noon, fluthered after it, and comatose by dusk.

She had never exchanged more than a few conventional words with him, a wary smile or two. She saw him as a frail old gentleman who walked around as if he had a hundred and one bruises. You looked at his ever-weeping eyes and marvelled at the purple reticule of veins on his nose and cheeks, and you'd sort of sidle past him as best you could.

Yet now, just the fact of cradling him in her lap that day – the day of revelations – and listening to the confused and startled love in him fighting with the whiskey . . . it had altered her whole perception of him.

Had she changed, or had he?

For her own peace of mind she decided it was mostly herself. She was still fearful enough of adulthood to want a world in which everything and everyone else remained more or less constant – otherwise how might she measure her gains?

It being her school holidays, she was free to ride over to the castle every day and spend an hour or two at his bedside, reading poetry to him – he had a great liking for Dryden – and generally talking about this and that. Dr Morgan said he was dying, but it wasn't the first time he'd said that.

To make sure he'd couldn't smuggle in any more whiskey, they locked him in the old nursery, which could be reached only through the nanny's old bedroom, which was also kept locked. And just to make certain, Swan herself moved into the castle and took charge of both keys.

'You're an absolute brick,' Madeleine told her. 'It'd be altogether too much for Mama. The pater's a full-time occupation for her these days.'

Swan smiled graciously and replied that, since she'd be one of the family soon enough, it was time she took her share of the responsibility. She was delighted that Caro seemed to want to help. 'How she puts up with all his scribble-chatter, I do not know,' she commented. 'D'you know, he told me yesterday that old Annie gave him the whiskey.'

'But she's been dead for years,' Madeleine objected.

'Quite!'

Caro couldn't believe that Uncle Cornel was dying. True, his mind rambled a lot, but her Mammy said that could be the laudanum. There were other times, however, when he was quite lucid, and she began to glimpse the fine man he might have been. He had no memory for recent events. He couldn't recall her finding him like that and cradling his head in her lap; but, just as on that occasion itself, he could remember earlier times – like when he had ridden his bicycle down the foot pavement and bowled her over as she was coming out of the school. He remembered that the justice hadn't fined him because he was a Lyndon-Fury. He chuckled when he remembered, further, that the justice was none other than Sir Lucius Lyndon-Fury, who often rode down the same pavement on the same bicycle!

His incoherent confession that he loved her, when he seemed to imagine she was Aunt Swan, intrigued Caro; she wondered if there was anything behind it or was it just the rambling of his disordered mind? She racked her brain for some way of raising the subject but every wheeze foundered on the fact that he still treated her as a child, with that gallant archness old bachelors keep especially for girls of her age.

One day, taking the risk of her life, she said, as casually as she could manage, 'By the way, I suppose you know that Uncle Napier is really my father?'

He just smiled at her and said, 'Families!'

It was hardly the response she had expected. If he had denied it, or remonstrated with her, or laughed and gone on to add whatever he knew on the topic . . . any of those reactions she could have built upon. But that enigmatic, one-word comment deprived her of any reply.

'How did you find out?' he asked.

She was too nonplussed still to do anything but tell him the truth.

'Ah,' he said when she had finished. 'And what did your parents have to say about it all?'

She stared impassively at her hands. Dirty fingernails. Not real dirt, only horsey dirt.

'You haven't told them?' he guessed.

Still not looking at him, she shook her head.

'Why not?'

'I don't know.'

He sniffed. 'I don't believe that.'

She smiled against her will. 'It sounds so silly.'

When she volunteered nothing further he prompted, 'Perhaps I won't think so.'

'Well . . . in a way, it feels almost as if it's nothing to do with me. Except by sheer accident.' She chuckled grimly. 'I mean, I *was* a sheer accident, wasn't I!'

After a pause he said, 'D'you really think so?'

'Well, of course I was! You don't imagine Mammy . . . really . . .' her voice tailed off, '. . . intended . . . or did she?'

'Isn't it possible?'

Caro shook her head in bewilderment. 'I can't imagine her at twenty or whatever it was. Christopher!' She stared out of the window. 'I never thought of that! Now I certainly can't talk to her about it.'

His smile seemed to show that he understood. 'Even if you were a sheer accident,' he said, 'I still don't see why you feel . . . aloof. Or unconnected – however you want to put it.'

'Because it's all feuds and battles and strife,' she said, becoming agitated. 'O'Lindons versus Lyndon-Furys. And us against all our rivals in business. And Mammy wanting to be on more committees than . . . oh, you know yourself now, the sort of thing! When I first heard Napier was my natural father – well, of course, I was too shocked to think anything. But one of my first thoughts, when I was capable again, was, "Good! Now I'm on both sides, so I needn't take part at all!" '

'And wouldn't you tell your Mammy *that*?'

Caro shook her head. 'She wouldn't understand.'

He nodded. Then a further thought struck him. 'Talking of feuds and strife – you omitted to mention one of the combatants: your Aunt Swan. You realize she *wanted* you to overhear it?'

The moment he spoke, Caro realized it was true and that some part of her had already reached the same conclusion; at least, his words came more as a confirmation than a surprise. 'Oh yes,' she said confidently. 'But I don't know why.'

'Don't you?' he asked, as if that did surprise him.

'Well, I suppose I do, in a way.' She remembered Napier telling her about the days at the Academy School and so she took an inspired leap at it. 'I think it must go back to when they were all in Dublin together.'

'You see!' He beamed at her.

She suddenly found herself wishing she'd made better friends with him when he'd been a better man; there was a whole raft of goodness and gentleness in him, when everyone else seemed consumed by strife and wanting to do each other in the eye. He was outside of all that.

She took a further step into uncharted waters. 'Uncle Napier tries to make it seem as if there was hardly anything between him and Mammy and really it was Aunt Swan all the time.'

'Your Aunt Swan,' he told her, drawing a parallel rather than a tangent to her thought, 'will be Cleopatra yet.'

'I see.' Caro nodded solemnly and stowed the comment away for later dissection. 'I think Uncle Napier really wanted to marry my Mammy, but she was the one who turned him down.'

He nodded. 'Even though you were already on the way. You know about all that, I suppose – babies and so on?'

'Of course,' she assured him lightly.

'So it was a very brave thing she did. But she always knew . . . about Napier . . . in her heart of hearts she always knew . . .' He glanced uneasily at her and then thought better of it. 'Families!' he sighed.

He continued to make such a good recovery that it surprised her one day when he said he was going to die quite soon. She knew him well enough by then to tell him not to be such an eejit; wasn't he getting better and better every day.

But he would not be cajoled into his usual playfulness. 'It has nothing to do with getting better or getting worse,' he said. 'It's as sure as next month's moon.'

'But how d'you *know*?' she protested.

'I know what I know, and that's enough for me. You may take it whatever way you want. But listen till I tell you. The distilled wisdom of a lifetime.' He smiled. 'Did I say distilled? Anyway, for what it's worth. First let me tell you about people. If a man says to you – or a woman, mind – if either man or woman tells you they want something for the simple reason that they want it, you may believe them. But if they tell you they want it for the good of the country, or the faith, or the grand oul' cause, or most especially for your *own* good, you may put a bullet between their eyes and rid the world of a scoundrel.' He grinned at her foxily.

'Don't be taking that too literally or there'd only be you and me left.' He frowned. 'That's people for you. What was the other thing?'

'Families?' she suggested, being now rather good at inspired leaps.

His face lit up. 'You're right! Ah, girleen, there's little fear for you! Families. They are without doubt the most destroying, vengeful, flesh-consuming, spirit-quenching institutions ever to come out of the mind of man. But as long as you know that – and don't forget it now – as long as you know that, it's worth the fight to preserve them. And d'you know why?'

She shook her head and hung on his every word.

'Because the alternative,' he said, 'is worse.'

He lay back and closed his eyes. 'Would you ever read me a bit of Dryden now. From *Oedipus*. You know the bit I mean.'

She did. She took down the book and read:

'Of no distemper, of no blast he died,
But fell like autumn fruit that mellowed long.
Ev'n wondered at because he dropp'd no sooner.
Fate seemed to wind him up for fourscore years
Yet ran he freely on ten winters more;
'Till, like a clock worn out with eating time,
The weary wheels of life at last stood still.'

She paused and looked up. A single tear coursed silently down his cheek. 'That's what I want on my grave,' he murmured.

She was still child enough to blurt out, 'But it isn't true!'

Without opening his eyes he smiled and said, 'Sure, a hundred years from now – who'll know the difference? That's another thing I meant to tell you. A hundred years from now . . .' He sighed and did not complete the sentence.

She left him shortly after that. It was the last time she saw him alive.

81

Doctor Morgan had no qualm in signing the death certificate. 'Didn't I warn him?' he asked in lugubrious triumph. 'He was sitting in that very chair when I told him. One more drop, I said, and your soul's on its own.'

He raised a helpless hand at the folly of those who tried to live beyond the reach of medical prophecy. No one was tactless enough to point out that his recent warning had merely been the last of a long line, reaching back almost twenty years.

Sir Lucius took the news of his second son's death more philosophically than he had Trapper's. When Napier went to see him he managed to get his clotted tongue and flaccid lips to convey the words: 'All up to you.'

Napier nodded morosely and murmured, 'Yes, Pater, of course.' But he did not consider it a promise.

That night Lady Lyndon-Fury awoke to hear her husband crying. She rocked him in her arms and dabbed away the tears until he settled back to sleep. When she awoke in the morning he lay cold at her side.

Rosina came at once from Waterford, thinking that she and Madeleine should take charge of the castle and all the arrangements. Madeleine explained that Swan and Napier would soon be married . . . and he was now the heir. But Swan resolved the dilemma for them. 'What would it look like,' she asked, 'with the pair of you here and me giving out marching orders right, left, and centre? And we can't announce our engagement until the funerals are over.'

They thought it showed great delicacy on her part.

She did, however, tentatively suggest that an inquiry be instituted among the servants to discover which of them had smuggled the second bottle of Bushmills to poor dear Cornel despite the double-locking of the doors. But Napier put his foot down at that. In the first place he wouldn't even entertain the suggestion that any of the castle servants could be so utterly disloyal; in the second, everyone knew how cunning a drunkard could be. If they went through all the nooks and crannies in the castle, they'd probably find a dozen bottles of this and that, all craftily purloined by Cornel whenever the drinks were brought out for guests and hidden there for just such an occasion as the one that had killed him. He pointed out that Bushmills had been served at Trapper's wake, and when it was over there had been an argument over whether ten bottles or a dozen had been ordered. 'Obviously it was a dozen,' he observed, 'though only ten empties were found. Now we know where the other two were.'

The two sisters were a little surprised when Swan insisted on inviting Caro. The old woman's feelings about the girl, and her mother, were well known – and so strong that not even Caro's devoted nursing of Cornel had been able to soften them. But Swan had a private talk with her, and after that her objections ceased – even though Caro was too young to invite without her parents.

The first shock as they came stamping into the ballroom out of the cold and the wet was to see a number of new canvases hanging where before there had been gaps. These were no fusty old history paintings, either, full of saints in togas or smug, bourgeois merchants challenging you to put one over them. They were bright, richly textured, intensely observed scenes of modern everyday life – a French goose girl, mushroom pickers, an orchestra tuning up, jockeys at a weigh-in . . .

It took Daisy about half a second to exclaim, 'They're by Napier.'

Swan, who had been hovering around, waiting for her to come in, clapped hands in delight and hugged her warmly. 'I knew you'd see it at once, darling,' she said. 'What d'you think of them?'

Daisy studied them briefly. How odd, she thought, that something like this could slip under her guard. She was sure, absolutely sure beyond a shadow of a doubt, that she had not the smallest pick of a romantic feeling left toward Napier. And even the anger that had supplanted it was also dead and gone. He was now just a person she had known quite well a long time ago and had lately encountered again.

But seeing those paintings on the wall, letting her eye run over the colours that only he could have chosen, reviving in her imagination the heady aromas of turpentine, linseed oil, beeswax, and copal varnish – so powerfully that she'd almost swear they were in her nostrils at that moment – it resurrected not so much her feelings for Napier as her remembrance of herself, the happy, naïve, trusting, romantic, giddy young girl to whom every day had been such a grand and glorious adventure. She felt keenly the losses that all the gains of her life had brought her.

Swan giggled and, coming close to her ear, said, 'There's one I don't know where to hang. I'm looking for a really good place for it. A portrait of Saint Joan of Arc.'

Daisy stared at her in horror. All she could think to say was, 'Sure St Joan was no saint in those days.'

Swan almost choked on her reply: 'You'd know more about that than me, my dear!' Then, to satisfy the curious near by, she added, 'I was never great on Roman Catholic theology.'

'Hagiography,' Napier corrected her, hoping the sternness in his voice would convey his displeasure at her unseemly levity.

Swan appeared not to notice. She put an arm around Daisy's shoulders and hugged her warmly once again. 'There's only one place for a heretic,' she commented.

'The flames?' Daisy asked hopefully.

'The dungeon, anyway.'

Caro, watching them, only half took-in their banter; she wondered how they could possibly chatter away so light-heartedly when less than half an hour ago they had laid to rest that wonderful, wise, and tragic man and his father. She wandered from them and gravitated – quite naturally it seemed by now – to the top of the tower.

Stephen watched her go, gave her a few minutes start, then followed her up. He found her standing beside the chimney, staring out over the park toward the Lyndon-Fury cemetery. She must know he was there, or someone was there; he'd made enough noise coming up.

'D'you think we're only terrible to be laughing and chatting the way we do?' he asked.

She turned round and smiled, having little other choice. 'D'you know what he wants on his gravestone? He told me, the very day he died.'

She repeated the lines of the poem.

As he watched her lips forming the alien, slightly archaic words, he realized how much she had grown up those last few months. She'd pass him out in many ways soon enough.

His response was the same as hers had been: 'It wouldn't be the truth.'

'In a hundred years,' she said. 'Who'd either know or care?'

'They wouldn't need to know,' he pointed out. 'They'd just look at the date of birth and the date of death and they'd see it wasn't true.'

She was glad she hadn't thought of that. 'All the same,' she said vaguely.

'Talking of inscriptions on stones,' he went on, 'you've seen the one in this chimney, I'm sure. The O'Lindon Stone, as they call it.'

'Yes!' She dragged the syllable out wearily.

'I can remember the shock I got the first time I saw it.'

'Like finding a cardigan at school with your name tag sewn into it – and you absolutely *know* it's not yours,' she offered.

He caught the sarcasm and raised his eyebrow. 'Is that how it struck you?' He felt something like panic at the thought that she was becoming a stranger to him; he would never have supposed her capable of throwing out such a telling question. The child had gone for ever and he had missed the moment of her passing.

'Didn't it you?' she asked.

He smiled ruefully. 'It was different. I was with two other lads,we were all apprentice joiners, and they knew it was here. They thought it a great joke. It made me angry.'

'Aunt Swan says it ought to be pulled out. It doesn't belong there any more.'

He was shocked. 'She said that to you?'

'Not to me. But I heard her say it to Uncle Napier.'

'And what did he say?'

'He just laughed. He laughs at a lot of the things she suggests.' As an afterthought she added, 'But he sometimes does them all the same.'

'Has anybody told you anything about him?' he asked.

It was on the tip of her tongue to say, quite casually, '*That he's my real father, you mean?*' but her courage faltered at the last moment. 'No,' she said. Then, realizing that was a little improbable, she added, 'Well, Uncle Cornel did sort of hint that Uncle Napier might have been sweet on Mammy once, but I'd guessed that already.'

His fingernails were hurting the palms of his hands; he had to force himself to relax and smile. 'How could you guess a thing like that?'

'Well – her staying at the Lyndon-Furys' villa, where you told me you met her.'

'Did I?' He had forgotten the incident.

'I couldn't think why else she'd be staying there unless Uncle Napier had invited her. And Aunt Swan wasn't there, so Mammy couldn't have been there to chaperone her.'

'Ah. I see. Well, you're quite right. That was the way of it.' He stared at her, smiling vaguely, suddenly at a loss. He had come up here intending to tell her the truth – and suddenly found he could not. It had something to do with his panic earlier, that the child had gone without his noticing it. He could not face the loss of whatever remained.

'Why did you bring that up suddenly?' she asked.

'Oh . . . because of the world and the way people are. Have you heard the latest – that Trapper Lyndon-Fury's death wasn't quite an accident? They're saying Flynn "assisted" it.'

'Killed him you mean?' she asked excitedly.

'Ah, well, they wouldn't go that far. They wouldn't say he killed him. But they wouldn't *not* say it, either. D'you see what I mean? They'll go round three corners to get at it. The reason I bring it up is just so you'll remember it if you hear anyone blackguarding me or your mother . . . or even yourself, now. You're getting old enough to be thought fair game yourself. That's all. Just hold it in mind.'

He could not tell whether she had heard him or not; she just stood there staring out over the park, her face quite devoid of expression.

'What can you see?' he asked.

'Nothing.' She smiled at him and held out an arm for him to slip his about her. 'I was just looking at the family burial ground. The Lyndon-Furys.'

His heart swelled with happiness at her gesture and at the comfort of feeling her beside him. 'Ours, too,' he said. 'There are O'Lindon graves there as well.'

'I didn't see any.'

'They're in the corner opposite where we were today.'

'That's where Mammy saw the stag escape.'

He laughed uncomfortably, as if he were aware of being slightly high-flown and not his usual character. 'It's where we'll all escape one day.'

'Not us,' she said. 'Not from *that* burial ground.'

There was a pause before he replied, 'Who can tell?' He eased his light clasp on her and took up her hand instead, to lead her back inside. 'It's getting dark.'

He gave the O'Lindon Stone an affectionate kick as he passed. 'She'd have a job shifting that, I can tell you.'

As they crossed the south battlements she suddenly asked why he and Mammy had decided to call her Caroline.

'For luck,' he replied light-heartedly.

'So it was nothing to do with the O'Lindon Stone,' she insisted.

'Well, wasn't it a lucky name for her, too?'

'To marry a Lyndon-Fury?' She laughed. 'There aren't any left for me. Uncle Napier is the only bachelor and he's going to marry Aunt Swan.' As soon as the words were out she could have kicked herself; it was such common knowledge within the castle she had forgotten it was supposed to be a secret until a week or so after the funeral. 'Nobody's to know that,' she added shamefacedly. 'Don't say I told you.'

'How is it you know it then?' he asked.

She didn't want to admit it was Napier himself who had told her. 'Uncle Cornel let it slip,' she replied. Once again she felt a dreadful traitress, but it appeared to satisfy her father. 'Anyway,' she went on, 'it means I certainly can't follow in the other Caroline's footsteps.'

As he ushered her into the stairway ahead of him he said, 'Well, there's always two ways to shave a pig.'

When they rejoined the company Daisy raised her eyebrows and drew him aside. 'Did you tell her?'

He shook his head. 'I couldn't. In the heel of the hunt, I couldn't.'

Daisy smiled. 'I never thought you could.'

'But you let me try.'

'What did you tell her? You were gone some time.'

He quickly summarized their conversation. The news that Swan and Napier were to marry did not appear to surprise her. 'I guessed as much,' she said grimly. 'The way she's been lording it over this household. Still, it's good to know where we are.'

'Where *we* are?' he echoed in surprise.

She stared at him with some asperity. 'You may come down off of that horse, Stephen. You covet this place every bit as sorely as me.'

His answering grin was slightly twisted, as if she had forced it from him against his will. ‘D’you think we dare?’ he asked.

‘Dare!’ She made a contemptuous exclamation of the word.

At that moment Swan’s eyes and hers met across the crowded room.

Swan beamed at her.

Daisy twinkled back. ‘By God but it’ll be a rare oul’ battle,’ she murmured to Stephen.

Part III

To have and to hold not

82

Madeleine, knowing that Caro was coming to tea that day, decided to ride out and meet her half way – not that she had a hope of following the girl over the sort of ditches she chose to jump, for Maddy, like most decent women, still rode side-saddle.

She enjoyed being able to ride again. In the days of their deepest poverty she had told herself she missed nothing about the old, privileged way of life as the daughter of the castle – and had even believed it, too. But the moment Thomas began to be collected, after Napier took him up and got the New English Art Club to accept him, it was only amazing how life's small luxuries began to creep back one by one. They'd never be rich, of course; Thomas would never be a fashionable painter like Napier. But the trappings of good, solid comfort had slowly returned: the cook, the tweeny, the daily nanny, the calling cards, the annual, then quarterly, then monthly, shopping trips to Dublin, the seaside holidays . . . It was amazing, too, how people to whom she had been transparent for years had begun to find her visible again.

She rode out towards the end of the old railway line, knowing that Caro would almost certainly come down the former railbed, which now made a superb bridle path over the bog and through the estate. Farther east, toward Simonstown, the farmers had claimed it all back, even though the lawsuit was still in progress. They had put fences across it – but then fences meant nothing to Caro, especially with her new horse, Shalimar. It was mainly to watch him in action that Madeleine had come out to meet them; she had hopes of making a killing on them at Simonstown races next month.

It was a bright, raw January day, verging on a frost and with a feeling of snow on the breeze. Local people said that when you could see every window across the lough in Linford, and count every tree on the County Clare horizon, six miles away – as she herself had done that morning – it was generally a poor sign. The exceptional clarity of the air, however, enabled her to espy Caro when she was still a mile up the line.

She still had to remind herself it was not a man riding like that – only Caro, scandalizing the countryside once more. Dr Morgan had warned her she could do irreparable damage to her internal organs and would certainly never be able to bear children; she'd be a cripple before she was thirty and would die soon after – but it made no difference to her determination. She just said (after he'd gone) that if God paid heed to Dr Morgan, there'd be no need for emigration from County Keelity. Daisy and Stephen had given up trying. Madeleine suspected they were actually rather proud of her waywardness; they often said, in other contexts, that she was 'a real O'Lindon'.

She was riding in a half-standing position, which must be murder on her back Maddy thought. She sat down only when she wanted to gather him for a change of pace or some other movement. She cantered down the line at a fair lick, too. The horses whinnied at each other when the gap was a furlong or so and Maddy's mount grew restive when it seemed as if Shalimar must come crashing into them. But Caro pulled him up at the last minute with a laugh.

'Whooo!' She was as breathless as Shalimar. She fanned her face with her hand and tucked a few stray wisps of hair back under her cap.

Madeleine looked her up and down and smiled. Jodhpur breeches, hacking jacket, cloth cap . . . how could she possibly remain so feminine? And yet she did. The 'New Woman'.

'Happy New Year!' Caro said. 'If it's not too late.'

'Same to you, my dear. I don't know how you do it.'

'What? You ought to let that bearing rein out another notch, you know – over country like this.'

'How you ride standing up like that for mile after mile.'

'Good training for me. How's Aunt Rosina? How are they all in Waterford?'

'Oh, I've masses to tell you there. Aren't you going to leap a few ditches? That's what I came out to see. I'm hoping to win a fair fortune on you next month. What about that one there? Would he refuse?' She nodded toward a particularly high patch of hawthorn.

Caro, pretending to be horrified, covered Shalimar's ear nearest Madeleine. 'Sure, he doesn't know the word exists. I have to be careful not to ride him at something the size of Coolderg Castle. He'd have a crack at it. Watch this.'

Sitting deep into the saddle she rode him off into the pasture and turned him to face the highest part of the ditch, which was a shade over six foot. Madeleine's heart rose into her mouth. If she were to face such a jump – which she would if certain death were the only alternative – she'd want twice as long a run-up as that, and she'd spur her mount on to a full gallop, and she'd close her eyes ten paces out and give the fella his head. Yet there was Caro, starting no more than twenty strides out, sitting deep, holding him back, cantering so slow you'd wonder he didn't drop off to sleep . . . he was surely never going to make it. Five paces out she lengthened his stride; with only two paces to go she gathered him sharply again so that on the final stride he got right under himself and then simply flew it. He didn't stir a twig. The grunt of exertion he gave out on landing sounded like a single *hah*! of triumph.

It was a straggly ditch and there was a three-foot-high gap not five yards from where Caro had jumped. Madeleine took a good run at it and got over, leaving it still at least two foot high behind her. 'That was a sight,' she told Caro. 'Don't do that where too many can see you. I'll make a fortune.'

'It's what Mammy calls a typical Lyndon-Fury ditch,' Caro said, running her eye up and down its monstrous unevenness.

'I don't know how you get him to face the highest part like that, when there are three-foot gaps so close.'

'That's where he's special.' She patted Shalimar's mane. 'He likes a challenge, don't you, old fella.'

He shook his head and champed at the bit.

'But that's enough for today. I'm thinking it's me needs the exercise, not him.'

They trotted down to the cottage, leaping the lowest parts of the ditches in their path. Their conversation was desultory since neither wanted to squander the best news until they had a cup in the hand and a fire to warm them.

'God, I reek like a goat,' Caro said as they went indoors, leaving Shalimar well blanketed. 'And I had a bath only this morning. You've done something to this room. Wait now, don't tell me.' She stared about her and decided: 'New curtains.'

'And antimacassars,' Madeleine said, pleased she had noticed. 'Tom's Christmas present to me.'

'Lord, aren't you both so romantic!' Caro teased. 'I got a new saddle and bridle from Callaghan's. And Mammy gave me these boots. Will I take them off?' She surveyed the trail of mud behind her and added, 'Bit late.'

Madeleine smiled bravely; from a hunting family herself, she was used to it. 'Never mind that.' She rang for the tea. 'What else has happened? You went to the hunt ball, of course. I hear you turned every head in the county – the madonna with the beautiful Italian shawl!'

Caro clapped hands at the memory. 'That was Uncle Napier's present. I'm in bad odour there because Aunt Swan found it hidden away and thought he'd got it for her!'

'And what had he actually got her?'

'Three Oriental fans for her collection. She didn't consider it anything like as good as the shawl. Oh, Maddy, it is only *sumpshus*! You should see it!' Caro still felt slightly awkward in calling her just Maddy but she was getting used to it.

'Everyone's talking about it. But it's the way you wore it, I'm sure. You have the face and figure to carry it. Who did you dance with?'

'Oh . . .' Her eyes raked the ceiling. 'George Danforth, Patrick Hamilton, two of the Trenches – don't ask me which, they're all mad – Oxmantown, and what's Inchiquin's youngest called? Him, anyway. D'you want me to go on? I never stopped all evening.'

'And no proposals?' Madeleine asked with arch curiosity.

Caro closed her eyes, made a grim arc of her lips, and nodded. 'You can think yourself lucky you were never an heiress.'

'I was,' Madeleine protested. 'Only the pot was empty. I take it there were no acceptances.'

'Mammy was furious – and still is. She wants me to accept Oxmantown, though anyone with a title would do.' She smiled suddenly. 'Did you know Dervla's expecting a baby? Sometime in August, she says.'

'Goodness, that was quick! They only married . . . when?'

'Last November. Ah, but Mammy has us all bet when it comes to speed in that department!'

Bridget, the tweeny, came in with the tea. During the pause Madeleine became aware that, from the moment Caro had seated herself, she hadn't been still. She crossed and uncrossed her legs, her hands fidgeted with her hair, the carving of the arm of her chair, the buttons of her jacket . . . everything within reach. She laughed, she smiled, she bubbled with good humour, but she was not at ease; she was not a contented girl.

'You haven't said a word about Waterford,' Caro prompted. 'Was your mother there?'

'No. I don't think she ever wants to come back to Ireland. Except for funerals. Pity, but there it is. The others are all in the pink, especially Gwendolen, who sends you her love and says . . .'

'Why don't I write? I know.' Caro covered her head briefly, as if from shrapnel. 'I will, I promise.'

'As for what we did – we went for walks. We overate on Christmas Day and repented on St Stephen's . . . what else do families do?'

'Quarrel,' Caro said glumly.

'That, too, of course.' She passed Caro her tea and waved an invitation toward the sandwiches and Madeira cake. 'What's *your* latest quarrel?'

Caro stared into the embers for a while. 'The same as ever,' she said at last, 'only it's made worse now because Uncle Napier wants to paint my portrait.' She took up the bellows and reddened the fire before she added, 'They made life hell on earth for me when I used to go over and tutor his riding. I can just imagine what they'll do if I go over to sit for him.' She closed her eyes. 'It's not fair.'

She braced herself, took a large bite of tongue sandwich, and pretended to be jolly again. 'How did I get into such a mess!'

'How did *you* get into such a mess?' Madeleine echoed.

'Well, I know they started it, but their mess is nothing compared to

. . .' She sighed without finishing the sentence. 'I keep forgetting what I'm supposed to know and not supposed to know, and it changes depending who I'm with.' She laughed without humour and began to tell it on her fingers like a schoolchild repeating a lesson by rote. 'When I'm with Uncle Napier, I know he's my father. In fact, I don't call him Uncle when we're alone, just Napier. And I also know Mammy used to pose in the altogether at the Academy School and there was a famous painting of her as St Joan . . .'

'Have you seen it?'

'Oh yes! Dear Aunt Swan made quite sure I blundered into the "locked" room, ha ha, where she keeps it!'

'Were you shocked?'

Caro shrugged. 'For a second or two. Mainly because I had no idea it was there. No idea it existed, even. Then I laughed. D'you know why?' She laughed now at the memory.

Madeleine shook her head.

'Because my very next thought was, *If Mammy goes and chops down that lovely pinewood by the villa, the first thing Aunt Swan will do is hang this over the fireplace in the ballroom and invite the whole county to a grand buffet-ball.*'

Madeleine laughed with her; the observation was so accurate.

Caro's humour died. 'It's not funny really, though,' she went on. 'That's what I mean. There you have a beautiful painting – and it really is a beautiful painting. And what do they do with it? They go and turn it into a loaded pistol to threaten someone with. They're so . . . *obsessed*! They ruin everything like that.' She looked up at Madeleine, who saw real pain in her eyes. 'Don't you agree?'

Madeleine nodded unhappily but thought it best to say nothing yet – just to give the poor girl the chance to get everything off her chest.

'All I want to do,' Caro went on, 'is to be friends with everybody, to feel free to walk into Coolderg and have a bit of crack with Aunt Swan or admire Napier's latest painting or go for a drive with them – and then go back home and talk about it just as if I'd been out for a drive with . . . I don't know, one of the Trenches or anybody else. Why can't they just forget the past?'

'Too painful still?' Madeleine suggested.

'But it needn't be. It's just because they keep fanning it back to life. They don't really care about family history and all that, you know.'

It seemed such an odd tangent to what had gone before that Madeleine asked her what she meant by it.

Caro glanced at her slightly warily. 'You know the room at the very top of the tower?'

'The pigeon loft?'

'Well, it only became a pigeon loft when the windows got broken and nobody bothered to repair them. It used to be the courthouse. There's a little dungeon, or a sort of prison cell to one side.'

'Is that what it was? Good heavens.'

Caro smiled at last and remarked that she wished everyone had Maddy's approach to the history of Coolderg. Then, serious again, she went on, 'I found an old locked trunk in the back there, and I picked away and picked away until I got it open.'

'How exciting! When did all this happen? While we were in Waterford?'

'No. Last November, while everyone else was being driven to distraction over Dervla's wedding.'

'You young slyboots! And you never said a word. What was inside? Any jewels?'

Caro smiled and shook her head. 'It's all old bills and letters. D'you know they used to write letters out in the old days and make copies! Where did they find the time?'

'Some people nowadays can't even find time to . . .'

'All right, all right! Most of the letters were about the estate, to and from the steward – whose name was Stephen O'Lindon, believe it or not!'

'What did your father say to that?'

'For God's sake don't tell him! Don't tell any of them. Don't ever breathe a word of this – please?'

'Why ever not? It sounds very exciting.'

'I've locked it again. I can pick it fairly easily myself now. But I shake dust back over it and everything. If they knew what was in it, they'd only ransack it for ammunition to use against each other. Exactly like Napier's painting of Mammy, you see? It can't be enjoyed just for what it is.'

'Is it all simply bills and estate business?'

'I don't know. I've only got about so far down. But what I was going to tell you was I found a copy of a letter from Caroline O'Lindon, the one who married the first Lucius Fury, d'you remember?'

Madeleine glanced heavenward. 'Could I ever forget! What does she say? Who was it to?'

'It was to her mother in Flaxmills. Her family lived in a house called Sharavogue! Sometimes when I'm reading it I wonder what century I'm in! It's not our Sharavogue, mind, but it was roughly on the same site. In fact, it's the hill that's called Sharavogue, not the house.'

'It means dandelion pasture, you know. Or so Thomas says.'

Caro chuckled. 'It's well named, so. Anyway, this letter is all about Lucius putting up the O'Lindon Stone with Caroline's name on it after she died. Obviously he discussed it with her while she was still alive. I think he must have been a bit like Napier. He intended it as a sort of gesture of reconciliation between the the Furys and the O'Lindons. That's exactly the sort of thing Napier would do, don't you think?'

'Soft, you mean?' Madeleine said sweetly.

Caro hunted for a better word but conceded. 'Yes. But Caroline knew her own clan better. She knew they'd take it the other way – as if Lucius were crowing, "I've gotcha now!" In her letter to her mother she describes how she's tried to talk him out of it, and failed, so now she wants her mother to explain to everyone that it's really like an olive branch. Hah!'

'Hah, indeed. What a pity you can't tell anyone now, though.'

'They wouldn't be interested, Maddy. That's what I'm saying. They're not interested in history. They don't give a damn about religion. They only want Home Rule because they think they can lord it over Ireland better than the West Brits ever did. They just use everything for themselves.'

Madeleine bridled at her ferocity. 'Aren't you being just a little sweeping there, dear?'

But Caro would have none of it. 'I *told* them, but they just weren't interested. I didn't say *I'd* found the letter. I told them Oxmantown mentioned he'd seen a letter from Caroline in the muniment room at Birr Castle, and then I said what was in it, in the one I found. Well, I might as well have been talking about someone who lived two thousand years ago in Patagonia. They don't want to know – because it isn't ammunition, you see. It was the same when Mammy got the College of Heralds to trace back her mother's descent, hoping to find some great anti-English hero who'd go down well at the next Home Rule meeting.'

Madeleine grinned, anticipating the general drift of the tale. 'And what did they actually find?'

Caro smiled maliciously. 'Her mother's family goes straight back to Hardress Waller and the Cromwellian army! They only turned Catholic in the eighteen-twenties. She said thank you very much, you may stop now. And she paid them off. And she burnt the lot.'

Madeleine let a silence grow, giving her a chance to simmer down; the poor girl was trembling like a sally in spring. 'I can see why you need to ride so hard,' she said.

Caro nodded. 'The same way as Mammy used to have to scrub floors and clean windows and do all these *furious* things. But she wanted to be . . . *consumed* by it all.'

'By what?' Madeleine asked. 'I've known your mother since before you were born. She never appeared to me to be particularly . . . I mean, she's always been perfectly friendly to me. She's not two-faced, you know. I couldn't let that pass.'

Caro sighed at the impossibility of explaining it all. 'I'm sure she'd agree with you, and quite sincerely. I don't think she knows what's really going on . . .' She tapped her own forehead. 'I don't think Aunt Swan does, either. They both dress it up in some other way. Historical costume!' She laughed and grew morose again at once. 'They'd be appalled to hear what I think of them. Napier's the only one I can talk about it with, but I don't because it only upsets him.'

'And there's me, too.'

Caro leaned forward and squeezed her hand impulsively. 'Yes, I'm sorry. How boring it is when people go on and on about their own troubles!'

Madeleine tilted her head in accusation. 'I didn't mean that, and you know it. I hope you'll always feel you can come here and tell me . . . anything you like. At any time.'

Caro's grin grew even broader as she assured Maddy that she did and she would, and really it was all just a storm in a teacup. But looking deep into her eyes the older woman could see that, if the girl's anxieties had been a mile high when she came, they were now shorter by a mere few yards.

And the forces that increased them were, she knew, gathering pace by the week.

83

A short while after Caro's visit, Madeleine went over to Coolderg Castle. She found Napier in the drive just outside the main gate to the keep; he was admiring Stephen's latest limousine. Stephen was admiring it, too, but trying to look as if he wasn't. 'It's for the Knight of Glyn,' he said nonchalantly, 'but we always give them a good road test first.'

'Lucky you.' Napier touched the badge on the radiator. 'It's the first Rolls-Royce I've seen in the flesh. They look even better than their photos, which is a surprise.'

'The coachwork is ours,' Stephen pointed out hastily. 'The customer buys a chassis, what we call a rolling chassis – engine, wheels, and petrol tank. Everything else is ours.'

Napier ran a kid-gloved finger over the lacquer and expressed his admiration all over again. 'I didn't realize. I thought you just supplied the upholstery and paintwork. Your firm can do all this? Even the nickel-plating on the lamps?'

Stephen crouched in front of the bumper. 'You see the chrome plate on this? I have a man who can start with a lump of chrome and beat it out as thin as paper. Then he swages it over the steel, laps it at the back, solders it, and polishes it flat. Take a good look at it and tell me where the join is.'

Watching them on their knees at their devotions, Madeleine thought they were like two little boys lost in fairyland. Stephen especially. She suspected that even if the bespoke-coachwork business did not pay as handsomely as it obviously did, he would still have let himself get caught up in it. She had seen him go into raptures over a well-cut gearwheel the way most other people would praise a great work of art.

'You should come up to Dublin to see the one we're doing for the Maharajah of . . . somewhere I can't pronounce. It's like a four-poster bed made of barley-sugar sticks.'

Napier gave up the search for the solder join. 'And you can find enough craftsmen in Dublin to do this sort of work?' he asked. 'Well, obviously.'

'Finding craftsmen in Dublin was never difficult. But "good engineers is hard got," as Peter Shaughnessy said the other day. That's why I'm moving part of the business to England. Did you know we're going to make our own cars, too?'

'Indeed and I didn't.' Napier glanced at his watch. 'Listen, are you sure you won't stop for a bite? It'll only be cold ham and pickle or something. Now Maddy's here you can tell us both all about it.'

Madeleine's heart fell. She could think of better pastimes than eating cold ham and listening to every chromium-plated detail of a new factory in England. 'Yes, do,' she said. 'Kill two birds with the one stone.'

It proved even worse than she feared, for Swan was away in Dublin all day and there was no one who'd even understand her occasional heavenward glance. But she did gather that Stephen was not aiming to build cars like the magnificent monster outside – and she had to allow that it was an extremely elegant equipage. He was going to start at the very opposite end of the business, building the cheapest possible car 'without compromising the engineering standards'. She had heard of young ladies being compromised; the idea that anyone might attempt to seduce something as forbidding as an 'engineering standard' only showed her how grotesque the world was becoming. Still, it would amuse Caro to hear of it.

As the ghastly luncheon progressed it became clear that Stephen was on his way to Limerick with the car, where he was to meet the Knight of Glyn and hand it over. He was then continuing to Cork by train, where he had some kind of commercial appointment. It became even clearer to her that Napier wanted to join him for the Rolls-Royce part of the trip – except that it would give him an awkward journey back. Madeleine saw it was a golden opportunity to get him alone for an hour or two and so offered to drive the Renault down behind them.

'But you've never driven in your life,' he objected. 'You've always said you hate cars.'

But she was familiar enough with her own brother to know he was going to agree.

'Sure, can't you teach me?' she scoffed. 'It has four wheels. It can't fall over like a bicycle. Bring me the first five miles, to the main Borrisokane road, and I'll fly the rest of it.'

Napier glanced uneasily at Stephen. 'What d'you think yourself?'

He shrugged. 'Sure everyone has to learn sometime. If Coutts sells a few more paintings we might have a customer here.'

And so it came about that Madeleine learned to drive a car – or, perhaps it would be more accurate to say 'to avoid crashing a car,' for she still couldn't avoid crashing the gears by the time they bowled into Limerick. She lost her hat in Castle Connel, but she noted where it had fallen and intended to retrieve it on the way back. Napier went off to get some more carbide for the lamps; she offered to fill in the time by helping Stephen to polish the 'Rolling Royce' ready for the hand-over. But he declined – whether because he didn't trust her or because he thought it no fit occupation for a lady wasn't clear. So she waited in the street and watched the soldiers marching between the port and the barracks. It was not an unusual sight for Limerick, which had always been one of the biggest garrisons in the west. But it was an unfamiliar spectacle to her, since the nearest army barracks to Coolderg were either at Portumna or Parsonstown.

After a while she turned her attention to the crowds who thronged the pavements. Their utter impassivity was most striking. What on earth were they thinking behind those mild, barely curious eyes? It was quite unfathomable. If you were looking for hostility, you'd look in vain, but the same would be true if it was a welcome you sought, even here in this land of a hundred thousand welcomes. And if *she* couldn't tell, how could the English ever know?

Napier returned with his carbide. They took their leave of Stephen and set off for home via her abandoned hat. Napier was still bowled over by his ride in the Rolls-Royce. 'By God,' he said as they negotiated the sharp bend by the Shannon, 'I wish I could afford one of those motors – even one with the standard coachwork.'

'Why, how much are they?' she asked, surprised that Napier would admit to being unable to afford anything.

'Three hundred,' he replied glumly.

'That's about a third of one portrait to you, surely?'

He nodded but said nothing.

'Well?' she prompted.

'Other calls,' he said vaguely.

'You think the lawsuit might go against you?'

'Yes, that too.'

'What d'you mean "too"? What else is there?'

He gazed uncomfortably around, clearly wishing he had not started this hare. 'Things. I haven't done so much painting lately. There've been so many other calls on my time.'

'You'll have to cut down on your hunting then, won't you,' she told him primly. 'Not to mention joy-rides to Limerick in Rolling Royces.'

He didn't correct her; he didn't say anything.

'Is it serious, Napier?' she asked after a silence.

'The market's changing,' he replied. 'They want slick, solid realism now. Sergeant and Orpen. Art for art's sake is dead.'

'It *is* serious.'

After a pause he said, ' 'Fraid so, old thing.'

'Why didn't you say?'

He peered at the road ahead. 'We must be getting near where you lost it.'

'No. It's another mile or so yet. Why didn't you say?'

He moved his head vaguely. 'What would have been the point?'

She let that one go. After a while she asked, 'What does Swan think about it?'

'Hard to say,' he replied evenly.

'Napier, you are the most infuriating person to try to hold a conversation with.'

'Especially when it's something I'd rather not talk about.'

'Oh well, if that's how you feel . . .' She tossed her hatless head and turned away from him to stare at the passing scene. A moment later she burst out laughing. 'It's all right,' she said. 'You may drive on at Castle Connel. I've just seen my hat.'

'Where?' He began to decelerate.

'No, go on,' she urged. 'It's on the ears of an ass in a field back there. I don't want it after that, thanks very much!'

They laughed and drove on, in an easier silence, for a mile or so. Then out of the blue, he said, 'Actually, Maddy, could I ask you your frank opinion of Swan? I know it's hardly good form and all that, but still . . . your candid opinion now.'

'Napier! That's a bit of a tall order. I mean there's so much I could say – almost all of it highly commendatory, I might add.'

'Why only *almost* all?'

Madeleine laughed. 'Because news of her canonization has yet to reach me. What has prompted this question? I mean what in particular?'

'D'you think she's entirely sane, for instance?'

The question took Madeleine completely aback. She laughed in astonishment and said, 'Oh that! I thought you meant something serious.'

'It *is* serious.' There was not the ghost of a smile on his lips. The leather of his gloves, where he gripped the steering wheel, was as taut as a drumskin. 'I wouldn't be surprised if, when she returns this evening, she hasn't spent a hundred pounds or more.'

'Good heavens! What on?'

'Nothing. I never met anyone who could spend so much and have so little to show for it.'

'A hundred pounds, Napier!' She felt sick at the very thought of it.

'Don't!'

'Has it been going on long?'

'Only since . . . well, since Dervla's wedding, I suppose. The O'Lindons are so tight with money they'd peel an orange in their pocket. But when they splash out they surely don't stint it. And that *was* a splash!'

'Wasn't it! Madeleine's eyes glowed at the memory.

'Well, Swan seemed to take that as a personal affront. Things have got so bad lately I've thought of putting an announcement in the papers – Mr Napier Lyndon-Fury of Coolderg Castle hereby declares he will no longer consider himself responsible for his wife's debts. You see them every week from some poor bugger, pardon my French. You never think you'll be there yourself one day.'

Madeleine closed her eyes and shook her head violently; it was too much to take in all at once.

But now that he was launched on the subject he seemed to need no comment from her to keep it going. 'There's a curse on that place, I'm sure,' he said morosely. 'It's never brought any good to anyone – certainly not to any Lyndon-Fury. Even the ones who died relatively prosperous died miserable. Their wives bolted or their children perished. I just want to lock the door sometimes and walk away from it.'

'Only sometimes?' she suggested hopefully.

'The rest of the time I don't even want to stop to lock the door. Oh God, I was so happy in Paris! Why did I ever come back? I was so bloody happy there.'

Madeleine realized there could be no half-measures in her response to this; she could either be utterly sympathetic, as she had been with Caro, and let him pour it all out, or she could be brutal. With Napier, she decided, there was a risk he might pocket her sympathy and later blame her for anything he did. So she was brutal: 'Why did you marry Swan?'

She saw the first sign of humour in him as he glanced at her and gave a guilty little smile. 'You know bloody well why. You saw me rowing up the lake that night – and going back down again the following morning.'

'Tom saw you the following morning.'

He accepted the correction with a little benediction of his hands.

'You still didn't have to marry her, Napier. Everyone would have considered Lucius to have been Mercier's – not that he'd have been called Lucius in that case, of course. The point is, you didn't have to marry her. She was left well provided for. You could have satisfied your conscience by giving her the villa at peppercorn rent.'

For a long while he said nothing. This time she did not press him – which, in a way, was the greatest pressure of all. At last he said, 'You know why I married her.'

'I'm pretty sure I do,' Madeleine conceded. 'But I'd still like to hear it from you.'

'I was frightened of her.' He gave out a sigh of relief, as if the utterance had been an ordeal. 'She was so . . .' He shrugged.

'Determined?'

'Yes.'

'More Lyndon-Fury than the Lyndon-Furys?'

'Precisely. It all goes back to when we were students, you know.'

'Did you do a line with her, ever?'

'No. We kissed a bit but that was all. I had a rag on every bush in those days.'

'And what about Swan?'

'Well . . . she wanted it to be something more. So did I, I suppose – until Daisy came along. I think it all goes back to then. And now she can't see anything Daisy does in its true light at all.'

'Really?' Madeleine did her best to mask her surprise at this assertion. 'What sort of thing, for instance?'

Napier heaved a great sigh, suggesting it was all far too complex to explain. Maddy, remembering a very similar gesture from Caro, smiled to herself. 'For instance,' Napier echoed her phrase heavily, 'Daisy's always played a sort of game with us – with the Lyndon-Furys. You must have noticed. First she pretended she was going to stigmatize us by staying in Keelity and having my bastard – leaving it to the last possible minute before she called her own bluff. And then to go and name the child Caroline! You know yourself how much that infuriated Mama . . . oh, there are so many things. Buying that pinewood, for example. As if she would ever really cut down those trees! It was just to torment us.'

'And always being there to buy up the distillery, the sawmills, the joinery . . . whenever we were strapped for cash?'

'If the O'Lindons hadn't done that, someone else would. That doesn't count. It was just commercial acumen, that.'

Madeleine suppressed her exasperated amusement at his extraordinary gloss on Daisy O'Lindon. 'And Swan can't see it like that? She can't see how essentially innocent and playful dear Daisy is being?'

'No. That's what I mean.'

They almost knocked an old woman over at that point. Napier stopped the car and got down to light the lamps. 'We'll have to go a bit easy now,' he commented. 'Where are we, anyway?'

'On the brink of the howling wilderness,' Madeleine commented. 'Actually, just about to turn off the Nenagh road to Rathtuagh.'

'Oh well' – his voice brightened – 'we've made splendid time.'

'Yes! Don't the hours just flash by when you're having fun.'

When they set off again, she returned like a terrier to the subject. 'If you want my opinion, Napier, I think Swan is closer to the truth of it than you – about Daisy O'Lindon.'

In his surprise he almost brought the car to a halt again. 'Not you, too?'

'I like Daisy enormously and always have done, right from the start. I thought you were an utter eejit not to have married her when you were in London.'

'Me too.'

'Yes. Well, that's just so much spilt milk now. Stephen and Daisy were always very good to Tom and me – when very few other people were, I may tell you. So it's not easy for me to say this. But I think Daisy has one big unfulfilled ambition left in her life – and that is to see the Lyndon-Furys out of Coolderg Castle and herself and Stephen into it. Or *back* into it, as I'm sure they'd put it.'

'They?'

'Yes, they! I think Stephen's as eager for it as Daisy. Whether he always was or whether he just took fire from her, I don't know . . .'

Napier began to laugh good-humouredly. 'Now I know you're unhinged! You're worse even than Swan. Stephen be like that? Never! You saw him yourself today. Not a hint of it.'

'Oh, I think he's very happy to leave all the "appearances" of it to Daisy. You talk about it to Caro sometime if you don't believe me. I wish they would talk to her about it, too. They'd get a bit of a shock, I'm sure.'

There! she thought and held her breath.

'Caro?' he asked. 'I don't want her mixed up in all this.'

'But she *is* mixed up in it, Napier, my dear. That's really why I availed of this trip today – to get you where you couldn't drop it all and run. Caro *is* mixed up in this, and she's one big mix-up inside herself, too. She can't stand all the pretence it involves.'

A near-full moon rose over Slievekimalta, which was now behind them. It far outdid the feeble rays of the carbide lamps, which were left to fill in the car's own shadow with their soft yellow luminance.

'I had no idea,' Napier said, shaking his head. 'She always seems so bright and cheerful.'

'She covers it well; like you've covered your worries, too. And like Daisy's kept you thinking she's only being playful. Oh, Caro's a true daughter to both of you. But she is in . . .' Madeleine wondered whether to soften her words and decided not to, 'some distress, I can assure you.'

Napier brought a fist hard down on the steering wheel and nearly put them in the drain. 'I won't have that,' he exclaimed. 'This nonsense has got to stop.'

'And how do you propose to do that?'

'Go and have it out with the O'Lindons, of course.'

Madeleine held her peace.

After a silence he said, 'Has either of them ever *told* her anything?'

'I gather you did?' she challenged.

'Not me. It was Swan. We were having an argument about it and she wouldn't keep her voice down. And Caro overheard.' He sniffed. 'Between you and me, I think Swan intended it.'

'No!'

He frowned at her. 'Are you trying to be sarcastic?'

'Oh, Napier! Dear, dear old thing! Of *course* Swan intended it. Just as she arranged matters for Caro to discover the Joan of Arc painting.'

'When?'

'I don't know exactly when, but Caro told me about it . . . and she's in no doubt Swan arranged for it to happen.'

Napier smiled. 'What did she think of it?'

Madeleine's anger at this selfishness was immediately tempered with the realization that Thomas would have asked precisely the same question. If she couldn't accept it, she told herself, she shouldn't have chosen artists for her brother and husband. So she laughed and said, 'Caro told me it's a lovely painting and she only wishes people could appreciate it for what it is and not use it as a weapon, the way Swan does.'

'No, she's wrong there,' Napier asserted. 'Swan herself promised me she'd never, never exhibit that painting. Unless, of course, Daisy did something outrageous – like chop down that pinewood.'

Madeleine raised both hands to heaven, silently offering his words as witness.

'Oh,' he said. 'I see what you mean.'

'Yes,' she sneered. 'Self-righteousness is the most effective blindfold.'

He accepted the rebuke with a dip of his head. 'You didn't say whether Daisy or Stephen ever told her the truth.'

'From the way she was talking, they obviously haven't. I'm only guessing – I mean, she was so distressed I didn't want to press her on the point – but my guess is she might have dropped a hint or two, as if some dear, sweet, good-natured friend had whispered something in her ear, and they pooh-poohed it, the way people do, and perhaps she said something a bit more definite . . . but now they were committed to the lie, and so they swore black and blue that Stephen is her real father and so on. I'm only guessing, as I say, but if she could be as honest with them as she is with you, there'd be no unhappiness, would there.'

'Then I'll go and have it out with them,' he said firmly.

'Don't you think it would be best to talk to Caro first?'

'Why? The quicker the better, surely?'

'Otherwise you'll be left saying, "Maddy says that Caro says . . ." And you'll sound like the town gossip.'

'Ah.' He nodded sagely. 'See what you mean.'

'I doubt it,' she sighed. But before he could take her up on it she went on, 'While this confessional mood is upon us, brother dear, may I ask you one more question?'

'Fire away.' He was cheerful now that he saw a definite course of action before him.

'You don't have to answer.'

'Get on with it.'

'D'you remember Mercier's funeral? The actual moment of interment?'

'Sort of. Yes. Who was the parson that day?'

'Never mind that. But at the moment Mercier's coffin was lowered into the grave, you and Swan smiled at each other. I've often wondered why.'

'Oh yes, that was most extraordinary,' he said at once.

'I certainly thought so.'

'You saw it, too, then?'

'I saw you smile.'

'No, no. The fish. The trout. At the moment Mercier's coffin went down, a trout leaped out of the lough. Tugs at the heartstrings a bit, eh?'

Madeleine began to laugh. She laughed so much he had to stop and slap her on the back.

84

Caro was entered for the third and biggest race of the day, the Slieve Derg Chase: three miles, for a ten-guinea purse, over a partly built course ending with a number of man-made obstacles in the field where the meeting itself was held. Madeleine was so confident of Caro, she'd put five pounds on her with Dessie Lynch, the race bookmaker, who gave her five to four; but when she saw Dermot Flanagan, Miley's son, on his great half-bred hunter, Mick the Finn, she began to worry. Seamus Devlin, too, on a high-spirited mare called Murphy's Maid, could not be ignored – such, at least, was the opinion being voiced around the course.

'Ah sure,' she told herself despondently, 'won't it give me something to scream about.'

It was an ordinary sort of meeting. A thousand others like it would be held up and down the country that year and every other year until Connaught froze over. A 'beer' tent sold stout and porter, duty paid; but a hundred pockets were stuffed with hipflasks that yielded something stronger, duty bound. There was a selling ring – five larch stakes and a bit of old rope – where those who'd made a lucky win with an old nag could capitalize upon it before the mood wore off. There was an Irish-dancing contest in another tent. There was a platform where the race officials and quality could get a chance at the rain before the *hoi polloi*. There were matchmakers, to be sure, men skilled in the bending of the two most unyielding substances in the universe – the careful Irish woman with a bit put by, and the wily Irish bachelor who had learned to relish his freedom. There were settlers who could shave a few guineas to a nicety when they were all that stood between a buyer and a seller of horseflesh. And, to round it all off, there were four thousand storytellers. And should anyone object that that is twice the number attending the entire meeting, the answer to the conundrum must be that every man, woman, and child there had at least two versions of every tale to tell. The hubbub would almost hold back the rain, which was more than could be said of the ineffectual little pipe-and-fiddle band hired to duel with the dancers.

Someone had promised to roast an ox, or at least the whole carcass of a beast, and sell portions in aid of the poor, but so far the men had not even turned up to dig the pit. Who could blame them in such weather? people asked.

But the the rain let up just before the big race at three and soon there was enough blue sky on the Tipperary horizon to make a sailor's shirt. Caro was disappointed. The land in the finishing field was very quick to drain and Mick the Finn was notorious in the mud, being so large.

There had been a great debate over whether she should be allowed to ride at all, because she would insist on wearing breeches and sitting astride. In the end they'd carried the decision to Father Horan, since it was a question of morality rather than of racing ethics. The priest, who had lately completed a new spire to his church with the aid of a generous donation from O'Lindon's Joinery, and who now had hopes of a splendid new altar of Carrara marble, which again would need a 'push' from the O'Lindons, saw no dilemma at all – which surprised everyone until they thought about it.

So now there was Caro, glancing at the sky and risking saddle-up, while

Jayjay O'Malley, the groom at Sharavogue, fussed around, bristling with last-minute advice.

'Get ahead at the first,' he said, 'and you have it in your pocket. The second you may lepp where you will – that's the rule. And a cunning one, too. For the straighter the line you make of it, the higher the ditch you'll face . . .'

She knew it all backwards, of course. She'd covered every inch of the chase on Shalimar a month ago and she knew exactly where she'd point him at that second ditch. But she let Jayjay ramble on because it calmed his nerves. She just said yes and no in the right places, judging by his tone, while she ran the course yet again in her mind. So when he went on to say, 'I have Dinny O'Toole with a good stout ashplant behind the ditch at the top of the hill beyond, where he won't blind the judges. He has instructions to encourage Mick the Finn if he's fading, like. Or Murphy's Maid, of course . . .' all she replied was, 'Yes, of course.'

Her casual acceptance of this blatant skulduggery both surprised and delighted him; he began to have hopes of her as a truly serious contestant at many a future meeting, rather than one of those incomprehensible eejits who'd let fair play stand in the way of a certain win.

'Good luck!' Dermot Flanagan held out his hand to her.

'Oh, thank you,' she replied, taking it. 'Same to you.'

He left it mangled to a pulp and bleeding under every fingernail – at least, that was how it felt. She had to take her glove off to make sure it was still all of a piece. He went off with a very smug grin on him.

'You have a lot to learn, girleen,' Jayjay told her, shaking his head sadly. 'Still, that's one thing you'll not do next time.'

'What should I have done?' she asked, favouring her wounded paw and trying to massage some life back into it.

'Sure, you could give him a good hearty clap on the back, where it would cure his cough for a year or more.'

'Good luck, Miss Caroline.' Seamus Devlin, smiling warmly, held forth his hand.

A moment later he went off with his cough well cured.

'You have the way of it, then,' Jayjay told her approvingly 'Remember now – first over the first and it's in your pocket.'

'What are you on for this one?' Swan asked Madeleine. 'I put a tenner on Caro out of loyalty but d'you see the odds have lengthened? Everyone's going for Flanagan's boy now.'

Maddy agreed uncomfortably. 'I put a fiver on when she was five to four. If I put a pound on Mick The Finn now and he won, I'd just cover it.'

'A Lyndon-Fury should bet in guineas, not pounds,' Napier said loftily.

Swan's face was a study in consternation.

'He's joking,' Madeleine told her.

'No, but he's right,' Swan said. 'I'd better go and see if I can change it.'
'Swan!' Maddy shouted after her.
'I'm coming straight back,' she called over her shoulder.
'She's mad!' Madeleine said to her brother – then, remembering his question to her on the road back from Limerick, said, 'Oh dear.'
'Quite,' he said.
The O'Lindons moved their carriage up to the edge of the course at that moment. 'Room for a little one beside you?' Daisy chirped, already driving in. 'Would you ever give him his bag, Mr Kelly?' she asked one of the bystanders, who leaped to comply. 'You're very kind.'
Sheridan, now eleven, got out at once and ran away almost bowling headlong into Swan on her way back. 'I saw your brothers going into the dancing tent' she told him as she fended him around her.
'He wants to get to the horses,' Daisy said. 'That's all he lives for. He's worse than Caro.' She greeted Swan, who returned at that moment. 'What are you on?'
'Caro, of course.' Swan smiled triumphantly. 'Ten guineas.'
'Hah!' Napier exclaimed.
'I put two on her myself,' Daisy admitted. 'But I have five on Mick the Finn.'
'Pounds or guineas?' Madeleine asked lightly.
'Shillings, to be sure.'
Swan smiled seraphically at the world in general, dipping her hat and its rain-bedraggled plumage at anyone with whom she was on hat-dipping terms.
Madeleine lowered her binoculars and passed them to Napier. 'I hope the judges are otherwise occupied,' she said. 'Look who's going up the ditch to the top of the course – and what's that in his hand?'
While Napier scanned the terrain she turned to Daisy. 'Is Stephen judging this?'
'He's disqualified himself. It's Ciaran Leonard.'
'Ah, you might get away with it then.'
'Get away with what?'
Napier handed her the glasses. 'That O'Toole blackguard. Just getting up near the top of the course.'
'Am I to be let in on the secret?' Swan asked.
The carriage on the other side of them belonged to a Mrs Robinson, who had an English cousin staying with her. He said, 'I thought this was supposed to be the three-o'clock race?'
'Yes?' she replied in a puzzled tone.
He held his watch to his ear and then shook it – the only man in two thousand who expected them to be off before four.

Napier explained the business with O'Toole to his wife, who, like the others, nodded her approval.

In fact, they were off at twenty *to* four, which was a record in the history of the event. Scratches and sales had reduced the field to fifteen riders, enough to give everyone a bit of elbow room without reducing the competition to a farce.

Caro knew exactly what would happen. The whole field would make one mad dash for the first jump, which was wide enough for ten but not fifteen. Some behind would have to pull back; some in front would refuse; others would go over and fall. And after that the race would be between the first six to get over safely.

She led the field by a length as they came up to the first ditch, half-standing in her stirrups as Madeleine had seen her that day. Five or six strides out she glanced under her arm and saw that the thundering on Shalimar's heels was from Mick the Finn, with Flanagan grinning at her like a gargoyle. She sat deep into the saddle and gathered him for the jump. To Flanagan behind, unused to such finesse in horsemanship, that sudden drop in pace looked like a refusal.

'Death and damnation!' he cursed as he hauled Mick the Finn to one side.

The next moment he was astonished to see Shalimar and rider in pure silhouette against the sky while he blundered half through, half over the ditch. 'How the *hell* did she do that? he asked as he spurred forward to catch her up. He might also have asked how the hell he got through without a worse scratching than he and the horse had received.

Caro looked around and saw that Murphy's Maid was also well up; there were about eight in serious contention now – though disaster could strike at any ditch and the prize had gone to a remount before now.

Down by the finishing line Daisy clutched a hand to her throat, which was already feeling the rasp of her cries at the first fence. 'She'll never jump *there!*' she exclaimed.

'You just watch,' Madeleine promised with relish. 'I've seen her jump higher than that.'

Caro took the fence in her stride at exactly the point where her mother had predicted disaster. It put her on a straight line for the gate at the top corner of the field, after which she would pass out of sight for several minutes – the middle mile of the course. She was now eight lengths clear of her nearest rival, who was still Flanagan on Mick the Finn – with Murphy's Maid trailing third.

'Just hold the gap, girl, hold the gap,' Napier muttered.

And then disaster struck.

Her course lay diagonally up the slope. About half way up, someone had left a cur of rope coiled up in the grass. Even so, all might have been well if that same someone had not first dipped it in bright yellow paint.

Shalimar did a sideways leap that left Caro lying in the mud. But Mick the Finn sailed past it as if he'd seen yellow snakes every day of the past month. Curiously enough, Murphy's Maid did not seem too put out by the 'snake,' either. She, with Seamus Devlin up, was now second.

When Caro at last remounted she was eighth in the field. Mick the Finn and Murphy's Maid were well in the lead, and between them were those, mostly from the back of the field, who had noticed the consternation caused by something up ahead and had ridden wide to avoid it.

'How beastly unfair!' commented the Englishman in the next carriage. 'Some careless blighter's left something in that field. Frightened the life out of them. They should start the race again.'

Such a novel suggestion caused a profound silence to settle for several dozens of yards around.

'That big fellow'll be way out in front now,' he added.

A few minutes later his prophecy proved absolutely correct. Mick the Finn came streaking down the hill as if the banshee rode him. Indeed, that might well have been the case, for there was no one else in the saddle to perform the service.

He was swiftly followed by another riderless horse, which a thousand excited tongues immediately identified as Murphy's Maid.

Then came Caro, still on Shalimar, riding now in the most stately extended canter down the hill. A great cheer went up, for she had still been the favourite, if only just, by the time they came under starter's orders. A furlong or more behind her was a rag-tag-and-bobtail of runners and riderless horses, content to fight for second place. Last of all, muddy, hatless, and on foot, walked Flanagan and Devlin. The crowd did not know it yet, but the pair of them were singing, for there was no point in taking these matters too seriously. The season wasn't half done. Sure, there'd be plenty of chances to get that girl yet. Let her have this petty triumph.

The cheering continued as Caro came down over the remaining ditches and entered the finishing field. It grew more excited as she took the man-made jumps in beautiful style. And it split they sky when she passed the finish at a gallop. Daisy, and Madeleine who had transferred to her carriage, were so excited that bystanders wondered how the springs stood up to it.

When Caro joined them, however, having collected the prize, posed for the *Keelity Vindicator*, and handed Shalimar into the care of one of the stable lads from Sharavogue (Jayjay being unaccountably absent in this moment of triumph), there was the gleam of battle in her eye. When the congratulations had died down she said, loud enough only for those in her immediate vicinity to hear, 'Just wait till I get Jayjay O'Malley back home! Where is he? Has anyone seen him?'

He was, in fact, at that moment behind the judge's tent pressing the second promised sovereign into the malodorous palm of Dinny O'Toole. 'Oh God be good to you,' O'Toole said, already licking the thirst from his lips. 'May your prick and your purse never fail your honour.'

A short while later Stevie and Finnbar O'Lindon came breathlessly back to the carriage.

'How is the dancing?' Caro asked pointedly.

They looked at each other and laughed. 'We only went in and straight out through the flap at the back,' Stevie replied.

'We went up the hill to see if we could help,' Finnbar added. 'But it was already organized.'

'In hand!' Stevie said as if correcting his brother. 'We should have known you wouldn't leave it to chance.'

'Yes, your father will be proud of you,' Daisy cut in. 'Well done!'

Caro stared from one to the other in horror.

What could have been an explosive moment was saved by the sound of distant singing. The two men whom all the world now believed she had outwitted at their own game were climbing the gate into the field and singing. The laughter rang around the field and soon everyone was joining in.

'Good Lord!' exclaimed the Englishman. 'I mean, I say!'

Caro closed her eyes, shook her head, and sighed at the impossible complexity of everything.

Madeleine leaned forward and patted her on her arm. 'No one is ever going to believe you, my dear,' she said with a smile. 'You might as well join in the race.'

Caro frowned in bewilderment.

'Which race?'

'Ours, of course.'

They stayed for the last two steeplechases and then left for a slap-up banquet at Dooly's in Parsonstown, which served the best food in five counties. As the crowd streamed out of the gate four men arrived to start digging the pit for the ox roast.

85

The bank first started bouncing Napier's cheques the week after Simonstown races. Suspecting such a thing might happen, he had picked carefully the recipients of those doubtful payments – choosing only those he could enjoin to silence if the blow should fall. Unfortunately, he could not so easily pick those to whom his select band might, in turn, endorse those same cheques. So when Harry Trench, who was a very decent fellow, endorsed one of Napier's cheques and passed it on to Miley Flanagan in payment for livery, and when Miley had it returned marked 'Refer to drawer,' the fat was in the fire. But Miley knew exactly what to do. He put the thing in his pocket and said nothing.

God would decide, he told himself. Either Swan Lyndon-Fury would walk through that door first or it would be Caro O'Lindon; whichever it was would solve his difficulty for him. There was good horseflesh in the Coolderg stables; but there was also a lifetime of good custom in the O'Lindon girl to consider. God would decide.

If that was the way of it, His finger fell on Caro – who was, of course, stunned when Miley showed her the evidence. 'I'm quite sure this must be some eejit mistake, Mr Flanagan,' she assured him. 'Someone at the bank is going to lose his place over this. Let me take it and discover what's what.'

He cleared his throat dubiously. He said he had no doubt but that she had the right of it. And he waited.

It was for eighty pounds, which she could just about cover out of her dress allowance, so she wrote him her own IOU. 'You'll accept that, I suppose?' she asked acidly.

He smiled very confidently and told her he had no fear of accepting any paper with the name O'Lindon on it.

After luncheon that same day she told her mother she was going over to see if Madeleine would ride out with her; otherwise she'd not try anything bigger than three foot, she promised. Then she rode straight over to Coolderg.

Swan was out, walking by the lough. Napier was sitting in his studio, staring at a blank canvas, his eyes quite expressionless. His whole face lit up on seeing her, though. 'Just the tonic I needed,' he cried out, rising and spreading wide his arms in welcome. 'Did you come to sit for your portrait at last?'

'No,' she said. 'That is, yes.'

'You're just what all the world needs,' he told her. 'A woman who *doesn't* know her own mind and is honest about it. Sit on the throne there while you decide.'

He put away the blank canvas he had been staring at and selected another, taller and narrower. 'D'you know what you looked like when you stood in the door there just now?' he went on. 'A Sergeant. He had one in the Academy last summer looked just like you. The Honourable Julia Something-or-other . . .'

It dawned on her that he was talking about a painter called Sergeant, not someone in the constabulary.

'That black jacket and the fawn breeches – typical Sergeant colours, especially with your burnished cheeks and flowing hair. You could be just what I've been needing. Do say you will?'

'Of course.' There was something wrong. When he said 'black jacket' it struck her that something was wrong, but it escaped her now. 'D'you want me cross-legged or what? Or,' laughing she snatched up a smaller chair and, reversing it, sat astride, 'like this? That's what seems to fascinate everybody.'

'No,' he said, not taking up her humorous tone at all. 'Standing, I think. Come down a step, so that your head's just above the level of mine. Look down on me. That's right. Higher. Tilt your head back a bit more. Really look down on me. I'm just a dauber, a tradesman, and you're the Honourable Caroline O'Lindon. I want to see half an acre of upper eyelid.'

He smiled at each of her efforts to oblige. 'Not bad for an Irish country colleen,' he said at last.

'It's that Ascendancy blood in me,' she assured him. She hadn't seen him so animated for months.

'The light'll be gone in half an hour,' he grumbled. 'Can you hold that without a rest, d'you think?' He smiled suddenly as a joke occurred to him. 'You have *that* blood in you, too. But I gather you already know that.'

'Are you talking about the Joan of Arc?'

'What else?' He picked up a stick of charcoal and began sketching in her pose with long, sweeping strokes.

'Did Aunt Swan tell you?' She saw him wondering whether or not to reply truthfully.

'It was Maddy, actually,' he said.

'I told her in confidence.'

'So she said.' He drew several more strokes and examined them critically before he went on. 'So what do you suppose might might make her break that confidence, eh? What would she consider important enough to override it?'

She closed her eyes and shook her head.

'Too much upper eyelid,' he told her.

She resumed her pose. 'I'm so tired of it all, Napier.'

'Me, too, Little Face. Will I do something utterly shocking? Will I just tell you the plain truth?'

'I think you always have, haven't you? I know why the others haven't, mind. It's not for spite, or because they think me too feeble-witted. They did it in my own best interests . . .'

'I mean the *whole* truth. Here goes, anyway. Just a mo. Tricky bit.' He drew several careful lines, gave a tut of vexation, drew out a gorgeous silk handkerchief, and flapped away the charcoal before he had another stab at it. That one pleased him better, for he relaxed, transferred his attention to some less important area of the canvas, and said, 'Maddy told me all about it – the day you rode over to see her after they came back from Waterford.'

'Oh, that was a terrible day. I hate January. I shouldn't have bothered her with it all. I'm much better now.'

'Are you?' He peered intently at her, as another human – as her father, perhaps – certainly not as a painter. 'Are you really?'

She lowered her eyes. 'No.'

'I thought not. What I want to do, my dear, is go and see your parents and have it out with them. Tell them all this pretence has to stop. It's poisoning your life. It's already poisoned mine. I don't know about them. I can't answer for them. Or for Swan, either. They *seem* to thrive on it. Perhaps there's something wrong with us.'

Watching him talk, catching the tone of his short, direct statements, she had a fleeting intimation that people like her parents and Swan would run circles round him and leave him tied in knots. He would just go on stating simple, obvious truths until – like anything repeated too often – sheer familiarity would rob them of any meaning. She knew it very well. It was what happened to her all the time.

But how could she stop him?

Nothing occurred to her. She said, 'I think it might be easiest for all concerned if I simply went away. I don't mean run away. Just go away.'

'Would they let you?'

That was one marvellous thing about Napier. He understood a statement like that at once. Anyone else would have said, 'Oh, are you sure? Have you thought it all out? Do you think it would be wise? What about this and that . . .' and a hundred other objections. But he just took it for granted that she meant what she said; and then he asked the next practical question: 'Would they let you?'

'In a way they would,' she replied. 'They'd take complete charge of it. Daddy would find one of his friends in England to give me a place. He'd send someone over there to vet my digs and pay six months in advance. And I'd come down to breakfast at Sharavogue one day and find tickets for the mail boat on my plate. Everything handed to me on a plate! I'll never escape Sharavogue.'

He looked up sharply. 'Now *I've* been told it was you wanted that house more than anyone else in your family.'

'I know! I can assure you I'm being much more frugal with my wishes nowadays.'

There was a pause during which he neither sketched nor looked at her. 'It would be better,' he said at length, 'if the truth were established between you and your parents first.'

She nodded glumly, unable to deny it.

'Or perhaps,' he went on, 'if *I* went away? They might find it easier to face the business fair and square if I weren't here.'

'But this is your home!' she objected.

'Hah! You've lost the pose. Just another ten minutes, eh?'

She resumed her position to the best of her recollection. 'You couldn't leave your home like that,' she insisted.

'Oh, Caro!' He swallowed audibly. 'If I don't, I think it'll kill me. It's ruined me already, you know? It's stopped me painting. It's consumed all my cash. I doubt we can survive another month. Any day now the bank will cry halt.'

It was the perfect opening. She felt in her pocket for the cheque she had bought – and then she remembered what was wrong with the black jacket: She hadn't been wearing it that morning. When she saw Miley Flanagan, she'd been wearing the gray.

86

If . . . if . . . if; it is the earthly trinity whose failure rules our lives. If Caro had not borrowed her mother's tortoiseshell hair grip . . . or if she had only returned it . . . if she had hung her gray jacket up neatly instead of leaving it for her maid . . . if the maid had not been given the afternoon off . . .

As it was, when Daisy went into Caro's boudoir to look for the hair grip and saw her daughter's clothing scattered between the door and the wardrobe, she emitted the obligatory tuts and sighs and bent to tidy them away. By long maternal habit – not because she was especially inquisitive or suspicious – she dipped a perfunctory hand in each pocket, turning them inside-out and nipping the fluff between thumb and forefinger. She hardly realized she was doing it; in fact, she was lost in a daydream, giving the girl up and down the banks for being such a slut, when she all at once found herself staring at a cheque marked 'Refer to drawer' in a bold copperplate hand. For one dreadful moment she thought Caro might have opened an account in secret and then got in trouble; but then she saw Napier's signature – and the whole day changed around her. The endorsements led her the rest of the trail.

Eighty pounds!

Napier Lyndon-Fury, shook for only eighty pounds!

Guiltily she folded it to her bosom, closed her eyes, and gave out a sigh.

Her immediate thought was should she wait and tell Stephen? He was in Dublin and might not be home until tomorrow. Obviously Caro had got this cheque off Miley that morning . . . had she bought it from him? Probably not. Miley would surely trust her. He was used to waiting for his money. But just a mo . . . eighty pounds . . . Trench . . . it must be for livery. In which case he'd been waiting for a year already. So he might have asked Caro to buy it.

A new line of thought struck her. That's where Caro was now, of course – with Napier. All that talk of going to the Couttses was malarkey. But why did she leave the cheque behind? Either she forgot it or she simply wanted to sound him out. Or perhaps she was never going to tell him – just take the loss herself. You'd never know with her. She could have a face like a plate of mortal sins and be happy as larry, or she'd sing like a linnet and be miserable as mud. A dark one.

She closed her eyes a moment to master her sorrow at the loss of her other daughter – that dear, sweet, innocent young Caro, as blithe as the day was long. Where had she gone? For the hundredth time she wondered whether some kindly 'friend' had told the girl a few home truths – and for a hundredth time dismissed the thought. She would surely have come to her own Mammy or Daddy and told them. It couldn't be that.

But what if Napier had told her? Or Swan, more likely. Napier wouldn't say a word, out of vanity. He couldn't admit the better man won. But Swan would let it slip somehow, or she'd arrange for Caro to discover it.

The fear – the near-certainty – that that was what must have happened, shrivelled her innards. Desperately she sought some counter-argument, and found it in the reflection that Caro had Stephen's word on it that *he* was her true father. Surely it would be be enough? The girl would never believe any of the Lyndon-Furys against her own father.

Reassured, Daisy returned her attention to the bounced cheque. This was no accidental discovery. It was *intended.* God works in mysterious ways, indeed, but He must have known she was going to come in here and find it.

The only thing that came to mind was the Joan of Arc painting. That must be it. Her prayers were answered at long last. Eighty pounds would be a fair price for it, seeing as the model was still owed her fee for the sittings! And if the artist was having his cheques bounced for the want of eighty pounds, he ought to leap at the offer.

She hung the gray jacket up carefully and, forgetting the tortoiseshell hair grip, went out to put on her bonnet. Just in case Stephen came back early, she left him a note. Half an hour later, with the dusk starting to fall, her gig was bowling down the castle drive.

At that same moment Caro was trotting back up the disused line. A mile short of Flaxmills Road she came across Bell-the-cat Dolan, walking slowly toward her, head bent, scuffling among the weeds with the toe of his boot. Looking for something, obviously. Shalimar was walking by then and what with the soft ground muffling his footfall and Dolan being so intent on his search, he didn't hear them until they were almost upon him. In the second or two before that he clearly found what he was seeking, for he gave a single *hah!* of triumph and bent to retrieve it. The light was poor by then, so Caro could not be certain; but it looked remarkably like a British army service revolver. He became aware of them at that moment and slipped it into his pocket.

'It is yourself, Mr Dolan?' she cried. 'Lord, you gave me a start! I was miles away.'

Reassured by this, he became genial, even effusive. 'I was out here wondering if maybe we didn't overlook a rail or two in our haste that time.'

'Like winnings on a horse,' she replied, falling in with his banter, 'it's soon gone.'

'Indade it is, Miss O'Lindon. Is it entered for the North Tipp point-to-point ye are? Ye'll have been out for a practice, so.'

'More than likely,' she agreed. 'It's easier now the days are drawing out.'

'He's a grand looking lad, that fella.' He patted Shalimar easily on the neck.

She tried to see what was in his pocket but the coat was old fashioned, with large flaps. 'More than good looking, I hope,' she replied.

'Indade and he is. I made a shilling or two on him at Simonstown, I don't mind telling you.'

'I saw you there. I thought you had a merry look!'

He chuckled. 'And I saw you, too, miss. And there's a quare thing I want to tell you. I saw you and I saw your Mammy there, and from that day to this I never saw neither one of ye. And today I see ye both again.'

She looked at him in surprise. 'You saw my Mammy this afternoon?' As far as she knew, her mother had intended to go through the accounts and minutes of some of her committees. Or had Dolan called to Sharavogue and seen her there?

'Sure I'm after seeing her turn in at Coolderg gates,' he told her. 'Not ten minutes since.'

She twisted round in the saddle to see for herself. It was a darkling world but she could make out enough of the landscape to know the gates weren't visible from here.

'I was up on Keenoge Hill.' He nodded towards the skyline to the south and grinned. 'Assisting Sergeant McNair in his delusions.'

She laughed. 'And what are they?'

'The poor fella's after persuading himself and half the garrison in Birr that there's great deposits of metal and Lord knows what up there.' He gave a triumphant little chuckle. 'Did you hear the dirt? How I got my house cleaned free of ivy – and free of charge, too?'

'I did not,' she said, settling for a good bit of crack.

'Sure, some eejit officer in Birr has lost his revolver and some eejit informer in Simonstown told the bold Sergeant it was me got it, and I was after hiding it in the ivy on my wall. So they cut it all down. For nothing, you might say. It certainly cost *me* nothing! There now, wasn't that great gas.'

They both had a good laugh at that, then Caro, seeming to remember his earlier remark, asked if he was sure it was her Mammy at Coolderg – which, indeed, he was. 'I've missed her so,' she said in mild vexation. 'I'd best go back, I suppose.'

She spoke as if it were a fearsome chore, but the moment she was well away from Dolan she asked Shalimar for a canter and held him to it all the way – hoping against hope that her fears were unfounded.

It was quite dark by the time she arrived. She rode him down to the stables, eased his girth and covered him before she approached the castle. She also threw a blanket over her mother's cob, still harnessed in the gig with only his nosebag for company. Some people *deserved* motor cars, she thought; they weren't fit for horses.

The big main door to the castle was wide open. There was no point in knocking, anyway; no one would hear her. They were too busy bawling their heads off at each other – or Swan and her Mammy were. Napier kept trying to say something more than 'Listen!' and 'Steady on!' and 'Calm down!' whenever they paused for breath.

Dearly as she would have loved to stand there and eavesdrop, Caro forced herself to walk in and join them. They were at the farther end of the ballroom, grouped around the fire, which provided the only light they had. The servants wouldn't come near them and they couldn't break off themselves to light the lamps. The scene was like something out of a medieval painting of Hell – the leaping flames, the screams of the damned.

They were so preoccupied with their quarrel they didn't notice Caro even now, though she took no care to be stealthy or quiet.

'You can't deny it's what you've always wanted,' Swan shouted at Daisy.

'I can deny it. I do deny it. D'you think I've had an easy life of it? I can tell you, I've had worries enough of my own, helping Stephen get where we are today without looking over my shoulder the whole time wondering how it is with the Lyndon-Furys.'

'And the pigs flew over the hill! You've had an eye on us like a travelling rat, waiting for the next crumb to fall from the Coolderg table.'

'Ladies . . . !' Napier protested ineffectually.

'God, but you give yourself airs!' Daisy sneered, looking about her – and still not seeing her daughter standing there in full view. 'There's nothing here I'd cross the street to buy if it was free.'

'Ah but there is!' Swan crowed.

'Oh, you suppose that just because you have that painting, you have a gun at my head . . .'

'For the love of God!' There was Napier again.

Caro could listen no further. Still talking no precautions to remain unobserved she walked to the grand staircase and went up. Two flights she went, not quite in the dark, for the servants had lighted a lamp on each landing. She took one to show herself down the passage to the room where she had last seen the Joan of Arc. The accusations and name-calling dwindled behind her but never to complete silence.

The door was locked, but she knew Swan's habits by now. She felt among the dust on the top rail of the doorframe until the key fell at her feet. She unlocked the door and went in.

The painting was still there, leaning face-in against the wall. She set down the lamp, turned the canvas round, and stared at it for a moment.

Her Mammy's face, with disturbing reminders of her own in its lines. Her Mammy's face, untainted as yet by rejection, anger, bitterness, and the poison of revenge. She stared at it a long while, trying to come to terms with the joy, the laughter, the carefree wildness that had once been there – which Napier had recorded so perfectly and then helped to kill.

How much of it had been inevitable? Could they have made it happen any differently? If Napier had married Mammy, would they have grown as sour with each other as he and Swan now were? Would their roles simply have been reversed, so that by some unimaginable life-lines they would all be here at Coolderg on this very evening, shouting at each other over some quite different argument but in precisely the same tones?

There had to be a way to break that cycle of doom.

She felt the key, still in her hand. After that it seemed only natural to use it to puncture four deep gashes in the canvas, marking the corners of a square around her Mammy's face. She joined them up with her fingernail and tore away the last tatters that held the square to the hole it now left. Then, taking up the lamp once more, she went back downstairs.

As she descended the last flight they all went quiet. She thought they had noticed her at last, but then she saw her father standing in the main doorway.

'Hello, Daddy,' she said lightly as she set down the lamp; then she turned and continued toward the others by the fire.

Now she used both hands to hold out the torn bit of painting where they could see it.

They watched her in bewilderment, not recognizing it or what she had done; then they were distracted by Stephen, who was striding vigorously down the ballroom toward them. In that way Caro reached the hearth without being stopped and without their guessing her purpose.

'Look!' she held it up for their final inspection, not realizing that – since the bright fire was all behind her – what they saw, apparently, was a handkerchief or a torn rag of some description. Then she tossed it into the flames and stood aside to watch.

It took several seconds to shrivel and catch fire – long enough for them all to see what it was at last.

'No!' Swan shrieked and dashed toward the flames.

'No!' Daisy's agony was no less intense. She arrived at the hearth at the same moment as Swan.

Swan was, naturally, astonished at Daisy's outburst – but so was Daisy herself. For that brief moment, between them, they accorded the doomed scrap of canvas and pigment its true status as a work of art. Their mutual surprise held them just long enough for any thought of a rescue to be meaningless; when they next turned to look at it, the only colours were black and bright red.

Napier had meanwhile run to Caro's side and thrown his arms about her. Utterly void of feeling she allowed him to fold her in his arms and half hug her to death. 'Thank God!' he repeated again and again.

Such was the scene that greeted Stephen as he reached the circle of the flames.

'He can paint it again,' Daisy said, still horrified at the destruction. 'Napier! You can paint it again, can't you? How much d'you want? I'll pay anything you want.'

Swan recovered during this extraordinary outburst. 'My God!' she shouted at Daisy. 'What are you saying? You can't even let him go! That's it, isn't it – you can't even let him go!' And she flew at Daisy with all ten claws out and bore her to the ground.

A moment later Daisy let out a shriek as Swan bit part of her ear off. Then their husbands pulled them apart.

And Caro, standing aside and watching them, wondered why the men bothered. They weren't solving anything; they were only postponing the final resolution of it all.

87

It was so obvious that Napier could no longer afford to stay in, keep up, or even own, Coolderg Castle that even Swan saw it at last. He had expected an almighty display of pyrotechnics when the truth finally dawned, but, God be praised, she took it quite calmly. Leaving him to pack up his studio, she went to Dublin, saw the auctioneers, and made all the arrangements to put the estate on the market.

Napier supposed she might stay up in the city that night. Mercier's parents always kept a bed for her, of which she often took advantage. So, filled with a wonderful sense of liberation – not only that Swan was away and so there could be no arguments tonight, but also that the long nightmare was now over – he drank rather a lot of whiskey and fell into bed. There he slept so soundly that even Swan's none-too-silent return failed to wake him. In fact, he did not awaken until the hammering began – and by then it was, of course, too late.

Swan got undressed and lay beside him in the large, cold bed. She left the lamp burning low. For a long time she stared at the ceiling, running her eyes up and down the maze of cracks, noting where the lath peered through, mentally repairing the broken cornices and mouldings. Then she thought of all the other ceilings in all the other rooms, most of them even worse than this. And it wasn't just ceilings, either. There were leaning walls, damp walls, mould-encrusted walls . . . and floors! Floors where whatnots and occasional tables covered the rot; floors where the carpets billowed like the sea whenever the wind blew; floors that bounced like a sprung mattress as you crossed them; stone floors that wept after every rain. There were windows you couldn't shut, windows you couldn't open, windows you couldn't see through, windows that had rotted away and gone.

Perhaps Napier was right when he said you'd want the key to the Bank of England before you'd buy a place like this. She hoped the O'Lindons were next. Rich they might be, but they weren't as rich as all that. It would suck them dry, too – and serve them right!

The sudden irruption of that hated name prompted a memory of the stone at the top of the tower, the O'Lindon Stone. It had always been her ambition to send the masons up there and have it removed. An immense sadness overcame her that she would never be able to fulfill it now. The tears began to stream down her cheeks.

And then, in the depth of her misery, it occurred to her that she could do *something* about it. If she couldn't remove the stone, she could at least deface it beyond recognition. Surely if she took a hammer to it, she could smash the face of it enough to obliterate the carving? Anyway, it was better than lying here, staring at the ceiling, weeping herself to death.

She rose, put on her dressing gown, and padded down to the kitchen in search of a hammer. In the end she found one in Napier's studio, which he used for putting together the stretchers for his canvasses. Then she began the long climb up the spiral steps to the top of the tower. On the way she peeped out into the corridor leading to their bedroom, to see if Napier was stirring. For a moment, indeed, she thought she saw him standing by one of the windows in the corridor leading to the second guest bedroom; but it was a trick of the moonlight, for when she peered more closely she saw nothing but the empty passage.

She was glad of the moonlight when she arrived at the top; it enabled her to leave the lamp at the stairhead and use her free hand to steady herself. The parapet where the defenders had once stood was in no better repair than anything else in the place – worse, in fact, since it took the full brunt of the weather.

She edged her way down the south parapet, holding her breath until her lungs threatened to burst. Then she stopped, clung like a leech to one of the battlements, and panted until she was giddy. When she had recovered she raised the hammer and gave one of the stones, an inoffensive one, a sharp crack. A satisfying splinter of rock spalled off the face.of it and went skeetering across the slates. Her heart rejoiced for, until then, she had not really supposed she would make much impression on that hated stone.

Down in their bedroom Napier stirred and turned over.

The parapet on the eastern side, where her target lay, was in better repair – except in the very place where she would need to stand. 'Isn't that the way of it!' she exclaimed aloud as, spreading her legs to span the gap, she settled to her stance and raised the hammer high.

The first blow took a large chip off the wrong stone. The chip, in turn, struck her a stinging blow on her shoulder and she realized for the first time what danger there was to her eyes. She raised the hammer again and struck a more accurate blow, closing her eyelids at the last moment. She hit the O'Lindon Stone this time but nothing broke from it; a small, starlike blaze showed where she had found the mark, but that was all.

Napier began to surface from his slumber.

Perhaps if she hit it in the same place? One blow to weaken it, a second to finish it off. She touched the spot with the hammer, to be sure of the length, then raised it twice as high as before and brought it down with double the force.

The metal sang like a bell and her wrist felt as if she had just dislocated it.

Napier came wide awake and sat up in bed.

The next blow would do it, she felt sure. Again she tested for length and raised the hammer, bringing it down with all the force at her command. It bounced off the stone like a steel tennis ball, ringing as before. The momentum, for which she was not prepared, carried it back to the top of the sweep. Her wrist was so shocked by now that she could not maintain her grip fully on the handle.

She watched the liberated hammer go spinning away in a moonlit arc, out over the battlements, down into the black silence beyond. Then there was the faintest splintering crash in the shrubbery below.

As in a trance she stood and walked to the space between the nearest castellations. Vaguely, at the back of her mind, lay the thought that she might mark the spot where it fell and then go down and retrieve it. But there was nothing to see down there, only a bed of dark leaves, some of them waxy enough to give back pinpoint reflections of the moon.

It was like a myriad eyes, all watching her.

Between them, a myriad dark mouths, silently laughing. *At her.*

If by that stage of her dementia she had been capable of words, she would have said that what had just happened was like a miniature re-enactment of her entire life. She had struck at the O'Lindon Stone with all her might. The resulting damage was trivial, and the rebound had dashed the weapon from her, casting it into the mocking darkness with its myriad eyes.

So it had been from the very beginning - futile - from the moment Daisy O'Lindon walked into the Academy and took Napier from her. No matter what she might wish for, some malevolent God immediately granted it to Daisy O'Lindon.

So it had been.

So it was now.

So it always would be.

Suddenly, the most easeful thing to do was to stand between the stones and step out onto the void.

She fell in absolute silence and died immediately she hit the ground.

Napier, who had mistaken the direction of the hammering sound that had awakened him, investigated the room below, the main guard below that, and, finding nothing amiss, went back to bed - not even knowing that Swan had returned from Dublin.

The sun was well up the following morning when he learned she had gone for ever.

The hammer rusted in the shrubbery for several years and was finally buried by a playful dog, pretending it was a bone.

88

Lady Lyndon-Fury came over for the funeral, of course. Napier wished she hadn't. All she seemed to want was to tear Daisy O'Lindon to pieces. When Daisy and Stephen came to commiserate with her at the funeral she just turned her back on them in the most ostentatious way and refused even to speak to them. And as for their coming back to Coolderg Castle after the burial, it was out of the question – even though they now owned the place!

'You've no idea how helpful they were to me,' he told her.

She gave a single sarcastic laugh. 'I think I may have a very good idea. You're a simpleton, Napier. You always were. She twisted you round her little finger once again. Swan saw through her, but you remain as blind as ever.'

He stared down at her frail old body and thought how dearly he'd love to hit her, to knock that arrogant conviction out of her. She thought she knew it all. Even now, when she'd been living for years in England, she would come back here and behave as if she knew the ins and outs of everything. He realized it was futile. He knew he ought not even to bother. He understood only too well that her ancient hatred of Daisy was unshakable. And yet he felt he owed it to her to try to get through.

'If it wasn't for Daisy O'Lindon,' he said, 'I'd be borrowing the fare back to Paris from Maddy. *And* travelling third instead of first.'

'If it wasn't for Daisy O'Lindon, you wouldn't be going at all.'

He ignored the jibe. 'Her husband would have beaten me down to sell at no more than our debts. I'm leaving because of *our debts*, Mama, and it was Swan who ran them up, not Daisy. Stephen O'Lindon's been a good friend, so I won't say a word against him, but he's also a man of business. He wouldn't yield a ha'penny where a farthing would suffice. When I told him I wanted twenty-four thou' for this place, he just laughed and said I'd have to come down on that. And d'you know what Daisy said?'

'I don't care a rap what she said,' his mother replied coldly.

'We were standing out in the park there, by that fallen a tree – where she and I once pelted each other with snowballs.' He stood a moment, lost in reverie.

'For God's sake!' she sneered.

Reluctantly he returned to his theme. 'And when O'Lindon said, "You'll have to come down on that," she just looked at him sharply and snapped, "He will *not*!" Just like that. And he said, "Oh, very well," and reached out his hand and shook mine on the deal. And that leaves me eight thousand pounds to restart my life with, all over again. But the three of us knew damn well he could have beaten me down to sixteen thou' – I mean, things truly were as desperate as that.'

He watched his mother closely for some sign that she might yield the point. She continued to stare blankly out of the window.

'If I've been able to forgive you for what you've done,' he added, 'don't you think you could find it in yourself to forgive her? Not that she did you any harm, but couldn't you forgive her for . . . whatever it is you *imagine* she did?'

That stung her at last. 'What have you to forgive me for?' she asked sharply.

'You lost me the only woman I ever really loved. You lost me my daughter – or at least her childhood years. You lost me all the happiness I might ever have had. Yet I have managed to forgive you every last . . .'

He faltered when he saw her staring at him, shaking her head in a kind of weary sadness. 'Oh, Napier, my darling boy,' she sighed. 'D'you really imagine *I* lost you those things? Daisy O'Lindon may be a hard, cruel, vindictive little witch but she's no fool. She saw through you the moment she came here that winter. The only thing that kept her by you after that was wishful thinking.'

'What d'you mean – saw through me? Anyway, you haven't answered my . . .'

'Why, she saw that you're that kind of sainted simpleton who has no place in the real world. Art is all you're fit for. Just listen to yourself now! In the face of all evidence, you go on standing there, braying out how *good* she is! The moment she met O'Lindon, you lost whatever chance you might have had. He was just the ticket for her.' She laughed as she remembered his earlier remark. 'He was her first-class ticket. And her destination,' she tapped her foot on the old stone floor of the main guard, 'was *here*!'

He picked up a half-burned pinecone from the hearth and hurled it into the cold gray ashes. 'Now I know just what Caro means,' he said bitterly.

Her ears pricked up at that. After a pause she murmured in an experimental sort of tone, 'She's another.'

He rounded on her at once, shaking with fury. Stabbing his finger at her like a dagger – almost wishing it *were* a dagger – he shouted, 'Don't you dare! Don't you dare!'

A slow smile broke over her face. 'Well, well, well,' she murmured. 'You, too!'

89

The dawn of that great day saw Daisy and Stephen already up and dressed. Indeed, she had not slept all night for the unending lists of things that tumbled through her mind. There were the repairs she had already noted; the sticks of Lyndon-Fury furniture she had bought but would not keep; the hiring of new servants and the dismissing of old ones who had fallen into bad Lyndon-Fury ways; the work to be done in the gardens and out in the park; the setting of Sharavogue . . . it was only amazing how the crowning of her life's ambition had become a mere doorway into a new phase of work and worry.

By seven o'clock that morning she and Stephen had cajoled and bullied their offspring – the four who had not yet flown the nest – into rising and getting themselves around some breakfast. By eight they were off, Daisy and Caro in the gig, the menfolk behind them in one of the phætons, down the road to their new home at Coolderg Castle.

It was a crisp morning in April, with the sun already up above the trees and fair-weather cumulus as far as the eye could see. The list-making worries of the night were behind her and Daisy's heart sang at the way everything had turned out. 'Isn't it exciting?' she asked Caro, who gave a shy sort of shrug and said, 'Yes, of course.' What else could she say in the face of such enthusiasm?

'You don't sound too convinced,' her mother chided. 'I should have thought the old courtroom at the top of the tower was *boudoir* enough to melt your indifference.'

'I'm not indifferent,' she protested.

'What is it then?'

'I just wish . . . I mean, I feel so sorry for Uncle Napier.'

'About Aunt Swan? That was a terrible, wicked . . .'

'No! I mean about having to leave Coolderg.'

Daisy laughed. 'Oh, Caro, he's over the moon about that. If you could have seen his face light up when we offered to buy him out. Tell me – when did you last hear that man whistling?'

Caro had to admit it: Napier, despite Swan's tragic death, had seemed like a man with a new lease of life since the sale had been agreed.

'D'you believe in ghosts?' Daisy asked suddenly. 'I usen't to but I'm beginning to wonder. I think I saw a ghost the first night I spent at the castle. At the time I was sure it was Napier playing a trick, but now . . . who knows?' And she went on to describe the events of that night.

'D'you think it was Hugh O'Lindon you saw?' Caro asked incredulously.

Daisy shrugged. 'As I said – who knows?'

'Uncle Napier believes in ghosts,' Caro went on. She told her mother the story he had told her that day they drove round both loughs; and Daisy, though she knew that tale well, heard her out in silence, listening for clues as to the girl's true feelings about Napier.

In fact, she was listening for such subtle inflections of voice that she almost missed the sledgehammer blow that Caro delivered as an afterthought: 'That was the day I first learned that he's my real father.' She reached over and took the reins from her mother – who hardly seemed to notice.

Daisy had to listen to the echo of the words in her mind – and feel the blood draining from her face – before the impact registered. She swallowed heavily. 'Did he tell you that?' she asked.

'No. He and Aunt Swan were having an argument and I couldn't help overhearing.'

Daisy swallowed again, even more audibly. 'I see,' was all she could think to say. It suddenly struck her she was no longer holding the reins. She glanced at her empty hands and then stared at Caro, so unreadably calm at her side. What ought she to do now? How could you deal with someone who gave so little of herself away?

'I wish I'd heard it from you,' Caro said in that same matter-of-fact voice.

Impulsively Daisy flung her arms around the girl and hugged her for dear life. 'Oh, darling!' was all she could say. 'Oh, my darling, darling Caro!'

To her surprise, the girl let escape a huge sigh of relief. 'Thank God,' she murmured fervently. It startled Daisy into withdrawing a little, to see her more clearly. 'Why so?' she asked.

Caro's laugh was pure relief, too. 'I thought you might get angry. I feared you might try to bluster and deny it. I thought you might have forgotten how to . . .' Instead of completing the sentence she rested her head briefly on Daisy's shoulder and said, 'Thank you, anyway.'

Daisy knew what the unspoken words would have been: . . . 'how to be honest with me'. Their evocation in her own mind revealed to her how perilously close she had come to making the girl's fear come true.

'Ghosts!' Caro said. 'Those are the ones I believe in.'

'D'you wish me to tell you all about it?' Daisy asked nervously.

Caro smiled at her. 'Not now. One day, perhaps – when *you* want to.'

'I've been such a fool,' Daisy confessed. 'And to think you've known all this time! What age were you then? You weren't even sixteen. Didn't you go mad?

'No.'

Daisy chuckled. 'That's all, is it? Just *no*. Oh Caro, I don't know!'

They drove on for a while in silence. Then Daisy asked, 'Do you call *him* Daddy when you're alone together?

Now it was Caro's turn to be astonished. 'Of course not!'

'Or Pater, or Papa . . . nothing like that?'

'I just call him Napier. Daddy's my father. How can something you and Napier did before you even met Daddy change that?'

Daisy scanned the clouds while she tried to unravel the question – and then decided it were best left ravelled. 'Quite,' she said. 'Still, he'll be overjoyed to hear it.'

'Does he need to know?' Caro asked. 'I think he tried to tell me once. I didn't realize it at the time or perhaps I'd have helped him more. Or perhaps not.'

Daisy, intrigued by her uncertainty, asked why not.

'He was so relieved when he found he couldn't do it, so happy. That's what later made me realize what he'd tried to do.'

'And how did you feel then – when you realized that?'

'I was glad he hadn't said it. I mean, I'm proud of him, you know.'

'Well, of course, dear . . .'

'No, listen till I tell you. I'm proud he *chose* to be my father when he didn't have to. So, unless you feel you can't have secrets from him, I'd rather he didn't know. D'you mind?'

Daisy felt the pressure of tears behind her eyelids. She slipped an arm about the girl's waist and gave her another squeeze. 'You're the one I'm proud of,' she said. 'Oh, Caro! I want you to be so happy at Coolderg. It's *your* place, you know.' She felt a sudden, surprising tension in her daughter's body. 'Your rightful place,' she added. 'The day you were born I made a secret oath to myself that before you came of age, Coolderg Castle would be yours again.'

'Again?' Caro echoed in dismayed surprise.

'And now there you are – in the highest room of the tower – Queen of the Castle! We've done it with a few weeks to spare!'

When Caro made no response, Daisy assumed she was overwhelmed at the magnificence of the achievement. 'Happy now?' she prompted.

Caro turned to her and gave a radiant smile. 'Of course,' she replied and planted a fervent kiss on Daisy's cheek.

What else could one do, she asked herself, in the face of such *merciless* love?

90

When they arrived at the castle the three boys jumped down and barred the great door. 'What's the meaning of this?' Daisy cried with mock severity as she climbed down from the gig and faced them. 'Mutiny, Mrs O'Lindon, ma'am,' Stevie replied in an unconvincing mixture of Long John Silver and County Keelity yokel. 'We're not lettin' any of yous in until we have your solemn affydavy that there'll be . . .' He glanced at his brothers and conducted them in unison: 'No cleanin' windows!'

They all laughed at that. 'Those times,' Daisy promised them, 'are well and truly behind us.'

She slipped her arm around Stephen as the lads stepped aside to let them in first. 'Would you ever carry me across the threshold?' she asked. 'It's the one thing you forgot at our wedding.'

He laughed at her outrageous gloss upon that fateful day, almost twenty-one years ago now. 'Hadn't we enough on our minds then not to fret over that?' he asked, giving Caro a wink.

'Go on,' his daughter urged, 'or she'll think you too feeble.'

So he bent his back and lifted her up. He told her she was lighter now than she had been then, which was, indeed, the truth, and he put her down inside and kissed her. And that was the first romantic kiss the children had ever seen them take.

From somewhere in the gloom, halfway down the ballroom, Napier delicately cleared his throat. They all turned to him in astonishment. 'You!' Daisy exclaimed.

' 'Fraid so,' he replied awkwardly. 'Sorry and all that. Mater trouble. She refuses to leave.'

'We'll soon see about that!' Daisy cried angrily. 'Where is she?'

Stephen put a restraining hand on her arm. 'Aisy now,' he cautioned.

'She's in the studio, or what used to be my studio. Nanny's gone ahead with young Lucius. They'll be wondering.'

'Is your mother ailing?' Stephen asked.

'Fighting fit, I'd say. I've tried everything.'

'Is she hysterical then?' Daisy asked.

'Calm as you'd wish.'

'Let me see her,' Caro said, leaving before anyone could stop her.

'Ah!' Lady Lyndon-Fury seemed pleased to see her – which astonished Caro, for such a thing had never happened before.

She smiled and came to stand beside the old woman, sitting in the throne on the dais. Her shawl had slipped. Caro straightened it and then drew up a chair and sat down, facing her.

'Your big day!' her ladyship went on stiffly. She looked as if she'd taken a breakfast of ramrods.

Again Caro smiled. 'Yours, too, Grandmama.'

The other didn't bat an eyelid. 'So they *did* tell you about that! Cornel was right. I owe him an apology when we meet . . .' Her eyes flickered briefly heavenwards.

Caro's mask was unreadable. 'And *he* owes *me* one. It was a confidence. He shouldn't have told anyone.'

Lady Lyndon-Fury shook her head sadly. 'Uncork the whiskey and you uncork all.'

Caro sighed at the justice of that. 'It hardly matters now, anyway. Do you really want to stay on here, Grandmama?' She smiled again. 'You could if you wanted, you know.'

The old woman made no reply; instead, she licked her lips and surveyed Caro speculatively.

'Well?' Caro insisted, trying now to hurry things along.

The other drew a deep breath and squared her shoulders, as if she had just come to some monumental decision. 'And are *you* staying?' she asked in a tone of disbelief.

'Of course. What makes you ask?'

'You mean you're *not* going to Paris with Napier?'

Caro stared at her in blank amazement. 'Napier . . . Paris . . .' she echoed in something close to a whisper.

'You mean, he didn't even *ask* you?' Lady Lyndon-Fury pressed.

The girl shook her head.

'Oh, he is so spineless! No wonder he lost your mother – he didn't deserve to win her.' She looked pityingly at her granddaughter and added. 'He never really grew up, you know. He's like Lanna Mochree's dog – he'll go halfway with everyone.'

The hair bristled on Caro's neck. In those few words, spoken in contempt, Lady Lyndon-Fury had managed to crystallize everything she, Caro, felt to be most lovable in dear Uncle Napier. Dear Napier. He was the one person who stood outside this circle of hatred, envy, and revenge.

When Lady Lyndon-Fury rose, Caro was shocked to hear how her joints cracked. The woman saw it in her eyes and said grimly, 'Your turn will come sooner than you think – so make the best of it now.'

Caro took her arm, wondering when the woman had last washed.

'Poor Swan,' her ladyship said as they went toward the door. 'Do you really think she took her own life?'

After a moment of stunned silence Caro muttered. 'The coroner . . .'

'Fiddlesticks!' the other interrupted. 'Go up there where it happened and see for yourself. Look well at the O'Lindon Stone.'

'Why? What'll I see?'

'Never you mind. It's plain enough to anyone who knew her.'

'Have you been up there?' Caro asked incredulously.

'Why else d'you suppose I'm all creaking and groaning today?'

91

The most incongruous sight of the century was surely the tableau formed by the O'Lindons, standing at the ruined keep of Coolderg Castle, waving an apparently amicable farewell to the last of the Lyndon-Furys: Stephen and Daisy, arm in arm; Stevie, on the verge of manhood, beside his two younger brothers, and – nudged a little apart by the sky-blue finger of a puddled wheel rut – Caro.

She stole a sidelong glance at the others. Finnbar and Sheridan had already stopped waving. Even before the departing carriage reached the first gate they turned their backs to it and were surveying the castle – not so much as owners, more as prospectors of a new playground, a treasure island, an Aladdin's Cave. Stevie, too, rested his arm, caught Caro's eyes, and gave her a cheerful wink. Beyond him, savouring the event to its last moment, her parents waved with languid assurance. The bright sunlight, glinting on their eyes and teeth, gave them a raptorial gloss in this, the crowning of their triumph.

'Ill got and ill gone,' Daisy murmured happily; then, to Stephen: 'You were too many for them.'

Caro turned and walked toward the castle.

'Where are you off to, darling?' Daisy called after her.

'Just up to my room.'

After a pause her mother cried, 'Boudoir, actually!' and laughed.

Caro waved acknowledgement of the correction without turning round. She went through the ballroom and up the main stair to the first floor. She peeped into the passage, just in case any old ghost decided to manifest himself; in fact, she waited there awhile – though nothing happened. Her parents came indoors; she heard her mother say, 'I've a mind to knock all this Georgian wing and just leave the O'Lindon tower and the old abbey. Wouldn't that be fierce, altogether!'

Her father made some inaudible reply, or maybe he just raked the ceiling with his gaze; then her mother laughed and said she was only codding.

Caro went on up the spiral stair to her room – the old courthouse at the top of the tower. But at the threshold she paused remembering her grandmother's strange words. She looked up the remaining flight to the roof.

Sure it was only another turn and a half.

But that was where poor Aunt Swan . . .

Suppose *her* ghost was up there . . . waiting!

The threat of it decided her; she turned resolutely and made her way up that last flight to the roof. As one worn step after another vanished beneath the hem of her dress she felt a prickling sensation run from her neck to the pit of her spine. She imagined Aunt Swan taking this walk for the final time. Had she known it was for the final time? If the coroner was right, she had. But if the cause of her leap had been . . . what? Something nameless. Something *other*. Then what had been her mood as this step, and this step, and this step rose to meet her?

The day had changed by the time Caro emerged at the top. A thin veil of cloud turned the sun to a disk of pale silver; the softened shadows lent that familiar scene the airless unreality of an early photograph. As in a waking dream, then, Caro wandered round the parapet to the chimney in the eastern wall, where she bent to examine the O'Lindon Stone and discover what the old woman might have meant.

At first she thought it was lichen - a sort of blaze of pale, gray-green rays from a bright centre. But when she put a finger to the surface and gave it a hesitant rub, she saw that precisely the opposite was true. A thin smear of pale and dark mottling showed that the lichen was everywhere *else*; this was freshly exposed stone. She noted two more of those curious marks, all centred on the 'O' of the monogram. When it dawned on her what they were, her innards went suddenly hollow and she had to cling to the stone for support.

Then she rose and, leaning her forehead against the cool stone of one of the battlements, she wept till the tears ran dry. 'Oh, Swan!' was all she whispered, over and over again, 'Oh Swan!'

92

Daisy and Stephen wandered into the old courtroom. 'Caro?' Daisy called instead of giving a knock. There was no reply. Stephen ducked his head back into the spiral stairway and called her name louder. Again there was only silence - or the unending cawing of the rooks. 'Not there either,' he said. They went back into the courtroom. 'Boudoir!' Daisy said fondly. 'I think she's outgrown that at last.'

'I think she's outgrown a lot of things,' Stephen replied.

'Meaning?'

'I mean she's really grown up. Look at the way she handled the oul' woman. There'd have been blood if you'd gone in.'

Daisy nodded at the justice of that. 'We can't have missed her, surely?'

she said. 'There's only the one staircase after the first floor. Did she go down while we were in the library? Did you hear anything?'

He shook his head. Stirring a heap of old leaves with his foot, he said, 'The mess that's everywhere!'

'Slip up and see if she's on the roof. Sure it's the only place she can be. Maybe she never heard you.'

With a vaguely martyred air he went to do as she bade.

'Neither hide nor hair of her,' he said cheerily as he returned. 'She must have slipped down past us. What's that?'

'It's an old letter,' Daisy said, continuing to read. 'There's a box full of them there. I never saw it before. Relics of old decency.'

He stopped and rummaged among them, examining his trawl with shallow interest, and then went to her side. 'What's it say?'

'It's from Caroline O'Lindon – the first one who lived here. To her aunt, I think. All about the O'Lindon Stone. She says it was her husband's idea of a *peace* offering to the O'Lindons!' She laughed scornfully. 'Would you ever credit that?'

Ten minutes later, when there was still no sign of Caro, they began to worry. Stephen went back to the roof of the tower and shouted her name to all four corners of the county. Her brothers rioted through all the rooms to see if she'd accidentally locked herself in one of them. Daisy went out and called her name through the garden and down to the stables.

And it was there, in the cobbled yard, that the gardener's boy came to her, pale-faced and shivering, to tell her what had happened.

93

The guard walked up and down the platform, hefting his flag, fingering his whistle, and shouting 'All aboard!' No one paid him the slightest heed for they could see that the porters had a dozen creamery cans to load yet. The platform was still thronged with people who intended to travel, including Napier and his mother, who stood a little apart from the others and peered outward, through the railings.

'I remember the day *she* got off the train here,' she said. 'It was May Day, eighteen eighty-five. I was in my carriage, there, under the linden with the broken bough. It wasn't broken then. I saw her get off the train and I knew at once she wouldn't do. But oh, the anger in her eyes!'

'Mama!' He patted her arm. 'It doesn't matter now.'

'She wouldn't have it, you know.'

'Yes, you told me.'

'She came storming down here in the rain and argued with me! With *me*!'

'Twenty-one years, eh!' Napier pretended to fall in with her mood though his heart danced as it had not danced in years and he felt as carefree as . . . when? Truth to tell, he hadn't felt like this since the day he and Daisy had taken the mail boat to England.

'There were some workhouse girls going for the emigrant boat, I remember,' she went on. Then, with a descent into bitterness: 'You realize that's what we are now. Just as she wanted it.'

'Paupers!' he echoed with weary scorn. 'If she'd really wanted that . . . I mean, why did she tell O'Lindon to pay my asking price? I don't know why I bother.' He saw there were only two more churns to go. 'We'd better start thinking of getting in.'

At that moment a gig came racing up the approach, its horse lathered to a rag. 'Is that Daisy?' he asked, trying to make out the driver, whom he could only glimpse in brief snatches among the linden leaves. 'What's happened?'

'She's come to gloat, of course,' his mother told him.

'Stop the train!' came a cry from the gig.

'Caro!' He laughed.

'Ha!' His mother clapped her hands and raised them to her lips, almost as if praying – or thanking for an answered prayer.

'Napier! Tell them to hold the train.' Caro leaped from the vehicle, threw the reins at a man she knew, told him the lad from Coolderg would collect it after dinner, and ran to the station entrance. Half no-time later, she came running down the platform, where she threw her arms around a bewildered Napier and burst into tears. 'Thank God!' was all she could say, again and again. At last, when she had got some of her breath back, she expanded it to, 'Thank God I'm in time.'

'Thank God, indeed,' Lady Lyndon-Fury echoed.

'You shouldn't have bothered,' Napier said, patting her on the back and wondering why she was in such a state. 'But bless you all the same.'

The green flag fluttered, the whistle shrilled, and at last everyone knew the man meant it. The scramble for places was intense – except for Napier and his mother in the First Class splendour. They were a little uneasy when Caro joined them. 'Better stay outside,' he advised. 'We can let the window down and talk until . . .' He faltered when he saw her grinning and shaking her head. 'What d'you . . . what's . . . ?' he asked.

'I'm coming with you.' Her grin broadened as she flopped in the seat and sprawled back. Her breathlessness now was more emotional than physical. 'To Paris!'

'But you can't,' he exclaimed at once.

'Why not?'

He floundered for reasons. Lady Lyndon-Fury smiled as she watched his struggles.

'But you have no luggage. You haven't even got a hat. Do your parents know?'

'Ha!' his mother cackled.

Napier ignored her. 'But what'll you *do*? Have you ever been to Paris? I don't even have a place to stay.' His tone, however, was growing less strident. The notion was beginning to seem not altogether impossible.

'What'll I do?' Her eyes scanned the grimy ceiling. 'I expect I'll cook for you. I'll fight off your creditors. I'll teach dressage. I'll darn your socks. I'll sit at your side in the cafés and make eyes at all the handsome young painters . . . What will I do? I'll be *me*, Napier! *Me!* Not Caroline O'Lindon the Second!'

The tears welled up in her eyes again at the prospect of that wonderful, monstrous liberation.

But a moment later she was back on the edge of her seat. 'Why aren't we moving?'

Napier frowned. 'I was just asking myself the same question.' He rose and, lowering the window all the way on its strap, stuck his head out.

'Well?' she asked impatiently.

'Nothing.' He craned out further and added, 'Two men. Railwaymen.' He opened the door and stepped back onto the platform.

She followed.

There were two men squatting on the line in front of the train, taking it in turns to tap one of the bogey wheels with a long-handled hammer. In between each tap they had a little argument.

'Oh God!' Caro murmured under her breath and closed her eyes in dread.

'What?' he asked.

She opened her eyes again and fixed them on the entrance to the station approach.

'Ah.' He bit his lip. 'I take it they don't know, then.'

'They'll come after me. Mammy will never yield an inch.'

'An inch is a lot if it comes off your nose.'

'Oh God, would you ever go and give those men a thousand pounds to ignore whatever it is with the wheel?'

'Listen, Caro, I don't wish to distress your parents,' Napier told her awkwardly. 'They've been very daycent to me . . .'

'You're a thundering disgrace,' his mother shouted from the depths of their compartment. 'For the love of Christ, will you stand up for something, once in your life. Can't you see the girl needs your support now, more than she ever needed anything of you before?'

Napier looked inquiringly at Caro, who nodded once.

'Right.' He squared his shoulders. 'When do you come of age?'

'Next month.'

'It wouldn't be long to wait, Little Face. Will I get my things off the train? I can wait here in Simonstown . . .'

She closed her eyes and shook her head. 'I couldn't live through one more *day.*'

'Like that, eh.'

'Oh, Napier, you can have no idea. You especially can have no idea.'

He nodded calmly. 'Then get back on the train.' He extended an arm to help her in. 'Even if they come, I won't let them take you.'

'God love you!' She kissed him on the cheek as she passed.

'Are you really any good at darning socks?' he asked.

She laughed as she settled in her seat again, next to young Lucius. Suddenly it no longer mattered that her parents might have learned of her whereabouts from the gardener's boy; they could even now be galloping into Simonstown for all she cared. To make all certain, Napier bought her a ticket from the guard.

It took a third wheeltapper and another five minutes for the bogeys to be certified as fit for duty. Then, with a second flurry of whistling and flag-waving, the engine hissed mightily and hid itself in a great aura of steam. Infinitely slowly they began to gather speed.

And at that moment the O'Lindon phæton came skelping into the station approach and rasped to a halt halfway up. Daisy was alone at the reins.

'That's the very tree!' Lady Lyndon-Fury murmured.

The hair rose on Caro's scalp.

Daisy's eyes raked up and down the departing train, found her daughter at last, and then saw the face in the window next to her. She made no further movement after that. She simply clenched her fists and stood there in the most curious attitude, like death upon wires.

'What is she doing?' Napier asked.

Caro murmured, 'Watching a wish come true. And wishing she weren't. And heart-scalded she ever made it, I hope.'

Napier, unable to tolerate such raw emotion, sought desperately to lighten the atmosphere. 'I say!' he exclaimed. 'Hell hath no fury, eh?' Then, seeing the unintended pun, he added, 'Nor has Coolderg now!'

'It has an O'Lindon, instead,' Caro replied.

But she was referring to the first of his comments.

'Bye bye, Mammy!' Her voice broke on the words and the tears coursed down her face.

Finally, her breath clouded the pane so that she could no longer see her mother at all.

MAR. 1992

F
Macdonald, Malcolm
Hell hath no fury.

DEEP RIVER PUBLIC LIBRARY
150 MAIN ST.
DEEP RIVER, CT 06417
526-5674